Sue MacKay lives with her husband in New Zealand's beautiful Marlborough Sounds, with the water on her doorstep and the birds and the trees at her back door. It is the perfect setting to indulge her passions of entertaining friends by cooking them sumptuous meals, drinking fabulous wine, going for hill walks or kayaking around the bay—and, of course, writing stories.

Born and raised just outside Toronto, Ontario, **Amy Ruttan** fled the big city to settle down with the country boy of her dreams. After the birth of her second child Amy was lucky enough to realise her lifelong dream of becoming a romance author. When she's not furiously typing away at her computer, she's mum to three wonderful children, who use her as a personal taxi and chef.

Also by Sue MacKay

Brooding Vet for the Wallflower
Wedding Date with the ER Doctor
Parisian Surgeon's Secret Child
A Fling with the ER Doc

Also by Amy Ruttan

Tempted by the Single Dad Next Door
Rebel Doctor's Boston Reunion
Their Accidental Vegas Vows
Snowbound with the Single Mum

Discover more at millsandboon.co.uk.

ENEMY ON HER HOSPITAL WARD

SUE MacKAY

SECOND CHANCE WITH HIS SUNSHINE SURGEON

AMY RUTTAN

MILLS & BOON

All rights reserved including the right of reproduction in whole or in part in any form. This edition is published by arrangement with Harlequin Enterprises ULC.

This is a work of fiction. Names, characters, places, locations and incidents are purely fictional and bear no relationship to any real life individuals, living or dead, or to any actual places, business establishments, locations, events or incidents. Any resemblance is entirely coincidental.

Without limiting the exclusive rights of any author, contributor or the publisher of this publication, any unauthorised use of this publication to train generative artificial intelligence (AI) technologies is expressly prohibited. HarperCollins also exercise their rights under Article 4(3) of the Digital Single Market Directive 2019/790 and expressly reserve this publication from the text and data mining exception.

® and TM are trademarks owned and used by the trademark owner and/or its licensee. Trademarks marked with ® are registered with the United Kingdom Patent Office and/or the Office for Harmonisation in the Internal Market and in other countries.

First published in Great Britain 2026
by Mills & Boon, an imprint of HarperCollins*Publishers* Ltd,
1 London Bridge Street, London, SE1 9GF

www.harpercollins.co.uk

HarperCollins*Publishers* Macken House, 39/40 Mayor Street Upper, Dublin 1, D01 C9W8, Ireland

Enemy on Her Hospital Ward © 2026 Sue MacKay

Second Chance with His Sunshine Surgeon © 2026 Amy Ruttan

ISBN: 978-0-263-41987-0

03/26

Printed and Bound in the UK using 100% Renewable Electricity at CPI Group (UK) Ltd, Croydon, CR0 4YY

ENEMY ON HER HOSPITAL WARD

SUE MacKAY

MILLS & BOON

To all the medical staff and volunteers driving vans and providing other necessities, a huge thank-you for being there for my husband. You all rock.

CHAPTER ONE

TAMARA FROST SCANNED the people waiting to board the flight to Vanuatu. There he was, standing talking to a couple in casual summer-weight clothes, looking as striking as ever. More so if she was seeing clearly. The other two people were likely who she'd also be working alongside. As for Mr Full of Himself, her mouth tightened around her old name for him. She would not let Fergus Collier get to her with his arrogant attitude. It might've been many years since their college ball when his friends had found them kissing and been derogatory about her wearing a thrift shop dress, but she hadn't forgotten. Fergus hadn't joined in with their mockery, but nor had he stepped up for her despite the sparks firing between them after a mind-blowing kiss.

He'd always been able to wind her up in a blaze of heat with his steady, grey-eyed gaze whenever she saw him. When he'd asked her to go to the ball with him, she'd turned him down flat, despite fancying him like crazy. He ran with the wealthy, privileged crowd who only dated the beautiful, popular girls, one after another, whereas she and her friends were the quiet, study-hard group. Turning him down had taken all her willpower, but she'd refused to become just another of Fergus's dating statistics.

On the night of the ball, she'd stepped outside to take

a breath of air and get away from seeing Fergus dancing with every pretty girl available while deliberately ignoring her. He'd rattled her more than ever that night, and when he'd followed her outside, taking her hands and locking his intense gaze on her, sparks had ignited. And when he'd leaned down to kiss her, all resistance had flown out of her head. Pressing into him as his mouth took hers, not in a demanding, see-what-you've-been-missing way, but in a gentle, giving, almost careful way. Her first proper kiss. One she still remembered to this day—along with the humiliation that had followed. 'Want to dance with me out here, instead?' he'd whispered. 'Please,' she'd groaned in reply. Then his mates had bowled out through the door, laughing and joking, and surrounded them, teasing Fergus, taunting her about her cheap dress. And he'd hesitated, then stepped away from her.

It had taken a couple of attempts to lift her shoulders as though she didn't care, and tell Fergus he was an arrogant arse who didn't deserve her, before turning and heading inside to join her true friends. But she had done it—stood up to him in front of his disgusting mates. That was what mattered. Not the pain and mortification of being ignored, the embarrassment over her cheap dress and how worthless she'd been made to feel.

She was still staring at Fergus now, almost wishing she hadn't come.

Right then he glanced around and instantly spotted her. His face gave nothing away, as though he'd been on the lookout for her and was prepared for anything she might say. Surprise, Fergus. She wasn't here to talk about him to him, or to anyone else. What had happened between them in the past was well and truly behind her, she decided, though she couldn't help feeling a little cautious since she didn't know him anymore and would be working alongside him during the coming weeks. Who knew what was going on behind that same decimating gaze? If only she wasn't so aware of him!

When she'd seen his name on the list of medical people heading to Port Vila to help the island locals for a month, she'd briefly considered pulling out of the volunteer programme, but more than anything she wanted to help the people there. Besides, Fergus was in her past. He hadn't ruined her life by not supporting her when his mates had jeered that they reckoned her op-shop dress was deliberately two sizes too small just so she could flaunt her pathetic figure. One of her friends—no longer a friend—had even joined in the teasing, just because she'd been jealous Fergus had asked Tamara to the ball. Tamara knew if anything good had come from that night, it was that she'd learned never to let anyone treat her like mud on their shoes ever again.

Dodging around people and carry-on bags, she headed over to the small group. 'Hello, Fergus.' She held out her hand to shake his. 'Seems it's a small world as far as you and I are concerned.'

His head jerked back a fraction as though she'd surprised him.

Good.

Get over yourself, Tamara. You're tough. He can't hurt you anymore. Then why was she feeling so uncomfortable? She couldn't still fancy him after all this time. That'd be plain weird. It had been a lusty teen crush, that's all, not something that had stuck with her in the intervening years.

Fergus reached to shake her hand with a cool, firm grip. 'Hello, Tamara. It was a surprise to see your name on the list for this trip. I didn't know you'd become a nurse.' He looked genuinely impressed.

She blinked. Where was the arrogance? The hubris? He was a doctor, after all, and the Fergus she'd known would've rubbed her face in that fact. 'I hadn't expected to see yours either.' Helping people in a small country with few medical resources didn't match the guy she'd once known, but she knew life had thrown a huge curve ball his way during his final few weeks at college. His father had been arrested and then imprisoned for scamming millions of dollars from people under the guise of an investment company he'd set up. When the wealthy lifestyle he'd been living had disappeared overnight, Fergus's outlook on life must've taken a huge knock. Maybe he'd gained some understanding of those less fortunate than he'd once been. She shrugged. Time would tell. 'Nursing was always my dream, right from the time I understood I'd have to get a job when I grew up.'

'I didn't know that.' He stopped, suddenly looking off balance. So unlike him!

'I don't suppose you did.' Why would he? They hadn't sat around talking and getting to know each other, merely ogled one another whenever they were in the same space, getting hot and confused. Well, she had, anyway. He'd been used to girls drooling over him. Especially at rugby games where he was captain of the college First Fifteen and played as a forward, with his rugby shorts emphasising a very sexy backside and muscular thighs.

'Tamara, I'm sorry, I'm being rude. I don't believe you've met Tim and Sarah McPherson. They're the other half of the team.' He smiled at the couple getting to their feet.

Turning to them, she smiled easily. 'It's nice to meet you both. You're from Hamilton?' So the notes said, but it didn't hurt to check.

'We are.' Sarah returned her smile. 'We've got a surgical practice there. Like you, I'm a nurse while Tim does the easy work.'

Tim grinned. 'You said it, babe.'

Sarah asked Tamara, 'Have you done this sort of work before?'

'Volunteering in offshore communities? No, this is a first for me and I'm really looking forward to it. You and Tim?'

'It's our second time. Unlike Fergus here. He's been to a fair few countries on the volunteer's scheme. Haven't you, Fergus?'

He was turning out to be nothing like she'd expected. If only he didn't still ramp up the heat when he looked at her. 'Have you been to Vanuatu before?' she asked him to distract herself from that rather disturbing thought.

'No, this is my first time. I've heard the locals are wonderful to get along with.' No smile for her.

Did she still annoy him? Strange how she hoped not. She shouldn't care. But then again, she wanted this to be a great trip with no complications. Getting along with Fergus would help with that. 'Sounds great.'

The speakers crackled to life. 'Ladies and gentlemen, we're about to begin boarding flight five oh one to Port Vila, starting with business class and families with small children.'

Here we go. A fizz of excitement tickled Tamara.

She was starting an adventure unlike anything she'd done before. The time had come to get out there and do something completely different in a place where she'd normally have gone to the resorts. Not because she was a snob, but when she took leave from work, all she usually wanted to do was unwind and relax. Not once had she known this sense of excitement filling her, though. Excitement that had nothing to do with Fergus. What could be better than a working holiday looking after people in need of medical attention? Nursing was in her blood, her way of looking out for others without getting too involved in their lives.

Except over the previous few months, when she'd been nursing her father as he battled with stage four bowel cancer. A battle he'd lost. It had been a very close and personal time, which had taken a lot out of her. But not for a moment did she regret taking an extended leave of absence from work and being there for her dad. Looking after the man who'd been there for her and her sister, Sashi, all their lives, especially after their mother died when a van had crossed the road in front of the long-haul truck she'd been driving. In an attempt to avoid the van, her mother had swerved to the roadside, which gave way, causing the truck to roll down the bank. Her mother had been crushed in the cab by the container on the back.

'Coming?' Fergus asked with a hint of amusement.

'What?'

'They've called our rows to board.'

He knew her seat number? 'Sorry, I was miles away.'

'Obviously.' A genuine smile came her way, not as relaxed and friendly as what he'd given the other two, but she'd accept it.

You haven't been very forthcoming, either. True. Working with Fergus would be awkward if she didn't do everything possible to turn things around enough to get along with him without complications. He appeared to have changed somewhat since they'd left college. It must've been incredibly hard to face everyone after what his father had done. The story had been headline news across New Zealand for weeks. Just about everyone in Nelson had something to say on the subject, true or not. Her stomach knotted for Fergus. How had he come through that while still managing to look sane and sensible? It wouldn't have been easy by any stretch, when he'd never held back about his wonderful lifestyle. Had he truly changed or just become better at hiding his arrogant nature? Until she knew for certain, she'd cut him some slack.

'Let's do this.' She joined the queue of people getting their boarding passes scanned and waited her turn. She'd been overreacting to the heat he caused to roll through her, letting old memories from long ago get in the way of sanity. A waste of time and energy. They might become friends, but that was as far as it'd go. She didn't trust men anymore—for very good reasons, she reminded herself.

She turned to look at Fergus standing behind her. He hadn't boarded with the business-class passengers, which once would've been a given. Now that he'd matured into a man, he was better looking than ever. There was a new quietness about him, along with a steadiness that suggested he'd settled into a life that suited him. A life where he wasn't handed everything on a plate? A life where he didn't rub other people's noses in his wealth and privilege? Even as a doctor, he probably wasn't anywhere near as well off as he used to be. His father's money and properties had all been seized so money could be returned to those who'd believed Jim Collier would make them a big profit. No one got all their investments back, though. There'd also been rumours that Collier had hidden most of his ill-gotten gains, but that had never been proven, and then he'd died in prison some years later, after a short illness. From the odd comment she'd heard from friends, Fergus had apparently turned his back on his father and made his own way through university and medical school. If so, it said a lot about how much he'd changed—something she admired. It would've taken guts and sheer determination to get where he was today.

Fergus followed Tamara down the aisle to their seats, unable to ignore how those cream Capri pants accentuated her curvy backside. Some things hadn't changed. His mouth dried as he placed his bag in the overhead locker then reached for hers. Seemed she could still get to him, even after all this time. 'Let me do that for you.'

'I can manage.'

'I'm sure you can.' He tugged at her backpack and smiled to himself when she finally loosened her grip and got a book out of the side pocket before handing it over. 'We're in the middle seats, Tim and Sarah beside us.' For the next three hours he had to sit alongside this woman who'd intermittently messed with his mind for years whenever he thought about his past. She'd made him so damned confused at times because he didn't know how to face the mix of emotions she caused in him. Had always caused.

He'd longed to learn all there was to know about her. She'd kept the same friends throughout college, had fought for them if someone hurt them, something he hadn't done for her, hence him deserving her vitriol. He used to get a kick out of winding her up so she spat sharp words at him while her eyes gleamed bright. It was something she never seemed to do with anyone else, suggesting he got to her as much as she did him. He'd wondered from time to time what might've happened after their illicit kiss if they had danced together the night of the ball, and his friends hadn't ruined his chance of holding her in his arms for the first time.

But then a bare month later, the news about his father's scam had landed hard and heavy, and his life became unrecognisable. There'd been little room for anything but the attempt to stay upright. Thank goodness for Kelvin, because he was the only friend to stick with him throughout the horror that came after the arrest of Jim Collier.

Wealth has made you so arrogant you don't care about anything or anyone else but yourself.

Tamara's words had rattled around in his head on and off since the night he'd let his mates get away with insulting her because she couldn't afford a perfect gown for the ball. She'd come straight back at him with that, and more. She'd been hurt, then angry when he didn't stand up for her. When she'd called him arrogant, he'd shrugged and walked away. No girl had ever said that to him before. But he had started to wonder if she had a valid point. Had he become too big for his boots? Not that he'd changed how he went about getting onside with the prettiest girls so he could have fun. *That* came later, when his father was arrested for conning people out of their hard-earned money when they were looking for safe investments. Millions of dollars had disappeared somewhere offshore while *he'd* been living the life of Riley thinking nothing could touch him. Why would it have occurred to him that Jim Collier was a scammer? His father had always come across as a caring man who he'd hoped to emulate. Until he could no longer believe in that. He hadn't forgiven his father for what he'd done and never would, even though he was now dead. Hell, he still couldn't forgive himself for how readily he'd accepted what rightly wasn't his, nor his father's to give. Which was why nowadays he did whatever he could to help people in need.

Fergus sank into his seat and buckled up, his mind still on the past. The consequences of that time had been huge for everyone involved. He'd stayed in Nelson only to finish the school year, then went to Dunedin to find a job to earn enough to go to Otago University to study medicine the next year, as he'd always intended. The main difference being that before the truth came out about his father, he'd planned on going to Auckland University, a place he couldn't afford after what had happened. Not that Dunedin came cheap, but it was easier. He'd felt more comfortable there, away from the guys he knew were going to Auckland and had given him loads of grief about his father after the truth had come out. So much for trusting his so-called mates. His grandparents had supported him as much as they could throughout that time, and he'd love them forever for that. His mother left Nelson within weeks of his father's heinous crimes hitting the headlines, and had moved to Auckland, where she quickly found another rich man to live with while she waited to obtain a divorce. That was another scenario he hadn't been keen to become a part of, and when she'd offhandedly suggested he join her, he'd said no. Oh yeah, it had been an absolutely wonderful time in his life.

But he'd got through it and was proud of himself for that. Now he was heading to Vanuatu for a month to help as many as he could—along with the woman seated beside him. She obviously still had no time for him. He couldn't blame her for that, though. He'd behaved despicably towards her, and despite how long ago it had been, she had no reason to think he might've changed. The one thing he admired about Tamara was that she'd always given back as good as she'd got. So unusual. He'd never had a problem attracting female attention; girls had always flocked around him, wanting to be the one. Was that why he'd never forgotten her? Nothing to do with how she turned him on with merely a glance? Couldn't be, surely? But then he saw people differently these days to how he did back then, when he'd believed he was invincible. Now he knew only too well how untrue that was and, as Tamara had said, just how arrogant he'd been. He hated to think what he'd be like now if he hadn't been dealt such a huge lesson. It'd clearly been a necessary experience to make him turn out to be a decent guy.

Beside him Tamara opened the book she held.

He got it. Conversation was off the table. He'd have to try changing her mind about that. After all, they did have to get along well enough during the coming weeks working together. 'I see you're still living in Nelson.' The notes everyone had received about this trip included who was going, their qualifications and where they currently worked.

'I am at the moment.'

'You're a theatre nurse?'

'Currently, yes.'

'Tamara, I understand you'd rather I got off the plane and headed straight back home, but that's not going to happen.'

'I know.'

She sounded withdrawn rather than snippy, but he couldn't let it go. 'We're part of a team, one that has to at least get along.' Not necessarily totally at ease, in their case.

She sighed, closed her book and looked at him. 'You're right. I apologise for being terse. I've also spent a lot of time on surgical wards and occasionally on gynaecology.'

'All of which fits in with what we're going to be doing in Vanuatu.'

'Yes, it does. How long have you been in Auckland?'

'I moved up there after I finished training in Otago.' He and Kelvin, plus another med school friend, had decided to go into practice together once they'd qualified. They'd agreed to give Auckland a try, and it was working out well being in a large city where no one knew him or, more specifically, who his father was—unlike in Nelson, where it was impossible to be anonymous. 'I worked in various hospitals around the country while specialising. Now I live on the North Shore, where I'm a partner in an obstetrics and gynaecology practice.' The North Shore wasn't a destitute part of the city by any means, but he hadn't gone there because of the middle-class residents. There'd been a need for specialists in their field and the three of them had decided to fill the gap.

She blinked. 'Good on you.'

'Did you train in Nelson?' This was a bit like pulling teeth, but now he'd started he didn't want to stop. If they were to ever move on and maybe become friends, they had to start somewhere.

Her thick, dark blond ponytail flicked over her shoulder as she shook her head, sending his hormones into overdrive. Just like he used to react to her all those years ago. 'I got out of town and went to Wellington.'

Why had she done that? 'Needed to spread your wings?'

Was that a smile? 'Heck, yes. Most of my friends headed to university, going in all directions, and I figured that after I left school it would be the freest time of my life to do whatever and go wherever I chose.'

'Yet now you're back in Nelson.'

Her face closed down. 'Yes. It's where home is.'

Something bad had happened. It was there in the way she'd just mentally pulled back, in how her fingers tightened around her book. Not his place to ask. Anyway, he doubted she'd answer even if he did. They weren't anywhere near close enough. He'd got further than he'd expected, so it might be time to sit back and relax, make the most of whatever was on offer from Tamara. They'd both grown up in the intervening years, had long-since changed from hormonal teenagers to sensible adults. At least *he'd* become sensible. She always had been; had a part-time job at the local supermarket throughout college, and was a member of a close group of friends who'd always studied hard, so he'd bet his last month's pay she was still sensible and would take nursing very seriously. There'd always been an undercurrent of serious determination to be good at anything she did, he recalled. Even when it came to telling him where to go. A smile slid over his mouth. Intriguing, to say the least.

Pushing in an earplug, he went through the available movies. Anything to pass the hours before touchdown in Port Vila. After the plane took off, that was. The door had been closed so they couldn't be far off leaving Auckland.

'Ladies and gentlemen.' A flight attendant interrupted his thoughts.

Knowing almost word for word what she'd say, he selected a movie instead, then had to wait until she'd finished her safety spiel before he could begin watching it. While he waited his eyes drifted sideways to Tamara. She'd been a stunning girl who'd caught his attention far too often. She hadn't been one to play on her looks, though, instead coming across as wanting people to like her for who she was on the inside. Yet he doubted there'd been a guy at college who hadn't had heated thoughts about how her curvy figure filled out the clothes she wore. She was always friendly and lots of fun—except with him.

She'd become even more attractive as an adult. Not quite the same daredevil look in her eyes as there used to be, but that could be because she was currently with people she didn't know—and him. One thing he could tell her was that he was no longer arrogant. She might've been the first to say he was, but she hadn't been the last, and he'd eventually taken it on board and done something to prove everyone wrong.

After his father's transgressions came to light, his friends had been quick to tell him the same and more, when once they'd been his best buddies. It had been gut-wrenching when they'd turned their backs on him. He'd struggled getting out of bed every morning to go to college, but had forced himself to, so he could become a doctor. Other than his grandparents, that goal had kept him on track more than anything else. Grandma and Grandad had been shocked over what their son had done, and had struggled to believe he was capable of conning people out of their hard-earned savings for his own benefit. They'd had nothing more to do with him right up until his death in prison from pneumonia.

The plane began to taxi out to the runway. Fergus settled further into his seat. There was never enough room for his long legs in cattle class, but he put up with the discomfort. First class was no longer his choice. He could afford it now, but after taking it for granted when he was younger, he wasn't prepared to be seen striding down the aisle to sit in a space that back here would hold nearly two people.

So, Tamara, I have learned a few things about myself and sucked up the lemon called arrogance. But he still owed her an apology and wouldn't feel entirely at ease around her until he gave it to her. Even then he doubted he'd be comfortable around her. It wasn't possible with everything that had happened to him in the years since he first saw her playing college netball, raising his hormone levels off the chart.

'Would you like something to drink with your lunch?' the flight attendant asked Tamara as she pressed the brake on the overloaded trolley.

'A glass of bubbles, thank you.' A celebration to this new adventure despite the man sitting beside her. Who knew? They might end up getting along perfectly fine. He hadn't been unfriendly so far.

Fergus paused the movie and removed the earplug. 'Salad looks all right.'

For airline food it looked passable, but then she wasn't too picky. 'Hopefully. At least the bubbles will be enjoyable.'

'I'll have a lager, thanks,' he told the stewardess, taking the tray she passed across. 'What made you decide to come on board with the medical volunteers, Tamara?'

He was full of questions. She'd go along with it for now. Anything to make things more comfortable between them. 'I thought it might be fun to do, instead of charging off to another country to go sightseeing for days on end.'

After her father had died, she'd been lost, and for a while had felt ambivalent about returning to her normal working life as though nothing had happened. Sashi had suggested she should get away and do something for herself. Something that meant more than having a cocktail on the beach. Something she could put her heart into.

'So I dug into information on medical volunteers, and here I am.' The photos of kids with their wide smiles as they were being treated for numerous problems had drawn her in and made her rush to apply to work for the aid program. When she was told she'd be working with a gynaecologist and not the children, she wasn't unhappy. She'd still be doing what she loved best—caring for people who needed her help. Then came the notes with Fergus's name, snagging her attention the moment she'd opened the letter. Was someone playing games with her? Stirring up trouble when it wasn't necessary? If so, it was up to her—and Fergus—to keep trouble out of the picture. They both had far more important things to do than get in a pickle over something long over.

'Be aware it's hard to say no after you've done it once. The people get to you with their gratitude and stoic attitudes.'

'I'm not surprised.'

'Done lots of travelling, have you?'

The questions were endless. What was he trying to do? She wasn't about to give him her life story. They'd never been friends, just circling teens using sharp retorts to try to put each other in their place. They were complete opposites in character. *Opposites attract, don't they?* Not in this case!

'I have.' She filled her mouth with chicken and salad and chewed slowly. She'd been to a few countries, worked in some of them since her marriage fell apart four years ago, when John had blamed his affair on her. Apparently, she was cold and unloving, so he'd had to look elsewhere for pleasure. He hadn't wanted their marriage to be over, he'd assured her. Tamara was the perfect woman to be the mother of the children they had started trying for, but he'd needed some fun on the side and he'd found that with an ex-girlfriend who didn't want kids. She'd finally accepted their marriage was over and, feeling grateful for not falling pregnant to John, she'd packed up her possessions along with her broken heart and walked away. Four years of marriage to a man she'd once adored, and she had nothing to show for it except a lot of distrust and a deep fear that John was right about her not being a warm, loving woman. Sashi and Dad had vehemently disagreed and said she was the warmest person they knew. But what did they know about her intimate life? Nothing.

It had been lonely adjusting to being single again. Her dreams and hopes for a happy future with John and their children had disappeared in an instant and she'd struggled with the transition.

Returning home to nurse her father had come at a time when she'd needed a change of direction. Her biological clock had started ticking. At thirty-five she was still young enough to have a baby, but she wasn't looking for a man to love because John had already proved she couldn't trust him to love her back. Neither did she want to be in her forties when, or if, she started a family. Her sister's children would be leaving high school by then.

'Favourite place you've visited?'

Weren't there other movies he could watch if the one he'd chosen wasn't to his liking? 'Paris.' She sipped her drink. 'No, actually—Sydney.'

'So you're a city girl at heart.'

'Not always. I worked in Sydney for a year and lived in the burbs.'

He smiled. 'Burbs. Now you're speaking like an Aussie.'

That smile struck hard where she least needed it. Right behind her ribs. *Warning, Tamara! This man still cranks up the heat like crazy.* She forked up another mouthful of chicken, determined not to continue this pointless conversation. Nor to be on the receiving end of another of those devastating smiles. They were trouble, which was the last thing she needed. She was here to look out for her patients, not get tied up in complicated knots with the one man she should only want to know as a colleague. Because he really was nothing like the type of man she was usually attracted to.

Of course, she wasn't giving him a chance to show how different he was now. It was obvious he wasn't the arrogant prat she'd once labelled him. That guy wouldn't be sitting cramped in the seat beside her sounding as though he wanted to know her better. He'd have been looking down his nose at the cargo pants and plain pink

T-shirt she wore. Fergus had changed and, so far, it seemed to be for the better. 'Did you go offshore when you were specialising?' A lot of Kiwi doctors did as part of their training.

He nodded. 'I went to Edinburgh. My grandmother's a Scot who came to New Zealand in her twenties,' he added as an explanation. 'I had an amazing time and was very tempted to stay, but—' He paused, staring at the back of the seat in front of him. 'My grandparents are getting on and they've done so much for me that I want to be around for them.'

Her determination to keep him at arm's length backed off some. 'Good on you.'

Fergus slid the earplug into his ear and pressed the screen in front of him. 'Thanks.'

A softness Tamara never expected to feel around Fergus slipped through her. This was definitely a different man to the one she remembered. He might've been able to turn her on with a look back then, but she'd never heard him speak with such affection about anyone before. Obviously, his grandparents meant a lot to him. She finished the bubbles and picked up her book, holding it awkwardly over the tray. Who would've thought she'd be thinking that? Were his kisses still as sensational? Nope—she definitely shouldn't be thinking *that*!

Fergus nudged her, his earplug in his hand. 'You do realise you're going to be working with me?' The earplug went back in place and the movie started again.

She nudged him back, waited until he was looking at her. 'It's fine.' She'd make sure of it for a comfortable working environment, if nothing else.

CHAPTER TWO

TAMARA HOPPED OUT of the van that they'd ridden in from the airport with Fergus at the wheel. She stared around. The hospital was single level, with hibiscus plants growing along the front wall, and lawns spread out to the sides with bushes and flowers swaying in the light breeze. 'It's lovely,' she sighed. Prettier than the photos had suggested. Hospitals weren't designed to be pretty. They usually had a severe 'this is where people help you through your pain' look.

'Our accommodation's only a couple of streets away,' Fergus said as Sarah and Tim joined them. 'I figured it wouldn't hurt to do a drive-by before going there.'

'As tempting as it is, I'm not going inside right now. Might get nabbed to help with something,' Tim said. 'Though I know that's why I'm here.'

'Tomorrow's soon enough to get started,' Tamara agreed.

'Let's sort out our rooms, then go for a wander around town,' Sarah suggested. 'I need to stretch my legs after sitting in the plane all that time.'

'Me, too.' Tamara clambered back into the van, thinking Fergus looked disappointed that they weren't going inside the hospital. 'You can drop us off and come back,' she said to him.

'No way. Despite the information I've read and the photos online, I expected something a little bigger.'

'Does it matter?' The notes had said the local medical service was basic, hence why they were here. There were waiting lists for minor to moderate surgeries that stood little chance of being shortened without outside help.

Fergus shrugged. 'Not really. I should've known better after other places I've volunteered at. I feel for the locals, although from what I've seen, they often don't seem too worried and just go along with what's available.'

'We don't know how lucky we are at home.'

'No, Tamara, we don't.' He got into the van and turned on the engine. 'Let's do this, guys.'

Two levels above the main street, the accommodation was basic but clean and spacious. Sun pelted the windows. Tamara gasped and opened them to let in what little breeze was available before opening her bag to grab a pair of shorts to change into. 'Unreal.'

'Keep the fly screens in place.' Fergus stood in her doorway. 'The mozzies will drive you nuts. You don't want to get malaria either. It's awful.'

She'd been vaccinated. 'You've had it?'

'Afraid so. I was vaccinated for it, but either the mozzies ignored it or the vaccine was out of date. I was in Thailand at the time.'

'Working?'

'I did one of my medical aid stints there.'

'Seems unfair you got malaria.'

He smiled. 'I agree.'

That blasted smile. She preferred he didn't look at her kindly, then she wouldn't get in a knot over him. 'What do we do about meals? I see there's a kitchen downstairs, but it doesn't look like it's been used in forever.'

'We'll mostly eat at the hospital during the day. I don't know about you and the others, but I like to eat locally for dinner.'

'Count me in. Um, what I meant was I'll probably do that too.'

'I get it, Tamara. I'll see you downstairs when you've changed into those shorts. The others will be there soon.' He was gone.

Leaving her feeling out of sorts. She'd started out thinking she'd be on edge around Fergus, and that he'd be rude and unpleasant all the time. So far that wasn't true. He was going out of his way to be friendly. How was she supposed to deal with that? *You could move on.* They didn't have to become best buddies, only needed to be civil at work and even away from it. Zipping up her denim shorts, she figured there was nothing to lose going with the friendly approach. It wasn't as though Fergus could belittle her. She was strong, knew her capabilities and got help when she wasn't managing something.

Swinging her bag over her shoulder, she locked the room and headed down to join the others. She was going to make this work. Four weeks wasn't forever, so why waste time being uptight and looking for trouble that might not exist? It would only spoil the enjoyment she planned on getting from being here.

As they wandered along the pavement where racks of clothes and other temptations for tourists stood outside shops, Fergus thought about the last volunteering trip he'd done in the Cook Islands. He'd enjoyed meeting the locals at the hospital and at the various markets he'd frequented for meals. It'd been hard to pack up and leave, but he'd needed to get back home to New Zealand. The easy lifestyle had really appealed, but he knew he'd soon tire of it and be looking for more to keep him occupied. Anyway, part of setting up the clinic with his friends was so he could settle permanently for the first time since leaving Nelson to go to Dunedin.

Keeping busy when not studying or working had been what'd got him through the years after his world had been turned upside down. His grandfather had pointed out that while he was not responsible for his father's crimes, or the life his father had given him, his future was his to sort out, no one else's. His grandparents had been there for him whenever he stumbled, as he was certain they'd have been for his father when he was growing up. He'd never found out why his father had done what he had. He came from a middle-class background, never wanted for much, and yet obviously it hadn't been enough. Had it been greed? Or a desire to be admired for being wealthy?

Even now, thinking about those months after he'd learned what had been going on and all the lies his father had told anyone who'd listen to him, Fergus shuddered with horror and remorse. Not because his life had changed so drastically and fast, although that had been shocking at the time, but because of the people who'd lost so much because of Jim Collier's actions.

Despite not knowing where the money that'd paid for his lavish lifestyle had come from, when it became clear what had been going on, he'd wanted to raid a bank and pay everyone back. He grimaced. If only it could've been that easy to rectify everything. One night before he went to trial, his father had said that if people were foolish enough to hand their money over to him, then they deserved to lose it. The next day, when Fergus had asked him if he'd meant it, his father had denied saying anything so stupid. In fact, he'd always denied all the accusations, and had until the day he'd died. Hence why Fergus had refused to have anything more to do with the man who'd sired him. If he couldn't even admit what he'd done, then he hadn't deserved his son's support.

As for his mother, it wasn't an easy relationship either. He believed she'd been so embarrassed she'd married a criminal that she couldn't face anyone she knew. On the other hand, she'd quickly found someone else; they'd been married nearly ten years now and seemed happy.

All of which made Fergus wonder about love and how anyone could really be certain they'd found it. Or how it could last through thick and thin. Caution was his middle name when it came to getting too involved with women. He'd once come close to being married, had actually believed he'd found the *one*.

He'd met Harriet at university in Dunedin and they'd hit it off straight away. She'd said his past didn't bother her one iota when he'd opened up about it, that it was Fergus she loved, not his father. When he proposed two years later, Harriet accepted. He couldn't believe how lucky he was. Until Harriet took him to Wellington to meet her parents. They recognised his family name and immediately knew who his father was. Appalled, they'd convinced Harriet that by marrying Fergus, her career in media would be badly affected, and that any children they might have would need to learn to live with what their grandfather had done. Harriet had returned the engagement ring he'd had specially made, unable to look him in the eye. He'd felt vulnerable ever since. Another mark against his father.

He'd let Harriet go without an argument. No point trying to hold on to her when he wasn't right for her. She'd further rubbed salt into his broken heart when she quickly found a new partner, who was a CEO of an international forestry company, and married him.

Once again, he'd misread the person closest to him. Harriet's desertion had hurt him as much as, if not more than, his father and his former friends had. It showed how useless he was at reading people correctly, at understanding them. He obviously couldn't see past the faces they wore to what was really going on in their heads.

There were exceptions. He knew he could love and trust his grandparents. Same went for Kelvin. But could he trust anyone else ever again? He wanted to. Big time. He knew he'd missed out on so much by protecting himself, but there were only so many knocks he could take. Nowadays his relationships were only about fun and were always short-lived. Nothing long-term in the cards for him. He was certain of that.

Light, happy laughter caught his attention. Tamara.

She stood at a stand of sunhats wearing a wide-brimmed straw hat.

Sarah held out another one. 'Try this. No pink elephants in sight.'

'Aww. I like elephants.' Tamara swapped hats, tugging her ponytail through the fastening at the back. 'What do you think?'

'Suits you,' he said instinctively, and winced. The question hadn't been directed at him.

Tamara grinned. 'You reckon?'

'He's right. It does,' Sarah agreed.

He'd said his bit; he wasn't saying any more. But—'Go on, buy it. The shop owner's looking hopeful.'

'You've got me.' She headed inside to pay for the hat.

Watching her, he felt unusually warm. No surprise she'd put her hand in her pocket to help a local. What was a surprise was how much he still liked her, even though their relationship was touch and go at the moment. She'd always been a friendly girl ready to give a hand to anyone needing it, so nursing was right up her alley. Why hadn't he understood what that meant all those years ago? He might've been a horny teenager, but letting his ego get in the way of getting to know a girl properly, beyond a kiss or two, had caused problems with Tamara. Because there hadn't been any kisses for them. She'd made sure of it. Until the ball, when they'd both imploded with long-suppressed desire. If his so-called friends hadn't turned up when they did, who knew what they might've got up to. He badly regretted not sticking up for her. He also regretted not apologising to her at the time. Yep, definitely an egotist back then. Not so much now. Did he show Tamara that or let her think he hadn't changed? Keep her at a distance? Somehow, he felt he might need to do that if he was to get through the coming weeks without becoming drawn to her all over again.

Tamara walked out of the shop wearing the sunhat, with a wide smile lighting up her face. 'Who's next to buy something?'

A challenge if ever he'd heard one. He didn't need a sunhat. Or anything else, really. He travelled lightly. Had done since he'd left school and Nelson behind him. But he was here to support the locals.

'I'm going next door to look at T-shirts.' Tim had beaten him to it.

'Me too.' He followed the other doctor.

'We've only just arrived. At this rate we'll need extra suitcases to get everything back home.' Sarah laughed.

'There's a shop selling those too,' Tamara replied with a grin.

Turning around, Fergus sucked in the sight of her happy face and wanted to freeze it in place. She looked stunning when she relaxed. Not that she didn't look lovely any time. An image of her in that aqua-coloured, floor-length, body-hugging dress at the college ball popped up. She'd mesmerised him. No other girl had made the sparks fly as high and bright as Tamara had when he'd kissed her. Why hadn't he stood up for her and told his mates where to go? He'd hadn't forgotten the hurt in her eyes, followed by fury, before she'd told him exactly what she thought of him. It had been the first time he'd realised he wasn't a gift to all females, that they weren't all going to fall for him in a blink. Yes, he had been an egotistical know-it-all, but he'd improved. Hopefully, a lot. Over the years he'd certainly worked hard to turn himself around. Being with Tamara for the next few weeks would soon show him if he'd succeeded or not.

After strolling the length of the street before heading to the sea front with everyone carrying shopping bags, the four of them turned into a café bar and sat at a table on the covered deck overlooking the harbour. 'This is magic,' Tamara commented, looking around. To think last night she'd been staying in a hotel at Auckland Airport with a view of the terminal, and now here she was, looking out over the boats tied up to jetties and moorings with people she was just getting to know. That included Fergus. She didn't know him, not this version, anyway, and she had to admit she wouldn't mind changing that. If she could trust him to be different.

'What does everyone want to drink?' he asked.

'Beer.'

'Beer.'

'Beer.'

'Guess that's four beers then,' Fergus teased with a grin. 'I'll get these.'

'You don't have to do that,' Tamara said. 'I'll get mine.' She wasn't going to be obliged to Fergus for anything.

'I'd like to, okay?' The grin was gone, replaced by a stubborn look.

She hadn't meant to cause trouble and felt like she'd been put on the back foot. 'Thank you, Fergus. That'd be lovely.'

'Good answer.' He headed for the bar, leaving her feeling awkward with the other two obviously wondering what was going on.

Dredging up a smile, she said, 'I overreacted. Must be more tired than I realised.'

Sarah nodded. 'It wasn't a long-haul flight, but with getting up so early, along with the time changes, it does affect us. I struggle with flying no matter what the distance.'

'Not good.' She had to relax and make the most of this trip. Learn to cope with losing her dad after he'd lost his fierce battle to beat the cancer. It was hard pretending she could manage without him to talk to whenever she needed a shoulder to lean against. He'd been the best dad she could ask for, always supporting her and Sashi, no matter what. Even when he'd been grieving for Mum he'd given them both so much of himself. They'd been very lucky, and she hoped she'd been as strong and good to him in the last months of his life. She shook her head. She was deliberately getting sidetracked when she should be enjoying Sarah and Tim's company, *and* Fergus's.

'Here you go, folks.' Fergus was back, placing ice-cold bottles of beer before each of them. 'Do either of you ladies want a glass?'

Tamara shook her head. 'Not for me.'

'Me neither,' replied Sarah.

Fergus sat on the only available stool at their table, beside Tamara.

She smiled. Of course it was the only stool available. Though he could've taken it to the other end of the table, she was glad he hadn't, which didn't make a lot of sense, other than she did want to get to know him better. Who knew? She might come to like him a lot. Wouldn't that be interesting? Only hours ago at Auckland Airport, she'd been in a knot about seeing him and remembering all his awful traits, and now here she was, thinking she wanted to learn more about him. A laugh spilled out. She was bonkers.

'What's funny?' Fergus asked.

'Nothing.' Like she was telling.

'So you just laugh for the hell of it?' There was a twinkle in his eyes, so he wasn't getting uptight with her.

'Sometimes. On the good days anyway. Today is one of those.'

'What really made you decide to volunteer?'

She hesitated. How far did she go in revealing herself? Did she tell him about losing her father, the need to rediscover her mojo?

'You don't have to answer if you don't want to.'

Looking at Fergus, she saw he genuinely meant it and wasn't trying to play nice. 'I lost my father four months ago and needed to do something different to get back on track. I hope this will help towards that.'

Fergus made to lay his hand over hers, then abruptly pulled back. 'I'm sorry to hear that. It must be hard waking up every morning knowing he's gone.'

'Very.' *Stop. That's enough.*

'So that's why you're still in Nelson.' His hand wound around his bottle.

'Yes. I'd been working in Greymouth before. After Dad died, I stayed on in Nelson to be near my sister. She's got a husband, and kids too.' But old habits didn't go away. Supporting Sashi came naturally.

'You're lucky to have her.' He took a long mouthful of beer.

'I am.' She and Sashi had always been close, and were brought closer together when their mother died. They'd missed her beyond description and had remained close ever since. Being the big sister—by eighteen months—Tamara had stepped into their mother's shoes. Sashi had been comfortable with Tamara being the boss. Their father had given her space to do so while making sure she didn't get too carried away. He also kept them safe and strong and able to cope. How she missed him. There was a constant ache in her chest now. But she'd come here to get back on her feet, not dwell on her loss. Picking up her beer, she followed Fergus's example and got on with enjoying the company.

* * *

The pain in Tamara's eyes when she mentioned her father made Fergus hurt for her. They'd obviously been incredibly close. There'd been no mention of her mother. There could be any number of reasons for that, but he wasn't asking. If he'd known about her father, he wouldn't have asked why she'd come to Vanuatu, thereby causing pain to surface when she'd been relaxed. Hopefully she'd get back to enjoying herself soon. He tapped her bottle with his. 'Here's to Vanuatu and doing all we can for the people who need us.'

She tapped back, giving him a small smile. 'I agree.'

'So do we,' Tim said from the other side of the table.

Fergus swallowed. For a moment, he'd forgotten Tim and Sarah were here as well. Showed how much Tamara distracted him. 'Sounds like we're all on the same page.'

'As if we wouldn't be.' Tim grinned. 'We didn't come here for an island holiday.'

'I wonder what the resorts are like,' Tamara said. 'I understand this is quite a popular tourist destination.'

'Judging by the number of people in here, I'd say you're right.' If Vanuatu was similar to the other island nations he'd been to, the locals would rarely come to the bars and cafés. These people would be tourists or on short-term contracts for road works and the like.

Sarah stood up. 'I know it's early, but I'm getting some menus. The airplane food wasn't exactly wonderful and I'm feeling peckish. Not to mention exhausted.'

'You're always peckish,' Tim teased.

'No menu for you, then?'

'Bring me one in case I change my mind.' He laughed.

'Or I could just order the burger and chips you always have.'

These two had a great relationship. He'd known them for a couple of years and had never seen them snap at each other. Naturally, like any couple, they'd have their moments, but nothing to suggest either one had to prove they were better than the other. Exactly the sort of relationship he'd want if he was ever game enough to try again. Which he wasn't, he reminded himself as he took a sideways glance at Tamara. Small and neat with boundless energy, she could snag his attention even when he wanted to ignore her. Odd how that was the last thing he wanted to do at the moment. They were getting along just fine, not too close, not too distant. If they kept this up, work would go well over the coming weeks. It might even help him come to terms with how Tamara still made him look at her twice when he least expected it.

She was very attractive with her long blond hair tied in that ponytail, and those aqua eyes drew him in in ways he used to ignore but wasn't rushing to do now. She was still short, barely coming up to his shoulder, which suddenly made him yearn to swing her up into his arms and hold her tight, to protect her from anything life threw her way.

'What are you ordering, Fergus?' Tim asked in a welcome interruption. What on earth had he just been thinking?

He hadn't looked at the menu. 'I'll have a burger.'

'Fish, beef or chicken?' Tim asked with a wink, knowing damned well his thoughts were miles away. He probably had a good idea what Fergus had been thinking about too.

'Fish.' With another cold beer. He was getting far too hot, and it wasn't all to do with the tropical temperature.

CHAPTER THREE

NEXT MORNING, FERGUS DROVE them to the hospital in time for their meeting with the CEO. When they walked into reception, a crowd of staff was waiting for them.

A tall, well-built man stepped forward with his hand extended. 'Welcome to our hospital. I'm Kaikea, the CEO.' He shook hands with Fergus, Tim, and then the women. 'We are so happy to have you all here.'

Let's hope that continues, Fergus thought as he looked around. He knew from previous experience that most staff would be pleased to have the voluntary service working within their hospitals to help them catch up with a backlog of patients. But not all would feel that way, thinking their abilities were in question, which wasn't the case. 'I think I can speak for the four of us when I say we're also pleased to be here.' He glanced around and found Tamara surrounded by women in scrubs, most likely nurses she'd work alongside. She wore a wide smile, reminding him of when he'd first seen her at college, laughing and chatting with a group of girls. Immediately he'd felt interested, which, as a teenage boy, had meant pretending he hadn't noticed her. There wasn't much he'd forgotten about Tamara, though. Why? It wasn't as though he'd carried a flame for her ever since.

The problems he'd faced after the ball had squashed any hope of repeating that kiss they'd shared.

Kaikea clapped loudly. 'Okay, back to work, everyone. I'm sure these people want to see where they'll be working before the first patients start arriving for their appointments.'

Sarah and Tamara headed towards Kaikea, eager to get on with what they were here for. Fergus knew that feeling. The urge to get stuck in helping the women who needed his attention to turn around their lives was strong. The resident gynaecologist had taken ill six months ago and hadn't returned from treatment in Australia, so when the volunteer's commission had called him for help, he'd been quick to come on board.

'I'll talk to you in my office first, then Aisi here can take you through to Theatre and introduce you to the anaesthetists.' Kaikea headed for a door on their left. 'Aisi is our head surgeon and runs Theatre.'

They followed Kaikea, who appeared to be in a hurry to get this over with.

'Is this how it usually goes?' Tamara asked quietly.

'It's different everywhere I've been. The one common denominator is that we're needed and not resented.'

'That's a relief. I'd hate to be working with people who didn't want us here.'

For him that wasn't always so easy. 'My biggest concern is having to get very personal with women who aren't used to male doctors prodding their anatomy.'

Tamara's eyes widened. 'That never occurred to me.'

'That's because you're a woman,' he said. 'They'll be fine with you. You might have to make things a little easier for me as we go.'

'No problem. I hope I get along with them well enough so that everything goes smoothly.'

Good answer.

'What did you expect?' she asked.

'Did I say that out loud?'

She smirked. 'You did.'

'In here.' Kaikea indicated an office large enough to hold a banquet. 'Take a seat.'

Once seated Tim said, 'I'm the general surgeon. I understand we're meeting our first patients this morning.'

'That's correct. There're offices available near the reception area for you.' Loud knocking interrupted him. 'Come in.'

A woman burst in. 'Kaikea, is the ob/gyn guy here? A girl giving birth has lost consciousness in the labour room.'

Fergus was on his feet in a flash. 'Coming.'

Tamara was right behind him. 'So am I.'

Of course she was. Go Tamara. 'Sorry, Kaikea, but this comes first.'

'No problem. Catch up when you're free. Joena, please take these people to your patient.'

'I'm a midwife,' Joena told them as they hurried along the corridor. 'Nurse Isa's with my patient, but she doesn't often work with women in childbirth.'

'Fill me in on everything,' Fergus said. 'Was the birth going normally until she lost consciousness?'

'Pretty much. Inina's seventeen and had been complaining of extreme pain for hours. I couldn't find anything out of order and put the complaints down to her age. It's not uncommon with the younger mothers.'

'Where is the pain? In the birth passage? Or the abdomen?'

'Both. I wondered if baby was the wrong way round but when I checked I found the head in the right position.' Joena pushed open a door. 'Isa, here's the doctor from New Zealand.'

Fergus nodded to the woman standing at the side of the bed watching the monitor closely. 'Hello, I'm Fergus, and this is Tamara, a nurse with our team.'

'Hello. Thank you for coming so quickly.' Isa stepped back to allow him nearer the patient. 'Inina, here's a doctor to help you.'

The girl didn't move.

Still out of it, Fergus presumed. He raised her eyelids. Definitely unconscious. Why? Syncope? Quite possibly.

On the other side of the bed Tamara was taking the girl's pulse. 'Slow.'

That went with syncope, as did the low heart rate showing on the bedside monitor. 'How long has she been unconscious?'

Joena looked at her watch. 'Nearly ten minutes.'

'It could be she's suffered a syncope. If so, she should start coming round any minute. In the meantime, I'd like to check baby's position.' He went to the end of the bed and lifted away the thin blanket covering the girl before crouching down. 'Nearly there.' He looked to Tamara. 'Any change?'

'Pulse is beginning to rise.'

He nodded. 'Good. We'll let nature take its course.' He'd be keeping a steady watch over things until baby popped out. Straightening up, he turned to Joena. 'You know about syncope?'

The worried nurse looked at her patient. 'I learned about it while training, but this is the first time I've dealt with it. I was frightened there was something terrible going on. That's why I ran to find you.'

'You did the right thing. Better to get help than not.'

'She's coming round,' Tamara said.

Inina groaned as her lower body tightened.

'Another contraction. How far apart are they?' he asked.

'Last time I checked they were just over two minutes apart,' Joena told him.

Inina gave another long groan.

'I think we can expect junior to make an appearance very shortly.' He stepped back. 'You see to the birth, Joena.' The midwife looked rattled. He suspected she needed a boost to her confidence after seeing her patient lose consciousness.

Glancing at Tamara, he saw a flicker of surprise cross her face. So she still thought he was that arrogant guy she'd known before. *Thanks a lot, Tamara. You sure know how to rub in the past.* He probably deserved it, but still. 'It's the right thing to do for both Joena and her patient,' he said rather curtly.

Tamara locked her eyes on him. 'It is. I like that you understand. Not all doctors do.'

She hadn't denied what she'd been thinking. He relaxed. 'Seems I'm not beyond surprising you.' There might be more surprises to come, hopefully even better ones.

Her eyes widened, then she smiled. A genuine smile aimed totally at him. 'Seems you could be right.'

He'd take those smiles any time. They lightened his heart and made him feel good about everything. 'Right, let's get on with delivering a baby. What a way to start our time here.'

'The best, I reckon.'

As long as nothing went wrong, he would agree with Tamara on that. 'Joena, how do you want to do this? You happy taking over the birthing?'

The midwife looked surprised, no doubt also expecting him to assume the lead. Well, they both could think again. He was no longer that guy.

'I think that's best, as Inina knows me,' Joena agreed.

'Is there someone to be with her when baby arrives?' Tamara asked.

'Her mother had to pop out but should be back soon.' Joena replaced Fergus. 'Inina, can you hear me?'

'It hurts a lot,' she murmured.

Tamara took the girl's hand in hers. 'The mothers I've been with when they had their babies told me that you forget the pain the moment you hold your baby in your arms.'

Inina's eyes widened. 'Is that true?'

'I think so. I haven't had a baby myself, but I saw a few births while I was training to become a nurse.'

Fergus watched Tamara calm the girl as easily as he'd seen a mother giving her child an ice cream when they'd been stung by a bee. The ice cream had been a huge lure, and so it seemed was Tamara's quiet confidence.

Inina tensed and cried out as a contraction gripped her.

'Push, Inina,' Joena urged.

Tamara held the girl's hands. 'Come on. You can do it. Push as hard as possible.'

Fergus felt useless. There was little to say or do except keep an eye on the screen where Inina's heart rate was being monitored. After the syncope episode, he wasn't going back to the meeting in case something went wrong. It shouldn't, but he'd been a doctor long enough to know that didn't mean it wouldn't.

Another contraction. They were coming fast now.

'Deep breaths, Inina,' Tamara said quietly. 'You're doing brilliantly.'

Her voice was soft and encouraging. He could listen to it for ages. It was new to him when it came to Tamara. But then he didn't usually obsess over women's voices. He was starting to see her quite differently in many ways. She still got fired up at him as she used to when he said something she disagreed with, but he couldn't remember her ever smiling at him so beautifully as she had earlier. A strong reason to remain aloof, he warned himself.

'You're nearly there, Inina,' the midwife told the girl.

'Do you know if it's a boy or girl?' Tamara asked.

'Boy,' gasped Inina.

'Have you got a name for him?'

'No. Ow!'

'Here we go. Push hard as you can, Inina. Baby's nearly here.'

'It hurts too much.'

Fergus watched Tamara brush Inina's hair back from her sweaty face. 'Deep breath, then push. That's it. Keep pushing, more and more. That's it. You're doing great.'

'Baby's here,' the midwife said just minutes later. 'A beautiful little boy.'

Tamara handed her a handful of wipes to clear the boy's face so he could breathe freely, then he watched her awed expression as Inina held out her arms for her son, her eyes almost popping out of her head.

'My baby,' Inina cried.

The door burst open and a woman rushed in. 'Is that my grandson? Oh, he's beautiful.' She rushed to the side of the bed and sat close to her daughter, gazing in wonder at the baby.

Time to get out of here. They weren't needed anymore. He looked to Tamara and received a nod.

'Well done, Inina. We'll see you later,' she said quietly and joined him at the door.

They walked out together, closing the new family in the small room. 'That was great,' he said.

She pinched her wrist. 'I always get goosebumps when I witness a new soul arrive in the world. It is the best part of nursing, though I usually have little to do with babies in my work.'

'It's not a field you'd choose to go into?'

'No. I'm not sure why. I like helping people get better, and usually babies arrive just fine.'

'I hate the days when they don't. Even when I've handed over responsibility to a paediatrician, I can't stop worrying about the outcome.' He was talking too much, but then why not? They had shared a good experience, so there was no reason to go on alert while chatting with Tamara.

'Is that why you chose gynaecology over obstetrics? Most specialists do both.'

'I'm trained in both but lean more towards the gynaecological side.' A lot more. 'It involves more surgical procedures and less getting up in the middle of the night to deliver a baby.' He'd gone for light-hearted, suddenly aware he had no qualms about that around Tamara. If she thought he was being flippant, then so be it.

'Why that field over any other one? You could have chosen anything.'

She thought he could be an expert in whatever he'd chosen to do? His shoulders lifted slightly. 'How well do any of us know what's out there until we're in amongst it? I got a kick out of seeing babies come into the world, which made me realise I liked working in a positive field, though I still didn't want to be a full-time obstetrician. Cutting out fibroids or doing hysterectomies doesn't sound like fun for patients, but I'm helping them improve their quality of life, and I like that.'

Of course he'd be helping patients in any area of medicine, but something about motherhood and mothers he'd seen in his first years of training had snagged his attention and made him think about what he really wanted to qualify in. He'd initially considered cardiology, but that had been the other version of himself, who'd only wanted to be a cardiologist because they were widely thought of as the crème de la crème in the medical world, not the Fergus who was struggling to overcome his father's betrayal and find himself. Finally, he'd woken up and gone for what he'd felt was right for his new persona.

'I'm glad. It would be terrible to put all the effort required into qualifying in a field you weren't suited to.' She opened the door and stepped inside.

He followed, his head spinning and his eyes on those rounded cheeks filling Tamara's light trousers. She understood him. Not something he'd expected so soon after meeting up with her again, if at all.

Sarah looked up from a file she was reading. 'How'd it go? I presume all good or neither of you would be here.'

'As I thought, the girl had suffered a syncope episode

but came round not long after we joined them,' Fergus told her. 'Then she gave birth to a lovely wee boy.'

'An absolutely beautiful boy who I wouldn't call wee, though for an islander he might be a tad on the small side.' Tamara was grinning like someone had given her a bar of chocolate. 'It's a great start to being here.'

To be followed by surgeries on women who were no longer having babies for all sorts of reasons. But he'd be relieving them of pain and discomfort, which had to be good. He pulled out a chair. 'Has Kaikea handed over his office to us for the rest of the morning?'

Tim shook his head. 'He had urgent business in town so suggested we remain here to go through files and get up to speed on what's ahead for us.'

'While you're doing that I'll go and suss out the hospital, get the idea of the general layout.' Tamara turned to him. 'Unless you need me here?'

'No, you do that. I'll make notes on each patient. You can get up to speed before we see them. While you're working with me most of the time, Tim might occasionally need your assistance too.'

'No problem. I like to be kept busy.'

No surprise. This woman used to be constantly on the go whenever he'd seen her at college events. Some guys had called her the energiser. Watching her on the netball court had been like witnessing a whirlwind tearing up leaves on the lawn. Horny teens that they were, he and his mates were often there to get a look at the girls in their tight sports shorts and T-shirts. Tamara had stood out as one of the hottest. His pants were tightening just thinking about her now. How crazy was that? Many years had passed since he'd seen her in her sports gear and he was still getting hard? Hell, he was thirty-five. Those memories shouldn't be revving him up now!

Grabbing a pile of files, he opened the top one and focused on the information in front of him. He had to shove those ridiculous thoughts away, not just for now but for the month ahead.

Isa Bule, thirty-three, large fibroid over uterus.

Focus, man. It took a little while, but finally he did.

Tamara couldn't deny the skip in her step as she walked along the corridor looking for the Theatre suite. Seeing that baby boy arrive had been awesome. Inina had looked stunned, then thrilled as she reached for her son. What would it be like to bring a child into the world? Your own child. Not that it could be anyone else's, of course. One day she was going to have a baby and raise him or her with all the love that was in her heart. One day.

She slowed down, caught by a longing so deep it frightened her. She'd been thinking about having a family quite a bit lately. Since John, she hadn't considered finding another man to love and have a family with. After John telling her she lacked sexual creativity in bed, the thought of anyone else saying the same thing had scared her, so remaining single had kept her from being hurt again. She also believed having a child on her own wouldn't be fair. She knew what it was like to grow up without her mother around, but she'd at least had seven years with her and had some wonderful memories to go on with. Hugs and kisses when she'd hurt herself, stories at bedtime, hot cocoa when she got home from school in winter, being told off for eating too many biscuits before dinner. The images were endless and had often helped her to go to sleep in the years after her mother had died. Her father had also been so loving and helpful, teaching her how to find her way through life's mishaps. Her child could not miss out on having a male role model. So, no baby for her, despite the need filling her.

'Are you Tamara or Sarah?' A young woman in scrubs stood in front of her. 'I saw you when you arrived in reception with the doctors. I'm Carrie, a nurse.'

'Hi, Carrie. I'm Tamara. I'm going to look around and familiarise myself with Theatre and wards. Sarah's joining me shortly.'

'Let me show you where everything's kept. I work in Theatre most of the time. It's fairly straightforward.'

'You're not a local, are you?'

Carrie's fair skin and blond hair gave it away, and if Tamara had any doubt, Carrie's accent sounded Australian.

'I grew up in Darwin. I came over here for a holiday with some nursing friends and never went home again. I met and married a tourist operator who'd come over from Queensland to start up a fishing tours business. We intend returning to Oz someday, but it's been five years since we first said that, and we've got no plans to do anything about it yet.'

'Hey, if you're happy, why change anything?'

'I agree. Right, in here.' Carrie led her into a small room off to the side and handed her a set of scrubs. Once dressed, they headed into the operating room, where two operations were underway. 'I won't introduce you to anyone at the moment.'

Tamara agreed. 'They wouldn't thank us for interrupting. Show me where all the equipment's kept and where the recovery room is. Here's Sarah. Perfect timing.'

An hour later, after checking out every last detail and then learning where the wards were and which was which, Tamara and Sarah went to find the men. They were in the canteen eating sandwiches and mangos.

Fergus glanced up as she approached, his serious face in place. 'Grab yourself something to eat. We've got a busy afternoon ahead, starting shortly.'

'Yes, boss.'

His head shot up, a frown appearing. 'Tamara, I'm serious.'

'So am I,' she retorted, wondering why the mood swing. 'Are you still meeting patients to discuss procedures with them?' He had indicated that he'd be doing that earlier but something might've changed.

'Yes, there're ten on today's list.'

That was quite a few when he had to discuss with each woman what he'd be doing and what came afterwards for them. It meant a heavy Theatre schedule in the following days. From what she'd been told when being interviewed to come over here, their patients wouldn't be as prepared as those back home and everything took longer. But, 'We'll manage.' Though it wasn't up to her how he got through the list. She was here to take in the details and reassure each woman they'd be fine, along with helping Fergus in Theatre.

Fergus stared at her as though she was an alien.

'I'll do all I can to help,' she snapped.

'I know you will.' The frown intensified. 'Get something to eat. It's been a while since breakfast.'

Many hours if her growling stomach was an indicator. When she returned to the table, the others were in deep conversation. Not wanting to interrupt and receive another frown from Fergus, she concentrated on eating.

'What's Theatre like compared to home?' Tim asked as she cut into a mango.

Since Sarah had a mouthful of sandwich, Tamara answered, 'Basic, but as far as I could see, everything you need is there. Two ops were going on and the areas were constantly being cleaned.'

'I'm going to take a look before I see my first patient,' Tim said. 'It's important to know where everything is in case something goes wrong.'

'I'm coming with you.' Fergus stood up to follow Tim out of the room.

Licking her fingers, Tamara savoured the delicious flavour of the mango and waited, suspecting Sarah had something to say about Fergus.

Pushing her plate aside, Sarah put her elbows on the table. 'You all right to work with Fergus? Or should I swap places with you tomorrow?' Straight to the point.

'I'm fine working with him.'

'Why the sudden atmosphere? He got uptight a few minutes ago and you tensed up in reaction.'

'We knew each other a long time back, but I'm sure he's told you that.' She had no idea what he might've said to Tim and Sarah, but she doubted he'd have gone into depth about how they'd reacted around each other at college.

Sarah nodded. 'He mentioned it in passing.'

So he hadn't said a lot. She'd keep it brief too. She wasn't looking for trouble. She liked Sarah, and Tim. *And* Fergus. Despite his recent grumpiness. 'We had a falling out at college that wasn't easy to put behind us, but it's in the past and now we're working together, which is good for both of us.'

'Glad you see it that way because you're both special. Having a problem between you wouldn't be great for anyone.'

'Thanks, Sarah.' Sarah's comment made her feel better considering how little they knew each other. 'When Fergus was short with me, I wondered if something had stressed him when he was going through his patients' files.'

Sarah drained her glass of water. 'From the last time I did this, I know the first days are often stressful for the doctors. The systems are different in lots of ways to what they're used to back home, and so much relies on getting it right. The staff can be wary because they think we might put them down over any little thing. Maybe Fergus is on edge about that.' Standing up, Sarah collected her plate and glass. 'I'm joining Tim and his patients. See you later.'

Leaning back in her chair, Tamara watched Sarah leave the room. The other woman had been open and friendly but obviously didn't suffer tiffs and nonsense at work. 'Not that I can blame her.' She didn't either. Tamara downed the last of her orange juice. Now she'd caught up with Fergus and spent some time talking, eating, shopping with him and the other two, she knew she didn't want to return to thinking he was an arrogant know-it-all. He had changed. To the point she barely recognised him. Except for those good looks. They were the same, though better.

Back in Theatre she found Sarah with the men discussing details with an anaesthetist.

'Ian, this is Tamara,' Fergus said at one point. 'She's a nurse and will be working mostly with me.'

'Hello, Tamara. Saw you sussing things out in here earlier. It's very basic but everything you need is available.'

'Hello, Ian.' She nodded. 'From what I saw it all looks shipshape.'

'We're seeing our first patient in ten minutes,' Fergus told Tamara. 'Let's find our office and see what's there.'

'Sure.' *We*, as in their patient, not only his, which he'd be entitled to think as he was the doctor. 'There're two rooms near the reception area that are for the team to use.'

'Good. How are you finding things so far?'

A lot better than she'd expected. 'It's pretty basic, but everyone's eager to help us, which goes a long way to making me more comfortable.'

'There might be a bit of one-upmanship going on. It's not uncommon in most hospitals. I doubt it'll be any different here.' Fergus turned to her with a small smile. 'I try hard not to be one of those people, Tamara.'

'I'm sure you do.' Totally. From what she'd seen he was relaxed around everybody. What's more, it came naturally. 'I mean that.'

His smile widened. 'Thanks. It took some work, but I think I've made it.'

Now *her* eyes widened. Did he really say that? 'You've really changed, Fergus.'

'For the better?'

'Absolutely.' As far as she could tell, anyway.

'I'll buy you a drink for that.'

She couldn't help it. She laughed. 'You're on.' So much for considering backing out of coming here once she'd learned Fergus was on the team. It was turning out to be the best thing to happen to her in a long while. He was quite the man to tickle her interest now he wasn't all about himself She had to admit he'd always drawn her attention, but now he was waking her up in ways she'd never expected. Not only because he was a hunk. Sexy as all hell, good looking, and his smiles were decimating. Kissed like the devil. Not that she'd kissed one of those, but that night of the ball had showed her what she'd been missing out on by deliberately ignoring him.

She had worked hard to deny how he made her want him. She wasn't used to retreating from people, other than back when they were sparring with each other. Sparring? That fit perfectly with what had gone on. Some verbal jabs had been harder and hurt more than others, but they had been set on pressing each other's buttons for a reaction.

This trip was turning out to be interesting in more ways than she'd expected. She hadn't thought about her father for hours at a time, which gave her room to breathe. She'd never stop thinking about him on and off, but since his death she'd hoped to finally be able to shake the fear that she wasn't ever going to have someone special in her life again. Sashi was there for her, as were her friends, but to have someone at her side permanently would be wonderful. If he could accept her for who she was and love her back equally, a man to be partners in life with.

'These the rooms?' Fergus stopped outside an open door off the corridor and waved his hand at the row of doors.

'Yes.'

'Let's bring our first patient in and get things underway.' He held out a stack of files. 'That's the order I'm going to see them in. Everything's on computer, but they like handwritten notes here.'

'Okay.' She took a quick look through the first file to get a general idea of why the woman was here. 'Fibroids?'

'Yes. They seem to be the most prevalent cases I'll be dealing with. A downside to not having a permanent gynaecologist on site.'

'Surely that's the same for everyone you're seeing?'

'You're right. Again. Okay, let's get this show on the road. You can bring in Mrs Tari now.'

Out in reception, Tamara looked around at the expectant faces and saw a couple of nervous-looking women at one end of the long seat. 'Mrs Tari?'

Sure enough, one of the two women stood up. 'Hello.'

'Hello. I'm Tamara, and I'm a nurse. I'm pleased to meet you. I'll be with you all the time you're talking to Doctor Collier.'

'Thank you.'

'Do you have someone here who you want to come with you?'

Mrs Tari nodded to the woman who'd been sitting beside her looking just as nervous. 'Emele.'

Tamara stepped nearer to her. 'Hello, Emele. Pleased to meet you too.'

'Thank you.'

'Let's go to the room where Doctor Collier's waiting for you. If you have any questions, don't hesitate to ask.

He's very kind and will explain everything so you understand.'

The women followed her in silence, Mrs Tari obviously not looking forward to being examined—possibly because the doctor was male. She'd do her best to help dispel any discomfort the lady had. After introducing Fergus, she closed the door and indicated the women should sit.

'Call me Fergus, ladies. Now, Mrs Tari, I understand you have a big fibroid on your uterus. Do you know what this is?'

'Yes. My doctor told me, and my daughter looked it up on the internet.'

Fergus smiled, though Tamara knew he'd be wishing they hadn't done that. It might've made everything appear worse and frightened them. 'I'm going to operate to remove it. Are you all right with that?'

'Yes. I want the pain gone.'

'I have to tell you that you will have some pain for a few days after the operation while everything settles down and the wound heals. You will also have light vaginal bleeding for up to two weeks afterwards as the wound repairs, then everything will come right and you'll feel so much better.'

Mrs Tari nodded. 'It will get better, then? The pain really will go away?'

'Yes.' Drawing a breath, he continued. 'I need to look at your tummy and feel the fibroid to see how big it is and exactly where it is. Tamara will help you get partially undressed and onto the bed. I'll be as quick as I can, but I have to do this examination to save time later.'

Tamara closed the curtain around Mrs Tari, and when

she'd removed her trousers, she covered the patient's lower body with a sheet. 'There you go. I'll be right here if you're worried about anything.'

'You're very kind.'

'I don't like patients feeling uncomfortable. It's not good for them.' She placed a hand on the woman's arm. 'Doctor Collier will be very careful, I promise.' She was certain of that.

'Are you ready, Mrs Tari?' Fergus asked from behind the curtain.

'Yes, Doctor.'

'Right. Remember, ask anything you want. Sorry if my hands feel cold on your skin.'

Mrs Tari laughed lightly. 'In this heat?'

'It's the vinyl gloves,' Tamara told her. 'They always feel cold.' She kept chatting, asking questions about Port Vila, and within minutes Fergus was tossing the gloves in the bin.

'I've seen the X-rays and the scan you had, and now I have felt the fibroid I'm ready to make you right. We're doing this first thing tomorrow morning.'

Mrs Tari paled. 'I know.'

Tamara squeezed her arm. 'At least you won't have days to think about it. Is Emele staying with you in the ward this afternoon?'

'She is.'

'Good. You can talk your heads off and relax.'

Finally, a big smile. 'We do that all the time. We're very close.'

'Nothing like best friends, is there?' Hers were amazing, and she'd do anything for them. Tamara helped her sit up and handed over her clothes. 'I'll wait for you on the other side of the curtain and then take you to the ward where you're staying.' The women probably knew better than her where to go.

Fergus was writing up notes. 'I'll see you again before you go into Theatre,' he told Mrs Tari from behind the curtain. 'If you have any doubts, then please tell me so I can reassure you everything's going to be all right.' He sounded confident that nothing would go wrong. Nor should it, but sometimes, in rare cases, something did.

Glancing at him, she found him watching her. 'It will be,' he mouthed silently.

In this situation she didn't mind his confidence. It would help calm Mrs Tari and make Tamara feel good about the surgery. Why, when she'd seen many operations being performed, she wasn't sure. Only that she was accepting Fergus was a good guy. Something she didn't want to change her mind about.

CHAPTER FOUR

'Clamp the uterine artery,' Fergus demanded. 'We're getting some serious bleeding.'

Tamara put a clamp in place, then swabbed the site. The fibroid was massive. 'You're not removing the uterus?'

'I'd prefer to, but Mrs Tari is adamant she doesn't want that. Something to do with being a woman.' Was that a smile behind his face mask? His eyes had lit up even as he focused on the procedure.

'As long as she's not at risk of cancer, I guess it's not a problem.' She continued to swab as Fergus made more incisions, oddly aware of his long fingers holding the scalpel precisely.

'No sign of cancer, and the X-rays didn't show any growths. I'll take a sample to make certain.' He cut around the fibroid, nodding to her when more clamps were needed. His hands were steady, his moves efficient. His patient couldn't ask for a better surgeon.

Fergus was the clever guy he'd always said he was, only this was for real. He knew what he was doing, did it carefully and competently. She was impressed. He was quite something beyond how easily he caused a sexy heatwave to roll through her.

'There, done.' Fergus placed the fibroid in the bowl she held out. 'That's heavy. No wonder she was in so much pain.'

Tamara shuddered. 'I wonder why she didn't get something done long ago.'

'She might've seen a GP, but there hasn't been a specialty surgeon to do anything about it for some time. That's why we're here to catch up on the backlog of surgeries.'

Another shudder wracked her. Wait times for procedures at home weren't perfect, but no one would have to wait for a fibroid to get this big before being removed.

Fergus said, 'Prepare needles for suturing.'

'Done.' She handed Fergus the first one. 'Here you go.' After she threaded more needles and removed clamps whenever he told her to, they were soon stepping back. 'Job done.'

'One down, three to go.'

Tamara stretched up onto her toes and rolled her head in a circle. 'It'll be a long day.' Each operation would take two hours or more. 'Then there's tomorrow.' And the rest of the week, including Saturday. Sunday was their only day off.

'You're an excellent nurse, Tamara. You did a great job with Mrs Tari.' Was he being condescending, as though he'd thought she'd be incompetent?

Or was she overreacting? The uncertainty made her tense and annoyance instantly flared. 'Why wouldn't I? I put everything into my nursing.'

'Whoa. I was paying you a compliment, not looking for trouble.' His head flipped up and his eyes were stern above his mask.

She stared at him. To be fair, what he'd said wasn't a putdown. She'd been looking for trouble, waiting to be criticised. Which she shouldn't have. There was no reason to. 'Sorry. And thank you, Fergus.'

'Let's move on. Grab a coffee before starting the next op.' He turned to the anaesthetist. 'That all right with you, Ian?'

'Go for it. Get one of the nurses in post-op to come in on your way out. Your patient will start coming round shortly. I'll join you in a few minutes.'

Tamara headed for the bathroom to divest herself of her scrubs and gloves before washing her hands thoroughly. What an idiot she'd been. The words had spilled from her mouth without thought about what she was saying, as though she was eighteen again. As she'd been continuously telling herself since arriving here, it was time to get over herself. If she didn't, she was in danger of being worse than Fergus used to be.

At the staff station she made a pot of coffee and got out mugs. When Fergus came through, she filled a mug and handed it to him. 'I *am* sorry.'

He leaned back against the bench. 'You're having difficulty thinking I've truly changed.' It wasn't a question. He was stating a fact.

She could do honest too. 'Sometimes.' She filled another mug and sipped the hot liquid.

'I don't blame you.'

Her eyes widened. Had he really said that?

A sad smile settled over his mouth as he stared at the floor. 'I mean it. I had some harsh lessons during my last term at college, but be assured, I did learn from them.'

While she had no idea how bad it had been for Fergus and how he'd managed to get through those final weeks at college, she'd heard enough gossip to know it would've been a horrific comedown for a boy who'd once been kingpin. 'It must've been a terrible time.' Everyone had been agog with shock and gossip about Fergus, even though it was reported that he hadn't had a clue what his father was up to. 'You lost so much.'

'What's that saying? Sometimes things are sent to try us? Until it all went pear-shaped, I'd have laughed at that.' His mouth was grim.

She couldn't believe he was actually talking about it, which rattled her to the core. He really and truly meant what he said. 'Fergus, I don't know what to say except the past is in the past, and I'm forgetting all about it and moving on.'

'Ahh, but you haven't truly forgotten any of it.' He looked her directly in the eyes. 'I'm not saying I blame you. I'm merely stating the obvious. There's not a lot I can do except carry on being who I am now.'

Sucker punch her, why not? 'Go you. I can't begin to imagine how you got through it.' She was struggling to get her head around who this guy really was now. She'd never expected him to be so open with her. Sure, he hadn't said a lot about what went on back then, but at least he had raised the subject. She did want to get to know this new version of Fergus. He piqued her interest in ways she'd hadn't experienced in ages. It could be exciting if she let him in. But... *Not happening*.

'Be glad you don't have to,' he said and drained his mug.

'I am.' After her mother died, her father had been the most important person in her life growing up, and for

Fergus not to have someone like Dad at his side must've been horrendous. From the little she knew, Fergus's father had egged him on to do better and better at college, to show everyone that he could have and be anything he chose just because they were so rich. 'My sister and I were very lucky to have our father.'

Rinsing his mug, he said. 'I'm pleased for you. I mean that, Tamara.'

'Fergus.' She paused. 'I know you do.' She truly did.

'Thanks.' He nodded, drew a breath. 'One more thing I should say and it's a long time coming. I am very sorry for how I treated you at the ball. I behaved appallingly in not defending you to the other guys.'

She stared at him, her mouth drying and a tremor starting up her spine. There was a steadfastness in his expression that cut through her like a blunt knife through butter. 'You did behave badly. But I retaliated and said some pretty awful things to you too.'

'Yes, you did.' He glanced at his watch. 'Right, I'm going to get scrubbed up and see my next patient.'

'Wait. Fergus.' She tried to swallow. Failed. 'That apology wasn't necessary but thank you. I really wasn't nice to you, either.'

'The difference being I fully deserved what you said.'

Strike her down. 'It's in the past now, Fergus. All of it.'

He gave her a tight smile. 'I agree.'

'I'll be with you shortly.' *And I vow to only look forward when it comes to you.* But no further than working together. Nothing Fergus could do or say would allow her to trust another man with her dreams.

The next operation was a hysterectomy on a thirty-year-old woman with a prolapsed uterus. When they'd met her yesterday, she'd sobbed as she'd accepted there was no other way round the problem. It was impossible to put her uterus back into place permanently. Having more children wasn't to be.

Tamara put on clean scrubs, her mind still going over how open Fergus had been. Never in a million years had she thought he'd be so frank with her. If he could do it, then she would too. It didn't mean they'd become best buddies, but they could get along well enough to be relaxed around each other while they were here. How he'd managed to face up to what his father had done, let alone how much his own life must've changed, was beyond comprehension, which was impressive. She'd heard a lot of his so-called friends had deserted him just when he would've needed them most. No wonder he didn't return to Nelson after leaving university. Other than bad memories, there wouldn't have been much there for him to stay for. What about his mother? She used to come and watch Fergus play rugby, always dressed to the nines and reluctant to mix with the other parents on the sideline.

Sarah popped into the changing room, tugging her scrubs top over her head. 'How's it going?'

'I'm in my element.' Nursing made her feel right at home, as though she'd been born to do it, comfortable in her own skin.

Even if it was only day two on the job, this adventure was already working out well. Nothing to do with Fergus making her feel more alive than she had in a long while. Exciting didn't begin to explain the bubbly warmth spreading throughout her. *Careful. John used to make you feel like that too.* Her shoulders sagged. *So did Fergus, once upon a time.*

* * *

Whatever had possessed him to say that to Tamara? Talking about his father never happened. Tamara probably felt smug right about now. Though she hadn't looked or sounded that way. More stunned. Guess he could still surprise her, after all. Long may that last, because he didn't want them falling out. He'd prefer to spend time getting to know her better instead of arguing.

He'd always enjoyed winding her up because when she got angry, she'd looked as sexy as hell. But he was no longer that guy. He didn't own the world. It was embarrassing to him now that he'd once thought so. He'd turned himself around and was no longer full of hubris. More importantly, Tamara was getting to him in unprecedented ways. She was smart. She was fun. She was honest—and always had been. She lit up any room she walked into. She was hot. Small and curvy, with amazing legs and a cheeky glint in her eyes when she wasn't having a poke at him. Which might be why he'd mentioned his past. He hadn't given much away, but he'd put it out there how hard that time in his life had been for him, something he never normally talked about. Except with Harriet, and in the end that had backfired on him badly. Having lost friends who'd said much the same, he knew there was nothing to be gained.

Not even his mother knew how he'd truly felt about those years. She became focused on maintaining the lifestyle she'd come to enjoy, while he'd concentrated on getting his life back on track in a way that didn't include being supremely arrogant to people. Especially to Tamara, he realised, as he looked back on it.

Tamara. What did she really think of him? She didn't

hold back on standing up for herself when she thought he was having a crack at her, like when he'd said she was a good nurse. She believed he'd been surprised she was as good as he'd said. He certainly hadn't been. One thing he'd always known about Tamara was that when she wanted something, she gave it her all and then some, and that would include being a top-notch nurse.

'Alani Leconte is waiting outside Theatre.' Ian stood in the scrubs room doorway. 'That was a massive fibroid you removed in the previous op. Don't think I've ever seen one that big.'

'It happens when there aren't enough resources to perform much-needed surgeries, sadly.'

'So they just have to grin and bear it, eh?'

'Afraid so.' He pulled on a clean top and straightened it down to his hips. 'And on that note, let's go.'

Ian smiled. 'Lead the way.'

Walking into Theatre, Fergus's gaze went straight to Tamara busy setting out the equipment he'd need during the next operation—the hysterectomy. 'You're way ahead of me,' he said, hoping she wouldn't take that the wrong way.

'I don't want any surprises like not being able to find anything you might require.' She gave him a small smile that helped ease his concern. 'I'm still learning my way around.'

Strange how he didn't want to get on the wrong side of her when that's all they'd ever done in the past, while pretending they weren't hot for each other. That could be why he felt this way. A lot had gone down in the time between then and now for him, and he knew that Tamara had faced some difficulties of her own, losing her father recently. Everyone did in one way or another. 'Looks like you've got it covered. Do you want to bring Alani in? I'll talk to her here.'

'On it. I've given her the pre-anaesthesia medication. She doesn't appear too stressed about what's ahead, which surprises me given how upset she was yesterday.'

'You can't always tell how people feel right before surgery. Some patients are good at hiding their emotions.' He'd learned that during his first time working in Theatre as an intern. A patient, a male in his forties, had come across as completely relaxed, only to start shaking and sweating when being wheeled into Theatre despite having had a pre-anaesthesia med. He began shouting that he didn't want the op. It took a lot of time and effort to calm him down. Afterwards, he'd apologised profusely, obviously feeling terrible about his reaction.

'Have you worked with Tamara before today?' Ian was at his monitors, getting ready for Tamara to bring Alani in.

'No, I haven't.'

'Well, I got that wrong. You both seem to know what the other's doing before you even do it.'

He hadn't noticed, but now hearing Ian say it, he knew that's exactly how it had gone during the previous operation. 'Tamara's good at reading situations.' Was she like that in other circumstances, or only as a nurse? He'd keep an eye out. Darn, he thought about her a lot. Too much, really, but when she made him feel so warm and comfortable it was hard not to. Now that they'd caught up in very different circumstances, he was coming to like her a lot. Tamara had turned into a mystery he'd like to unravel.

The door to Theatre swung open and Tamara pushed a bed through with his patient on board. As they came closer, she said, 'Alani, Doctor Collier's here to talk to you.' She smiled at their patient.

'What's wrong?' Alani looked worried.

Fergus quickly stepped up, working at ignoring the fluttery sensations in his gut brought on by Tamara's smile. 'Nothing at all. This is routine protocol. I'm here to reassure you and answer any last-minute questions you might have.'

'I am already uptight. Let's get it over and done with. You answered everything I wanted to know yesterday, Doc.'

'Then as you say, let's get underway. I'll see you after the op. In the meantime, you're in Tamara's capable hands.' Rubbing it in a bit, perhaps, but too bad. He liked letting Tamara know how he felt about her work, if not her. Yet. If ever. He didn't know her very well. He frowned. She could be married with kids, although according to the volunteer service CEO, she hadn't hesitated about coming over here when asked. She might be single and staying that way. For all he knew, she could spend her time travelling and working all over the world, or she might've become a hermit who never intended moving away from Nelson. Though that one seemed far-fetched, since she was already here in Vanuatu.

'You need to move over to the operating table, Alani. Think you can do that if I hold you steady?'

'Of course.' Alani swung her legs over the side of the bed and stood up, with Tamara holding her arm. Turning around she sat on the edge of the table.

Tamara lifted her legs up. 'There you go. Lie back

and we'll give you another anaesthetic through the cannula in the back of your hand to send you to sleep. Start counting to ten. See how far you get.'

'One, two, three, four, fi—' Alani was out.

Tamara wiped the spot where the cannula had leaked. 'It's a very trusting moment, isn't it?'

Fergus wasn't sure if she was talking to him or Ian, but he answered, 'Absolutely. From this moment on, the patient has no idea what we might do. We do explain it all, but it's completely out of their hands.' It still amazed him how people trusted him to open up their bodies and either remove parts or do whatever he'd gone in for and not harm them in any way. They were at his mercy, and he fully respected that. It kept him grounded.

Ian watched the monitors at the head of the OR table. 'All yours, Fergus.'

Tamara moved Alani's gown to expose her abdomen. Then she swabbed the site with antibiotic wipes and stood back, waiting for him to begin.

Picking up one of the scalpels she'd put into a stainless steel dish, he made the first incision.

'Surgery day one is over and done, and every patient seems comfortable.' Fergus stretched his arms above his head to ease the kinks from his muscles. Four surgeries had been time-consuming, not to mention tiring.

'I'm going to pop in and see them all before heading back to our accommodation for a long shower followed by a walk on the beach,' Tamara said.

'Can we join you on that walk?' Sarah called across Theatre from where she'd been assisting Tim.

'More the merrier.'

'Count me in,' Fergus said. 'Followed by a beer and dinner at one of the steak houses, maybe?'

Tim wandered across. 'Seems we have a plan.'

'How did your day go?' They hadn't talked much as whenever he was free Tim was doing a procedure and vice versa.

'Pretty straightforward. Four hernias, and a rectal procedure to remove a non-malignant growth.'

Fergus laughed. 'We call this straightforward. Mind you, I suppose airline pilots say landing a 747 is straightforward.'

Tamara was shaking her head at him. 'You're nuts. Though you're probably right.'

He shrugged. 'Let's see our patients and get the hell out of here.'

Everyone headed to the wards. Fergus and Tamara went straight to Alani, who was surrounded by four little kids and a large man. 'How're you feeling?'

'Not too bad.' She looked grey, but that wasn't unusual after two hours under anaesthesia. 'Did everything go all right, Doctor?'

'Yes. No problems at all. We'll keep you on pain meds for a while so you can move around carefully and hopefully get some sleep. Otherwise, you're already on the way to getting back to normal,' Fergus said reassuringly.

'This is my husband, Mike, and these are our four little ratbags.'

'They're gorgeous.' Tamara watched them with awe. 'Bet they keep you on your toes.'

'Oh, yes,' replied Mike. 'Most of the time it's impossible to keep up with them. They'll have me feeling old before long.' He laughed.

'You're so lucky,' said Tamara with deep longing.

At least Fergus presumed it was longing. So, she wanted a family, did she? Guess that meant she didn't have any children yet. 'They are,' he agreed, and felt an unusual sense of wonder. He visualised small versions of Tamara running around and leaping all over her as these little guys were doing with their dad, and the wonder turned to a longing of his own. For children and a wonderful woman to be their mother. And his all-time love.

Did he really want kids? Since he'd decided never to get married, children hadn't entered into the picture. If he did have another serious relationship, there were no guarantees it would work out any more than the last one had, so no kids for him. Both his parents had let him down. While his dad had showered him with gross amounts of money and bought him anything he wanted, Fergus doubted it demonstrated real paternal love; instead, it had been part of his obsession over appearing richer than everyone else. As for his mother, she'd thought more about how she was going to carry on her lifestyle than her only son's well-being.

Did any of that mean he wouldn't be a good father? Neither of his parents had been great examples of how to raise a child well. He hoped he'd do better because he'd learned the hard way how *not* to do it. Something to think about, perhaps—if he ever found the courage to risk his heart again. His gaze tracked to Tamara. No way. They'd barely begun getting to know each other, yet she kept popping into his mind like she belonged there. *No way*, he repeated silently. But since his apology, he'd found himself wondering if there was a possibility they could be more than friends.

Tamara chuckled as Alani and her husband talked about some mischief the boys had got up to yesterday. 'And you wanted more kids.'

Alani shook her head. 'I did, but having this surgery has made me realise how lucky we are with our boys. Not everyone gets to have a family. I've got nothing to complain about, really.'

'Aww, go you.' Tamara leaned down and gave Alani a quick hug. 'Take it easy and try to get some sleep. I'll pop in to see you tomorrow morning before we go into Theatre.'

'Thanks.' Alani looked over at Fergus. 'Again, thank you, Doctor Collier. I appreciate that you've come over to Vanuatu to help me, and others.'

Her husband stood up and held out his hand to shake Fergus's. 'Me too, Doc.'

Fergus returned his firm grip. 'You're welcome.' Making people better felt good and made him believe he was a better person for it. 'I'll drop by tomorrow to see how you're doing too.'

He crossed to another bed, where his first patient of the day lay dozing. He read the chart on the end of the bed and moved on to the next woman, a lightness in his step. He had turned his life around, and it might be time to think of the future and what he could achieve outside the medical world. Nothing to do with that laughter coming from Alani's bedside. Soft, silvery laughter that sucked him in was not going to change his mind about remaining single and safe.

The sand was warm on Tamara's feet as she strolled, sandals in hand, along the water's edge with Sarah. The guys were behind them, talking about cricket. 'I should've put on my bikini so I could go for a swim.'

'It didn't occur to me, either. Not used to doing this after work.' Sarah gazed along the beach. 'It's lovely.'

'How are you finding things here so far?' Tamara asked.

'I'm enjoying it. It's similar to working in Fiji. Everyone's so friendly that it's fun just walking down the street.'

'I'm glad I got the chance to come here.'

Fergus came up beside Tamara. 'Ladies, there's a bar overlooking the beach over there. Feel like a cold one?'

'Now that you mention it, I do.' Tamara wanted to dance on the spot. This place was magic.

'Looks like they do meals too, so this might as well be our stopping point.'

The sun had set and her stomach was saying it was way past dinner time. It would have to wait. A cold beer was first on the list! 'My shout,' she said.

Fergus shook his head. 'I owe you, remember?'

'Save that for another time.' Which meant she expected to spend more time with him outside the hospital. Of course she would, because there were plenty of hours to fill when they wouldn't be working. But doing that with Fergus? Was that wise? Men didn't fall for her and only her, did they? They sought pleasure elsewhere too. Air trickled out of her lungs. If only she could get past what John had done, she might find the happiness she longed for. She just didn't know if she'd be able to. At the bar she ordered four beers and grabbed a couple of menus for everyone to peruse.

'Are you on holiday?' the barman asked.

'Not really. We're helping out at the hospital for a few weeks.'

'You're those guys? Welcome to Port Vila. My friend is having his hernias removed by one of you next week. He's been in pain for a long time. I'm so grateful he's getting help.'

'I'm a nurse, and since that's general surgery I'd say Tim is your friend's surgeon. He's the brown-haired man sitting at that table.' She shouldn't have said that. This guy might go racing over and make a big fuss, which she didn't think Tim would enjoy. 'We're relaxing after a busy day.'

The man winked. 'It's all right. I know how to behave.' He picked up the four bottles of beer and headed around the end of the bar.

'Hey, I haven't paid.'

'This round's on me.' He placed a bottle in front of everyone. 'Welcome to Port Vila.'

'You don't have to do that,' Tamara said.

'I want to, okay?' He headed back to the bar with a smile lighting up his face.

'Then thank you very much.' She sat down, doubting he'd heard her, and placed the menus on the table. 'The barman shouted us this round.'

Fergus nodded. 'That happens when people learn why we're here.'

'Then I'll have to keep my mouth shut.'

'And spoil their fun?'

'I suppose not.' To think it was only yesterday morning when she'd first seen Fergus at the airport and hoped they'd get through the next few weeks without ripping each other's throats out. Seemed they were doing okay so far. Most of the time, anyway.

'Sarah and I are going to a resort after we finish work on Saturday afternoon,' Tim told them. 'Figured we might as well make the most of the beautiful spots around here. We'll be back early Monday, ready for another busy week.'

'Sounds idyllic,' Tamara sighed. She wouldn't mind doing something similar, but going on her own wouldn't be much fun. 'Have you got a resort in mind?'

'Port Vila Resort. We got lucky. They had a cancellation, otherwise staying only two nights wouldn't have been possible. They target long visits. More profitable, I imagine.' Sarah smiled lovingly at Tim. 'I bet you charmed them into letting us stay for such a short time.'

'Naturally.' Tim returned her smile.

If only, thought Tamara wistfully. Since splitting up with John, she hadn't experienced anything like this closeness. But then she hadn't been out there trying to find it, had she, afraid of having it thrown back in her face again. She still had dreams of the kind of marriage she remembered her parents having: strong and loving, there for each other all the time. Her sister's marriage was similar, so if Sashi could find that, so should she. One day. But it wasn't easy to let go of the feeling that John had been right about her—that she was cold and lacked sensuality and spontaneity. Sashi disagreed, but sisters were supposed to stick up for each other, weren't they? One day, hopefully not too far in the future, she might try again. Before her hormones dried up and she had to breed puppies instead of having babies!

'What do you think you'll do on our day off?' Fergus asked.

'I've been too busy to give it any thought. I would like to see as much of the island as possible over the coming weeks. Also, I want to go kayaking and give paddle boarding a go.'

'How about we hire a motorbike and do a trip around the island? I do have a license,' he added with a grin. 'In case you're wondering.'

It wasn't the license filling her mind, but the fact he'd offered to spend the day with her. On a bike. With her arms around that sensational body. *Do it. What could go wrong?* A lot. So what? She was here to have fun when she wasn't working. But fun with Fergus? *Give him a chance. Give yourself a chance.* All right. 'Sounds like a plan.'

'That's a yes?'

She dipped her head in agreement.

Fergus looked pleased. Had it been difficult for him to suggest they spend time together? Did he have similar thoughts about something going wrong between them?

'We'll have a blast,' she promised. She'd make sure they did. Then she could at least say she'd tried.

'Been on a motorbike before?'

'A few times. I knew someone who owned one.' An unpleasant memory of John presented itself. 'He liked to shock me by going too fast. In the end, I refused to go with him at all.' Another point against her, apparently.

'Trust me, I won't be doing that.'

Funny but she did trust Fergus. This Fergus didn't appear to want to show off all he was capable of, instead seemed to prefer giving others a good time. 'Perfect.' When he didn't smile, she added, 'I believe you.'

His head dipped to one side as he watched her. 'Thanks.'

'Seems we've all got Sunday sorted.' Tim stood up. 'I'm going to order. I'm starving. Must be the warm air and working in a new place. Would everyone like fish and chips with salad? It's trevally tonight.'

Tamara's mouth watered. 'Count me in.'

'Me, too.' Fergus got to his feet. 'I'll get another round of beer.'

Sarah leaned back in her chair. 'You and Fergus seem to be getting along better now.'

'Yes, we are.'

'Was it that bad whenever it was you didn't see eye to eye?'

Not going there. 'We had some issues, but I'm not talking about them. They're over and done with now.' Fingers crossed. 'We worked well together today and outside of work we are getting along. I want it to stay that way.'

'In other words, I should mind my own business.' Sarah smiled. 'I didn't mean to sound nosey. It's just that we know Fergus a little but have never heard anything about his past.'

There was a good reason for that. 'He's very focused on the here and now, and seems happy with what he's doing.' That's all she was saying.

'You're sticking up for him. I like that.' Sarah glanced at her phone. 'I haven't heard from anyone at home yet. Do they think we've gone off the planet?'

'They're probably jealous and don't want to hear what a wonderful time you're having.' Sashi had texted earlier to ask how it was going. Her sister had been referring to Fergus as much as Port Vila. Tamara had messaged back saying everything was working out better than expected and got a thumbs-up in reply.

'I'll take a photo of the view from here and send it to everyone. That'll really get their backs up.' Sarah grinned. 'I can be a bit of a stirrer when it suits.'

'Here you go.' Fergus placed a beer in front of her. 'The fish and chips look awesome. I saw a plate being taken across to the table at the other end of the deck and immediately my mouth watered.'

'Excellent. This is turning out to be the perfect end to a hard day at work.'

'We'll probably do this most days we're here.'

'Don't say that. I might not want to go home again.' Though the food wasn't cheap by any means. Nothing was from what she'd seen so far, but she'd been warned about that before leaving home. Lunch was provided by the hospital, as was all the coffee or tea they could drink. Other meals were theirs to sort out. As they were a volunteer team here to help because people couldn't afford the medical expenses, she wasn't complaining. It was part of the deal she'd happily signed up for.

'I asked the barman where to hire a motorbike and he's given me two numbers to call. Both mates of his, but that's fine.'

'So we're on for Sunday.' It was exciting to think about riding around the island and discovering beaches and waterfalls and resorts with dining facilities. 'Great!'

Fergus frowned. 'You really are looking forward to it?'

She sat back. 'Have you changed your mind?'

'Not at all. I just didn't expect you to be this willing.'

'You're sounding like a wet blanket, Fergus.'

He instantly looked contrite. 'I didn't mean to be. I don't know you well, that's all.'

'At least you're honest. I think we've done okay so far. We haven't lost our cool too badly with each other.'

'You're right, and it's refreshing. If I may say so,' he added in a hurry.

He seemed more worried about their past than she was, and that said a lot because she'd been in a ball of knots for days before flying over here. 'As I've already said, despite what went down between us, I'd like to think we've moved on and can at least be friends.' That came out a little abruptly, but she wasn't apologising. He needed to understand she wasn't playing games here.

'We can, and we are.' Although a little forced, his smile was devastating. He could still charm the pants off anyone he wanted to.

Her pants were still in place despite how he made her feel. But her face was heating up and sitting under the deck roof, she couldn't blame the sun. She hated to imagine what he might be thinking about that. Nothing sensible, or even inane, came to mind, except memories of how he used to tease her and make her feel hot and needy, so she took a swig of beer in an attempt to calm her brain. But damn it, he was getting to her in ways she'd never have believed possible. Not when it came to Fergus Collier.

She wasn't falling for any man. Especially not this one. Turning her back on him, she stared out over the water, seeing nothing. *Fergus, I am not letting you in.*

CHAPTER FIVE

ON SATURDAY MORNING, Tamara leapt out of bed bright and early. Despite a busy week with a heavy workload, she felt energised in ways she hadn't since her father became ill. Nursing him had been exhausting, knowing she was losing the one person who'd always been there for her and her sister throughout their lives. But today she felt alive, ready for the world and whatever it brought. Starting with a fast walk.

Throwing on shorts and a T-shirt, then walking shoes, she headed down to the beach. At six, the sun had barely risen. The beach was empty except for a couple of fishermen on the jetty. Setting a fast pace she headed for the far end.

'Tamara, wait up.'

Spinning around, she saw Fergus jogging towards her. How had she missed seeing him? Couldn't she have a quiet walk by herself? Then, noticing those long legs eating up the distance between them, she decided being alone wasn't necessary. He was good looking in every aspect. *Shut up, brain. I don't need to hear that.* 'Morning, Fergus.'

He slowed to stop beside her. 'Hi. How far are you going?'

'To the end and back.' Obviously. She wasn't going to spend the day sitting at the far end.

'Want company?'

'I guess.'

'I can go in the opposite direction if you prefer.'

She shrugged to hide her mixed feelings and started walking. 'Come on. Let's do this. It's a great way to get psyched up for the day ahead.'

'You don't walk along Tahunanui Beach every morning?'

'I don't live within walking distance, whereas rolling out of bed to walk out the door almost onto the beach is perfect.'

'It does take the fun out of it when you have to find car keys, drive a distance to the beach, all the while keeping an eye on the time because you've got to get to work in rush hour.' He was laughing at her. Rush hour in Nelson was a doddle.

'Cheeky blighter.' She picked up her pace.

He stayed beside her all the way. She didn't waste breath on talking, just kept pace and looked around as she went. When she stopped at the end of the beach she rolled her shoulders. 'That feels good.'

Hands on hips, Fergus stared out to sea. 'It's a beautiful place, but most island nations are.'

'Been to many?'

He nodded. 'I've done similar work in Suva and Rarotonga.' Then he clammed up.

She decided to open up a little. It might lighten things between them further. 'Dad took my sister, Sashi, and me to Rarotonga when we were young teens. Absolutely loved it. I want to go back one day.' When she had time and one of her girlfriends was available to join her. It wasn't really somewhere to go alone.

'It's a special place.' He began walking back the way they'd come, slower this time. 'You've mentioned your dad, but not your mother.'

Hmm, true.

'Don't answer if you don't want to.'

She shrugged. There was no reason to hold back. Friends shared stuff like that, didn't they? 'It's all right. Mum died in a trucking accident when I was eight and Sashi seven. Dad raised us on his own, the best dad ever.'

'What happened? Did a truck hit her car?'

She smiled wryly because a lot of people thought that. These days she didn't get upset thinking about what had happened. There was nothing she could've done to change it. Besides, she'd learned to live without her mother a long time ago. 'The other way round. Mum was a truckie doing long haul between Nelson, the Picton ferries and Christchurch. A car crossed the median line in front of her. She tried to avoid hitting it to her detriment. The truck rolled over a steep bank. She didn't stand a chance.'

He touched her shoulder. 'How did you deal with that?'

She shook his hand away. This wasn't a moment to get all hot and tight. 'I didn't at first, but as I said, Dad was there, helping us get through it all while coping with his own grief.'

'What a man.'

'Absolutely.' That was all she was saying, nothing about the cancer and how it had felt watching her dad fade away in pain. Too soon. It had been such a horrible time. Even knowing it was impossible, all she'd wanted was to make him better. Watching his life slowly drain away and knowing he would never recover had broken her heart. He'd done all he could for her, and she'd done all she could for him. It hadn't been anywhere near enough.

Fergus glanced at her and opened his mouth to say something, then closed it again. Had he seen her anguish?

She hoped not. She didn't like to appear too vulnerable. They might be getting along, but she wasn't up to showing her feelings about a lot of things. She'd learned that when her mother died. Everyone was helpful and friendly for a while, and then they'd moved on and she'd discovered they expected her to do the same. They had a point, except it had taken her a long time. Possibly because she'd been so young. Anyway, she was here now, on this beautiful island, and was supposed to be enjoying herself, right? Why spoil the moment?

She looked at the closed cafés along the beachside. 'Too early for breakfast.' She could do with something more exciting than toast and honey at the hospital canteen.

'How about the cafe next to where we're staying? They open early.'

'Fine. I could go for eggs on toast. Along with fresh fruit. Tropical fruit here's to die for.'

'I agree. Getting it straight from the tree makes all the difference.'

'How many patients are you seeing today?'

'Four. Nothing major since we've got tomorrow off. Who knows? We might even finish early.'

'If we do, I'll go for a swim.'

'I've booked a motorbike for tomorrow. You're still on for a ride?'

'You bet.' She'd said she'd go, and wouldn't change her mind without a strong reason, which so far hadn't occurred.

'Great.'

The cafe owner was putting out the open sign as they walked up the road. 'Hello, you two. Feel like some brekkie?'

'That's our plan,' Tamara said.

'We're still getting organised but take a seat and I'll bring menus. The cook will get on to whatever you want straight away. I know you've got to get to the hospital to start work.'

'We're getting known around town,' she commented.

Fergus sat opposite and picked up a menu. 'It feels good, like we're a part of the community for a while.'

'Different to Auckland.' Large cities didn't do that.

'Completely, which was why I moved there.'

Her eyes widened. He was admitting that? Honestly he'd been admitting a lot of things over the past couple of days. 'Did it work out?'

'Yes.'

She looked at him. 'I've never seen you look so at ease.' When he'd been hamming it up as the smartest, sexiest guy around, there'd always been a tightness about him. Now he looked more relaxed, as if he'd found his true self. 'It suits you.' Oops. Picking up the menu, she studied it intensely, wishing her words back. What had come over her? Fergus was going to think she'd lost her mind and needed locking up.

'You certainly know how to surprise me, Tamara.'

Glancing over the top of the plastic-covered menu sheet, she found him watching her with something like amazement darkening his slate eyes. 'Thought I'd always done that?'

'True.' Then, 'You don't care about that night anymore?'

Maybe they couldn't fully move forward without putting some things straight. 'No, I don't.'

'Excuse me, what would you two like for breakfast?' The café owner stood by the table. 'I'm Max, by the way.'

'Tamara?' Fergus asked.

'Poached eggs on toast, please, plus a pot of tea.'

'Bacon and eggs, and a long black, and I'm Fergus.' He sat back watching her. Waiting for her to continue what she'd started?

Best to get it over with. 'Holding a grudge after all this time is pointless. When I first learned you'd be working here, I confess I thought about pulling out but then figured that was stupid. If we couldn't get along well enough to look after patients, then we shouldn't be doing what we do for work.' She sipped the water Max placed in front of her. 'A lot's happened in the intervening years. Why waste time over something that seems almost trivial now? You had a lot worse to deal with back then.' She wasn't mentioning her father again. 'How you got through, I have no idea, but you've survived and grown a lot.' Time to shut up, or the Fergus she used to know would get up and walk off.

He didn't say anything for so long she began to expect him to do exactly that. Finally, he drew a deep breath, and said quietly, 'Thank you. I have changed. It was a dreadful time, but I do wonder if it hadn't happened, would I still be an arrogant arse? Or worse.'

Not a lot wrong with his backside these days, but she wasn't saying that! 'Nothing's ever straightforward, is it?'

'You can say that again.' He held his hand up in a stop sign. 'Don't bother.'

'Spoilsport.'

'One tea and one coffee.' Max placed mugs on the table.

'Nothing like tea to start the day.'

'After a walk on the beach.' Fergus smiled, truly at ease now.

She was coming to appreciate him more and more. They were getting along just fine, and, if any hiccups arose, hopefully they'd get through them without any difficulty.

Don't let the reins go too soon, Tamara.

A loud screech sounding like metal on metal rent the air, followed by a loud bang as though something had hit the floor in the direction of the kitchen. A scream sent a shiver down Fergus's back.

'What the hell?' He leapt to his feet, quickly followed by Tamara, who headed towards the door the staff used.

'Sounded like it came from through here.' She carefully opened the door, looking behind it before going all the way.

Over her shoulder Fergus saw a man sprawled on the floor between a bench and the ovens. 'Hey, mate, what happened?'

'Tyler was prepping steak and slipped over. Had a knife in his hand,' Max called from the other side of the kitchen. 'Don't know where that went.'

By the look of it, into his upper body, if the blood beginning to stain his white apron was any indication. 'I'm going to check him over, all right?' Too bad if Max said no, he'd do it anyway.

'Go for it, man. Glad you're here.' Max had come around to stand at Tyler's feet. 'I'm not good at this stuff.'

'Not many people are,' Tamara said as she knelt down beside Fergus. 'Roll him over, do you think?'

'Only way to get a look at what's going on. I'll take his upper body while you move his hips and legs.' It wasn't going to be easy in the narrow space but essential if they were to help Tyler.

Max knelt down. 'I'll shift his legs when you tell me to.'

'Thanks.' That'd make things easier for Tamara. He put his hands on Tyler's shoulders. 'Tyler, this might hurt, but we have to get you on your back, okay?'

Something sounding like *yeah* came from the guy.

'Right, you two ready?'

'Yes,' Tamara and Max answered.

'On the count of three, turn him towards Tamara.' He drew a breath, aware they knew nothing about what they'd find. It could be a nick in the skin or a serious internal injury. 'One, two, three.'

Tyler groaned as they eased him onto his back. The knife was embedded below his ribs, blood seeping out slowly. Removing the blade could exacerbate the bleeding. Best leave it where it was until they got Tyler to hospital.

'His breathing's rapid,' Tamara pointed out.

Due to a pierced lung or shock? 'Max, call the ambulance. Tell them it's urgent. Then grab your first aid kit if you have one.'

'Sure do.' His phone was already in his hand and he was punching in the emergency number while moving towards a cupboard at the back of the kitchen.

Fergus had seen Tyler wince when he mentioned this being urgent. 'Tyler, we're being cautious here until we find out what injuries you've sustained.'

'Okay.'

'Did you bang your head on the floor when you fell?'

'I think so. Slipped on something.'

'Looks like oil to me,' Tamara noted. 'There's a skid mark near his feet. We need to watch out for that.'

Another man in an apron appeared at the end of the bench. 'I'll clean it up now. I was outside in the chiller and didn't know anything happened. Is Tyler all right?'

Gently pressing around the area where the knife was, Fergus couldn't feel anything to gain any more knowledge, but he kept pressure on the area to slow the bleeding. 'Too soon to say.' Bowel damage or a punctured rib were on the cards. 'Tamara, can you keep pressure around the entry site while I check Tyler's head for injuries?'

'Sure. Pulse is slightly elevated,' she told him. 'I hear a siren. Thank goodness the hospital is close by.'

'Yes. I want to wait until we're in the emergency department before dealing to that knife injury.' The blood loss could increase drastically if he moved the knife even a little. His finger found a soft spot above the right eye. 'You landed face forward, Tyler?' He figured that was the case given where the knife went in but could be wrong.

'Yeah,' Tyler whispered. 'Feel dizzy.'

'You've taken quite a knock to the head which is why you feel like that. How's that wound, Tamara?'

'The pressure I'm applying has slowed the bleeding. Think I should remain doing this on the way to hospital?'

'I do. It'll be awkward getting you into the ambulance at the same time, but if at all possible, you should stick with it.' At least she was small, unlike him, and with everyone working carefully they'd hopefully manage to get Tyler and Tamara inside the vehicle unscathed. Then they'd have to reverse the move once they reached the hospital.

'Through here,' he heard Max saying. 'There's a doctor and a nurse with him.'

Two men in uniforms came through the door carrying a stretcher and a medical kit. Fergus shuffled sideways, remaining on his knees as he explained the little he knew about the injury. 'The sooner we get him to hospital, the sooner we can do something about the bleeding.'

The older of the paramedics nodded. 'That's best. Staying here and checking everything you say you've done is wasting important time.'

'Tamara's keeping pressure around the knife wound. Do you think we can move Tyler without her having to remove her hands?' It wasn't his place to tell these guys what to do, but he could put the idea out there.

'We'll find a way.'

And they did. Once Tyler was moved onto the stretcher, Fergus and one paramedic carried him outside with Tamara walking carefully beside the stretcher, her hands firmly in place. Taking slow steps, she got inside the ambulance with Tyler and knelt on the floor beside him, continuing to focus on what she was doing.

Fergus joined her and the senior paramedic for the slow trip to the hospital, where he went to find the HOD and explain the case, before handing over after the paramedic agreed Fergus had it in the bag.

Ten minutes later, a nurse replaced Tamara and she joined him. 'I hope he's going to be okay. It was one of those odd accidents that I can't quite get my head around.'

'Did you hear Max as we were carrying the stretcher out of the building? He was tearing into the staff over who'd spilled the oil. I wouldn't like to be the guilty one.'

'Can't blame him. It could've been a lot worse.'

'Don't say that until we know how serious the injuries are.' He didn't like tempting fate.

It wasn't until the head of the ED came to tell him Tyler needed surgery for a small cut in his bowel but otherwise would be fine that he finally relaxed. It never mattered how much he put into looking out for a patient; he never stopped worrying until it was all over.

Later that day, Tamara changed out of her scrubs for the last time and grabbed a quick shower in the women's bathroom. Saturday's roster had been tight after starting late because of helping with Tyler's operation, since there'd been a shortage of staff that early in the day. Now she was looking forward to her day off tomorrow.

As long as she and Fergus didn't get snippy at each other it should be fun riding around the island on the back of a motorbike. She shivered. Holding on to that gorgeous body was not a good idea when they were still feeling uncertain around each other, especially since he excited her too much at times. Losing control of her careful side and letting rip with what her hormones were demanding—hot, satisfying sex—would not be right, though it might be awesome to finally have sex with the guy she'd always had a thing for. Like finally laying to rest the intense desire he'd always lit within her without a single touch. Those feelings of need for him hadn't gone away. Instead, they were raising their heads faster and stronger than ever. If she didn't want to see where this went, then she needed to tell him she'd changed her mind about the motorcycle trip and she'd go paddleboarding by herself instead.

Coward.

That was one thing she could honestly say she wasn't. She always stood up to whatever was thrown at her. Except when it came to handing over her trust. When she walked out of the bathroom, Fergus was coming out of the men's room looking good in denim shorts and a white T-shirt. Her mouth watered. He was extraordinarily gorgeous. She couldn't—wouldn't—deny it. 'Hey, there.'

'Want to grab a beer and a bite to eat?'

Was that wise when they'd already be spending the whole day together tomorrow? A distraction, remember? 'Sure. I'm planning on an early night, though.'

'You having doubts?'

Her hair flicked around her shoulders as she shook her head. 'About what?'

'Tomorrow.'

He read her far too well. 'No.'

'Good. Sarah and Tim have already left on their trip. Tim couldn't wait to get away.'

'Sarah was pretty excited too. Time alone with Tim, not having to think about work is apparently the perfect break.' Hopefully riding on the back of a motorbike would be just as relaxing for her. Outside, the heat slammed into her. 'Whoa. That's the hottest we've had so far.'

'There's rain on the horizon. Could be why it's so hot and humid.' Fergus grabbed her arm and tugged her out of the way of two youngsters on skateboards racing towards them. 'Watch out, guys.'

The young boys dodged around them, one bumping her as he went.

Tamara shook herself and straightened up. 'That was close.'

'You all right?' Fergus looked her up and down.

'All good. He banged my hip, but I'd probably have been flattened if you hadn't grabbed me.' Her skin was cooling where his hand had heated her up, in complete opposite to the rest of her body as the humidity took hold.

'Boys will be boys. Come on. I could do with a cold drink right about now.' He tossed the van keys up in the air and caught them again.

'Me too.'

Fergus parked outside their accommodation building. 'Might as well walk.'

'Fine with me.'

He glanced at her. 'You're very obliging.'

'You don't expect that?' She winked to show no hard feelings.

'It's another side to you that I've never been familiar with.' He smiled.

Which got to her because it made him look way too open and friendly and adorable. She wasn't used to feeling like this about Fergus. Except she had once, hadn't she? Now the need for him was getting stronger, overtaking her reticence about getting too deeply involved with him. Some of the feelings Fergus evoked in her now felt far too similar to how she'd felt back when she was a teen and he'd teased her with that wide grin and fiery eyes, except now there was a growing, deeper sense of longing for him. 'We've never spent time together on our own. I like it.'

'You think we might've got on better in college if we'd taken time out to talk to each other without looking for reasons to cause trouble?' His smile dimmed.

Time to get back on track. She didn't want any tension between them. 'We'll never know, will we? All I can say is that it's good getting to know you now.' Leave it at that. 'Shall we go over there?' She pointed to the Port V Bar and Grill on the other side of the road.

'Might as well. Looks like half the island's come to town. Just as well I made a booking.'

'You thought ahead while at work?' He must have really wanted to spend the evening with her.

'Kaikea warned me it would be busy.'

Hopefully her shorts and T-shirt were smart enough for what felt a little like a date. No doubt she was deluding herself, but there was no harm in thinking that as long as Fergus didn't know. Was she desperate or what? Her dating life was non-existent. Her father used to tell her all the time to get out and have some fun after her divorce. She'd stuck to hanging out with Sashi and friends. So her reactions to Fergus were surprising. The desire and wonder she'd known around him all those years ago couldn't have been lying dormant, waiting for him to come back into her life. That'd be crazy. But true, perhaps? She huffed out a breath. What was going on in her head and her heart? No, not her heart. *Sure about that?* an annoying little voice asked.

Fergus nudged her. 'You still with me?'

Very much so. 'Yes.' Too much.

Walking into the bar, she was relieved to see she didn't stand out for wearing shorts. Since when did she worry about what to wear? Another new experience. Surely it had nothing to do with the company she was keeping? He looked good enough to eat, and he was dressed casually. See? They were a team. A sigh escaped. Not once during the days she'd prepared to come over to Vanuatu had she ever believed they'd become a team. Not even in the hospital, since Fergus was the specialist and therefore her boss. Proved how wrong she'd been. Again. They were good together, most of the time.

'You want the usual?'

No, tonight was different somehow. 'I'll have a chardonnay, thanks.'

'No problem.'

While Fergus headed to the bar, Tamara wandered onto the deck to gaze along the street at the shops. One was an outdoor clothing shop with racks of T-shirts and shorts with touristy logos printed on them. She'd make a note to go there to buy a few tops and shorts before going home. It was summer back home, and she was short on outdoor clothes.

'Here you go.' Fergus held out a glass. 'That's our table in the corner.'

'Cheers.' She followed him across the crowded deck. 'Are you sure they don't mind us sitting here? Someone else could use it before us.' Though she didn't want to be here all night.

'It's ours for the evening.'

She tried the wine. 'Not bad.'

'It should be good. It comes from New Zealand.'

She laughed. How could she not? Fergus looked so relaxed she felt totally comfortable. 'You're being loyal.'

'Only way to be.'

They sat for a while saying nothing, enjoying the atmosphere and warmth as they watched people wandering up and down the footpaths and stopping at shops. Sipping the wine, Tamara thought about coming here for a holiday. She'd need someone to come with her, and for once asking a girlfriend along didn't hold the usual appeal. It was being with Fergus that made her relaxed and happy. Yes, happy. With Fergus. Not that she was thinking of anything more involved than sharing a meal and being tourists tomorrow. That was enough. She still wasn't looking for anything deeper. Except the ticking baby-clock was getting louder all the time. Glancing at Fergus, her heart squeezed. Imagine little boys who looked like him? *Stop it, Tamara. You're way out of line.*

They would never get together. Fergus had the potential to hold her heart so tight that if she didn't measure up to his needs, the pain of losing him would be huge. Something she didn't want to go through ever again.

Fergus leaned back in his seat, watching Tamara while trying not to stare at her. He didn't want to rattle her, but he enjoyed taking in the sight before him. He'd always thought she was a looker, and these days she went beyond that. She was stunning and gorgeous, and made him heat up in places he needed to control.

This was not how he'd believed working with Tamara

would go. He'd supposed they'd be focused on patients so they wouldn't have to try too hard to get along. He'd stopped recalling her words from that night at the ball. Instead, every time he was with her now, he wondered how he could've been so awful to her. These days, if she or anyone else uttered those words to him, he'd stop and take note, think about it and see if there was some truth in what they'd said.

He had changed. He was beginning to think that even more so than he'd once believed. Throw in how Tamara now calmly approached situations and there was a high chance they could go back to New Zealand on good terms. They probably wouldn't keep in touch, but at least the past would be well and truly buried, something he'd wanted for a long time but had kept away from doing anything about, because the first thing he saw in the faces of people from the past was the disdain that his father was a criminal. The next was the suspicion that he'd done well out of his father's ill-gotten gains and therefore wasn't to be trusted.

That really hurt when he'd put so much effort into turning himself around and not being the arrogant prat he'd once been. But he couldn't blame people for their reactions. Two of his classmates had had grandparents who'd lost money in the scam, and they'd never forgiven him for being his father's son.

Tamara wasn't holding his previous arrogance against him. He didn't know what that meant in terms of being friends, but he wasn't jumping in expecting much more to come of this time than where they were at now. Hopefully, tomorrow would be all fun and no difficulties.

About tomorrow. 'Tamara, I've changed the motorbike

to a four-wheeler. I figured it would get too hot wearing protective jackets and trousers. What do you think?' He was also preventing her from wrapping her arms around him and holding on throughout the day as they rode around the island. Truthfully, he had wanted that so much that he'd decided to make sure it couldn't happen. Hard to fathom why he'd been looking forward to having Tamara so close. He wasn't open to the risk of showing his feelings—even to himself, hence changing the bike to a four-wheeler.

'I haven't been on one before,' Tamara replied.

'It's different to the two-wheeler, but I hope you'll like it. Are there any places in particular you'd like to see, or shall we take it as it comes, stopping off anywhere that interests us?'

'I like that idea best. I'm going to pack my bikini in case we come to a spot where I can get in the water. I've heard it's possible at some waterfalls.'

Tamara in a bikini would play havoc with his mind as much as her arms around his waist on the bike would have. Maybe she'd wear a bathing suit that came down to her knees and elbows. It was hard not to laugh at his own ridiculousness, but if he did, she'd want to know what was funny. He laughed anyway. He couldn't help himself. Showed how much she stirred him up.

One of those neatly plucked eyebrows rose. 'What's so funny?'

He shrugged exaggeratedly. 'You and I going for a bike ride. Who'd have thought?' Tempting her to change her mind?

'It's a bit odd, I suppose, but I'm not bothered.'

'Me neither.' The hell he wasn't. He downed the last of his beer to moisten his mouth. 'Want another wine?'

She gave him a bewildered look. 'I've hardly started this one.'

'I could line them up for you,' he said, trying to cover his confusion. He was losing the plot here. 'I'm getting another beer, so I'll grab some menus while I'm at it.'

Tamara's face tightened. She was starting to look annoyed with him.

'You did say you wanted an early night.'

'I did.'

'Then what's the problem?'

'I'm not rushing my wine.' She wasn't messing around with playing nice, instead getting straight to the point. Nothing new there.

'I didn't mean it to sound like that.' She always seemed to have him on the back foot!

'Okay.' She sipped her drink slowly. Rubbing her point in?

He waited, sure there was more to come.

Finally, 'We're doing better than I expected.'

That was it? Understanding Tamara didn't come easy. 'We are. I'll tell you something for nothing. I'm pleased that we are. It's a surprise and yet it's not, if you know what I mean.' He wasn't sure he did, but he had to get it out there so she might understand him better.

'I get what you're saying, but occasionally I admit I can still get a little edgy. Which is plain silly after all the time that's gone by.'

'Can't be helped. We were pretty horrible to each other.' He held up his hand. 'I'm not suggesting we have another heart-to-heart about it, only saying we've both moved on with our lives and it would be petty to drag everything up again now.'

The stiffness in her shoulders melted away and a smile appeared on her lovely mouth. 'Agreed.' She raised her glass to him. 'To friends.'

Friends was good, but despite that edgy moment the feelings filling him went beyond friendship. Something to keep to himself. He tapped his empty bottle against her glass. 'Friends.'

Taking another sip, she smiled tentatively.

More like sucker punched him. He grinned, hoping to give her the same thump in the belly as he knew his smiles used to.

She gulped.

Yes! He wanted to cheer. With difficulty he refrained and leaned back in the chair to savour the moment. Who knew what lay ahead? Finding out could be fun.

Tamara fought the urge to grab Fergus's hand and swing their arms between them as they strolled back to the apartment block. The steak and chips had been yummy, as had the cheesecake she'd finished with. As for the company, she couldn't have wished for better.

Fergus had interesting stories to tell about training to become a doctor. He hadn't spent all the time talking about himself, though. He'd wanted to know more about her. They'd discussed places they'd travelled to and found they loved Europe and hoped to visit other destinations. After getting over that brief hitch, it had turned out to be a better evening than expected. Then tomorrow they were off to explore the island.

She couldn't wait. 'Are you checking on your patients before we head out in the morning?'

'Yes, I'll drop in early to see how they're doing, so

we won't be late leaving to pick up the bike and get on the road.'

'That rain didn't eventuate. I hope it's not waiting to dump on us tomorrow. Not that it would put me off going,' she added.

'Glad to hear it.' Fergus laughed. 'I'm going no matter what, and I'd like some company.'

'You're stuck with me.'

'Good.'

She wouldn't think too much about what he might mean by that, would instead take it as an indicator they were still on track to being friends. It was the easy way out; not her usual style, but with Fergus, she was finding it hard to stand up to him just for the sake of it.

'What does your sister do for a living?'

His question came out of the blue, knocking back some of the relaxed feeling. She didn't want to talk about family or personal matters. She preferred enjoying the moment, but ignoring him would create tension between them. 'Sashi's a beauty therapist when she's not busy with her kids. Who I adore,' she added for no reason. She was missing them heaps. 'They're full of mischief and love playing pranks on me.'

'Bet you give back as good as you get.'

She blinked. 'It's what crazy aunties do.'

'You're lucky to have them.' There was a wistful undercurrent to his words.

She remembered that Fergus was an only child. 'I'm very lucky.' With a bit of luck, one day she'd sort herself out and add to the family brood. Staring straight ahead, she fought the urge to look at Fergus and picture once again the little boys she'd imagined earlier.

'Not all families are close.' The wistfulness remained.

She'd like to ask about his mother but didn't want to spoil the comfortable feeling between them. 'That's what families should be about.'

'How true.' Suddenly Fergus spun around to face the way they'd come. 'Come on. I need to get back to my room and sort out a few things before we head out tomorrow.'

In other words, he was changing the subject. Fair enough. It could get intense discussing families. He was probably worried she might raise the subject of his father. He needn't. She had no intention of doing so. There was nothing to be gained by talking about Jim Collier. 'Hopefully, I'll get a decent night's sleep. The humidity makes me sweat a lot and keeps me awake.'

'Is this something that's only started since you arrived here?' Doctor to the forefront?

'Yes, Fergus, it is.'

'Glad to hear it. Can't have my nurse getting sick.'

She laughed.

CHAPTER SIX

So much for sleeping.

Tamara groaned as she rolled over in bed yet again, hours later. No blaming it on the humidity this time, either. This was a different heat, engendered by pictures of Fergus walking beside her on the beach, those long legs eating up the distance so comfortably. They'd made her feel even shorter. She barely came up to his shoulder as it was.

Her phone buzzed.

Fergus. Are you awake? the message read.

The time was five fifty. The sun must be creeping over the horizon. Yes. Had a bad night.

Shall we have breakfast here then get on the road?

He was keen. Hadn't he slept either? Was she getting to him as much as he was her? She grinned. See you shortly.

Leaping out of bed, she had a quick shower to wash away the sweat and threw on shorts and a T-shirt. After putting her wallet and a light jersey in a small backpack, she locked her room and went downstairs to the tiny kitchen.

The aroma of coffee filled the air. 'That smells good.'

'You want some?' Fergus asked.

'No, I'll stick to my usual tea.' Coffee would have her wanting to get off the bike for a trip behind the bushes.

'Toast's on.'

'You are organised.'

'I always am.' From what she'd seen while working with him this past week, she knew that to be true. 'It saves a lot of hassles later.'

While she often left things to chance. Not the serious things, but still, she wasn't always thinking ahead about what could go wrong. 'I suppose it does.'

The toaster popped and she took a piece. 'What time does the bike rental office open?'

'The bike's been left outside the office with the keys in the letterbox. I made sure they were there before texting you.'

'Sounds like you had as little sleep as me.'

'It *was* hot last night.'

'Yes.' Did that mean he'd been in a bit of a turmoil about taking her out today, or had something else got to him? She wasn't asking. He likely wouldn't tell her. Anyway, if it had anything to do with her, she didn't want to know. Better grab her swimming gear. A vision of Fergus in speedos whammed her in the head. He'd more likely wear swimming shorts, but she couldn't see past the thought of a tight brief-style suit outlining his male parts all too well. She groaned.

'You all right?' He looked concerned.

Not at all. 'I'm fine.' After using a teaspoon to squeeze the teabag, she tossed it in the bin. She'd better be, or this was going to be the day from hell. How could Fergus do this to her so easily? She'd once despised him— even when she had the hots for him, which was why she'd spurned him, not wanting to be yet another name on the long list of girls who gave him whatever he wanted—and here he was now, walking all over her determination to remain no more than friends as though there was nothing that could stop him.

He watched her like he didn't believe her. 'It's not too late to change your mind about coming with me.'

Coming with him? Heat swamped her face. Don't go there. 'Why wouldn't I?' she snapped in embarrassment.

'Because you suddenly seem uneasy.'

'Well, I'm not.' Picking up her tea, she said, 'I'm going to add a couple of things to my bag, then I'll be ready whenever you are.' She was suddenly feeling rather scratchy. She paused, oddly unsure of herself. Something else to blame on Fergus? She turned back to him. 'I'm sorry. I'm being a grump, but I promise you I'm looking forward to going around the island. If you'll still take me.'

'Absolutely. I was probably looking for trouble when it wasn't there.'

Make her feel worse, why didn't he? He really was a great guy, nothing like he used to be, and she needed to remember that at all times and stop judging him. 'Come on, let's go have a great day.'

'You're on. But I still have to check in on my patients first.'

'I'll come and say hello to them too.'

His smile softened her insides completely. Truly a great man. One she could get to more than like if she risked dropping her barriers and took a chance.

Fergus held his breath as Tamara climbed onto the bike behind him. This wasn't going to be easy. Over the day, she was bound to bump against him, and that was going to heat him up hard and fast. Even the helmet she'd put on did nothing to dampen the attraction he felt to her lovely face.

'Ready,' she said beside his ear.

His hands tightened on the handlebars as a rose-tinged scent teased his nostrils. Man, why had he suggested doing this? 'Hold on to the side bars whenever we go round corners or over rough patches.'

'Yes, boss.'

'If only,' he muttered. At the moment, he didn't feel in control of anything, especially with Tamara ramping up his hormones like he was a teenager again. The one she refused to acknowledge, remember? Could be good for both of them if she thought he hadn't changed because then she wouldn't want a bar of him. Except he wasn't that guy anymore. 'Here we go.'

Pulling out onto the road, he headed towards the coast and the first of the stops he'd looked up online. There were waterfalls along the way where people swam and dived in the deep blue, crystal clear water. He'd need to take a dip to cool off as soon as they got there. The way his skin was on fire, the water would no doubt start boiling fast.

He sensed Tamara sitting back and looking around at the trees and thick greenery on the sides of the road. Glancing over his shoulder, he said loudly, 'It's magical, isn't it?'

She leaned close. 'Absolutely beautiful. I can't wait to see everything.'

What the heck? If he was going to spend the day with Tamara this close to him, he might as well make the most of it. He breathed deep, drawing in her rose scent again. 'The first waterfall's not far. Ready for a swim?'

'It's a bit early.'

Damn. He'd hoped she'd say she was ready to leap in the moment she got off the bike. He could set the precedent and perhaps she'd follow. 'No such thing.'

'After you, then.'

Perfect answer.

When they arrived, he could see the sun hadn't reached the waterfall yet, but they were in Vanuatu and cold weather didn't exist. He kicked off his sneakers, stripped away his shirt, and jogged to the water's edge. Unsure how deep it would be, he held back from taking a flying leap and waded in. The level quickly reached his waist and he dived deep.

Pleasure filled him. It was wonderful being with Tamara. Popping up, he saw her coming towards him, the water covering her knees as she tiptoed over the rocky bottom. For the first time ever, he saw her body. Dressed in a lime-green bikini that highlighted her gorgeous shape and full breasts to perfection, she was all he had ever imagined and more. His chest tightened and he felt humbled. She was so lovely his head spun with a longing to get closer to her, and not only sexually.

'The water's very clear. I can see my toes.' She giggled like a six-year-old.

'Jump in. It's not as chilly as we expected.' He doubted he'd ever feel cold when Tamara was around.

Slowly sinking down she let the water come up to her breasts and then her neck before spreading her legs out as far as they could reach. 'Wow.'

Yes, wow. But he wasn't thinking about the water.

Leaning back, he tilted his head to stare up at the top of the waterfall where the sun's rays were sparkling on the edge. A dream moment. A simple pleasure, no one else about, and nothing pretentious about the area. No huts or parked caravans nearby. Again, he used his word of the day. Perfect.

He'd come a long way from the lad who went on holidays to swanky tourist towns with his parents and believed he was in an idyllic place with everything he wanted on hand. Now he knew something like this spot was far more special. Less was more. Except when it came to Tamara. There was a lot to her, and getting to know her properly was like unravelling many layers of wrapping paper with a surprise in each one.

'I could stay here all day.' Tamara laughed. 'Except I didn't bring any food.'

'There are other days for that, if you don't fall in love with the next place we stop at.' He knew what she meant. Lying on his back, he let the flow slowly take him further down the river, soaking up the view of the bush, and the bright blue sky above. Sometimes life was indescribably good.

Scrambling to his feet, he was surprised how far along he'd floated. Tamara was back in the same place, splashing around and ducking under the water. She appeared happy. Another reason to feel content.

Making his way back to her, he wondered if he'd ever feel this relaxed about falling in love and having the family he'd like. The idea of kids had always scared him. If he hadn't had his grandparents to look out for him in that horrific year, then he wouldn't have a clue how to be a good father. Other than be the complete opposite to his own Even then, knowing how people could taunt his kids about their criminal grandfather, it wouldn't be right to place that burden on innocent children, would it? Finding the right woman who'd stick by his side would be difficult, too, if not impossible, so he'd given up looking. He'd loved Harriet and had thought himself heartbroken when she'd left him, but now he wondered if he'd deliberately made himself believe she was exactly what he'd hoped for simply because he'd desperately wanted to be loved unconditionally.

His gaze drifted to Tamara. She was bringing far too many emotions to the surface that he'd thought long buried. She'd always got his attention but now appeared to be doing so in lots of ways he hadn't thought possible. Was he open to that? To letting her in? He couldn't be sure, and he wasn't prepared to think about that now, scary as it was. Wading through the water, he joined her.

'Thought you'd gone to sleep at one point.' Tamara laughed.

'It wouldn't have been hard to. It's wonderful lying back and letting the current take over. You should try it.'

'No, thanks. I like knowing where I am at all times.'

What would it take to distract her from focusing too hard on what she was doing? 'Shall we move on to our next destination?'

'Got something in mind?'

'There's a place where you can go zip-lining down the hillside. We should give that a crack.' Would that be pressing her worry buttons? She'd know where she was but wouldn't be able to do a thing about controlling the ride.

Her face lit up. 'You're on.'

'I really don't know you. I expected you to do a runner at the thought of flying down a wire.' Then again, Tamara didn't tend to run away from difficulties, did she?

She laughed.

A deep laugh that made his knees knock.

'That is so not me.'

He swung her pack over his shoulder. 'Let's get back on the bike.' Then he had an idea. 'Do you want to take the controls?'

'I wouldn't know where to start. Anyway, I'm happy being the passenger and gazing around at everything we pass.'

'I could be your instructor if you change your mind.'

Her sodden ponytail slipped back and forth over the back of her neck. 'Not likely. I prefer to sit back and enjoy the day.'

Fine with him. Enjoyment seemed to be the new word of the day. Long may that continue. Pulling on his shirt, he straddled the bike and waited until Tamara was seated behind him, then booted the accelerator. They were off to the next adventure. This time in the jungle.

Tamara held the zip line bar tight and waited to go whizzing down towards the bottom of the cliff face. It wasn't too steep. She couldn't wait to get started.

'Make every moment count,' the guide said. 'Your ride will be over almost before you've started.'

'Bring it on.' Looking around she found Fergus on the ride behind her, looking as excited as she was. Giving him the thumbs-up, she faced forward again.

'Ready, steady, go.' The guide released the harness holder and she was off, zooming down the cable towards the trees at the bottom. Air whooshed past her face and her hair flew behind her. 'Yahoo,' she yelled as everything sped by in a blur. Then she was rushing up to the platform, slowing as the pulley rose to where two men waited to catch her. 'That was amazing,' she babbled as they undid the harness for her to step out of. 'Thank you, guys. I loved it,' she said as she high-fived both of them.

Stepping aside, her body fizzing with excitement, she watched Fergus come flying down, his face split in the widest grin imaginable. Her fingers were tapping her thighs as she rose up and down on her toes. What a thrill. Talk about being on a high.

Fergus looked as thrilled as she was. When he reached the platform and the two men grabbed him, he was laughing.

She threw herself at him, winding her arms around his shoulders. 'It was amazing.'

'Incredible.' He grabbed her, spun her in a circle before pulling her closer and leaned down. His mouth covered hers and his tongue dived inside—hot, delicious, thrilling.

Her head spun. Her mouth opened wider as she tasted him and drank in his heat, the whole wonder of Fergus. Fergus kissing her after all this time. Was this for real? Pressing her body harder against him to feel his body against hers, she kissed him back as though her life depended on it. Yes, very real. Awesomely so. Those muscles under her hands were firm and hot. His mouth tasted of wonder with an intensity she'd only known the first time they'd kissed.

Deep laughter around them interrupted her sense of wonder. Reluctantly she lifted her mouth to look around.

The two guys who had unhooked her from the harness were watching them with wide grins lighting up their dark faces. 'That's the best reaction to the ride we've seen in a while,' said one of them.

Fergus kept holding her. 'It was incredible,' he repeated.

She glanced at him. *Kissing me or the ride?* she wondered.

He winked. 'Both.'

Was she that obvious? Too bad. She couldn't always keep her feelings under lock and key when it came to Fergus. 'I agree.'

'I'll have to do the ride again. I missed everything on the way down, only felt the speed and wind and didn't notice much else.'

She had to *kiss* him again. But she agreed about the ride. 'There wasn't enough time to look around. Do you want to do it now? Or another time.'

'Another time. Something to look forward to.' He put his arm over her shoulders as he stood on one leg and freed the other from the harness tangled around his ankle. 'It's quite an adventure, isn't it?'

'Sure is.' She'd got a high from the zip line ride followed with a top-up from Fergus's kiss. Both experiences had been filled with excitement and amazement. 'What's next?'

'How about lunch at the first resort we come to?' He stepped away from the harness and straightened up, all but towering over her.

She usually disliked being small, as it made her think she had to prove she was big on the inside, but Fergus made her feel good about her size. She fitted against him perfectly. Taking a step back, she looked him over and felt her stomach tighten in anticipation. Of what, she wasn't sure, but that kiss surely wasn't a one-off. Not if she had anything to do with it. This man was coming up to her expectations of who she'd like in her life, at her side, permanently. She took another step backward. That was so wrong it was ridiculous. But why was it wrong? She hadn't been looking for a man to love and share her life with, yet Fergus got to her in so many unexpected ways she was confused—and happy. He already had her thinking he could help her get over the worry that she wasn't good enough to be in a relationship again. He'd turned his life around in the face of what must've been an overwhelming experience, yet he'd come out as an honest, genuine guy. Could he help her regain her confidence and turn her life around, too?

'Tamara? You're not keen?'

'What did you ask?'

'About lunch.'

They were always having meals together. Like an old couple with a regular routine. As if. 'I'm all for it. I'm starving after all the excitement.' Hungry for more than food, but she wouldn't mention that. Going too far, too soon, wasn't a good idea. There was a lot to think about first.

'For a moment there, I thought you must've left your brain halfway down the zip line.' The twinkle remained in his eyes, filling her with more longing for another kiss.

'Seriously, I'm in need of food in a relaxed setting with nothing more important to do than enjoy myself. And the company,' she added for the hell of it.

'When did you turn into such a charmer?' Fergus grinned.

'When bluntness doesn't work, it's always worth a try.'

'Your kiss worked.' He laughed. 'I can't imagine you do that often.'

She did a little wriggle on her toes. She was getting to like him more and more, and wanted that feeling to continue. More kisses included. 'I'll change out of my wet bikini before we go anywhere.' There was a changing room back at the start of the zip line.

His grin slipped. 'Okay.'

Her turn to laugh. 'Not saying I won't go swimming again, but I don't want my shirt sticking to my damp bikini top while I'm having lunch.' It would accentuate her boobs, and she'd probably struggle to eat, thinking about what lay beneath his shorts and T-shirt.

The wide smile returned. 'Come on, let's get moving. Want to walk back up or wait for the guys to give us a lift on the trailer?'

'Walk.' She'd try not to think what that smile might mean. Surely she wasn't getting to him in a sensual way? Then again, why not? He'd kissed her like he meant it and was hungry for more too.

The track back to the top was narrow, with loose pebbles making it slippery. When Fergus took her hand to steady her, she didn't pull away. Keeping her balance wasn't hard, but having his fingers entwined with hers sent shivers of desire down her spine. The zip line ride had excited her but the kiss that followed had really turned up the heat. Time to take a breath and slow down? There were still three weeks to get through, and if anything went wrong between them because they'd gone too far, it'd be difficult, if not impossible, to remain in accord while working alongside each other. And first and foremost, that was why they were here, not to begin a relationship.

But she wasn't letting his hand go. It felt right. So good. She'd never have thought holding hands could be such a turn-on. Hopefully, that was why Fergus didn't let go until they reached the bike. Maybe he felt the same way.

Giving him a smile, she grabbed her bag to go change. 'Back in a minute.'

'No rush. We've got all day.'

That was the thing. They did. *I'm going to make the most of every hour with Fergus today.* If only to deepen their friendship. She laughed at herself. Who did she think she was fooling?

They spent the rest of the day at the first resort they came across. After helping her off the bike, Fergus kept his hands to himself, causing her to wonder if he'd been thinking along the same lines about how they had to stay on track if they wanted to get through their time here without any difficulties. Swallowing her disappointment, she stuck to her decision to make the most of being with him, enjoying the afternoon, swimming in the pool, sharing food platters and cold drinks. Like a real date. Being with Fergus was fun.

Even though her body was yearning for intimacy, her head worked hard to keep the desire in line. By the time Fergus parked outside their accommodation building at the end of the day, she was mentally exhausted but happier than she'd been in a long time.

'I'll take the bike back,' Fergus told her.

Stretching up on her tiptoes, she brushed a light kiss over his lips. 'Thanks for a wonderful day. See you in the morning.'

Placing his hands on either side of her head, he leaned in and deepened the kiss for a brief moment. '*Thank you.* I've had a lot of fun.' Turning around, he revved the motor and roared away.

Tamara watched him until the bike went around the corner. Her heart was beating hard, her face warm. 'So have I, Fergus. So have I.'

CHAPTER SEVEN

'THERE'S A TEAR HERE.' Fergus pressed hard on the vein leaking blood faster than a tap turned on full. He suspected there'd be more to come. A tree branch had rammed long-ways into the woman's abdomen when the ute she'd been driving went out of control on the coastal road and hit a tree.

'I'm getting more clamps,' Tamara told him, obviously thinking the same. She *should've* been a doctor.

'Good.' He continued investigating the damage in front of him.

Within moments Tamara was back. No messing around. Like the way she'd leapt up to kiss him on Sunday. No messing around then either. Heat ripped through him at the memory of her soft lips on his mouth. He couldn't deny she'd got to him. Was that good, or was it something to worry about?

'Here.' She slid the steel bowl onto the table.

'It's going to take lots of sutures to save the uterus,' he said. 'Even then I'm not sure if she'll be able to conceive. The damage to the ovaries is extensive.'

Tamara shuddered. 'That's really sad.'

No identity had been made yet, but the woman looked to be in her late twenties or early thirties. 'I'd say she's had at least one baby.' The abdominal muscles were soft, suggesting a previous pregnancy.

'I hope she's already got the family she wants, then.'

'I agree.' The sadness emanating from Tamara again had him wondering if she wanted children. He could imagine her small figure swollen with a baby inside, and he smiled. It was a picture that filled him with a similar longing, but he shook it away. As if that was going to happen. He needed to get real. Tamara knew what had happened and still spent time with him, even kissed him, but did she still have doubts about how he'd turned out? About who he used to be? He couldn't be sure, and that was the problem. But he wasn't getting a lot of say in how he felt about Tamara. She was taking over his mind all too easily. As well as other parts of his body, if he was being honest.

Suturing the internal wounds took time and care, and gave him something else to concentrate on rather than the gorgeous nurse on the other side of the table. When he finally straightened from the table, his patient was in better shape than when she'd been brought in by the paramedics. 'She's going to need blood,' he said.

Ian looked up from the monitors. 'We don't have a big blood bank, so I hope she's got a common group.'

'Surely O positive will be available?'

'Should be, but you'll have to get onto it sooner rather than later,' Ian warned.

'I'm O pos,' Tamara piped up. 'Happy to donate if needed.'

'I'll keep that in mind when I see the lab techs. Which'll be shortly. I want to make sure everything's all right here first.' He couldn't be too careful when it came to trauma cases. He hadn't known what to expect when he'd opened the already torn abdominal area, but he needed to be absolutely certain he'd done all he could. 'How's the blood pressure?'

'Eighty-six over fifty-eight,' Ian said.

'Could be worse considering the blood loss.' Fergus began to relax. Tossing his gloves in the bin, he said, 'You can start bringing her round. I'll go arrange the blood transfusion. Tamara, are you sure you don't mind donating, if needed?'

'Wouldn't have said it if I didn't mean it,' she retorted.

'True.'

Her eyebrows rose, then she appeared to smile behind her mask. 'Go get things sorted.'

'I'd like you to stay with this lady until I get back. Don't take her to recovery. She's bound to be in shock when she comes round and as she won't know where she is since she was unconscious when they brought her in, having you here to answer questions would be a help.' She could do that in recovery, but it was busy out there.

'No problem.' Tamara was watching the woman as Ian began reversing the anaesthetic.

As easy as that. If only everything was so straightforward when it came to Tamara. Like getting closer without worrying about the past coming back to bite his arse. Because everything kept coming back to his father, he often felt worthless as an individual despite holding his head high and fighting the consequences. But after Harriet's betrayal, he doubted if he could ever truly trust someone to love him for himself. If he did manage to put it all behind him.

Many people had deserted him when he'd needed them

most. To find the love he yearned for, he had to take another chance on being loved unconditionally. Was he capable of doing that? He just didn't know.

Tamara hoped no one noticed her yawning behind her mask. With the woman involved in the accident needing urgent surgery first thing, it had become another long day as they worked through the schedule. She hadn't had to donate blood as there was enough available in the lab. Fergus had refused to cancel any operations even after he'd learned they had an emergency to deal with as well. She'd been right behind him. They were here to do all they could for the locals. If that meant being exhausted at the end of each day, then she'd cope. There hadn't been a lot of sleep going on all week. Daydreaming about Fergus and what it would be like to have more of those kisses and to be held against his naked body had taken over from the humidity. Whatever was going on in her head and heart, she had it bad.

One more procedure to do before their day was done. Belle, their final patient of the day, was dozing while she waited to be taken into Theatre.

'Belle, it's time.' Tamara shook her arm gently.

Her eyes blinked open. 'Wish you were waking me to say the surgery was finished,' she said.

So do I, thought Tamara. 'You've been very patient,' she said.

'It's okay. I'm not an urgent case like Aria was.'

'You've heard about the woman in the accident this morning?'

'Her kids go to the same school as ours. Is she going to be all right?'

'She's had surgery and is resting quietly.'

'In other words, that's all you're going to say.' Belle nodded. 'I understand.'

'Let's get you into Theatre so the anaesthetist can have a quick chat with you.' Tamara released the brake and began rolling the bed through the doors. 'Doctor Collier's waiting for you too.'

'I am popular.'

Tamara laughed. She liked this woman. 'You've got their full attention. Make the most of it.'

'What's funny, ladies?' Fergus asked as she lined up the bed beside the table.

'Girl talk,' Belle told him.

'You're supposed to be half asleep by now.' Fergus chuckled.

'Belle, I'm Ian, your anaesthetist during the operation. Do you have any concerns about having anaesthetic?'

Thankfully, they were back on track or it'd be midnight before they were finished up. Tamara sighed. Tomorrow, five more ops were scheduled. Then it would be Sunday again.

So far, she had no plans for the day off. Lazing round on the beach was tempting. Also a second zip line ride. But she might save that for the last weekend here. Something to look forward to. Unless Fergus suggested they do it again tomorrow, and then she'd be buzzing. For another crazy ride and another knee-bending kiss or two.

Once Belle was lying on the operating table Tamara covered her with a sheet and squeezed her hand. 'See you soon.'

'Not too soon, I hope.'

'Start counting to ten, Belle,' Ian said.

'One, two, three, four—'

'Gone,' Tamara said as she tapped the back of Belle's hand to be certain. Placing the blood pressure cuff around Belle's arm, she pumped it tight and read the monitor. 'Normal.'

'Ready,' Ian said.

Fergus picked up a scalpel. 'Me too.'

Swabs in hand, Tamara waited as Fergus opened Belle's abdomen. 'You've done a few of these hysterectomies over the past couple of weeks.' The days were flying past. She couldn't believe they were already halfway through their time. The thought of returning home and not seeing Fergus was an increasing worry. He was coming to mean so much to her. Too much. She needed to be incredibly careful or she could get badly hurt again.

'*We* have,' he corrected her.

She liked that he didn't take all the credit, even when he did most of the work. She was the cleaner-upper and loved it. It was nursing at an intensity that kept her focused. When she was doing her nursing training, she'd thought she'd work on wards looking after people when they were recovering from an illness or surgery, but Theatre had drawn her in from the outset. She cared for patients at a time when they were worried about being put under anaesthetic and having surgery. Over here, she often saw them afterwards too, which she liked.

'Swabs, Tamara.' Fergus stood back for a moment to watch her clean around the opening he'd made.

When he removed the uterus, she held out a steel bowl for him to place it in, then put it aside to swab before handing him a suture threaded needle. It was a routine she knew well and found almost relaxing. Of course, she was aware things could go wrong fast, but she was ready to do whatever required if that happened.

Together they worked on Belle's abdomen until Fergus had closed the wound and she'd finished swabbing the area clean. Standing back, they both watched Ian reverse the anaesthesia. Then Tamara wheeled Belle out to recovery to wait until she was awake and feeling all right.

The day was finally over.

'You still think you'll do more volunteering after this?' Fergus asked as they drank coffee, overlooking the hospital grounds while waiting for Tim and Sarah.

'Definitely. I get a buzz from helping others less fortunate. As soon I get home, I'm putting my name down for next year. You're right. What we're doing is wonderful in a different way to how I usually feel about nursing. I feel more involved with these people.' Everyone was so welcoming and grateful, it was humbling.

'You found your calling, didn't you?'

'I certainly did. I'd say the same about you after seeing how you look out for your patients, whether they're awake or under anaesthetic.' He was always careful and gentle when operating. As were most surgeons she'd worked with, but Fergus seemed even more concerned when it came to surgeries. Maybe she was looking for all things good about him.

'I do my best.'

An understatement if ever she'd heard one. 'Was it always your intention to become a doctor when you were at college?'

'Yes, it was. Though back then, I thought I'd become a heart surgeon.' His smile was lopsided. 'Then one day in my first year at university, one of the women studying with me said her father was a cardiologist and that it was one of the most admired positions. That's when I took a long, hard look at what I really wanted from my career, and after listening to a friend talk about the problems she and her partner were facing trying to get pregnant, I knew I wanted to be a gynaecologist.'

The way he was opening up more and more suggested he trusted her not to give him a hard time about the past. 'You got it right. The patients you've worked with here all say you're wonderful.' There hadn't been one who'd complained about what he'd done for them. 'A lot of that's how you take the time to talk the procedures through and listen to any questions or concerns they have without looking at your watch.' She'd seen specialists do that in pre-Theatre rooms and it drove her crazy. Patients were vulnerable pre-op and deserved to be heard, even if the clock was ticking in Theatre.

Fergus smiled. 'You're saying not all surgeons are the same?'

'Sometimes, I think trainee doctors need to do a paper on how to be nice to patients, but I'm being unfair because most I've worked with are definitely kind and caring.'

'Like nurses.'

'You're on to it.'

'So why is nursing your dream job like you said at the airport?'

Tamara didn't have to think about it. 'I was always going to be a nurse. I've never regretted my choice. I wonder if I got Dad's compassionate gene. He raised Sashi and me so lovingly that we couldn't have asked for better. Other than to have our mother back,' she added quietly. Then shook her head. Where did that come from? She never said out loud how much she'd missed her mum growing up.

A warm hand covered hers. 'You've had your share of tragedy.'

'I have, but like I said, Dad was awesome.'

'You miss him a lot.'

Oh, damn and blast. Something else she didn't like to talk about. It was too soon and still raw.

Fergus squeezed her hand. 'It's all right. You don't have to say anything.'

It might be good to talk about it, let go of some of the pain. 'Dad suffered from stage-four bowel cancer. When he was told there was nothing more to be done for him, I took a leave of absence from work and nursed him at home, because he didn't want to be anywhere else but where he lived with my mum, and where Sashi and I grew up.'

Her hand was back in Fergus's. 'That's special.'

'It was.'

'I can't begin to imagine how you coped.'

He'd lost his father in totally different circumstances, and she didn't know anything about his relationship with his mother. They might've become closer while dealing with the situation. 'Does anyone know what they'll do in that situation?' she asked.

'No.' Blunt. And poignant. He sounded like he hadn't got over what he'd lost. Not completely anyway. Probably never would.

Her turn to squeeze Fergus's hand. She had no other answer without getting too deep, and that was something she wasn't ready for. Losing her father had been huge. After how John had treated her, the loss of Dad had only underlined what could happen if she gave her heart to anyone again. Sashi had said she was wrong to believe she should hold back on that score because love was everyone's dream, and essential for a fulfilling life. Seeing how happy her sister was with her man and their kids, Tamara knew she was right, but it didn't help to lift her caution. Losing a loved one hurt like hell.

'You all right?' he asked.

'Actually, I am.' She meant it. Whatever lay ahead, she'd relish this time with Fergus. 'I don't usually talk about Dad, but I'm glad I did.'

'I'm here any time you want to get anything off your chest.'

She liked that. In fact, she was liking everything about him. Scary and exhilarating all in one. Life could be looking up.

'You've got it bad,' Tim said when they climbed out of the van laden with takeout meals Sarah and Tamara had left them to take inside.

'You think?' Fergus shrugged, pretending a nonchalance he didn't feel. Despite warning himself more than once, Tamara dominated his thinking whenever he wasn't focused on work. Even then she managed to sneak into his head at times.

'Definitely. You're not very good at hiding your feelings.'

'Here I thought I was very accomplished at doing that.' What if Tamara was the one for him? She'd known him when everything had turned on its head and had never given him a hard time about his father. *No, 'the one' doesn't exist, remember?*

Tim laughed, shaking his head. 'Often, yes, but when it comes to Tamara, you're up the creek without a paddle.'

Wonderful. 'I hope she hasn't noticed whatever it is you think you have.' He doubted she had. She was too busy keeping her own feelings under control. There were moments when he knew she wanted to get close, to touch him, maybe repeat that kiss, but she always pulled her shoulders back and put on a straight face whenever he thought she might be letting go a little. Which wound him up harder than her dazzling eyes did. He *couldn't* risk falling for her. Not when love wasn't supposed to be on his agenda at all.

In the kitchen, Tamara handed him a plate. 'What are you doing for Christmas?'

Christmas was only weeks away. 'I haven't given it a lot of thought.'

'What do you usually do?' she asked.

'Spend it with my grandparents. Though now they live in a retirement home in Nelson, my grandma has given up making her hot ham and roast vegetables.' He smacked his lips together. 'Always my favourite.'

'Because your grandmother cooked it, I bet. I prefer turkey. It's the only time of the year I have it, and even then not every year. Depends on my sister and what she has planned.'

'Do you go to her place for the day?'

'Always.' Tamara's face dropped. 'It'll be different this year with Dad gone.'

He'd love to hug her, but after Tim's comment he stayed where he was. 'Your sister lives in Nelson, right?'

Maybe they could catch up when he went down to see his grandparents.

'Yes, thank goodness. It's always a great time with the kids excited about Santa and presents.' That longing in her voice when she mentioned her sister's children had returned.

He wanted to tell her she'd surely be a mum one day, but he wouldn't. What if the longing was brought on by the fact she couldn't have children? When it came down to it, he knew so little about her. Only one way to find out, though, and that meant spending more time together. 'I'll be in Nelson for a couple of days, so let's catch up,' he offered impulsively, which wasn't at all like him.

'You're on.'

An unexpected sense of relief filled him. He hadn't believed she'd say a flat-out no, but to hear her agreement felt surprisingly good. 'Great.' Looking across the room, he got a wink from Tim. *Thanks, buddy*, he muttered under his breath. Hopefully Tamara hadn't seen it. 'What have you two got planned?'

'Making the most of not working,' Tim said.

'A family get-together,' Sarah added. 'I've got three brothers who are married with kids so it's always a noisy, cheerful day.'

A yearning for children to celebrate all the wonderful events that happened throughout the year was rising again. Tamara was stirring up so many feelings he'd buried when he and Harriet broke up. But the idea of possibly having a partner and children made him remember what he'd risked all those years ago, which had nearly broken him when Harriet had walked away. A shiver went down his spine.

CHAPTER EIGHT

TAMARA JERKED UPRIGHT in her bed. 'What the hell?' It sounded like a freight train was rolling down the road below her window.

A familiar sound. She knew exactly what it was. An earthquake. A huge one. She leapt off the bed. The building started shaking violently. The walls creaked. The ceiling groaned as though about to implode. Staying upright on the heaving floor was a struggle. The noise grew louder as plates and mugs crashed to the floor. She needed to get in the doorway. Or down on her knees with her head under her arms. This was bad.

Crash. The bathroom door fell inwards.

She shrieked. 'Fergus.'

'I'm here, Tamara,' Fergus called from the other side of the wall. 'I'm coming.'

The floor moved up and down and sideways. 'Stop,' she shouted. Every second felt like a minute. Books fell off the table, then banged onto the floor. Her sandals slid across the room, then came back towards her.

'Fergus,' she screamed again. She was terrified. She wanted it to end. Now. Slip-sliding across the rocking room, she tried to open the door. No go. Jammed shut. 'I can't get out.' Panic filled her. She couldn't stay here. She was tugging with all her might, but it stayed put.

Suddenly the shaking stopped. All went quiet. Too quiet. The quake was over. Until the aftershocks started. Then they'd go through the same scenario many times more. With less intensity, if they were lucky. She'd been through the Christchurch earthquake years back and knew what lay ahead. Hell. The worst thing being there was nothing anyone could do to stop the quakes.

'Fergus, I need you,' she whispered. 'I don't want to be alone.'

'Tamara, are you all right?' Fergus banged her door with his fist. It didn't budge.

'No, I'm not. I hate these things.' The fear in her voice made his heart trip.

Tamara was tough, but this was something totally out of her hands. She wouldn't like that. Nor the consequences that could follow. He wasn't exactly enjoying himself either, but his biggest concern was Tamara. Her fear was gut-wrenching. He had to get her out so they could make their way downstairs and outside. 'Stand back. I'm going to kick your door in.' It could work or go badly for him.

'It's jammed,' she shouted.

'Are you out of the way?'

'Yes.' Were those tears in her voice?

He hoped not. They'd be hard to take. 'Here I come,' he called. She might've said she was out of the way, but he was making sure. Slamming the door into her was not an option. Standing back, he lifted his leg and went for it.

The door groaned and moved slightly.

'And again,' he called.

This time the door fell in, with him sprawled on top.

Tamara was instantly reaching for him. 'Fergus? Are you all right?'

'Yes. What about you? You weren't injured?'

'Apart from being terrified, I'm good. I loathe earthquakes. I was in Christchurch when they had the big one and this felt worse. The noise of it coming woke me and I immediately knew what was happening.'

'I've never been in one that big. We need a torch.'

'I haven't got one. Have you?'

'On my bedside table.'

'I'll get it.'

'No, Tamara, I don't want you going anywhere on your own. We stick together. I doubt we can trust any part of the building not to give way. Give me a hand up.'

She reached out her hands to take his. She was shaking hard. 'Come on. As much as I want to go get that torch, I don't want to move far from you.'

He wrapped her in a hug. For both of them. 'We got through it. We'll get through anything else that follows.'

Her head lay on his bare chest, her hot breath sharp stabs on his skin. 'I hate earthquakes,' she repeated.

'Probably because we can't do a damned thing about them.'

Her head moved up and down against him. 'Yes.'

'Hey, Fergus, Tamara. You guys all right?' Tim called from the other side of the hallway, a torch beam finding them.

'Think so. What about you two?'

'Sarah took a knock on the head when the mirror came off the wall. From what I can see, she's not seriously injured. We need to get out of here.'

'I'm going to find my torch and take a look around.'

What if they couldn't get out of the building? They'd find a way. They had to. There'd be aftershocks coming.

'Tell me where it is and I'll get it. Sarah, come out here with the others. We have to stick together.'

'It was on the bedside table. Could be anywhere now.'

Sarah quickly joined them. 'The sooner we're out of this building the better as far as I'm concerned. It's not very stable.'

'I agree. I imagine our services are going to be needed at the hospital after this. I'm heading that way once we've got out.'

'As if you wouldn't,' Tamara muttered.

Despite everything he grinned. 'I like that you believe in me.'

Tim returned. 'Here you go. One torch. Now what? Do we get our phones and other gear or try to make our way out of the building and hope we can get everything later?'

'I'm all for getting out,' Tamara was quick to answer.

The building creaked and groaned, and Fergus had to agree with her. 'Better to be safe than sorry.' He took a look at her, and then across at Tim and Sarah. 'Think we need to grab some clothes. None of us are dressed to go out on the street.' Fergus shook his head. Tamara looked so damned sexy in a pink singlet and white satin knickers, it was hard to focus on the mess they were in. Then he realised he wore only a pair of lightweight shorts that barely covered his butt.

Tim nodded. 'Good point. Let's do that. Might as well grab essentials while we're at it.'

'I'll come with you, Tamara.' She wasn't going into her room on her own. 'Don't argue. That'd only waste time.'

'I wasn't going to.'

Within minutes everyone had returned to the hall dressed in hurriedly hauled-on clothes and carrying tote bags. They moved to the stairway, Fergus with Tamara's hand in his, just as Tim had Sarah's.

The stairs looked all right, but caution prevailed. 'One of us should go down first to make certain they're safe.'

'I'll go,' Tamara said. 'I'm the lightest.'

She was right about that, but he didn't want her going first.

'Let's do this.' She removed her hand from his grasp.

'I'm right behind you,' Sarah said.

Someone shouted from below, 'Hey, Docs, you guys there?'

'We're making our way down now.'

'Go easy. Lots of damage to this building.'

'Great,' Fergus muttered.

The stairs creaked with every step they took. Eventually they reached the ground floor and hurried out onto the street to be greeted by a fireman.

'Glad you're all okay,' the man said. 'We've barely started checking on people, but some are already making their way to hospital with injuries. Many buildings came down.'

The ground started shaking again.

Fergus caught Tamara to him and held her tight. 'It's okay, Tamara. We're out of the building.'

'We're not supposed to stand out on a street lined with tall buildings. It's dangerous.'

The shaking stopped and he leaned back to look into her eyes. 'You're doing well. Want to go to the hospital and see how we can help?'

She straightened immediately. 'Of course.' Nurse to

the fore. Hopefully caring for others would help keep her focused and her mind away from the earthquake.

'Tim, Sarah, what do you think?' he asked.

'Same as you. We need to make ourselves available.'

The fireman stepped up. 'I'll give you a ride. We'll have to take the long way round.'

'Is there a lot of damage?' Tim asked.

He nodded slowly. 'From the calls already coming through the radios I'd say so. Our buildings aren't all as solidly built as they should be. Not enough money to go round.'

'It can't be helped,' Fergus told him. Sometimes they got it wrong back home too. Especially when it came to the older buildings.

The man shrugged. 'Come on, let's get you somewhere safer.'

They climbed into the fire department jeep and stared out the windows as they headed to the hospital. Collapsed buildings, huge cracks in the roads and people wandering around in a daze were all over the place.

Beside him, Tamara was shivering. He tucked her in against his side. 'Deep breaths. We'll get through this.'

'I know, but what about the families who live along the roads? All those cute little kids must be terrified.'

So she was thinking about them and not her own reactions. That would help keep her calm. 'It's unavoidable.'

'I remember after the Christchurch earthquake how people were too scared to go inside their homes for days, while others carried on as normal, allowing for the lack of water and other essentials as they went.'

'And you?'

'Did my best to carry on regardless. For four days I

worked all hours in the medical tents set up in Hagley Park.' She gave him a tentative smile. 'I know how this goes, but I did lose it for a bit back there in the apartment.'

'Shows you're normal.' He smiled, hoping to lift her spirits. If only he could swing her up in his arms and take her away from this.

'You weren't with us,' Tim said. 'Sarah's tougher than me. Despite the mirror whacking her, she insisted on checking me over when the shaking stopped.'

Finally, after a convoluted trip on destroyed roads, they reached the hospital, where crowds were gathering outside the main entrance. People lay on the ground, while others walked back and forth between everyone. Lights showed through the windows. Torches were being waved around. The clear sky made the darkness less intense. One plus in everyone's favour.

'Here you go, folks. For everyone's sake, I hope you don't have too many injured people to deal with.' The fireman pulled up as close to the door as he could get.

Fergus got out and looked around. 'They've obviously got a generator to make life easier.'

'Three, actually.'

'Well prepared then,' Tim commented.

'This isn't the first quake to strike Vanuatu, and no doubt won't be the last, but in my experience it's the worst.'

'Thanks for the ride.' Tamara got out and looked around at the crowd watching them.

'I'll see you all later. I'll find out more about the building you were using and let you know if it's safe to get all your belongings out. It might pay to see if you can sleep here for a night or two.' The fireman drove off slowly, stopping to talk to people as he went.

'Shouldn't he be rushing to see what needs to be done urgently?' Sarah asked.

'Talking to people might help calm them, and that's just as important as anything else,' Tim replied.

'Let's see what's going on inside.' Fergus took Tamara's hand again and walked towards the main door. There was nothing to be gained by standing out here. He was ready to get busy dealing with injuries because he didn't believe for one minute there wouldn't be plenty. The decimated buildings, some flattened, that they'd passed on the way had turned his mouth acidic. It was horrific. There was no way people had got out unhurt from some of those buildings. No doubt there'd be deaths.

'Slow down, Fergus,' Tim called.

'You tell him.' Tamara was holding his hand as though she never intended letting go. 'At least I'm experienced in the aftermath of an earthquake.'

Tamara shook her head. How she'd have got through the last hour without Fergus at her side, she'd never know. He'd been there for her from the moment she'd called out to him. Now she needed to toughen up and get on with being a nurse, not a woman relying on a man to get her through the coming hours. Reluctantly letting go of his hand, she followed him inside, ready to do whatever was required to help others. It was the only way to get over the quake. Focusing on other people and their injuries would shove her fright to the back of her mind, and with a bit of luck that's where it'd stay. 'Going to ED first?'

'Where else?' Fergus asked.

'You know me. I like to be sure.' She was walking close to him because she needed his strength, liked how he'd held her in the jeep and the other moments he'd touched her. He'd made her feel safe. She didn't feel ashamed for being afraid. She could pick up spiders, catch rats in a trap, go to the top of high buildings, but earthquakes were her uncomfortable place.

'In here.' He pushed open a door.

Raised voices slammed into them like a wall of noise. Doctors and nurses were rushing between beds and chairs where patients waited anxiously. Some lay on the floor as there was nowhere else to go.

'How did they get here so soon?' she wondered.

'They'll be locals from nearby. Plus, it's now an hour since the quake struck.'

She looked around for someone in charge. 'That man standing by the desk seems to be running the show.'

'I agree.' Fergus turned back to Sarah and Tim. 'What do you think?'

Tim nodded. 'Afu's the head man in ED.'

Afu spotted them. Relief lightened his taut face.

'Afu, we're here to help in any capacity you need us,' Tim said. 'This is Sarah, my wife. She's a nurse, as is Tamara. Fergus is a gynaecologist who can help in any way you require, though not major surgeries, other than for women with problems in the reproductive area, which I'm presuming won't be many.'

'Hopefully not, but we've got plenty to keep you busy, Fergus.' Afu shook hands with them all. 'There're fractures, minor head wounds and other injuries. There're also two people with internal problems yet to be sorted.'

'Currently our ED doctors are in different cubicles with a nurse each. I'd suggest you all take a cubicle. For safety reasons, emergency crews are setting up tents outside with beds and equipment, but until they're ready we're working inside. There's no other choice if we're to saves lives.'

'Makes perfect sense,' Fergus said. 'Tamara, you okay working with me?'

Try to keep her away. 'Absolutely.'

Despite the tense atmosphere, Sarah smiled. 'Who else is she going to work with? I'm going to stick with Tim as much as possible.'

Tamara hoped being with Fergus would make that safe feeling last the distance. She walked into the nearest cubicle with no medical staff attending the wee boy lying on the bed in his mother's arms. 'Hello, I'm Tamara. I'm a nurse. What's your name, little man?'

The boy blinked, then turned his head into his mother's breast.

'He's call Fuifui,' the woman told her. 'He fell out of the top bunk in the earthquake. His brother said he landed on his shoulder and head.'

Tamara crouched down beside the bed. 'Fuifui, does your head hurt?'

He nodded slowly without looking at her.

'Thank you for telling me. This is Doctor Fergus. He's going to check you over. Do you know what a doctor is?'

A more vigorous nod. His head couldn't be hurting too badly if he could nod like that.

Fergus stood by the bed. 'Hello, Fuifui. Does your shoulder hurt?'

'Yes.'

'It's a strange shape,' the mother said.

'Can you lie beside your mum so I can look at it, Fuifui?'

Tamara helped the boy move onto the mattress, his face screwed tight and tears leaking down his cheeks.

Tamara wiped his face gently. 'Bruising above his right eye,' she told Fergus.

'Same side as the shoulder.' He felt over and around the shoulder. 'Dislocated. I'll give him a local anaesthetic before I do something about that, but first I need to check his skull for soft spots.' Again those long fingers went to work, touching every part of Fuifui's head.

The boy yelped when Fergus touched behind his right ear.

'Sorry, mate. You're going to have a bit of a headache for a few days, otherwise I think your head's all right.' He looked to the mother. 'He's got bruises around his ear. The bigger problem is his shoulder. It's dislocated,' he repeated. 'Do you understand what that means?'

'Yes. Can you force it back in place or does he need surgery?'

'Since it's only just happened, I should be able to put it back into place without surgery. It's a painful process so I need your permission to give him a mild drug to make him sleep, followed by a light anaesthesia so he doesn't feel a thing.'

'Go ahead. Do I have to sign anything?'

'I presume so. It's normal to do that back where we come from. I imagine it's the same here. I'll go and arrange everything.'

Tamara began wiping Fuifui's face clean. He looked like he'd been swimming in a mud pool, not sleeping in bed. 'Kids, eh?'

'He's not good at doing what he's told.' His mum smiled lovingly at her son.

'He's a boy. That's how they're made.' And lots of girls she'd dealt with in emergency departments. 'Have you any daughters, too?' *Keep talking and forget the quakes.* As if.

'Two girls, two boys.' Her smile widened.

'All set to go.' Fergus strode into the cubicle with a dish containing pills and a vial of anaesthesia. 'Mum, we need you to sit on the chair while we do this.'

As soon as Fuifui nodded off, Fergus manipulated the shoulder back in place and bound it firmly against his body with a crepe bandage. 'There you go, little man. No jumping off anything high for a few days.'

'You need to tell him when he's awake.' His mother chuckled. 'He won't listen to me.'

'He might. It'll be very tender,' Fergus told her. 'We'll be back to check on Fuifui before you take him home.'

'Thank you very much for looking after my boy.'

'No problem.' His heart went out to these stoic people. 'Take care out there.'

'Let's find another cubicle and see who's next,' Fergus said to Tamara. She looked so much better now that she had other things to focus on. Her gorgeous smile was back and the tension in her shoulders had disappeared. 'It's going to be a long night.'

Fergus got that right, Tamara thought as she dropped blood-soaked swabs into a bin. She'd lost count of how many patients they'd seen. The last woman had come in bleeding after a window broke over her during a big aftershock. The shards had caused deep cuts on her face, neck, shoulders, arms. It had taken Fergus time to suture them but now he was done. 'I wonder what's next?' she said out loud.

'Coffee and something to eat,' he answered as he looked out the window. 'The sun's been up for ages. We need a break.'

'That's the best thing I've heard for hours.'

They found Tim and Sarah at a table in the canteen and joined them with sandwiches and mugs of tea. 'How's it going in Theatre?' Tamara asked.

'Busy, but it finally seems to be slowing down,' Tim said. 'Did you hear the quake was a magnitude seven point three?'

Tamara's mouth dried. 'That's humungous.' Her body tensed as she remembered the shaking as the floor rose and fell beneath her. There'd been numerous quakes since then, and she doubted they'd stop any time soon.

'It explains the strong aftershocks,' Fergus said.

He'd touched her every time one struck, helping her find her inner strength again. 'I wonder if that fireman has found us somewhere to stay.' Somewhere that didn't shake would be perfect. And impossible.

'I'm not going back to the apartments.' Sarah was adamant.

She shivered. 'Me either. But what options have we got if he doesn't come up with somewhere? He'll be too busy doing essential work. We can't stay here. All the beds and floor space are taken.'

Carrie, the nurse Tamara had met on the first day, was walking past. She stopped and came back. 'I overheard what you said. Jimmy, my husband, is the fireman who gave you a lift earlier. He's checking out places for you as he goes around the town. It'll most likely be a resort or hotel as no new visitors will be arriving for a while.'

'That would be great.' People around here were kind even in the middle of a disaster.

Carrie nodded. 'I'll go and call Jimmy on the radio to tell him you're happy with the plan.'

'The only problem there,' Tamara said, 'Is if tourists can't fly in, then the ones already here can't get out. There might not be any rooms available.'

More hours and many more patients later, Fergus went to find Tamara who had been assisting Tim and Sarah with a surgery on a middle-aged man who'd fallen off a roof onto a garden post while trying to fix broken roof tiles. She looked as shattered as he felt. Placing an arm around her waist he pulled her into a hug. 'What's up?'

'The man died. He bled out, despite everything Tim did.'

'Come on, everyone. Afu says to get away for a break while we can. We've got accommodation at a nearby resort and it's time to get out of here. We've done more than enough for now.'

Tamara sagged against him. 'Yes, please.'

'You're asleep on your feet, my friend,' he said, though it felt like she was something more than a friend now. He didn't want to go back to where he'd been before they'd caught up. It was rather lonely there.

'You don't look a lot better.'

'Let's get out of here before someone else asks for help.' He cared that Tamara was coping with everything while looking shattered beyond recognition. In the emergency department she'd been calm and confident, but whenever she stopped to take a breath, he saw her looking around as though wondering what was coming next.

Not once had he ever seen her so concerned about anything. He was going to stick by her until she found her feet again. Of course, if asked, she'd deny she'd lost them, so he'd remain quiet on that subject. They were doing better by the day, and he'd do nothing to wreck that.

He was so aware of Tamara that nothing else got to him, not even the continuing quakes or the endless stream of patients. She was sexy and he desired her. She cared not only for patients, but about them. She was sharp and intelligent, liked keeping fit and having fun. She also liked challenges. In other words, Tamara was his kind of woman. A wake-up call he hadn't seen coming. After Harriet, he'd dated quite a few women, but not one of them had him thinking beyond a fling. He wasn't even having a fling with Tamara, yet here he was wondering what it would be like to spend more time with her doing the things they both enjoyed.

They stepped outside and were immediately swamped with humidity. 'Just what we need,' he muttered.

A four-wheel-drive truck pulled up, Jimmy behind the wheel. 'Hop in, guys. I'll drop you off at your accommodation. It's at a resort nearby.'

'You're a champ, mate. By the way, I'm Fergus and this is Tamara, and Sarah and Tim. We didn't get around to introducing ourselves last time.'

'Don't worry, we had more important things to think about. I'm taking a break once I've dropped you off. It's hell out there, but I think we've dealt with the most urgent problems for now.'

'What about tourists? I presume the airport's closed,' Tamara said.

'It is and will be for a few days for commercial flights,

but it's open for humanitarian flights. The Australian Air Force is sending planes over with essential relief cargo and people to give a hand with roads and the runway, et cetera. New Zealand's arranging similar aid.' He carried on talking about what he'd seen and done over the preceding hours until they reached the resort. 'Here you go, folks. Try to have a comfortable night.'

At the reception desk the manager greeted them like long-lost friends. 'Welcome to the Beach House. I'm Harry. Thank you for what you've been doing for our people. It's much appreciated.' He placed key cards on the desk. 'We've got two units ready for you, and the kitchen's open and will provide dinner or any other food you need. Can't guarantee what you'll get, but it will be well cooked.'

Two rooms. Single or double beds? Fergus glanced at Tamara and saw the same question on her face. Which did she want? Or did she want a room of her own? 'Tamara?'

Her steady gaze locked on him. 'I'm fine with that.'

He knew she wasn't talking about the kitchen being open. Heat fizzed along his veins, knocking the exhaustion aside. It had been one hell of a twenty-odd hours with the quakes constantly reminding them what they had no control over as they faced a myriad of patients requiring all their attention. He had to let go and relax or he'd not be able to crawl out of bed in the morning for another round of injured people. And Tamara held the answer to that in her hand.

If she was on the same page as him.

'By the way,' Harry called. 'Jimmy retrieved your gear from your apartments and brought it here.' He indicated a stack of bags. 'No idea whose is whose.'

'The man's a wonder,' Tamara commented as she swung her pack over her shoulder. 'Glad I've got something to wear that doesn't smell of sweat.'

If he had his way, whatever she got into, it wouldn't stay on for long.

Tamara watched Fergus tap the key card against the lock, her heart pounding. She was about to share a room with the one man she'd never believed she'd get this close to. The man she'd once had the hots for and a longing to get up close and personal with, and she had done everything possible to hide from those feelings.

Not anymore. Not since arriving here, really. Time to get real about her feelings. Lying to hide them from herself was a waste of time and energy and had only created more problems than the truth. So honestly? She wanted him. Of course, she was tired beyond description, but that wasn't why she felt this way. Fergus had been there for her from the moment the apartment building began shaking and he hadn't gone far from her side since. Whenever fear had hit her, he'd been there, holding her or talking her through the moment. Whether he'd also been afraid, she didn't know. He hadn't shown fear, nor had he been tense when he held her.

'Tamara? It's not too late to see if there's another room for one of us.' Fergus was watching her with a longing she hadn't seen before. Not even back when they were teens pretending they didn't really care about each other.

Grabbing his hand, she tugged him into the room and kicked the door closed behind them. 'It's way too late for that.' Stretching up on her tiptoes, she found his mouth and kissed him. Long, and hot, and with everything she had to give. Oh, it felt so damned wonderful. He tasted exotic. Turned every part of her on fire with the need to forget the horrors of the past night and day. Had her aching to have him inside her, to finally know him intimately. To lose herself in Fergus would be bliss. And a lot more, no doubt.

He was returning her kiss as fervently. Which thrilled her to bits. There was no stopping either of them. He clearly needed this as much as she did. Perfect. She'd waited so long for this. Lifting one leg, she stretched it to curl it around his waist.

Fergus lifted her higher, making it easier to wrap both legs around him. His hands spread firmly over her backside as she nestled closer to his wide, firm chest and all the time he kissed her deeper, almost devouring her in his bid to get more of her. And winding her tighter than she'd believed possible. This was unbelievable. She'd never known sex could be this amazing, and they hadn't even got started yet. It was mind-blowing. Every cell in her body was crying out for more.

Any moment now she was going to explode with need if they didn't move to the bed. Lifting her head, she locked her eyes on his hot gaze. 'Fergus? I can't wait much longer.'

A slow, crooked smile widened his mouth and sent another wave of heat fizzing through her. 'Know what you mean,' he whispered hoarsely. 'But we're going to slow down and make the most of every touch, every moment.'

'I—I can't,' she croaked through the need filling her.

Fergus strode across the room and lowered her onto the bed before dropping his shorts and hauling his shirt over his head. Lying beside her, he held her close, his hands pushing under her clothes for his fingers to run over her skin, heating her up further, yet quietening her racing hormones so she assimilated more of him. Her own hands were working on his skin, touching him everywhere, feeling his muscles, his strength, then his erection. He was ready for her. She melted into him, savouring each touch, each moment, everything about Fergus.

Sprawling over him, his hardness pressing against her drove her to new heights of desire. 'Fergus, I want you,' she murmured.

His hands were making light work of removing her shirt, touching her breasts as he went. Shivers of pleasure rippled through her as his fingers stroked down over her stomach. Then lower and lower, sliding beneath her shorts.

Reaching for his length, she rubbed gently, slowly, causing him to strain against her.

'Tamara,' he groaned, then flipped her onto the bed and rose above her to remove the last of her clothing.

Her gaze fixed on his need for her. And deep inside something gave way, letting Fergus in more than ever. Letting her accept she could make this work, make him happy, because he wanted her as much as she wanted him.

Lifting her legs she wrapped them around him to keep him close, to feel his heat against her core.

He settled between her legs, his hands again working magic on her breasts, then her stomach and lower. Then finally when she couldn't take any more, he touched her where she was most sensitive. She cried out, 'Fergus. Please. Fergus!'

Lifting her hips she reached out to pull him closer to her heat.

As he slid inside her, she cried out again, 'Fergus! Yes.'

She climaxed instantly. Then he was with her, moving into her heat, pulling back, pushing in again. In, out, in, out, reaching his own pinnacle of release before they fell into each other's arms, bodies pressed into one another as though they were never going to let go.

Heat emanated from every pore as she felt Fergus all around her, inside her. Fergus. Unbelievable. It was as though she'd found her way home. She couldn't wish for anything else. Her body was so relaxed it felt impossible to move. Her head was filled with wonder, and her heart beat to a rhythm of happiness. Fergus.

Holding Tamara as though he'd never let go, Fergus closed his eyes and let the moment take over. His body had no strength left. He'd poured everything into her. He'd lost all sense of anything else but Tamara. He couldn't believe how wonderful she'd felt in his arms. Her body so receptive to his. She'd given herself to him without hesitation. As he'd given back to her, hopefully making her feel just as wonderful. It felt as though this was always meant to happen and finally they'd got there. Who'd have thought their lovemaking would be so intense? That they'd be so in sync? Instinctively she'd understood his needs. He might've wanted to have sex with her in the past, but not once had he imagined how amazing it would be. He'd been unwilling to revisit those feelings after learning Tamara would be in Vanuatu with him, sceptical that he might be hanging on to something that had never really existed. So life could still surprise him, make him feel great. Were there more surprises to come?

'Hey, are you awake?' she asked quietly.

'Wide awake. Though I doubt my body is up to moving at all right at the moment. I'm whacked.'

'Me too. It's been quite a day after a frightening night.' Then she chuckled. 'Which has nothing to do with how I feel right now. All soft and warm and cosy. And happy to be with you.'

He'd take that any time. Brushing a kiss on the top of her head, he said, 'If the earthquakes are still bothering you, you could catch a flight home when they're available.' He wouldn't blame her if she did, but he'd be disappointed now that they'd reached this stage in their wobbly relationship. They'd only just got to know each other intimately, and it was nowhere near enough. Having made love, he hoped the wobble was gone and they'd get on better than ever. There was potential for their so-called friendship to grow into something more. If he wanted that. If Tamara wanted that. His gut clenched. He had no idea what she thought. But neither did she know how he felt about her. Because he wasn't at all certain himself, yet. There was still a long way to go. But in the meantime, he'd make the most of being this close to her.

Up on her elbows, Tamara smiled down at him. 'No way. I came to do a job and I'll see it to the finish.' Her smile widened. 'Not to mention how we've started something I'd like to keep on with.'

'Phew. You know how to make me feel good.'

'You weren't doubting my enjoyment, were you?' By the sudden tight look on her face, it was a serious question. 'Because if you were, let me tell you that I want more as soon as I've recovered and had a shower.'

Was that her way of saying all was good? He wasn't

sure, but he wasn't going to stir up trouble by asking. 'Throw in a meal and you've got me.' She already had him, but it didn't hurt to play hard to get just a little.

Slowly the smile returned. 'Let's go, then. I'm starving.'

She'd said that often over the past two weeks. 'When aren't you?'

'When I'm making out with you.'

'That's better.' Way better. He'd take that anytime and oblige in making her happy—and satisfied.

Crawling off the bed, Tamara looked around the room. 'Oh cripes. We didn't close the curtains.'

His gut tossed up a deep laugh. 'Just as well the sun went down over an hour ago.'

'Plus we didn't switch on any lights.' Her grin struck him hard.

Tamara was beautiful. He couldn't get enough of her. Knowing that amazing body better, he hoped there'd be a lot more to come. 'Go have a shower while I close us in and straighten the bed.'

She wiggled her delectable backside at him. 'You could always join me.'

'I could, but then we wouldn't make it to dinner, and right now I know I have to eat or I'll lose it.'

'You get hangry?'

'I do.'

'Then I'll get that shower.'

Watching her walk to the bathroom while remaining where he stood turned out to be the hardest thing he'd done all day. He only managed because he promised himself they'd get together, up close and sexy again later. Life hadn't looked this good in forever.

CHAPTER NINE

'Liz, I need to examine you internally,' Fergus told the woman writhing in pain on the bed.

'No problem, Doc. I know what goes on. This isn't my first baby. But my daughter was born at full term, not several weeks early.'

Fear and tension due to the quake might've brought on contractions. 'When did you feel the first contraction?' Tamara asked.

'About an hour after the earthquake.'

Tamara reached for Liz's hand. 'You're like me? You were scared out of your mind?'

'You bet I was. I'd never been in one before. They're not common in Australia.'

'I was in a big one thirteen years ago and I still freaked out on Friday.'

Tamara felt the shudder that wracked Liz and fully understood what had brought it on. If she hadn't had Fergus there, she wouldn't have been feeling as relaxed. Add in all the lovemaking they'd got up to in the days and nights since the quake and relaxed was an understatement. Fergus was wonderful. He'd shown no signs of thinking she wasn't good enough in bed. In fact, he'd been vocally enthusiastic! But it was early days for sure, and she wasn't going to ruin everything by overthinking his reactions. Instead, she'd make the most of his exceptional lovemaking and leave the future alone for now.

He crouched down at the end of the bed. 'Liz, can you part your legs?'

As Liz did so, she looked to Tamara. 'Fun being a woman, isn't it?'

'Men have no idea how lucky they are.'

'How far along did you say you are?' Fergus asked.

'Thirty weeks.'

'Any chance you're out by a few weeks?'

'I suppose it's possible. I wasn't very regular. Why?'

'I think baby's bigger than I'd expect for thirty weeks.'

'That's got to be good news, isn't it?'

'Definitely. Every week helps.' Fergus stood up. 'But I also have to tell you that baby's stuck in the wrong position. As I can't move him or her, it means doing a caesarean.'

Tamara reached for Liz's hand. 'You'll get through this, Liz. You've got a superb surgeon on your side.'

Fergus's eyes widened briefly, and he smiled at her.

Liz was staring at Fergus as though he'd grown horns. 'You're serious?'

Fergus nodded. 'Unfortunately, I can't change what's going on. There could be further complications if I don't go in and retrieve the baby. I wouldn't do a caesarean if I didn't believe it was essential.'

Blunt, but it worked.

Liz sagged. 'Do whatever you have to, to save my baby.'

'Do you want me to go and find your cousin?' Tamara asked her. Liz needed someone close with her at the moment.

'Please. Tell her to try and get in touch with Jay.'

Glancing at Fergus as she headed out of the room, Tamara bit her lip. Would he leave her side if she was having their baby? After his actions during and following the earthquake, she thought he wouldn't.

What the heck? She shouldn't even be thinking that. Far too soon! More likely they'd never reach that point. She might be enjoying his lovemaking, but caution still prevailed about falling in love with him. Not because she and Fergus once hadn't got along, but because of how her ex had treated her, lying and cheating and blaming it all on her. She'd believed she'd come to terms with what he'd done, but now she was sleeping with Fergus, so content in his arms each night, the wariness was suddenly returning in full force. She had to take this one day at a time and not rush anything.

'Tamara, I want you in Theatre with me,' was the first thing Fergus said when she returned to the cubicle with Liz's relative in tow.

'Glad to help.' She needed something good happening to take the edge off the many hours they were putting in here.

'Thought you might be.' Fergus smiled. 'I'm going to find an anaesthetist and organise a bed in Theatre. Stay with Liz until I'm ready. She's more upset than she's letting on.'

'No surprise. She's determined to be strong, but not having her husband here makes it hard.'

'We're going to name him Fergus,' Liz's husband said later as he sat beside the crib where his son lay attached to monitors and an oxygen mask.

Fergus's face reddened. 'You don't have to do that.'

'Maybe not, but we're going to anyway.' Liz looked exhausted, but her face was alight with love. 'Don't think Fergus Tamara really works, though.'

Tamara burst out laughing. 'I couldn't agree more.' Though she might be happy to tie her name with Fergus's surname one day, if she could get over the panic that had set in earlier. Sure, it was fading a little now, but it had been a wake-up call, for sure. Her emotions were all over the place, one moment wanting to trust her heart and let loose, the next wanting to hunker down and hide. So far, there was no reason to doubt him. He'd changed so much it was exciting getting to know this new version. He still looked the world in the eye, but the arrogance was nowhere to be seen. He was kind and caring with his patients and other people he spent time with. There were so many things about him that warmed her and made her wonder if at last she truly had found the man she'd been looking for most of her adult life. But John had caused so much damage with his lies and cheating. Did she really know Fergus well enough yet to trust him with her fragile heart?

'Feel like going along the road for a meal?' Fergus asked Tamara when they'd finished up for the day.

'I'd prefer to go back to the resort and stroll along the beach, maybe take a dip in the pool before having dinner, if that's okay with you.'

'The resort it is.' They'd been lucky. People had been cancelling their holidays since the earthquake so there were rooms going begging all over the island. He wanted to pay for their room, but the owner wasn't listening to him, merely said he was pleased to have them there. It gave him something to do, he'd said with a cheeky smile. 'We're keeping the cook happy too. She likes preparing meals.'

'I don't eat that much,' Tamara joked as he drove away from the hospital.

'Want to bet?' For someone so slim, she managed to put away a fair amount of food. 'Where do you put it all?' That svelte body turned him on with only a glance. 'It doesn't show at all.'

'It's in the genes. My dad was lean, and Mum wasn't big either.' She eyed him up and down. 'I'd say you got your father's genes. Tall, slight without being skinny, and muscular.'

'Mum's tall and slim,' he said quickly, wanting nothing to do with his father. 'She has to work hard at keeping her weight in check, though.' He'd sort of admitted he was like his father. Only physically, but memories of his so-called mates saying he was going to turn out a con artist like his old man were never far away.

'I remember her being beautifully dressed whenever she came to watch you play rugby.'

'You were at most of those games, weren't you?' he asked, aiming to shift the direction of the conversation away from his parents.

'All the girls were. What better way to spend a Saturday morning than watching the hunky college boys playing rugby in their tight-fitting T-shirts and shorts?' Her grin was huge. 'Those were the days. All innocence and fun.' The grin dimmed a little. 'Mostly.'

'For us lads, it was watching you girls in shorts that accentuated your legs while playing netball that wound us up.' Hopefully that wouldn't give her a reason to bring up the subject of him being rude to her.

Thankfully, Tamara laughed. 'Typical teens. Something about those days was kind of carefree. We knew there was a lot ahead in terms of studying and getting serious about being adults and were probably postponing it by having a lot of fun.'

'You've nailed it.' Parking outside the resort, he turned to her. 'I am glad we've caught up again. I've always regretted what happened between us. We're getting on better than I'd ever believed possible.' He hauled in a lungful of air. 'I'm really enjoying spending time with you, Tamara. You're one amazing lady.'

She stared at him wide-eyed.

Had he shocked her with his honesty? Did she still have doubts about how much he'd changed? Please not that. 'I mean it.'

'I know you do.'

'But?'

'But nothing.' She leaned over and planted a kiss on his mouth, then locked her eyes with his. 'I feel the same as you. Spending time together here has been great, and I'm looking forward to more.'

Hauling her into his arms, he kissed her like his life depended upon it. Which, right at this moment, it seemed like it did. 'We're on the same page,' he whispered before plunging his tongue back inside her mouth, sending need spiralling throughout his body. 'Now let's get on the same bed.'

Fergus woke to loud knocking on the door. 'Why? Who?' He wanted to stay snuggled up to Tamara for another hour or so. Hauling himself out of bed, he wrapped a towel around his waist and opened the door to find Tim about to knock again. 'Morning.' Through the broken windows in the hall, he could see the sun rising over the hill.

'We're needed for an urgent operation. Twelve-year-old boy rode his four-wheel motorbike into a five-metre hole during the night.'

That would've caused serious injuries. 'What about the girls?'

Tim shook his head. 'Leave them sleeping. There are nurses preparing for us right now. I'll warm up the ute.' The vehicle they'd been lent since the van couldn't get through all the potholes on the road from here to the hospital.

'Be right with you.'

Throwing on shorts and a T-shirt, Fergus leaned down to brush a light kiss on Tamara's cheek. 'See you later,' he whispered.

She didn't stir. Showed how exhausted she was coping with the after-effects of the quake. As they all were. It would be too easy to slip back under the sheet with her, but at the moment he needed to tug on his doctor hat.

What had the kid been doing riding in the dark with all the damage out there? He should've been at home with his family. Not his problem. Putting the kid back together was his concern. He said to Tim, 'I take it I'm the lackey for this op.' It didn't bother him. They'd worked together a couple of times over the days since the quake, as there weren't many cases turning up that he specialised in. He was upping his basic surgical skills working with Tim. Never hurt to learn more.

Tim grinned. 'You bet. It's a boy we're operating on, remember?'

Fergus laughed. 'True.' He did enjoy Tim's company. The guy took his work seriously but could still have fun, which always helped when the case was serious. He enjoyed working with Tamara too. Not only because she was very competent and obviously got a lot from her work, but because occasionally she'd give him one of those heart-warming smiles that moved him deeply. Of course, the smiles were reflected in her gorgeous aqua eyes, and although he couldn't see those lips he enjoyed kissing because of the mask she wore, he knew what her mouth looked like. Yes, he was starting to think he might have it bad.

'You and Tamara are still getting on well,' Tim observed as he turned into the hospital grounds.

'We are.' *Leave it at that, mate.* It was far too soon to talk about how he felt or what he hoped for—if he ever opened up to anyone, which was unlikely. He hadn't been good at talking to others about his feelings since being jeered at about his father.

'I'll shut up about now,' Tim said as he parked.

'Good idea.' Fergus chuckled. Tim would do exactly that. From the times he'd spent with him he'd come to understand he wasn't one for stirring up trouble. 'Let's get this underway.'

As he scrubbed up, he spent a brief moment thinking about Tamara. Again. Seeing her lying curled up in the bed they'd thoroughly messed up making love before falling asleep in each other's arms. She was coming to mean so much to him, which was a worry. He wasn't sure he could easily hand over his heart again after what

Harriet had done to him. If he didn't take risks, he had nothing to look forward to—but it was such a huge, frightening step.

'You ready?' Tim called from the doorway.

'As ready as I'll ever be.' For work, if not love. He headed to Theatre. Time to get on with practicalities.

Tamara sat on the sofa, her legs tucked under her backside. 'I keep thinking about those kids racing around playing hide-and-seek and causing their mothers never-ending worry over the danger they might get into around the wrecked buildings.' They'd spent the day visiting small villages to offer aid.

Fergus placed a very full glass of wine on the small table at her elbow. 'I think it's the kids' way of coping with what's happened. They're terrified whenever there's an aftershock and get busy running away to hide.'

'At least the aftershocks have slowed down and aren't as strong.' She'd slept uninterrupted for four hours last night, before waking up—not to a quake, but to the absence of one. The quakes, along with the long hours they were working, had screwed with her mind to the point that she wasn't always sure where she was whenever she woke from a deep sleep.

'To think we're leaving here in two days' time. Home and comfortable while these people will still be struggling to get through each day.' Fergus took a mouthful of beer. 'I considered staying on, even though I have commitments back home. I talked to Kaikea, but he believes they have things under control and, if anything, he'd prefer I returned next year to continue the work I've been doing.'

'Do you think you will?' She knew she would—if they promised no earthquakes.

'I'd like to, but I've already told the volunteer service that I'd go where they needed next year. A second stint back here, away from my practice, would be asking a lot of my partners.'

'Didn't you say you're on the North Shore?'

He nodded. 'I never thought I'd move to Auckland once I'd qualified. It makes Nelson feel like a suburb. A beautiful one, though.'

'And friendly. It's a rare time I don't bump into someone I know when I walk down Trafalgar Street.'

'Know what you mean,' Fergus muttered darkly.

She'd clearly touched a sore point. He probably got bad-mouthed by people, but it was quite the opposite for her. 'I wasn't referring to things you'd prefer left alone.'

'It's all right, Tamara. It's over and done with.'

Except it wasn't. She could see the hurt and anger in his expression. He hadn't done anything wrong. He hadn't been the guilty party. She stood up and crossed to wrap her arms around his tense body. 'I am sorry.' She truly was. He'd changed so much that he deserved to be recognised for who he'd become and not the teen of the past. Another squeeze and she returned to the sofa.

He remained silent, but his back wasn't quite so tight and those delectable lips no longer looked grim.

Sipping wine, she stared out at the pool with the palm trees on the far side. Enticing, if it didn't take energy to get up and go change into her bikini before jumping in. Far easier to stay put, enjoying the company. Despite that little setback, she was relaxed with Fergus pretty much all the time now. Sometimes she had to pinch herself in case she was dreaming and about to wake up to find he wasn't half as wonderful as she believed. He listened whenever she talked about anything—as her father used to. Her ex never took the time to hear what she had to say about most things. And he'd thought she was cold. But she hadn't even told Fergus that she'd once been married, not wanting memories of John to taint her time here. Did it matter? It probably did if she wanted this to go anywhere.

'I checked out the zip line but it's closed. Not sure if it was damaged or the owners are being cautious. Whatever the reason I'm disappointed.' Now he was smiling. 'That was an awesome thing to do, and something I'll do more often in other places.'

'Count me in.'

Plonking himself down on the chair opposite her, he laughed. 'Have to find one that's handy. They don't pop up all over the place.'

'Shouldn't be too hard. There's one in Kaikoura. It'd be an overnight trip from Nelson.' Nothing wrong with that if they were sharing a room and a bed.

His smile backed off a little. 'I don't often go down to Nelson for longer than one or two nights.'

Of course he didn't. 'Fair enough.'

'I try to see my grandparents regularly, but I don't usually allow time to do anything else.'

'Where's the retirement village they've moved to?'

'In Bishopdale, on the hill overlooking Tahunanui and Tasman Bay. Grandad's got osteoarthritis and looking after the grounds and the house got too much for him.'

A very expensive place too. Guess they hadn't been

fooled into investing their money with their son. 'It's a lovely place.'

'They find it strange being contained—Grandma's word, not mine—in a small unit and not having to worry about a thing, but it's good they don't have to mow lawns or maintain the house they used to have.'

'You'll stay with them at Christmas?'

'Yes.' He hesitated, as if wondering how to say whatever was on his mind.

She waited, not wanting to interrupt in case he reacted badly. She still didn't know him well enough to read his mind.

'The other day I mentioned us getting together at some point.' He could've sounded more enthusiastic.

'I'll be disappointed if we didn't. I'll text you my address. Drop in any time you like, other than Christmas Day, when I'll be at Sashi's.'

'Will do.'

As easy as that? He didn't seem to get that she understood his problems and wouldn't try to make things more difficult. Hopefully, he'd start to see that soon and let go of his hang-ups. 'Good.' She wouldn't overplay her enthusiasm even when he'd shaken her about how well they were getting on. Could it be she was putting more into what they had going than he was? At the end of the day, they were just having a fling while they were both on this island. A fling she'd hoped might eventually grow into something deeper. But Fergus perhaps didn't see it that way. There could even be someone back in Auckland he spent time with. She'd never asked.

Tamara's heart sank. She'd been rushing in blindly, believing this Fergus was so unlike the old one that she could accept the feelings she'd once had for him were real and this time there'd be nothing getting in the way of them. Or she could just be overreacting and needed to get a grip on her emotions. Just because it had been a while since she'd felt this way about someone, it didn't mean she was fully ready to trust again. Not so quickly, anyway.

'Want a top-up?' Fergus asked, nodding at her nearly empty glass.

Why not? She wasn't working for the next twelve hours. 'Please.'

'I hear that the Last Resort Café has opened up again. Would you like to go there for a meal tonight? It would be a change, and good to support them.'

They were supporting the owner of this resort now that he'd finally given in and had accepted that they pay for their food and drinks at least. But Fergus was right. They did spend all their time at the hospital or in this bungalow, so a change would be good. 'Great idea.'

The relief in Fergus's face suggested he wanted to get away from here because it was almost too cosy. Another warning he wasn't as keen as she was for this fling to go somewhere.

Placing the wine on the table, he looked at her. 'Bet you're looking forward to catching up with your family again.'

'I am. Especially Sashi's little guys.' She couldn't wait to see their faces when they saw the trampoline she'd bought them for Christmas.

'Kids, eh? They twist your heart when you're not looking.'

She gulped. Fergus had said that? To her? 'They sure

do. I adore the boys. They're a great pick-me-up on the down days. But I don't have to be there for them twenty-four seven. Not that it would be a problem if I was. After how Dad looked after us all the time we were growing up, it's the only way I know how to be with children.'

'Is Sashi the same?'

'Absolutely. Sometimes she worries something bad might happen, that she won't be there to see them grow up, and goes overboard caring for them.'

'Better that than not at all.'

'I agree. I'll be the same if I'm ever lucky enough to have children.' It was her turn to say too much, but then wasn't that part of getting to know each other better?

'You'd like a family?'

'Of course.'

Fergus drained his beer quickly and stood up. Closing down that subject before they got too deep? Her heart twisted.

'Let's make a move and get to the café before it fills up. Many tourists who can't get off the island are bored silly and spending a lot of time in the bars and restaurants that have reopened,' he said.

'Shall I ring and make a booking?'

'I'll own up. I already did that in the hope you'd agree to go with me.'

'Why wouldn't I?' They were sleeping together, sharing meals here and having a drink, if not revealing everything about themselves.

He shrugged. 'I'm still reluctant to readily accept that we're at the stage where I can go ahead and make a plan without talking to you first.'

'Fergus Collier. The past is exactly that. I do not look

for the arrogant young guy I once knew. He's gone. Not completely, because that's impossible, and I wouldn't want everything about you to be different, but I like who you've become. A lot. Now I'm going to change my shorts for a skirt. Back in a moment.' She strode into the bedroom without looking at him. She'd said her piece and didn't want to hear any more about the subject.

With a rare warmth in his chest, Fergus watched Tamara charge into the bedroom. She knew how to wake him up while putting him in his place at the same time. She was the first, apart from his grandparents, to acknowledge he'd truly changed. It was as though the attraction that flickered between them when they were young had flared up bigger and brighter, making him see her for real. As Tamara appeared to be seeing him. Was there a future for them? One where they had those children she'd mentioned and obviously longed for? One where he could believe he was genuinely loved for who he was?

Accepting she liked him enough to spend most of her free time with him didn't come easily. A lot of which was in bed or at a table eating. Nothing to complain about there, but she'd just told him she liked the man he'd become. No wonder his heart was out of sync. It didn't have a clue what was going on.

She'd noticed how worried he'd been when he'd thought she was talking about his past and had been quick to reassure him she wasn't. He shouldn't have worried in the first place. It was a long-held habit, but he needed to trust her not to say things aimed at hurting him. If only memories of what Harriet had done didn't keep raising their heads. *She'd* sworn it didn't bother her about his father's crimes, that it was Fergus she loved and therefore had no issues with his past. Then she'd changed her mind.

Which was why he struggled to trust Tamara, even when she was aware of what had happened. She had tried to see the true picture. Yet she'd also had every reason to rub it in and mock him. But she hadn't. Something he'd been grateful for and kept tucked away in his head to take out and smile about whenever the going got too rough. In the beginning that was often. Despite that, his heart wasn't an object to hand around willy nilly. At the moment, he was in two minds over whether to toss caution to the wind and take a risk on finding out if they were meant to be together, or to remain locked down and safe.

Safe sounded boring. It *was* boring. He loved how he and Tamara were in bed. How she smiled at him as though he'd given her a gift every time they made love. How she curled in against him, seemingly without a care in the world. At least he hoped she wasn't wondering if he might hurt her in some way. That was the last thing he wanted, but it was difficult to be completely open and honest with her. Another bad habit, but one that had kept his emotions safe whenever he'd caught up with someone from the past. He also realised he still knew very little about what she'd done in the years since he'd last seen her, other than her nursing career, and losing her dad. She'd been just as close-mouthed about her romantic past as he had, but surely she had one. Didn't that signal a fundamental lack of trust between them?

Tamara skipped into the room. 'Ready as I'll ever be.'

Okay, this wasn't the time to be gloomy or question everything. He liked being with Tamara and, at the moment, that's what mattered. 'You look lovely.' Good enough to wrap up in his arms and carry her to the bedroom. He'd have to wait. They had a date first. Catching her hand, he let them out the door. 'Let's party.'

She beamed from ear to ear. 'Bring it on.'

They would enjoy wining and dining and for a couple of hours pretend everything was right with Vanuatu. Then they could return to their room and definitely wind up the tempo.

The restaurant was full to overflowing. 'Just as well you made a reservation,' Tamara said. 'Otherwise, we'd be going hungry.'

'We still might have to wait a while, but at least the wine won't need any working on.' Fergus nodded for her to follow the waitress to a table in a corner.

'I overheard what you said. The cooks are keeping up with the orders so not a long wait. Can I get that wine you mentioned right away?' the waitress asked.

Fergus nodded. 'Please. Tamara? What would you like?'

'Chardonnay, thanks.' It was the one wine they both liked. Slipping onto the chair he'd pulled out, she gave him a smile. She could get used to this.

Sitting opposite, he looked around before focusing on her. 'I'll miss this place. The time's gone quite fast, despite the earthquake.'

It was hard to believe she'd soon be back in Nelson catching up with Sashi and her family. Fergus had said he'd be in town for Christmas and that they should catch up. Hopefully, he meant it. 'I can't believe it, either. But then it's been tricky keeping track of hours and days with all that's been going on.'

The waitress arrived with the wine, two glasses, and menus. 'The menu's rather limited, but it's the best we can manage at the moment.'

'We're just happy to eat,' Tamara told her. 'And not have to cook,' she added. Something that wasn't her favourite pastime. She was okay at putting a meal together but no chef. Noting what Fergus liked to eat, she believed he had a taste for high-end food, not the everyday stews or chops she cooked.

'Glad you understand. Not everyone's as easy to please. But then, aren't you two working in the hospital?'

'We are,' she said. Was there anyone on the island who didn't know who they were?

'The other doctor with you helped my brother after the quake. He broke a leg falling off the balcony of his house.'

'How's he doing now?' Fergus asked.

'Apart from having to sit around and do nothing, he's fine.' The waitress smiled. 'In other words, grumpy as can be. I'll be back shortly for your orders.'

She was right. There wasn't a lot on offer. Tamara quickly decided on steak with whatever vegetables were available.

'Same for me.' Fergus placed his menu on the table and lifted his glass of wine to tap hers. 'To a quieter last couple of days.'

She tapped back. 'Agreed.' Yet a sense of finality was creeping in, and she couldn't put her finger on what was causing it. Did she ask Fergus whether he'd like to see more of her once they were home? Or did she sit back and enjoy dinner and leave tricky subjects alone? That was probably the easier option. No doubt the wisest. But she didn't always do wise. After taking a sip of wine, she placed the glass on the table and began twisting it back and forth between her fingers.

'What are you thinking?' Fergus asked.

'About life once we're back home.'

'Ahh. I see.'

Did he though? 'We will stay in touch, won't we? I want to.'

'Of course we will.' He reached for her free hand. 'I don't want to never see you again after we leave here.'

Meaning? That he wanted to see her a lot? Or just catch up whenever it fitted into his busy life?

'What would you both like to order?' The waitress was back.

'Medium rare steak, and the vegetables,' Tamara told her.

'Same for me,' Fergus answered, still focused on her.

'We live a long way apart,' she pointed out as the waitress disappeared.

Fergus leaned back in his chair. 'Less than an hour and a half by plane.'

'And almost that long to drive from the airport to your part of the city,' she said, but she felt a crushing sense of relief. So, this wasn't the end of everything. There was more to come. What that turned out to be was still to be worked through, but she'd go with the flow. After taking a mouthful of wine, she set the glass down. As long as she could stop worrying, she'd be happy. More wine might help there.

After dinner, they strolled barefoot along the beach, hand in hand. The closer to the far end they got, the more concerns about Fergus and what he might want from her began to rise again. So much for being happy. She was still tense. On edge. Nothing new there, after how John made her feel when he left. He hadn't ever liked her honesty; said she could be brutal when she wanted to know something. But for her it was the only way she knew how to be. She'd learned that when her mother died and friends of her parents began tiptoeing around her. She wanted them to be normal, not strange. She'd hoped being open and honest would resolve that. It didn't work with everyone, but it was her way.

So, here went nothing. 'Do you have someone special in your life back home?'

Fergus came to an abrupt halt. He dropped her hand as though it was on fire and turned to look at her with incredulous eyes that hardened as she watched. 'No, I do not,' he snapped. 'Do you think I'd have slept with you if I did?'

She'd gone too far. 'Not really. I'm sorry, but I like to know exactly where I stand with the men I date.'

'Subtlety was never your strong point, was it?' He wasn't calming down.

While she was starting to get wound up. 'I prefer to call it being frank.'

'I'm sure you do.' He began striding back the way they'd come.

She kept pace with him. 'Fergus, I'm sorry, but I wasn't looking for trouble. I wanted to be certain you were totally single, that's all.'

'Yes, Tamara, I am, and I'm likely to stay that way. I've been engaged before, and that was a fail; we never made it to the altar. Not something I'd like to repeat. Okay?'

No. Not at all. 'I've been married. It was so awful when it fell apart that I thought I'd never want to fall in love again. But now, four years on, I would like to try again, if I can put what happened behind me, which isn't as easy as I'd hoped.'

He spun around to stare at her again. 'You never mentioned being married. Why tell me now?'

'I'm being honest and hoping to get closer to you by opening up.' Right now, it looked like that was never happening. 'To show you that you can talk to me even when you're reluctant to talk about the past. I have to admit, I've wondered what else you don't want to talk about. Why didn't you tell me about your fiancée?'

'You want me to haul myself through all my past troubles again when I've finally managed to bury them.' Not a question, but a statement. 'Forget it. I'm not going there for anything or anyone.'

'If we're going to be in any kind of a relationship, then we need to talk about things that came between us, and other things that have happened to each of us since we last saw each other.' She was prepared to talk about why her marriage failed, explain how John had hurt her saying she was cold and unloving, and blaming her for his lies and cheating.

He was staring at her as though he wanted to see right inside her. 'Tamara, it's only been two weeks since we started sleeping together. I don't call that a relationship or anywhere near one.'

'Is that why you clammed up when I mentioned your father earlier?'

'Yes, damn it, it was. You know what happened, so there's no reason to talk about it.'

'I think there is. I'm not looking to cause trouble or stir things up for you. I want you to understand how much I care about you. How I admire you for working your way through all the backlash and coming out whole.' She mightn't have gone running to his side to help at the time, but he'd have shoved her away if she had. Anyway, she hadn't. Instead, she'd wished him well but never told him so. 'Partners should support one another.'

'So I thought until my fiancée proved otherwise.' He began walking again, slower this time but still with a determined step. 'Don't bother asking what happened. I'm not talking about that either. Neither am I asking what went wrong with your marriage.'

Then this was the end of the road for them. There could be no relationship of any kind if he refused to open up, to show her his vulnerabilities, to take the risk and try to love her. Tamara gritted her teeth. She might've been called cold and uncaring by John, but she did truly care about Fergus and what happened to him. There was a warmth within her that had risen as she got to know him since arriving in Port Vila. A warmth that made her feel whole again and rekindled her need to love and be loved. A warmth that now seemed to be fading. She did want to share her heart with Fergus, but only if they could talk about anything and everything. Trust one another fully. 'What's really eating at you? What's wrong with asking for the truth?'

'Like I said, I've done that once and it cost me everything. I lost the woman I loved, who I believed I'd be spending the rest of my life with. I am not prepared to go through that again.'

'We're on the same page there. But for different reasons.' If she understood him correctly. 'Having said that, I might be willing to try again if I met the right man.' *I have, but it seems he doesn't want the role.* In fact, he didn't seem particularly interested in the fact she'd once been married or why she was now single again. So, he could go take a leap. For them to go forward together, they had to at least listen to each other!

'I wish you all the best, Tamara. I really do.' He remained silent until they reached the ute, which he unlocked, then held open her door. 'Maybe we were never meant to be more than a brief fling. It didn't work out between us the first time and I did want to get to know you, then. This time, we've got on great, but there are problems that we can't ignore. I don't trust any woman not to let me down, and from what I'm hearing, I doubt you trust any man not to walk out on you again, either. Let's face it; it's not a recipe for success, is it?' He closed the door and walked around to the driver's side.

There was nothing to say about that. Fergus was right. She had struggled badly with trust issues, had wondered if she'd ever truly, fully be able to fall in love again. She knew she'd been falling deeper and deeper for Fergus every day, but did she trust him not to walk away without a backward glance when it wasn't working for him? She wasn't sure. And if she wasn't sure, then she had no right to insist he give her a chance.

So much for a hot, sexy night of lovemaking after dinner. Fergus removed his clothes from the bedroom they'd been sharing. The couch was his for the remaining two nights. He couldn't lie beside Tamara and not reach for her, and that would be what he'd do when her scent filled the air around him and the heat from her body drifted his way.

He was a fool. He should've talked to her about his feelings regarding his father—and his mother—and got them out of the way. And he should have told her about Harriet, although the fact that she'd kept her own marriage a secret was a concern too.

Tamara was right; partners should stand by one another. If he wanted more time getting closer to her, then it was the only way to go. But what if, like Harriet, Tamara ultimately decided he wasn't worth the risk? Didn't want to be Mrs Collier? Didn't want to have his children, who might be tainted by his family name? He wanted to accept that just because Harriet had walked away from him, Tamara wouldn't, but it was beyond him. There'd been one too many knockbacks in his life to be able to accept a person into his life so easily. Even someone who'd known him for so long.

He couldn't deny Tamara got to him in unexpected ways. She always had, if he thought about it, which was why they'd always pressed each other's buttons back then.

Here in Port Vila, she'd tripped every button in his body, and in his head, in completely different ways. He wanted her even more than he'd wanted Harriet, and that was what totally scared the pants off him. Making him run from a chance of love, turning him into a coward.

'Goodnight, Fergus.' Tamara stood in the bedroom doorway, watching him with a guarded look on her face.

It would be so easy to walk across and haul her into his arms, hold her, kiss her, make love to her until all the pain disappeared. But that wouldn't solve a thing.

There were some serious problems standing between them. Ones he was afraid to push through in case there was no happy-ever-after waiting for them on the other side. 'Goodnight, Tamara.'

The door shut with a bang. As did his heart. Time to toughen up and get on with his real life. One with no dreams of the impossible. It was far safer all round.

Stretching out on the couch with his legs hanging over the end, hands behind his head, he stared up at the fan rotating above. There'd be no sleep for him tonight.

'Bring him round, Ian.' Fergus stepped back from the operating table after opening and cleaning wounds made by rusty nails in the boy's thigh.

The kid had been playing in a shed that had partially collapsed after the quake and had fallen onto a board with nails sticking out. Six years old and very fidgety, Fergus had preferred to put the lad under for the time it took to clean and stitch the wounds rather than use a local anaesthetic.

Tamara wiped the last of the blood from the boy's thigh and tossed the swabs in the bin. She looked tired, as though she hadn't had any more sleep over the last forty-eight hours than he had. 'I'll stay with him,' she said quietly.

No chirpiness in her voice today. Nor yesterday as they'd worked side by side. 'He won't take long to come round and will probably be in a hurry to get out of here and see what his friends are up to.'

She nodded. 'He's an energetic wee guy.'

At least they still agreed on some things. 'Our next patient is a man with appendicitis.'

'You did appendectomies during your training?'

'Yes.' Otherwise, he wouldn't be doing this one. But Tamara would know that and was probably only making conversation, as it was awfully quiet between them most of the time. 'I've already explained to Kaikea that I haven't done one in years, but he says it's urgent and another doctor won't be available for a long while.'

'Makes sense. I feel for the other women we came to help who didn't get their operations because of the quake.'

'Me too.' Who knew when they'd get help now? He might make an exception about doing two trips in one year, or tell the volunteer committee that he wanted to return here to finish that list.

Tamara looked thoughtful. 'I'll come back if there's someone available to do the surgeries.' She didn't lock eyes on him.

His gut sank. They were in a mess. But he made up his mind about one thing bothering him. 'I'm definitely going to volunteer to come back.' Did that mean they'd be a team again? Could he manage that after all that had happened? What was more important? His heart or helping those in need?

Tamara's mouth flattened as she pushed the bed up to the table. What did that mean? She didn't want to work with him anymore?

He couldn't blame her. He'd shut down on her when she'd mentioned her marriage and had flung the news about Harriet at her, without properly explaining that disaster, either. She'd have suffered when her marriage broke down. No way she wouldn't have done. This was Tamara. She gave her all when she was involved with other people, and he doubted she'd be any different when it came to a partner. And while they'd managed to work together efficiently, there had been uncomfortable moments which, on reflection, he now realised showed him that she didn't trust him easily. Now hurt and anger hung between them, and there was no way to fix it without opening up completely, something he'd struggle to do. But he would tell her what he planned to do here. 'I can't leave those women wondering what's going to happen now that I've met them. It's not in me to do that.'

'I know.'

Knock his socks off. She hadn't let their break-up get in the way of that. Why couldn't he be the same? Say what was on his mind, see how she reacted and learn how she felt about him? If only it was that simple. *It could be, if you truly want to find happiness.*

There was the problem. He'd realised he did want love. Without all the fears, without looking over his shoulder waiting for the axe to fall. It was hard to believe Tamara would do something awful to hurt him. But. There was always a huge *but* holding him back. Would he ever be free of it?

CHAPTER TEN

STANDING AT THE luggage carousel in Auckland International Airport, Tamara shivered. It might be summer here, but it was a lot cooler than Vanuatu. It wasn't the weather making her shiver though. It was Fergus. This was the last time she'd see him, and that hurt beyond anything she'd imagined. As bad as when her marriage had ended.

No, worse. She and Fergus hadn't cleared the air between them. Fergus had remained withdrawn from her since the night he'd refused to talk about himself and had ended their fling. She hadn't been any better, though, because she'd believed he wouldn't want to know about John and her trust issues.

'Your bag?' Fergus pointed to the carousel.

'Looks like it.' She stepped forward to grab it off the conveyor belt but Fergus beat her to it.

'I've got it.' He swung it up and placed it beside her, then reached for another one. 'Guess that's it then. I'll catch a cab and get back to reality.'

Reality? She couldn't even imagine what that was anymore. Her life had been turned upside down and inside out since Fergus came back into her life. 'I'll walk out with you.' Her flight to Nelson was two hours away, so she'd walk across to the domestic terminal to stretch her legs. The problem being, she wasn't ready to say goodbye to Fergus. Never would be. If only she knew what to say that might have him giving her a chance to talk and tell him what he'd come to mean to her. Could she tell him he held her heart in his hand? If she could be certain he'd listen, then yes, she'd take that risk.

Outside the sun was low in the sky and the air was still. Night-time was approaching. Taxis were lined up at every vacant spot, and people were bustling in all directions. Her heart was heavy. Her head in a spin.

Fergus turned to her. 'Bye, Tamara.' Then he walked away.

Staring after him, she knew she wasn't letting him go that easily. 'Fergus, wait,' she called and ran after him.

He stopped and turned around. 'Yes?'

She paused in front of him. Licked her lips. This wasn't easy. All the things she wanted to say weren't coming out. Her mouth was dry. Her heart pounded as though she'd just run a marathon. 'Fergus—' Sucking in a big breath, she knew she couldn't say what was in her heart. He wouldn't want to hear it. Which would only hurt her. So instead she threw her arms around him and hugged him tight.

His arms lifted slowly, hugged her back, but lightly. It wasn't quite a rejection, more a goodbye.

Pulling back to look at him as her heart began shattering, she said, 'Fergus, you're amazing. I wish you could believe that, and I hope you get everything you want for the future because you truly deserve it.' Placing a light kiss on his chin, she stepped away and headed back to her bag lying on the pavement. Time to get away from here before she fell apart completely.

* * *

Stunned, Fergus watched Tamara walk away. She believed in him. She truly did. No one had done that since he was a teen, and even then, he always questioned their motives.

His phone rang. One of his partners at the clinic. 'Hey, Matt, what's up?'

'I'm parked behind the shuttle buses waiting for you.'

'That was close. I was about to grab a taxi. Be right there.' Placing his bag in the boot, he got into the car. 'What brings you all the way over here?'

'Kelvin's in hospital after some fool driving erratically crashed into him on his cycle. His leg's fractured, as are six ribs. Otherwise, he's okay.'

'When did this happen?' Kelvin was injured and nobody had told him?

'Calm down. It only happened three days ago and with everything you've been dealing with in Vanuatu, Kelvin insisted no one tell you till you got back.'

'Of course he did. But I wish you'd ignored him.'

'What could you have done? Swum home to see him?' Matt could do sarcasm as easy as a bird could fly.

'Fair cop. Is he really going to be okay?'

'Yes, though it was a close call. It'll be a while before he's back at work.'

'Just as well the clinic's closed for three weeks.' Oh, yeah, he got it. 'Kelvin's on call for that period.' And Matt was heading to London to see his parents immediately after Christmas. 'I'll be here.' Hopefully, his grandparents would understand he'd have to cut his stay short. What about Tamara? He'd thought he'd stay away from her so as not to raise her hopes, but after what she'd just said to him, he wasn't sure he could remain aloof from her much longer. She was tugging him closer and closer, and he didn't know how he could keep resisting. Or if he even wanted to anymore.

Tamara stared at the self-check-in kiosk. This was it. The final stage of her trip home. The one she didn't want to make because it meant accepting Fergus wasn't going any further with their relationship—the one he'd told her wasn't a relationship. It had been for her, though.

His goodbye had been final. He was never going to open his heart to her. It was too damaged from the past. She had walked away after hugging him. She did know he wanted nothing more to do with her. But— There was always a but!

What if she tried to talk to him once more? She wasn't one to give up easily on something important, and what could be more important than the man who'd stolen her heart? Absolutely nothing. Except to try to win him round would make her seem needy, and as much as she wanted Fergus in her life, she wasn't going to beg. If he wasn't interested, then it would never work out, and she'd be back where she'd started. Heartbroken.

'Do you need help?' an airline assistant asked.

Shaking her head, Tamara looked around and saw the couple standing behind her waiting patiently for her to check in. 'Sorry, I'm thinking about changing my flight plans.' Moving away, she found a row of seats and sat down to consider her options. If she changed her flight without knowing if she could see Fergus, then she might end up forking out for another expensive ticket because the airline wouldn't let her change flights without paying. It would be worth it, though. If Fergus refused to talk to her, she'd at least know where she stood.

You already know that.

How true. She did. She'd been in denial. Not anymore. Jumping to her feet, she grabbed her bag and joined a queue in front of one of the check-in machines. No more wasting time thinking of ways to get around the pain in her chest. She and Fergus had had a wonderful time and now she had to move on, get her career back on track, forget about love.

Fergus wandered around the house feeling at odds with himself. He usually felt comfortable here. It was his space. No one could throw him off centre. Except tonight it was chilly, as though something—someone?—was missing. Loneliness poured through him. Strange when this was the last place he ever felt that way. Even after an exhausting night working with a patient in labour where everything went wrong, coming home always lifted his spirits. This house was his pride and joy, obtained through his own hard work. No sucking up to strangers to help him obtain his goal. Tonight, though, nothing felt right.

Tamara. She was behind this loneliness. He'd walked away from her at the airport just because he was afraid to lay his heart on the line. Gutless. That's what he was. Now here he was, two hours later, and he was wound up even tighter. He couldn't accept that he'd let her go when she'd come back to hug him without complaint. He didn't deserve her. Yet he wanted her. So much that the pain was unbearable. What was he going to do? If his heart was broken again at some point in the future, could it be any worse than this?

His phone rang. Hope rose. Tamara? Tugging the phone from his back pocket, he sighed. 'Hi mate. I hear you had a bit of an accident on your bike.'

'That bastard needs to be locked up forever,' Kelvin growled.

'Take it easy,' Fergus muttered. He should've got Matt to drop him off at the hospital to go see Kelvin instead of coming home to feel sorry for himself. 'Matt filled me in on what happened. Just glad you're okay, buddy.'

'Cheers,' he said. 'How'd it go with Tamara?'

If Kelvin wasn't lying in hospital with several broken bones, Fergus would've hung up on him. 'Better than expected.' He could've lied and said she'd been a pain in the butt and he was glad to get away from her, but Kelvin knew him better than that. 'We got along well, really well. But now I'm home and everything's back to normal.' There was a hitch in his voice when he said that.

Sure enough, Kelvin latched onto it straight away. 'You don't understand normal, Fergus. Stop wasting time procrastinating. You've already wasted too much time trying to protect yourself. If Tamara's ringing your bells, then do something about it. You've always had a soft spot for her.'

'You finished?'

'No, but I'm too tired to carry on.'

Fergus tried to laugh. Failed. 'Kelvin.' He paused, then ran with honesty. 'You're right about everything.'

'What are you going to do about Tamara?'

He was already looking at the bag he'd unpacked the moment he got home. 'Go talk to her.'

'At last, the man has seen sense.' The phone went dead.

Fergus stared at it, a smile starting to spread across

his face. He might not have a chance in hell of winning Tamara back, but he was going to give it all he had and more.

The doorbell rang, cutting through the silence enveloping Tamara as she sat at the counter nibbling half-heartedly at a slice of toast. Who could that be? The only people who visited her usually just walked on in, calling out to her.

She didn't recognise the car in the driveway.

The bell rang again.

'Coming,' she muttered, though she'd prefer to ignore it and pretend she wasn't here. There'd been little sleep going on last night, her head a miserable whir of Fergus and what she'd lost.

Hauling the door wide, she did a double take. Couldn't be. She was hallucinating. 'Fergus?'

'Hello, Tamara. Can I come in?'

Had he come to tell her he wanted no part of her in his life? That they wouldn't even be catching up at Christmas? She'd already assumed that to be the case, and surely, he could've done that on the phone, anyway. But she didn't think he'd come to open up and be completely honest about his feelings. Not after he'd walked away from her yesterday like she didn't matter at all. She looked at him as he waited patiently for her answer. Could she let him in and listen to what he had to say when she doubted it was for her own good? She had no choice. Despite everything, she loved Fergus with all she had.

Her hands were shaking as she stepped back. 'Come in.' He looked tired, as though, like her, he hadn't slept all night.

Stepping past her, he waited until she closed the door. He still wasn't saying much.

'Come through to the kitchen. I've just made coffee.' She led the way, aware of him right behind her every step. Pointing to the stools at the counter, she said, 'Take a pew.'

Fergus hesitated. 'I'm sorry to turn up unannounced, but once I made up my mind to see you, I had to come.'

She hadn't tied back her hair, and it flicked from side to side as she shook her head. 'You didn't want me doing a runner, you mean.' It was there in his wary eyes, in the way he clenched his jaw.

'I had to see you.'

'Had to? Or have to?' Yes, she was being blunt, but how else could she protect herself? She had no idea why Fergus was here. He'd said his bit at the airport. Or so she'd thought.

'Have to,' he conceded, raising a hint of hope in her heart.

But until he said what he'd come for, she was going to hold on to her emotions, not spill them out in a rush for him to walk away from—again. She poured coffee for both of them, then paced back and forth behind the kitchen counter, not knowing what she was waiting for, only that it was going to be big, one way or the other. Finally, she stopped and locked a steady gaze on him. 'Fergus, this waiting is hard.' Then she went back to waiting. Afraid to say another word in case she said the wrong thing and he walked out.

Fergus's shoulders rose and his chest lifted as he drew a long, shaky breath. 'Tamara, I love you.' There, he'd done it. Told Tamara he loved her. So far, the floor was still under his feet.

She was staring at him. 'You what?'

'I see you for who you are, and you're amazing. You always were. I admit that back when we weren't exactly the best of friends, I had the hots for you, but for some reason I've never worked out I didn't want you to be just another notch on my bedpost and nothing else.' Bile soured his mouth. He had been awful to her. 'Tamara—'

'Wait. My turn.' She looked flustered. About to tell him to take a hike and don't come back?

His heart crunched. Not that. He'd finally opened up. There was a lot more still to come. 'I understand I need to be open with you about everything if we're going to make this work.' He stopped. Then the words spilled out, almost unbidden. 'I am so afraid of being hurt again by someone special to me. Apart from Kelvin, all my friends became nightmares, taunting me about my father and what would I do since the money I loved to flaunt had gone. Worse, my mother didn't know how to handle the situation, and apart from offering for me to go to Auckland with her, she got on with her own life by finding someone else to marry and support her. I can't blame her, but I needed her. I'd lost my father, who wasn't the man I'd believed in and loved. That man hadn't ever existed. He'd been a dream, and the dream was gone, destroyed forever.' He gulped down a mouthful of the coffee she'd poured him. Couldn't look at Tamara for fear of what was showing in her face. 'Then I met Harriet and everything was wonderful again. I truly believed, when she agreed to marry me, that I had moved on to a new, more loving life. I was so wrong. Harriet's parents refused to accept that my family history wouldn't destroy her life or those of any children we might've had. At first, she denied that was true, but after a constant barrage from her parents, she gave in and agreed they might be right about us ending our engagement.' He wasn't stopping now. 'I closed down after that. Haven't wanted a relationship since, because I didn't want to go through that pain again.'

'Fergus—'

He held his hand up. He had to finish what he'd started. 'Wait. Then you came back into my life and everything changed. I mean *everything*. I started to feel again. To hope I could love and be loved. To start longing for children and watch them grow up to be stable adults, the best versions of themselves. All because of you, Tamara. I fought it. But I lost. I love you with my heart and soul. You are incredibly special. You are the one. The only one for me. If you'll have me.' He finally puttered to a stop, unable to utter another word.

Sinking onto a stool, she looked at him with what he thought might be love in her warm gaze. 'I haven't told you much about my past either. When my husband left me, he said I was cold in bed and uncaring about his feelings. I tried not to believe him, but sometimes it was so hard, thinking that was why he didn't love me anymore, and why he cheated on me with an old girlfriend of his.'

He couldn't listen to her pain. Moving around the bench he went to hold her, but she pushed him back with her hand. 'I haven't finished. I loved John, and thought we had the dream life. I was wrong. For a long time, I didn't want to try again, didn't want to have my face rubbed in my own failure.' Another deep breath before she continued. 'Then I caught up with you and like you, I started to look at things differently. Especially you. You have changed and that took guts and determination. Then there're all the other wonderful things about you, like how you treat me, and how you stuck by me during the days after the earthquake. How you worship me in bed. I could go on and on, but it's probably best I shut up now. Other than to tell you—I love you, Fergus Collier. Maybe I always have, though I didn't recognise the heat you created within me as love.' She sat watching him, like she was waiting for an axe to fall.

He couldn't take his eyes off this wonderful woman. She'd always been honest, but this took the cake. She loved him. Unbelievable. Yet true. He stepped up mentally. 'Tamara, I've been falling deeper in love with you every day since we met again at the airport just over a month ago. And for the record, you are not cold, in bed or out of it. You are hot and sexy and gorgeous.' He'd throttle the bastard if he ever met him.

Relief filtered through Tamara's eyes as she took in what he'd said. Coming round the bench, she wrapped him in her arms. 'Take me to bed, Fergus.'

'That's it?' He couldn't stop the smile widening his lips. 'You have nothing more to say?' No wonder he loved her.

'What is there to say? You can trust me to always love you as I trust you to do the same.'

There *was* one more thing to say. It felt so right after all this time holding on to his heart. Taking Tamara's hands in his, he got down on one knee. 'Tamara Frost, will you marry me? Be my forever woman? Have children with me?'

She blinked and a tear slid out of the corner of her eye. 'Yes, Fergus. I will.'

He was on his feet and reaching for her. 'Thank you. That's the best thing I've heard in a long time.'

'We took our time getting here, but I believe that's been for the best. I love you, and probably always have.' Tears were gushing down her face now. 'I can't imagine a life without you now.'

'Then what are we standing around here for? Where's the bedroom?' He scooped her up in his arms, his heart going so fast there was an actual, physical ache behind his ribs. A good ache. His life had come full circle and he was happy beyond belief.

EPILOGUE

Two years later...

TAMARA SAT ON the beach at Port Vila, keeping a constant eye on her daughter, who loved nothing more than to toddle down the few metres to the water's edge and sit down in the water. 'Izzy, be careful, sweetheart.' As if eighteen-month-olds knew what being careful meant.

'Good luck with that.' Fergus grinned. 'She's a water baby.'

'Don't I know it.' Glancing over at the man she'd married seven days ago at the resort where they'd made love for the very first time, she felt her heart go all mushy. 'I can't believe we're here again.' They'd been back once to finish the list interrupted by the earthquake, and then again last year to help more women with gynaecological problems, so when it came to their wedding, it was a no brainer where to hold it.

'This time it's all about wedding bells.'

She nudged him. 'And children.'

Fergus laid his hand over her slight baby bump. 'Wonder if he knows he was just at his parents' wedding?'

'You can ask him in five months' time.' She still struggled to get her head around the fact she and Fergus were married and expecting their second child in the middle of next year. Life had really proved to be wonderful. She couldn't be happier.

'Izzy, come and give your dad a hug.' Fergus was watching her as she sat smacking the wet sand. 'I want her away from the water while I kiss you.'

Tamara laughed. 'Good luck with that. It's as though Izzy knows exactly what you're doing.'

'She's no slug. A lot like her mother.'

'And her father.' Izzy had stood up and was starting to race up the beach towards them. 'Quick. We've about ten seconds before we're interrupted.'

As Fergus's lips covered hers, she sighed with pleasure. When he lifted his mouth, she murmured, 'I love you, Fergus Collier.'

'Love you back, Tamara Collier.'

Izzy jumped on Fergus's back shrieking, 'Dada!'

Darn, but life was perfect.

* * * * *

If you enjoyed this story, check out these other great reads from Sue MacKay

A Fling with the ER Doctor
Parisian Surgeon's Secret Child
Wedding Date with the ER Doctor
Brooding Vet for the Wallflower

All available now!

SECOND CHANCE WITH HIS SUNSHINE SURGEON

AMY RUTTAN

MILLS & BOON

This book is for one of the most sunshiny people
I know, TL! You always brighten my day,
even on some particularly cloudy ones.
Thanks for forcing your way into my life
and deciding I was going to be your friend.

CHAPTER ONE

I FEEL LIKE he's watching me.

Although, Dr. Emile Moreau felt that way every time he passed his father's venerable portrait that was hanging on the Moreau hospital wing of Hôpital de Ville-Marie. One in a *very* long line of Moreaus that adorned the memorial wall. Each and every one of his ancestors staring down at him with an almost righteous indignation. Even though Emile walked these halls every day, for most of his life, and even though his father had died while he was still in medical school, he could still feel his father's eyes boring into the back of his skull from that damnable photograph.

Judging him.

Displeased with him.

And disappointed.

"If you want to be the best and save lives, you have to toughen up. Your work is your life. It comes first. Nothing else matters." His father's voice echoing in his mind. It weighed heavy on him. A burden he just couldn't escape.

It didn't help that Hôpital de Ville-Marie's cardiac wing only existed thanks to his late grandfather's philanthropic endeavors. Then his father's brilliance in the cardiothoracic surgical field had built the reputation that meant people came from all over Montreal to get the very best in care.

Emile's care now.

He stiffened his spine and adjusted his tie.

His late father and he had not had a loving relationship, but Dr. Moreau Senior had been brilliant and that was why Emile had followed in his footsteps. Really, there were no other options for him. He was a Moreau and the only possible path for a Moreau was cardiothoracic medicine.

Emile had even surpassed his father in one way, by becoming the youngest head of cardiothoracic surgery at Hôpital de Ville-Marie.

Not that it would have pleased his father. No matter what Emile did, nothing had ever seemed to make him happy.

So he ignored the photographs and continued his brisk pace to his office. He knew exactly why he was feeling the weight of their gazes so strongly today; that was no mystery. And it wasn't only because he was still reeling from what he'd just seen on the imaging of one of his younger patients.

It was the fact that after ten years, he was going to have to call the only woman he ever loved, the one whom he had to let go, and ask her for help.

He passed a resident, who greeted him politely. Emile nodded stiffly at her and the group of nervous interns who were moving together quickly with her. He didn't give them a smile, but inside he was laughing slightly, remembering what it had been like when he was in their shoes.

That was when he'd been with Chloé. Those had been some of the happiest moments of his life.

And he'd never forgotten them. They just stayed buried, deep in his heart. His first love was and would always be Hôpital de Ville-Marie. Just like it had been for all those Moreaus who had come before him.

His mother still cursed this hospital's name.

Emile didn't blame her for that. There had been times as a young boy he did, too.

But he had learned where his cold, aloof father hadn't. There was no time for love, friendship, marriage or a family when you were running an illustrious cardiothoracic wing. And there was no way Emile would ever think of having a wife and starting a family just to ignore them or put them second because of work.

He couldn't pretend that he wasn't lonely sometimes, but he wasn't selfish. Sometimes you just couldn't have it all.

"These scans are in, Doctor Moreau," his assistant said as he entered his office. Donna had been his father's assistant before she'd been Emile's right-hand woman. She must be close to retirement now. He didn't know what he'd do once she left; she was the only one in this hospital who didn't shrink back in fear from him.

Not that Emile was a heartless person. His patients trusted him, and he always tried to be warm with them, but to run an efficient unit, he expected perfection and demanded respect from his staff. And it was easier to keep most people at bay, rather than forge relationships with people who were most likely to leave as soon as a better opportunity arose.

Just like Chloé.

Emile shook that thought from his head. "*Merci*, Donna. When the call comes in from the hospital in Ottawa, please patch it through straightaway."

"I will, Doctor Moreau."

Emile retreated to the safety of his closed office and sat down at his desk, pulling up the images from the scan that had taken place last night. The premier of the province had brought in her child yesterday. The little girl had been presenting all the symptoms of heart failure, but there were irregularities—something else at play.

Emile had seen to the scans personally, so he'd known the moment the images came up what was happening.

Heart cancer.

It was rare and he didn't see many cases. He'd seen them in pathology in medical school, but not in the case of a child of six. The truth of the matter was he hadn't done many heart cancer surgeries in the first place and definitely not on someone so small. It was a risky surgery at the best of times, especially for someone without much experience.

Thankfully, he knew someone who had plenty.

The phone buzzed. He picked it up. "Yes, Donna?"

"Doctor Chloé MacDonald is on line one," Donna replied.

"*Merci.*" His pulse was pounding between his ears as he took a deep breath and connected to the call. "Doctor MacDonald."

"Oh, that's so formal," came the bright voice he knew all too well on the other end. "How are you, Doctor Moreau?"

He tried not to smile, although he could almost hear the air quotes as Chloé said his last name. "I am well. I trust by now you've seen the scans and my report?"

"Getting down to business, eh?"

"My time is…limited." He would've said *valuable*, but given Chloé's expertise as a surgeon, he knew her time was just as precious as his own.

"Limited. So obviously, we're done with pleasantries or friendly chatter."

Emile sighed and rubbed his temple. "It's a pressing issue."

"I'm well aware," she responded. "That's clear from the details you sent over."

"What do you think?"

"The child is six?" Chloé asked with some trepidation.

"*Oui.*"

"She's young for someone with this type of tumor."

"I know. You have worked on a case like this before, though."

"You keeping tabs on me?" Chloé teased.

He rolled his eyes. She still had the same sunshine-y personality he remembered so well. When he'd first met her that bubbliness had vexed him, but at the same time it had drawn him in. It had been such a departure from the strict, humorless household he'd grown up in.

Right now, though, he found it somewhat annoying because he needed to keep her at arm's length. He didn't want to be sucked back in, to be enchanted by her and the promise of warmth and joy that he had found with her once. That was not an efficient way to stay at the top of his game.

"Your career is impressive. So yes, I have kept tabs on you."

In truth, he'd tried not to, tried to block her memory from his life, but it was hard when her name was everywhere in medical journals. Her work and her research were testament to her dedication, as was her role as a persistent advocate for a better health infrastructure in remote northern communities.

It was what he'd always loved about Chloé; she had huge goals, just like him. The only difference was that he knew she wanted an equal partner, a family. They'd discussed it before, when they were dating and things had seemed like they were starting to get serious. Emile had told her then that he didn't want a family—a slight lie, but also not. Though part of him longed for one, he just couldn't commit to it. Work would always be more important and he couldn't ever hurt a child, a partner, by putting them second.

Chloé came from a loving home. He knew she had a supportive, happy childhood and wanted to provide the same for children of her own. That was a kind of life he didn't know how to give her.

The last thing he ever wanted to do was to make Chloé resent him the way his mother bitterly resented his father. As much as he was drawn to her, he had to resist. It would be painful, but it was the only way.

"I can hear your teeth grinding," she chuckled.

Emile relaxed. "Do you think you can help? I mean, does your schedule afford you the time to help us out in this situation? The child is very fragile, medically, and I don't know if transporting her would be in her best interest right now."

"No. You're right, if what I've read from her labs is correct," Chloé agreed. "It's best I come there."

"And you can fit this into your schedule?"

"I can," she replied brightly.

"Good. The board of directors has arranged a suite in a hotel where we often put our visiting physicians."

"You've already spoken to the board, eh? Seems like you've already decided for me," she teased.

"This is an urgent situation."

Emile heard her sigh down the line. "I do understand that. Well, send me all the information and arrangements and I'll hop in my car and make the trip. It's not a terribly long drive."

"No. It's not," he said tightly.

When their relationship had ended, it was partly because Chloé had taken her first job in Yellowknife and had been talking about moving back to her home city of Iqaluit. It had hurt him a little bit to see she only stayed in Yellowknife for six months, before moving to Ottawa, much closer to Montreal.

Maybe they could've worked things out had she gone to Ottawa in the first place.

Really? It wouldn't have worked out for plenty of reasons, and you know it.

Which was true. Emile needed to devote all his time and energy here, at the hospital. Proving he was the best, good enough to fill his father's shoes. Besides, he had never wanted to hold her back from her dreams. His destiny, his future, had all been planned for him. She had the opportunity to live out her life the way she wanted to. He didn't.

"Good, because the sooner I'm there, the quicker we can start treatment. This is an aggressive cancer."

"I will send the details over straightaway. I... I look forward to working with you again, Chloé." He hoped she didn't hear the hesitation in his voice, because there was a part of him that was nervous about seeing her again.

Just like there was a part of him that was excited about that prospect, too.

Don't think like that.

"And I you, Emile." Chloé disconnected the call.

Emile hung up the phone and sat back in his office chair, rubbing his hands over his face, before staring out at the city of Montreal spread out before him. From this vantage point in the hospital, he could see the gorgeous skyline of the city rising below him, and the St. Lawrence River winding its way from Lake Saint Louis—or really, its starting point at Lake Ontario over two hundred and eighty kilometers to the west—between the island of Île Notre-Dame and St. Helen's, under the Victoria bridge and eventually making its way out to the Atlantic Ocean.

Emile loved that sprawling river. When he was a child, his mother would always take him up the coast and into Québec City, where old-European style met with Canada. They would pick berries along the roads and always end up sharing a tortiere, picnicking under the roar of the Montmorency Falls.

Those halcyon days had come before his parents divorced. Before his dad got full custody and his mother moved to Beaupré. Before Emile and his mother became distant with each other. She didn't understand his passion for medicine, and he didn't understand her bohemian lifestyle.

Still, Québec had always been his home. He'd even gone to school here, but chosen to do his medical schooling in Toronto. Other than that, he hadn't wandered far from his roots, because what was the point of that? His father had set his path for him, right here.

Emile knew his place and yet, there were still times he wondered about the what-ifs.

What if he hadn't followed in his father's footsteps?

What if he had taken that fellowship in Vancouver?

What if he hadn't ended it with Chloé?

"I think it's for the best, cherie." It was hard to get those words out. He knew by the pain in his heart, the lump in his throat. "You want things I can't give you."

"Like what?" Chloé stood before him, her dark eyes moist with tears. The lips he loved to kiss, set firm in a straight line.

The body that had melted against his time and time again, stiff.

He'd hurt her.

"Family and career. You need someone to support your aspirations. I have my own goals. I have to be selfish."

"Selfish?"

"Oui."

"Why do you want to go to Montreal?" she asked. "And to your late father's hospital? Vancouver is offering you so much more."

It was a legitimate question, but one Emile didn't want to answer. "Why do you want to go to Iqaluit?"

"It's where I'm from. I'm needed there."

"Exactly."

"I'm not going there yet. I had an opportunity in Yellowknife. One that is offering me more so I can return home one day."

She was right, but there was no point in arguing or dragging it on. He took a deep breath. "Chloé."

She held up a hand. "No. Don't. I guess we really didn't promise each other anything. It was casual."

"Yes. Casual." He loved her, but he'd never told her that and now there was no point. It was time to let her go.

"I wish you the best, Doctor Moreau."

He nodded. "And I wish the same for you, Doctor MacDonald."

That was all in the past.

They'd gone their separate ways and forged the careers they wanted. Even though Emile had never forgotten her, this situation wasn't about that. This was about working together to save a young life, nothing more.

There was no way he was going to let those old feelings creep back in. He was over her.

Her time in his hospital would be temporary and then she'd be gone again.

Surely, enough water had gone under the bridge that he

wouldn't be tempted by her again. At least, that was what he had to keep telling himself. For however long Chloé would be here, he had to keep his walls up and his heart closed.

Like he did with everyone else.

It had taken a couple of days for Chloé to get everything in order and head to Montreal. She was still trying to wrap her head around the idea that Emile had called her and asked for her help. She hadn't heard from him, personally, since they went off in different directions after residency. And honestly, she'd never expected to. There were times she'd thought she might run into him at a medical conference, and she'd gone over multiple scenarios in her head about how cool and nonchalant she would play it, all "ha ha, I don't miss you at all."

Of course, it had never happened. He never seemed to attend.

And she really did still miss him. Even after all this time. She'd been so in love with him, even if they'd never said it. It had hurt so much when it all ended.

She'd gotten on with her life, but every once in a while she'd wonder about him. A fleeting thought from a song that they'd danced to, or a joke they'd shared.

It had taken her time to heal, to accept it, but she knew now that they couldn't have been together. He'd made it clear he didn't want a family.

Whereas she did.

Do you, Nuka?

She hadn't actually gone out and made that dream come true, but it was so hard to do when she was so focused on her work.

Saving lives.

Sure. That's the real reason.

She shook that little voice out of her head. Yes, she thought about Emile still, but never expected to see him again.

And then he'd emailed, asking her if he could call, and they talked.

He sounded the same as ever over the phone, but also different.

So formal.

Emile had always been a bit broody, when they'd been working together. The attendings and nurses liked to call them "storm cloud" and "rainbow." Chloé had never minded that, but over the phone his stormy, grumpy personality had seemed a bit grouchier than back then. Not grouchy... Maybe more hermit-like? Crabby?

Great. You're comparing the great love of your life to a crab. Not the best metaphor, Chloé.

Of course, it was not hard to let your mind wander when taking a late-night drive from Ottawa to Montreal.

The suite in the residence hotel that Emile's hospital had set up for her was amazing. It was within walking distance to the hospital, had a gorgeous view of downtown Montreal and the bed was a huge king. Bigger than the bed she had at her sparse apartment in Ottawa, and definitely more luxurious than her lodgings when she stayed in Iqaluit every three months.

Montreal seemed way over-the-top.

Though she tried to get a decent night's sleep in that large bed before her first day at the hospital, she just couldn't. All night she tossed and turned, because she was completely nervous to see Emile again. Which was so silly, right? They had parted ways fairly amicably, even if every time she thought about it, it still felt like a knife had been jabbed into her heart and twisted. Those were just feelings. The facts were they both had wanted very different things and it made sense that they didn't end up together.

She could see that now. It really all made sense.

Nuka, you're being foolish. You loved him.

Immi's words in her head made her smile. Even though they'd been twins, Immitaq had been older by five minutes and liked to rub it in by calling Chloé "little sister."

Immi had been her other half. Now she was Chloé's guiding voice and she missed her fiercely. And even though Immi had never lived to meet Emile, Chloé knew how Immi was a romantic at heart. *You loved him.* That was exactly what she would say to Chloé if she were still alive.

She'd died at sixteen; she'd had so many big dreams she hadn't gotten to live out, but Chloé had done her best to live her own. Maybe Immi would have berated her for not falling in love or having a family by now, but Chloé couldn't help others like her late sister if she wasn't spending her time learning and researching. It was important.

So love and romance took a backseat. She'd find time for it. Eventually. The most important thing was to save as many lives as she could right now. There was no way other families would suffer like hers had when Immi died. Not on her watch.

Chloé knew her sister would have understood.

Sort of.

I'm doing this so others won't lose their loved ones. So others won't lose the Immi in their life. I'm not squandering anything.

As she made her way down the street toward Hôpital de Ville-Marie the next morning, her heart was hammering a steady pound between her ears. All she could think about was not putting her foot in her mouth when she saw Emile again.

I've got to be cool.

The thought made her roll her eyes. That in itself was so not cool. She had nothing to worry about. There were no romantic intentions here. It was all work.

Besides, surely by now, Emile had married some francophone socialite. Whereas, she had stayed married to her job this past decade. Too focused on saving as many lives as she could and bringing more skilled physicians to the north so that no one would have to die needlessly without the proper health care access, just like her twin.

Immi was her whole reason for doing what she did every day. And now as she stared up at the gorgeous hospital where

Emile was head of cardio, all she could think about was her twin and what she would say to her right now.

Dang, Nuka, stop standing there. Get a move on you and do your job. Ailiruk eh!

Chloé smiled, lifted her head high and marched right into Hôpital de Ville-Marie like she belonged there, because she did. She was a surgeon and a damn fine surgeon, too. However much she sometimes still felt like that little girl from the north, lost in the big city.

I've got this.

She closed her eyes and took a deep, calming breath. When she opened them, she got her first real look at the modern, open-concept foyer. The glass walls rose high and covered the old brick wall of the original hospital facade. Windows from the seven floors overlooked the space. As she gazed up through the glass roof, she could see white fluffy clouds treading across the blue sky.

"Beautiful, *non*?"

Chloé's pulse skipped a beat because she recognized that voice. She turned around and tried not to gawk at the man she'd been so head over heels in love with a decade ago.

There were some subtle changes to Emile. His jaw was a bit more defined, none of the baby fat of youth. His hair was still that same dark ebony, but with some thick silver strands in the mop of carefully trimmed curls on top. His dark eyes didn't sparkle and there were a few lines on his face, marking the passage of time, but she had to admit she really liked the Van Dyke beard he had going on.

Then she realized she'd been staring too long at him and tried to plaster on the most suave and sophisticated smile she could. And answer him calmly. Professionally.

"Lots of glass. It *shatters* my expectations." And then she winked exaggeratedly, before cringing inwardly at the horrible pun that just slipped past her lips.

Emile's eyes widened slightly, like he was alarmed. He didn't smile. An awkward tension settled between them. Chloé could almost hear the *badum-ting* following the epic failure of that pun.

It's lack of sleep. That's why I'm making bad jokes.

Except, she didn't think that was it at all. She could almost hear Immi groaning at her.

So not cool, Nuka.

"Get it?" she added, desperately, giving Emile a slight nudge in the ribs, hoping it would make it better.

It didn't.

No, Nuka. No.

"I do," Emile agreed, but still didn't smile or acknowledge the humor in any way. "Still a joker, I see. That hasn't changed."

His tone stung, but Chloé couldn't really expect anything less from him. "Still on a serious streak, are we?"

She half expected a comeback or some witty repartee, like they'd shared in the old days.

Instead, Emile's eyes narrowed. "Well, how about we get your identification cards and then we can chat about the case?"

"Sure."

Emile turned and Chloé followed him.

Nuka, easy with the jokes.

She was already off to a great start. If she didn't pull herself together, this whole situation would drag on forever, which was the last thing she wanted. She was half tempted to turn round and run.

Except she couldn't. There was a life on the line.

It was clear Emile had changed, that was all. And that wasn't a problem. This was a working relationship and this Emile, for all intents and purposes, was a stranger.

CHAPTER TWO

EMILE DIDN'T MENTION her epic failure of a pun at all. Actually, he didn't really say much as they walked in awkward silence side by side. He seemed to move through this hospital on autopilot, which wasn't surprising. She knew he'd been working here since they finished their residency in Toronto, and that this was the place his father had worked at before that.

Emile had mentioned enough times that generations of his family had been involved in or worked at Hôpital de Ville-Marie.

In fact, the whole cardiac unit was named after his family. Once they'd gotten all Chloé's identification and passes set up, they made their way over to the Moreau wing, where she could see the line of photographs and plaques, all with Emile's last name etched into the gold plates below.

She couldn't even imagine such a family legacy.

She was the first doctor and surgeon in her family, the first to go to university. Her sister hadn't even been allowed to make it past sixteen.

A pang of guilt washed over Chloé and she swallowed the lump in her throat. Though they'd been twins, she'd never been sick, always healthy, whereas Immi had struggled all her short life.

Life was so unfair.

Walking through the long hall to Emile's office, Chloé got

a kind of creepy feeling that all of Emile's ancestors were watching them, judging them. She couldn't help but wonder if he felt it, too.

If she had to live with that every day, she might be a bit formal as well.

When they'd been interns and then residents together, she'd always felt like he was a bit too hard on himself. A bit of a perfectionist. Now, walking down this hallway to a wing named after his family, she could see why.

"After you, Doctor MacDonald," Emile said, holding open the door to a small meeting room.

"Thank you." Chloé stepped inside.

Emile shut the door, then pulled out a leather high-backed chair for her. She nodded, thanking him again as she sat down and set her computer bag on the floor. Emile took the seat next to her, lacing his fingers together and resting his hands on the table, his back ramrod straight. No expression on his face. No warmth in his eyes.

It made Chloé sad.

"I'm so glad you were able to come and assist me, Doctor MacDonald."

Still with the formality, eh?

"You can call me Chloé. I like to keep it informal."

"It's a bit different here in the city."

Chloé frowned. "I also work in Ottawa, in the capital of Canada, a city. I like to keep it informal and would prefer if you call me Chloé. However, I can call you Doctor Moreau if that's what you prefer."

Emile's lips pressed together in a firm line and she knew that tight expression meant she was bugging him. That was sort of how their relationship had always played out. Classic grumpy/sunshine. Except this went beyond a mere rain cloud. He was like a massive, pressure-filled storm front.

"Very well, but around patients I would prefer to keep things formal," he agreed grudgingly.

"I can do that." She leaned back, relieved he'd given her that concession. Maybe there was hope for him yet. "I have looked over all your files."

"Good. I expected no less."

She bristled at his tone. "You expected no less? I'm not an intern."

"I know, you're a professional. That's why I didn't doubt you would prepare."

Part of her wanted to scream that it was her, that it was Chloé, and they didn't need this frosty formality! But she swallowed that urge. "Oh. Well, yes. I have gone through what you sent over."

"Is it what I think?"

"Heart cancer?" she asked.

"Oui."

"Then yes. You said you haven't had much experience with heart cancer?"

"No. I haven't. I also don't typically get pediatric patients. I am one of the best cardiothoracic surgeons in the province, though. I have worked on small hearts, but I haven't removed cancer from them. It seems…delicate."

"It is," she replied gently. "I've worked on three patients of this age. Younger even."

A smile crept across Emile's lips then; that twinkle that had been missing a moment ago sparked back to life in his blue eyes. "I know. It's why I reached out. You're talented. But then I've always known that."

No one stood up to Emile. It was refreshing that Chloé did. Frustrating, but he actually didn't mind it.

He was trying to keep a very professional wall up between them, because the moment he'd seen her, he'd realized she hadn't changed at all. It was like time hadn't passed and he was still staring at the same woman he'd fallen for all those years ago. Her dark brown hair was weaved into a long braid that hung down her back. Her luscious lips were painted red and her warm brown eyes were full of awe. He remembered the way her long lashes would brush against his face when they kissed.

The only difference was she now had traditional Inuk tattoos on her fingers.

That was something she had talked about getting done when she finished residency, and he was glad to see she had followed through with that tradition. But then when she said she was going to do something, she usually did it.

Like Emile and his determination to work here at Hôpital de Ville-Marie. They were similar in that way.

And as much as he wanted to keep that professional wall up, it was hard to do that when he was in her presence, because he remembered all those times they were together. The way they worked together, totally in sync, the fun they had and how much he missed her when it all ended.

Then she'd made that terrible pun.

He'd actually gotten a kick out of it, but couldn't acknowledge it. He didn't want to get too chummy with her. Working together on a case was fine, but having her slowly creep back into his life would not be acceptable. If he started goofing around with her again, then it was a slippery slope indeed.

Yet, it was so easy to forget himself when he was around her. He was already kicking himself for giving her that compliment about her talent. Then again, it was the truth.

Pink tinged Chloé's cheeks and she dipped her head slightly. "Thank you."

"There's no need to thank me, Chloé. Your reputation and work is admirable. I have only seen one heart cancer patient in my time here at Hôpital de Ville-Marie and it was an adult male. Not in a heart tiny like this. I would like to learn, so please keep me informed and include my residents and interns whenever possible. We are a teaching hospital here."

"You want *me* to teach your students? Are you sure?"

He frowned, annoyed that she would doubt herself. "Of course. That is why you're here."

"Well, I'm happy to teach, if you think they can learn from me."

"*Bonne*. So, how do we proceed?"

"Well, there's a few steps we have to take before we can do the surgery." Chloé reached down and pulled out her laptop, opening it. "I find shrinking the tumor with a combination of chemotherapy and radiation is effective. Also, immunotherapy."

"That is a lot to put a child through."

"I understand, but we have to shrink this tumor. It's quite large for someone so young." Chloé sighed. "We have to. It's nowhere else in her body? This is a primary malignant angiosarcoma?"

"*Oui*," Emile replied. "The CT scans I sent you were the most recent. It's just a very large malignant angiosarcoma in her heart. She presented with back pain, shortness of breath and extreme fatigue. It was during her initial exam that she began to cough up blood and the scans were ordered."

"Poor kid," Chloé murmured. "I would like to see her. I assume she's been admitted?"

"Of course. We can see her right away. Her mother is the premier of the province, and is most anxious to have a plan of attack."

Chloé smiled. "An attack on cancer? I like this mother's way of thinking."

"Well, again, she is premier..."

"I've dealt with my fair share of politicians and I know how they can be. Especially when it involves something personal to them."

Emile cocked an eyebrow. "Oh?"

Chloé laughed nervously and shook her head as she typed in some notes on her laptop. "Just bureaucratic stuff. Trying to get more surgeons and physicians in the north."

"I'm surprised that you are in Ottawa."

Her eyes narrowed. "What do you mean by that?"

"Well, when we left you were off to Yellowknife. You stayed there for a few months."

"Keeping tabs on me?" she asked slyly.

"Maybe, but I keep tabs on all the residents from our class." *Liar.*

"I worked there for a couple of years actually, flying back and forth, before I was offered a place at Ottawa, which meant that I could be put on rotation to work in Iqaluit. Ottawa is closer to Iqaluit than Yellowknife. It's geography, Emile."

"I didn't mean to offend."

Chloé shrugged with indifference. "I understand. I just mean not all of us can stay in the same hospital."

Emile knew it wasn't an insult, but it still stung just the same. There was a part of him, one that existed a long time ago, that wanted to travel and work in different hospitals. The old him regretted giving up that opportunity in Vancouver to come here to Hôpital de Ville-Marie. And then there was another part of him that wished he could go far north, to work in those remote communities like she did. He'd always been fascinated with remote medicine and the north since he was a child.

I did my duty to my father. This is where I belong. I upheld the legacy.

Except, looking at her and all the opportunities she had, the different cases she got to work on... It had certainly given her experience, room to grow, like seeing more heart cancer than he ever did in the city.

"Well, we should go visit the patient and maybe you can request the labs you require and come up with that plan."

This was the part of the job he'd always enjoyed with her, and he could enjoy it again now. He just mustn't let himself get sucked into thinking about the "what-ifs" with her, no matter how tempting it might be.

He was where he was meant to be. Just like she was. All he could hope was that she found happiness there.

"I'm hoping you'll help me, Emile. With the surgery. You say you want to learn. Well, I'll need your skills in the operating room."

Her request caught him off guard. "Of course."

"It's a delicate surgery, and it's complex. It's a team effort and this is your case and your hospital." Chloé smiled warmly, which made his heart skip a beat. She'd always had a way of including him, bringing him joy. It made him want to soften to her, to relax his control…

Keep those walls high, Emile, an inner voice reminded him.

"Of course, I will assist you. It's a rare surgery and a tough case. I would like to learn and assist."

Chloé nodded. "Good."

"I will make sure I get you set up with a workspace and if you need to see patients… I mean, if any of your patients are willing to drive to Montreal to see you then we can give you clinic time."

"No, I was getting ready to do a rotation in Iqaluit. So Montreal is a little far to travel. I might have to disappear for a couple of days to head up to Nunavut, especially if I'm needed, and I might have to head back to Ottawa to see extreme cases."

"Can your patients fly here? Can we transport them here instead of Ottawa?"

Her eyes widened. "I suppose. Would the board of directors be willing to do that? Some of my patients can't afford commercial flights. There's a fund to help in Ottawa…"

"Hôpital de Ville-Marie has a significant fund for that. I'm sure I can speak to the board about allocating some of those funds to accommodate your patients while you are here."

"I would appreciate that."

Their gazes locked and he could feel his wall crumbling again. She had always been able to get under his skin, no matter how serious he was trying to be, and it appeared that time hadn't changed that. He would have to be more careful around her.

Yes, he would be working with her, but he had to remember that her time here was short.

Nothing could happen between them.

They were colleagues and nothing more.

Even if there was part of him that wanted, right in this moment, to have just a *little* bit more.

CHAPTER THREE

EMILE GOT CHLOÉ a space to work and left her to go through some paperwork before she had to meet with the patient and her parents later. Once she was alone, Chloé was able to get herself settled and take a few deep breaths to calm down. She was still in disbelief that she was even here.

Why had she thought this job was going to be easy?

Not the case—heart cancer was never easy—but she really had thought that enough time had passed under the proverbial bridge that she wouldn't be drawn to Emile the same way that she had been before. Instead, even though he was very aloof and closed off, there was a part of her that wanted to try to warm him up, to break past that facade.

She couldn't let herself get sucked into anything with him again. They'd made it clear when they broke up that they were on different paths, wanted different things.

Except, all she had pursued since was medicine. Not a family or a partner, like she'd claimed to want.

How can I have that when there are patients like Immi who need me?

Chloé ignored that little thought. It was clear that the circumstances that had triggered their breakup were still in play and unlikely ever to change. Emile was the head of his department here at Hôpital de Ville-Marie; Chloé never expected him to give that up. And her life wasn't going to change, either—she was happy with her work.

She was exactly where she wanted to be, except for the fact that there could be better health services in the north. At least she was making a difference. She was helping people.

People like Immi.

Just thinking about Immi made her heart twinge. It was a grief she always carried, but never spoke of. It was easier to hide it all, put on that happy face. Her family had been through enough; she didn't want them to have to worry about her, too.

When Emile knocked at her office door, Chloé realized she'd lost an hour to her thoughts, which was so unlike her.

"You all right?" Emile asked as he stepped into her office.

"Why wouldn't I be?"

"Well, we were supposed to meet out in the hallway ten minutes ago."

"Oh?" Chloé glanced at her watch. "Right. I was getting caught up on some work and I didn't sleep the best last night."

It was an excuse and one she hoped he bought.

Emile cocked an eyebrow. "Was the room not to your liking? The hotel is one of the best residence short-stay hotels in this area."

"No, it's not that. The room was fine. It's just..." She trailed off. When they were residents, she would have said that she could talk to him about anything. But had that been true? She hadn't told him everything about her life. She'd never talked about Immitaq and she knew there were things Emile had never told her.

It was something she had often wondered about after their breakup. Had they really known each other at all, or had it merely been just physical attraction and the stress of the residency that brought them together?

Still, he was someone she could usually confide in about work, at least. But right now she felt something holding her back.

"It's just what?" Emile asked softly, the formality slipping just a bit.

As their gazes locked, for one brief moment, Chloé could see the Emile whom she had fallen for all those years ago; the Emile who loved surgery and wanted to make a difference. It was like he was still hiding there under the surface.

Then the moment passed, and he was gone. This was not that Emile, not the one she thought she knew. There was no intimacy there. No trust. He was a stranger with a familiar face.

She wasn't going to talk to him about Immi or the fact that she still felt that troubling pull of attraction toward him. He didn't need to know those things. All she had to talk to him about was the case.

That was it.

"I have a lot on my mind. My own patients back in Ottawa and in Iqaluit. Now this young child with heart cancer."

They were colleagues and nothing more and she'd have to keep reminding herself of that fact. And it was true; she was thinking about her patients and this child whom she was here to see.

Work was her life.

It always had been.

There hadn't been time for dating or really a social life. All her focus had been on her career; her energy and her drive completely centered around that, so that no one would have to lose a family member the way she had. She had a life. Immitaq didn't. Chloé had to use the time she'd been given for good.

"I've been thinking a lot about this case, too," Emile said. "I find it vastly frustrating that a child has cancer and that I cannot solve the issue on my own."

"Heart cancer is rare. Especially primary angiosarcoma in a pediatric patient. Don't beat yourself up over the fact you haven't worked on enough cases. Be thankful you haven't."

Their eyes met again, and again for a second she could

see the empathy, the pain, the drive to eradicate this disease in him. Warmth spread through her and she smiled. It was that passion for medicine that had brought them together all those years ago.

His lips pursed together in a thin line and he tore his gaze away, the brief spell broken once more. "Well, when you put it that way, I suppose you are right. Still, I don't want to let any patient down. There is a reason they come here to Hôpital de Ville-Marie and not somewhere else. We are the best here."

"No doubt." Chloé mustered a fake smile, because she wasn't sure what else there was to say to that. The boast annoyed her. He wasn't wrong; his hospital did have that reputation, but they'd had to bring her in to help. The way he'd always placed this hospital on a pedestal even in their days in residency was one of the reasons they broke up. There had only ever been one path for Emile.

She'd kept an eye on his work, too, over the years, and Emile was just as talented as she was and had achieved everything he'd wanted. If he'd been pigeonholed here at Hôpital de Ville-Marie, then he'd been the one taking every step possible to make it happen. So why did she get the feeling that he wasn't actually happy about it? Like what he'd achieved still wasn't enough.

He'd always been chasing something here, something more than the department head role. Chloé just didn't know what.

It's not my concern.

"Well, we better go and meet with the patient and her parents."

"Yes. Let's do that." Chloé stood up and followed Emile out of her office.

They didn't say anything to each other as they made their way down to the pediatric wing of the cardiothoracic unit. The hallways were brightly colored; there were beautiful sunflowers and other happy paintings on the walls, but as Chloé glanced through windows, the sight of tiny bodies in the beds or walking the floor made her stomach twist in a knot.

In those little faces, all she could see was Immi.

It was the same whenever she saw sick children. And it was why she always worked doubly hard when it came to the youngest patients.

"Right here," Emile said, stopping and opening the door.

She nodded quickly and followed him into the room. Emile began speaking rapid French but she could follow most of it.

A woman with dark circles under her eyes stood up, extending her hand. "It's a pleasure to meet you, Doctor MacDonald. I'm Agathe Paquette and this is my husband, Tomas."

Tomas just nodded and didn't get up from where he was sitting at his daughter's bedside.

"A pleasure to meet you," Chloé greeted, but she couldn't take her eyes off the tiny girl, so little in that big bed. Her face was sunken and she was hooked up to far too many monitors for someone who was six.

"This is my daughter, Céline," Agathe introduced. "Céline, this is Doctor MacDonald."

Céline's gaze latched on to hers. Chloé could see immediately that she was wary of doctors and being poked and prodded.

"You can call me Chloé," she said.

Céline smiled slightly. "I like your earrings."

Chloé reached up and touched the beaded earrings she was wearing. Immitaq had made them for her, but she couldn't bring her sister up in this room or she might cry. "They were a gift. I got them a long time ago."

"They're pretty." Céline coughed; it sounded a bit raspy, like even the mere act of a small cough was too much exertion for the child.

"Do you mind if I listen to your heart?" Chloé grabbed

the stethoscope that was lying on the table with some other medical instruments.

"Sure," Céline consented.

Chloé smiled and then sat down gently on the edge of the bed while Tomas helped his daughter to sit up. She could see on the monitors that the vitals weren't great and as she listened to her breathing and heart, it was clear that Céline's heart was failing.

Way too young.

"Thank you, Céline," Chloé responded and helped her lie back down. "I'm going to talk to your mom and dad and then they'll be right back."

"Okay," Céline said.

Chloé stepped out into the hallway with Emile, Agathe and Tomas.

"So," Agathe said as the door closed, "what is the plan?"

"I would like to get another scan with contrast. I want to see if the tumor has grown in the last couple of days."

"You think it could have grown?" Agathe asked, her breath catching in her throat.

"It's a rare cancer," Chloé explained gently. "And before I make my plan, I want to be sure. I would like to shrink it with chemotherapy and do immunotherapy on her before I operate. I want her to be as strong as possible."

Agathe looked at Emile, which Chloé could have been insulted by, but it wasn't surprising. They trusted Emile. He was their doctor and she was the stranger here.

"It's a good plan," Emile agreed.

Agathe nodded. "Do what you can, Doctors."

"We will," Emile assured gently. He may be standoffish with Chloé, but she was pleased to see he was still caring with his patients.

Agathe and Tomas headed back into Céline's room.

"When do you want the scan done?" Emile asked, turning to her and getting straight to business.

"As soon as possible."

Emile nodded. "We can make that happen."

"Good. Once I have that, I'll know the proper dosages to order chemotherapy from your pediatric oncology team here."

"*Bonne*," Emile stated. He looked at his watch. "It's almost lunchtime."

"Do you keep on a schedule?"

He cocked an eyebrow. "I try, but I meant that you might have to wait for a scan. Radiology does close for an hour, unless a trauma case comes in through the emergency room."

"Ah. Right. Lunch. Where can one get a bite to eat around here?"

"There is a cafeteria. Or you could walk to a nearby bistro."

"That sounds like fun! Care to join me?" The invitation came out before she could stop it.

Emile took a step back from her. "Why?"

"To eat?" she asked carefully. "You do eat, yes?"

"I do. Alone usually."

"Well, why don't you eat with me?"

Nuka, what are you doing?

Say no.

Only, Emile didn't. Couldn't. "Very well." He cleared his throat. "I think we have some more things to discuss, after all."

Chloé's eyes widened. "Do we?"

"About the case." What had come over him? He never went out to lunch with anyone. Actually, he never really took a lunch break at all. He would eat something at his desk. So he wasn't sure what compelled him to say yes to a lunch outside the hospital, with Chloé of all people. It must just have been habit, because when they'd been residents they always ate together.

"Great," Chloé said. "I wouldn't mind trying something local to this area of Montreal. It's my first time here."

"This is your first time in Montreal?" he asked, surprised.

"Yes. I've been mostly everywhere else in Canada, but haven't had the pleasure of visiting Quebec. I don't come to the east coast much."

"We're not part of the maritimes."

"I know. I'm just saying that I'm either north or out west but…anyway, yes, let's do lunch out to discuss the case. With you. In case I didn't make that clear."

He tried not to smile. It was hard not to when she was rambling. He'd always thought she was so cute when she was flustered. "You did. How about we meet downstairs in the main foyer in about thirty minutes? That way you have time to set up the testing. Just don't be surprised if they don't get to it right away."

"Good. It's a date." Pink bloomed in her cheeks. "I mean… lunch. Business lunch."

"*Bonne.*" Emile turned on his heel and left, quickly, putting some distance between them. He wasn't going to change his mind about lunch, but he was annoyed that he agreed to the invite anyway.

Falling back into old habits, letting himself be enchanted by her quirks again…

This was not how to maintain a working relationship.

This was not keeping his distance.

CHAPTER FOUR

THERE WERE A few times over the next thirty minutes that Emile considered coming up with some sort of excuse not to go out to lunch with Chloé. Unfortunately, every story he could think of was absolutely ridiculous.

Which made him feel a bit foolish. And irked.

His father had never stood for half-truths or lies and Emile couldn't stand them, either, so the temptation to hide behind one now was frustrating him all the more.

In the end, there was no getting out of it. He'd accepted her invitation and he had to go.

I have a lot of work. I could tell her that.

He always had a lot of work. Usually, he would eat by himself, because that was the way he liked it. He preferred to keep to himself for the most part.

This is why you don't have much of a life, a little voice reminded him. *This can be just business.*

He'd taken other people out for a meal before. This wasn't a foreign notion. He'd wined and dined board members, VIP guests, prestigious donors, so why was this so different?

Annoyed with himself and his thoughts, Emile stood up and pulled off his white lab coat, then grabbed his suede bomber jacket from where it hung on the back of his office door, so that he could leave before he went through another cycle of self-deprecation, trying to convince himself to change his mind.

Again.

Even though Chloé and he had agreed to meet in the foyer, he headed straight for her office where he found her just leaving.

"You ready?" he asked.

Chloé startled, then spun around. "I thought we were meeting downstairs?"

"We were, but I decided to pass by to see if I met up with you." What he didn't tell her was that he'd taken this route so he wouldn't have time to talk himself out of going to lunch with her. He was facing his trepidation head-on.

Her eyes widened. "Oh."

Emile got the distinct impression that she wasn't thrilled by his catching her leaving. Maybe she was having second thoughts about asking him and had been planning to sneak away?

"Oh?" he asked, slightly amused. "Were you going to run out on me and then send me a text, feeding me some excuse?"

That was exactly what he'd thought about, too, but there was no way he was going to tell her that.

"No!" Except Chloé wouldn't look him in the eyes and there was a blush on her cheeks.

Busted.

He chuckled. "You were always a bad liar."

"How so?"

"Remember the time you were late to rounds and you came up with that ridiculous excuse about the squirrel on the subway?"

She smiled and rolled her eyes, tossing her hair over her shoulders. "Fine. I was going to text you my regrets."

"What did the text say?" he asked, enjoying seeing her squirm.

"It doesn't matter."

"It most definitely does."

Chloé pursed her lips together in an adorable expression of playful frustration. "You're a pain."

"And you are stubborn."

"How am I stubborn?"

"You just won't admit that you were going to cancel on me." He grinned, smugly pleased with himself.

Chloé pulled her phone out of her purse. "Fine. You were right. Happy?"

He leaned over to read the half-typed text. "Very, though I'm disappointed there was no squirrel involved."

"There really was a squirrel on the subway car and it was a menace!"

They both laughed and he felt himself relax. He couldn't remember the last time he'd actually done that; the last time he'd laughed and joked with someone. It had probably been with Chloé. She always had a way of making him feel at ease. It felt nice to be smiling with her again, just like old times.

Unlike old times, though, he had to remember that they were colleagues only. Nothing more. He couldn't let his guard down. As much as he wouldn't mind falling back into bad habits around her, it wouldn't be fair to Chloé.

Their lives were so vastly different. Even if they appeared the same on the surface.

She wanted things he just couldn't commit to giving her. Like children. And time.

"So do you still want to get out of this lunch?" he asked solemnly.

"No. I'm an adult. A professional, and a VIP here. I think the head of the department *should* take me out to lunch." She nodded for effect, mock-serious.

She was so adorable.

Time apart hadn't changed that.

Don't think about her like that. I can't think about her like that.

That sort of thinking would lead him down a very slippery slope, with no possibility of a positive outcome. Nothing had changed about their lives. He wasn't going to hold her back by keeping her here, and he couldn't leave this place.

Why not?

Emile ignored that little voice, the small one inside that made him think about other paths, ones he hadn't taken. "I believe *you* invited *me* out."

"I did, but that was only because you weren't polite enough to offer. After all, I am a guest."

He rolled his eyes. "Indeed. Let's go."

There was no backing out now. They were going out for lunch, even if both of them in their own ways had tried to get out of it. The only difference was that Chloé didn't know that he'd been grappling with his own indecision, and it was going to stay that way.

When they stepped outside, the sun was shining and it was warm.

June was one of Emile's favorite months in Montreal. Warm, but not too warm or humid like the summers could get. The leaves were on the trees and flowers were blooming. It wasn't officially summer yet, still spring, but it felt like a summer's day.

Chloé sighed and closed her eyes, smiling brightly, just like a sunbeam. "Don't you love it?"

"What?" he asked.

"The sun on your face."

Emile shrugged. "I suppose. I mean, it's a nice day..."

She looked at him with exasperation. "Still so enthused, I see."

"What do you mean?"

"It's beautiful out."

He shrugged. "I suppose. It's a typical June day."

"Still can't see the bright side, eh?" she teased.

"And you're still all super sunshine."

Chloé smiled. "And why not?"

He sighed, because he didn't really have much of an answer. How could he have that upbeat attitude when he'd always been forced to hide any sign of emotion? His whole life, he'd had to be serious.

Get good grades.

Be the best.

Become a surgeon. A heart surgeon.

Marry the right person.

Uphold the family name.

That was the course of his life as laid out by his father. Those were the tenets he followed, because if he did, then his father would praise him and see that he was worthy of his name. The only place he'd fallen down was marriage; he refused to marry or have children if his workload meant he'd just have to ignore them.

The family name would die out with him.

Just thinking about his father made a dark cloud settle over him.

"The bistro isn't far from here. Just a short walk," he said, gruffly trying to change the subject as he headed off down the street toward the little restaurant he had in mind. It had a small rooftop patio where they could sit outside and maybe catch a glimpse of the river.

"Sounds good," Chloé replied. "Lead the way, MacDuff."

Emile cocked his head and looked at her quizzically as they walked. "That's not the quote."

Chloé rolled her eyes. "I know, but it's what my father always said when we were out on the land and he wanted me to lead the way. He was teaching me how to navigate out on the tundra in the snow."

"Ah, I see. Well, as long as you know the actual quote from the cursed play."

She grinned. "I took a lot of English literature in my undergrad. The actual quote is 'Lay on, MacDuff,' but has been reinterpreted to *lead on*, which is what my father would often say to us."

Her expression changed then, just a brief flicker of what looked like regret and pain.

"Us? I thought you were an only child?"

"Slip of the tongue," she replied quickly.

There was a part of Emile that wanted to pry, learn more about her family, her childhood. But if he did that then he'd be opening himself up to her again. He had to keep this a working partnership. Once this surgery was done, she was going back to Ottawa. Montreal was not her home.

They didn't say much else during the short walk to the bistro. The waitress took them to the upstairs rooftop patio, to a small wrought iron table with an umbrella at the far corner. Ivy crept up the old stone walls and they could see a glimpse of the St. Lawrence through the tall modern buildings that dominated the Montreal skyline.

"Gorgeous," Chloé sighed, leaning back in her chair. "I do love how old and modern meet here."

"*Oui*. I do, too. It's *tres bon*. If you really like the old, then you should take a trip to Quebec City. The Chateau Frontenac poised on the cliffs about the old city is formidable."

"I might have to make a weekend getaway there. Anywhere else I should see?"

"The *chutes de Montmorency* and *Sainte Anne de Beaupré*."

Chloé made a face. "Might have to think on the church, given the history."

"Of course. My apologies for not thinking about that."

"It's okay. I did ask about sightseeing, and I have heard of that church before. So *chutes de Montmorency* is a waterfall, yes?"

He smiled. "*Oui*."

"I do remember some of my French. Like *tabarnak!*"

Emile's eyes widened. "Don't shout that around here. That's a terrible word. You're cursing."

"Really?" Her eyebrows shot up, then knit into a frown. "I'm going to murder Jerry Aglook if I ever run into him again," she growled. "He taught me that in grade six."

"And what did you think it meant?"

"Tabernacle. Like a building."

Emile smiled slightly. "Well, technically, that's what it means, so Jerry Aglook is not wrong. It's just one of the worst *sacres* or swear words used in Quebec. So, maybe try to keep that word to yourself?"

"Noted."

The waitress approached their table. *"Bonjour et bienvenue!* What can I get for you today?"

"I'll have smoked meat on rye and espresso," he ordered.

"I'll have the same," Chloé replied.

The waitress nodded and took their menus, before disappearing again. A silence descended between them and Emile just stared at Chloé, sitting across from him in the sun. She was still as breathtaking as ever. She always was so hard to resist.

"So," he said, leaning over, "now you know a cuss word in Quebecois, you need to tell me one commonly heard in the north."

Their gazes locked, her eyes widening in surprise. "We don't really have swear words."

"I find that hard to believe."

"Believe it! I suppose you could use the word *huqutaunngittuq*, which means terrible and basically is used to indicate a good-for-nothing." Chloé laughed to herself.

"What?"

"Well, here we are, two surgeons at a business lunch talking about swear words instead of the case. I find it funny."

Her comment reminded him how easy it was for him to

forget himself, to let down his walls around her. He couldn't do that, no matter how good it felt.

It had nearly broken him all those years ago when their relationship had ended. He wouldn't hurt himself again that way, and he wouldn't hurt her by starting anything when he knew he couldn't give her what she really wanted. The last thing he wanted to do was cause her pain.

"You're right. We should talk about the case."

Chloé shrugged. "Well, there's not a whole lot to discuss. Not until I have the results of those scans. Once I know if the tumor has grown, then I will know how to proceed."

"Then why did you ask me out to lunch?"

Pink tinged her cheeks. "Habit, I suppose."

"I could be working." Instead of sitting here and being tempted by her.

She sat up a little straighter, tapping her hands against the table. "You're right. We need to talk about the case. It's a business lunch, so yes, let's draw up some battle plans."

He felt bad for calling her out, so he smiled at her to soften the criticism. "Like Macbeth calling into MacDuff to fight? Lay on, MacDuff."

She nodded. "Exactly."

There were some other words in Inukitut Chloé could've taught Emile, but again, they weren't really curse words in the way he meant. It was more about how one used a word, contextually, that could make it an insult. Like the way she often called him an *aiviq* or a walrus in her head whenever she thought about their breakup years ago.

Then again, that wasn't really fair to walruses in general, because she liked them. They didn't deserve to get caught up in the mess between her and Emile.

Still, it was funny how, after the awkward silence that had fallen on them as they'd walked from the hospital to the bistro, the moment they'd sat down at their table it had been as though no time had passed at all. It had felt like they were those two silly residents in Toronto again.

In truth, she'd forgotten about the squirrel incident.

There was a lot that she'd tried to put out of her mind when they'd broken up. It was just easier on her heart that way. Pain was something she'd learned to easily hide. It was good to mask the pain and just keep it to herself, instead of burdening others.

And as much as she didn't want to let Emile in, it was so hard to remember the walls she'd built to keep him out, because he was so easy to talk to and he always had been.

"Chere, you should be studying," he whispered in her ear as they sat on the couch of her tiny little apartment, his arm draped over her shoulder and his breath on her neck. Studying was not what she was thinking about and it was clear that wasn't on his mind, either.

"Oh? And what are you doing? I thought we were going to watch this surgical procedure on the television. I mean, it's studying an important surgical technique."

He sat up straighter. "Then why do you have popcorn? I assumed you were going to put on a movie."

"Well, it's a surgery movie type of thing."

He looked at her curiously. "You eat popcorn and watch surgeries?"

"Not live." She grinned and then picked up the remote. "What movie were you thinking of?"

"I don't care." He smiled lazily and then ran his finger down her neck.

"Right, so why are you pestering me about studying when all you want to do is make out to a bad movie?"

"Well, studying anatomy is important," he teased, his voice low and husky.

"Is it?" Her pulse began to race. *"I thought you aced anatomy in medical school?"*

"I did." He kissed her then, tantalizingly slow, making her melt. *"I could use a refresher. How about you?"*

Chloé's cheeks heated and she tried to chase away that memory of him, of their impromptu anatomy class on her couch that was probably the best she'd ever attended.

The one she'd taken in medical school had involved a lot of heaving and gagging as people couldn't stand the sight of their first cadaver.

Chloé, though, had stood the test.

She'd had to, because there was no way she could let her average drop, lose her scholarship to the Northern Ontario Medical School at Lakehead and have to go back home having failed her family. Having failed Immitaq.

"You okay?" Emile asked, intruding on her thoughts.

"Yep. Why?"

"You zoned out there."

"Just...thinking." Which was true. Thinking about his kisses, the way he made her feel safe, how much it had hurt when things ended.

It had been for the best.

Was it?

"About the rate of immunotherapy?" he asked.

Huh?

"Yep. Totally."

He looked at her dubiously. Before she had to explain herself further, the waitress returned then with their food. The steaming smoked meat was piled high on the marbled rye. The scent made her stomach growl with complete appreciation. She'd had smoked meat before, in a deli in Toronto, but she knew Montreal was the home of the spiced treat, and she couldn't wait to sink her teeth into it.

"Bon appétit," the waitress said.

"*Merci*," Chloé responded. The waitress left and she picked up her sandwich, savoring that first bite. "So good."

"It is the best," Emile agreed.

"Tomorrow I want a bagel. And then I want poutine and then tortiere."

He chuckled. "You're making quite the list for Quebec."

"You know it. I'm not here for a fun reason, but I'm going to also enjoy my time here." She took a sip and looked out across the city. "Maybe I'll take the train to Quebec City, so I can enjoy the ride along the river."

"You could... Or I can drive you."

The offer, though it sounded a bit forced, made her heart skip a beat. "What?"

"There is a bookstore I like to frequent in the old city, so I don't mind going with you to show you around. I mean... we can be friends, right?"

Startled, she said, "I would like that. Friends is good."

It was true; she would like it. She just wasn't sure they could do it. They'd tried to be friends before, but that turned into friends with benefits, which then turned into something more and then, ultimately heartache.

She didn't think she could survive another heartbreak with Emile. So if they were going to try out this friend thing, which she was highly suspicious of, she'd have to be careful.

"*Bonne.* Then, before you leave, we'll plan a weekend to go to Quebec City and the falls, but no church." He took a sip of his coffee. "Hopefully, it will be soon."

"You want me to leave that fast, eh?" It was just a tease; she knew he was being optimistic about Céline's case.

"No, but...you know why."

"I do. I want to win this for Céline, too. No parent should have to lose their child." Chloé only hoped her voice didn't catch in her throat.

She could hear her mother sobbing from her bedroom.

Her now-empty bedroom. Not completely empty. She was still there, but there was a hole, a space that still belonged to Immitaq, and it felt like this great chasm in her heart.

"I have to be strong for anaana and ataata. I have to be brave for them. Strong for them. They need me."

No one had been there to be strong for her. Now she was here, to be strong for those who couldn't be. It was the least she could do. Why else had she survived?

Every life she saved was an Immitaq saved for a loved one, so that person didn't have to experience that pain and that grief her parents had felt.

The excruciating pain Chloé had felt, and still felt to this day.

Both of them sat in silence, eating their smoked meat sandwiches and staring out over the city. She was trying to formulate the right words to continue a lighthearted conversation and keep the emotion of Immi from leaking out.

Her phone buzzed, notifying her of an email. When she picked it up, she could see that it was from the radiologist.

"Well?" Emile asked.

"It's from Doctor Garneau and it's the results of Céline's scans. I guess they worked through lunch."

"I'm glad they did. What does Doctor Garneau say?"

"I'm reading," she mumbled as she read through the report and then opened it up. The images were small on her phone screen; she'd analyze them more closely when she got back to her office. But the report told her everything she needed to know and it was hard to control her expression in the face of such disheartening news.

She knew that Emile would know instantly what was in that email, and his stony tone confirmed it. "Tell me."

"The tumor has grown. It's rapidly progressing."

"I see."

"I know how to attack this. When we get back, I'll order

the correct protocol and we'll get her on some strong chemotherapy and radiation to stop the growth and shrink the tumor before we operate."

Emile frowned. "Aggressive. It sounds so wrong for a small child."

"It is, but the good news in all of this is it hasn't spread. Of course, it's just a matter of time before it does, but in all honesty, with the rate the tumor is increasing in her heart, it will kill her before it metastasizes anywhere else."

"How about I pay this bill and we head back—if you're done, that is?"

"I'm done. And I did invite you out. I can pay."

"No," Emile stated. "The hospital will."

"Okay, thanks. I want to get back, too, and start the protocol. This whole process is just going to be a bit of hurry-up-and-wait for the foreseeable future."

Emile nodded and headed downstairs to the main part of the bistro. Chloé finished the last bite of her sandwich and chugged her espresso, staring at the bleak images one last time. There was a part of her that had been hoping the tumor hadn't grown and that the course of treatment wouldn't be as complex. Not only because it would be better for Céline, but also, selfishly, because then Chloé wouldn't have had to remain so long in Montreal, putting her own heart in danger. Instead, it was looking like Montreal was going to be her home for some time.

But all that really didn't matter in the grand scheme of things. All that mattered was making sure that little Céline came through this, so that she had a chance to grow up and live a normal life.

Chloé's heart could handle the threat.

For now.

CHAPTER FIVE

THEY WALKED BACK to the hospital in silence. Something had shifted since Dr. Garneau sent over that report. There had been a few moments during lunch where she saw snippets of the Emile she remembered, but when reality had hit and those scans came through, his demeanor had changed.

It was like all that old familiarity had been left back at the bistro. Chloé was trying to chalk it up to the urgency of the situation.

"Would you like to come to my office and we can review the scans there?" she asked as they stepped back into the atrium of the hospital.

"No. I have too much to do." Emile barely looked at her. "I shouldn't have gone out."

The last sentence was a bit of a mumble that caught her off guard.

"For lunch?" she asked quizzically.

He frowned. "I am the chief of cardiothoracic. Again, my time is limited. I should've been at my desk when the scans came in."

"They were sent to me."

He wasn't looking at her, but checking his phone. "Send me your report."

"I thought you want to learn?" Chloé asked. "This is a hands-on moment." An increase in professionalism was one thing, but this total shift in his personality had her stunned.

"I do. I can read and learn as well."

Before she could argue any further, he quickly walked away.

She rolled her eyes and headed back to her office. He was acting a bit like his father. She'd only met Dr. Moreau Senior once, when he came to the hospital in Toronto. She hadn't liked the energy he put out then, and had been glad Emile was so different. Now, though, it felt like he was trying to be like his late father.

It wasn't her concern, though. Emile could act however he wanted. As long as it didn't interfere with his work.

When she got back to her office space, she pulled the images up on her computer to study them. It had been one thing seeing the images on her phone and reading Dr. Garneau's report. It was another thing entirely to see the tumor on a larger screen and realize what a fight it was going to be. There was going to be a *lot* of medication for Céline to handle.

Carefully, she started to put together the plan of attack to present to Céline's parents. Just from her brief meeting with Céline's mother, she knew that Agathe was going to want all the facts—not that she would do less for any of her patients.

She wanted all them to have every option available. Especially the littlest and most precious ones like Céline.

Chloé's parents hadn't always been in the know about Immi's diagnosis and they had cycled through an endless revolving door of doctors, depending on who was doing their rotation up north that month.

"But we were told the stage of heart failure wasn't so bad," her mother said softly, completely confused.

"Who told you that?" the new doctor asked.

"Doctor Gerrity," her father answered.

The new doctor scoffed. "Well, no offense to Doctor Gerrity, but I'm a heart specialist."

Chloé wandered away from her parents and down to her

sister's room. Immi was lying in bed, oxygen cannula in her nose, her little beading loom on her lap. She looked exhausted, just from the act of living.

"What're you making?" Chloé asked.

"Earrings," Immi gasped. "For you."

Chloé smiled. "They're pretty."

"Thanks. I want you to wear them. Always."

Chloé reached up and touched her earrings now. Céline had liked her earrings. Maybe Chloé could make some for her. She often did that for her pediatric patients.

Céline was lucky to be in Montreal, and Chloé was thankful that Emile's hospital was going to allow her patients to come here, too.

It was a kind gesture.

Proof that he could still be kind, even though he was keeping Chloé at an arm's length. No matter how cold he was to her, she could still see the remnants of the man she fell in love with years ago. There was an empathy that was still lurking under that aloof exterior. It was almost as if this hospital, this place, was weighing him down.

It wasn't so much Montreal; she had been able to see the love he had for the city when they'd gone out for lunch and eaten on that beautiful ivy-covered terrace. So if it wasn't that, then it must be this hospital.

Which seemed odd, given how this had always been the plan for him. Always the endgame.

"But why your late father's hospital? He's no longer there. You can go anywhere," she said. She could tell how sad he was about turning down Vancouver.

Emile frowned. "It's a legacy."

"Ah, legacy shemgacy," she joked, trying to make light of it. Clearly, this was the wrong thing to do. His face hardened.

"And look who is talking," he snapped. "You're going to

go to Iqaluit. That plan hasn't changed. What is so different about my plans compared to yours?"

Emile had had a point. And now Chloé couldn't help thinking of that painting of his father and all the others that had come before him, glaring down at him... She couldn't even begin to imagine that kind of pressure. She also knew that Emile was stubborn and wouldn't walk away from something he had worked so hard to achieve.

Why should you worry?

The answer was simple. She shouldn't. They were colleagues, friends, that was it. They weren't lovers, and given the way their lives were going and the fact that they lived in completely different worlds, she didn't really see them ever getting back together. Ever.

Even if Emile was still as dishy and tempting as he'd been all those years ago when they'd first met. The same smile, the same laugh, that made her feel so comfortable—when he let her see them. When he was himself. The closed-off workaholic he'd become, she wasn't too keen on. If she ever decided to get married and have kids, she wanted an equal partner. Someone who could be there; someone to rely and lean on.

Emile was not that person.

And no amount of desire or wishing would change that.

Chloé groaned in frustration and ran her fingers through her hair.

What she needed to do now was focus.

"Come on. You can do this," she grumbled to herself as she stared at her report.

"Do what?"

Chloé glanced up to see the very man who was distracting her from her work, hovering in the door to her office.

"Work," she replied and then sat up straighter. "What're you doing here?"

Emile sighed. "I came to apologize. I got...distracted. I like to be here when news like that comes in. Also, it's been about an hour since we came back, so I'm looking for the report."

Chloé leaned back in her chair, crossing her arms. "I was just going to send you my report."

"I appreciate it, but I'm here now."

"Well, then by all means, come on in." She pulled up the images, mumbling about finicky behavior.

"What?" he asked.

"Nothing. Just muttering to myself." She smiled, glad he hadn't heard her complaints.

"I'd forgotten you talk to yourself."

"I don't do it that often!"

Emile smiled, his blue eyes twinkling briefly. "You do. You have full conversations with yourself. And you talk in your sleep."

Heat bloomed in her cheeks. "Well, I can't confirm or deny that..."

"I assure you, you do. 'Kill the elves' was my favorite of your nocturnal shouting matches. It scared me half to death when you sat upright in bed, screamed that and went back to sleep. I always did mean to ask what you were dreaming about that night."

Chloé groaned. "Can I help you with anything *medical*, Doctor Moreau, or is this visit merely to discuss my unconscious effort to go marauding on innocent fay folk? I honestly don't know if I'm coming or going with you."

He looked away, shoving his hands in his coat pockets like he was a bit on edge. His lips pressed together in a firm line. "I'm aware. My apologies. I keep to myself mostly."

"People who want to be friends usually are a bit more social."

"I'm out of practice," he admitted.

"Indeed. Well, you're forgiven. Now, tell me what you think of these scans."

Emile leaned over her, close. She closed her eyes, drinking in the scent of him; she always did love the way he smelled.

Nuka, seriously?

"That is a nasty tumor," Emile remarked.

"It is."

They shared a look. Chloé realized her pulse was racing. Then Emile abruptly stood up, taking a step back like he was pushing her away. "You have a course of action?" he asked.

"Working on it."

Emile nodded. "Good."

She thought that was going to be the end of it, but he lingered.

"You know, I can't think with people hovering over me," Chloé teased. "Something else is on your mind."

"Indeed. You know, I have a very unique ventricular septal defect repair in about an hour, and I was hoping you'd like to join me."

Chloé was definitely intrigued by the prospect. A VSD repair was a simple enough procedure and she'd done the operation herself countless times, but the fact that Emile said it was unusual had her interested.

"What makes it so special?" she asked, curious.

"Well, the patients are conjoined twins. This is the first step in determining their eventual separation. One of the twins has a ventricular septal defect and in order to get them strong enough to be separated, both their hearts need to be strong."

"Conjoined twins?" It was true; that was very rare. She hadn't seen many cases in the north at all. Well, not in her jurisdiction. And she was very tempted. He might be learning from her about heart cancer, but this was an opportunity for her to learn from him.

"Well, are you interested in joining me in the operating room?"

"Yes. I would like that. Thank you for asking me. You're right—I don't get a lot of cases like that in Ottawa or in Iqaluit."

"Good. The procedure is in an hour and in operating room four. I'll meet you down there."

"Yes."

Emile nodded and slipped out of her office just as quietly as he entered. She was so thankful for the opportunity, but there was a part of her that was a bit concerned about where this could go. She'd fallen in love with him the last time over surgery, the way they'd always worked together so seamlessly in the operating room. Sure, they bantered outside, but it was in that moment of surgery, staring at a heart, when it had felt like they were truly one.

There was a deep connection. Wouldn't this be just setting herself up for something similar? Put her in danger of falling for him again?

Not if I don't let it.

She would only be observing, really. A VSD didn't require many hands. Besides, Emile would be right there with her when they did Céline's surgery. This would be a good test of her willpower.

Emile had sent over the file, so Chloé had a chance to look at it all before she headed down to the operating room.

The conjoined twins were connected by liver and bowels. They both had separate hearts, but there were parts where they shared a blood supply. Twin A's heart had the VSD and that hole in the heart was affecting the blood supply to Twin B. So before they could be separated, Twin A had to have their ventricular septal defect repaired. And then when it was safe, the separation surgery would occur. Chloé wished she'd be around then to watch or lend a hand, but that was at least a year away, maybe more. Conjoined twins were never separated surgically until they were at least a year old.

She wouldn't be here then.

Montreal was not her endgame.

Maybe she'd be able to come back and watch it?

Do you think that's a good idea? Immi's voice questioned.

It probably wasn't.

She got a pair of scrubs, changing quickly in the locker room, tying back her hair under a generic scrub cap—she'd left her personalized ones in Ottawa—then she headed into the scrub room to wash and get masked up. As she scrubbed in, she could see Emile was already in the operating room and she paused for a moment to admire him. She'd forgotten how good he looked in his dark blue scrubs.

Sometimes, back when they were residents, she'd stand in the gallery to watch him work, mesmerized by his focus and trying not to think about the fact she knew exactly what was under those scrubs.

Her face heated under her mask, thinking about a few times when things had gotten hot and heavy in the on-call room.

Oh, my God. I'm doing it again.

Friends don't usually lust after one another, Nuka, Immi's voice reminded her.

Chloé groaned quietly under her breath and shook off her hands before stepping into the operating room to get gloved and gowned by one of the OR nurses. The moment she stepped into that room, she just shut out all those thoughts about Emile and the past and focused on the surgery and this amazing opportunity to see a complex VSD repair.

The operating room was a calming place for her, where she was able to just focus on her work and clear her mind. As she approached the table, though, she had to look twice to take in the sight of the two tiny babies, joined together and hooked up to so many lines and monitors. There were scans and fluoroscopy imaging on the screens around the room so they could see how the blood was moving through the arteries, the structure of Twin A's heart and the ventricular septal defect. And just by looking at the twins on the table she could see that Twin A was the more robust of the two.

This repair would definitely make Twin B stronger and more able to withstand the eventual separation when the twins were older.

"What do you think?" Emile asked, coming to stand beside her.

"Twin A is larger," Chloé remarked. "Not knowing all the facts, I can only surmise the situation from your notes, but I think it should be a simple enough repair, even though it's a large VSD. I assume you're doing open chest?"

Emile nodded. "That is the only way to ensure that it will be successful and beneficial for both twins in the long run."

"What're their names?" She hated thinking of them so clinically as Twins A and B. Sometimes it was better to compartmentalize things, but she found she worked better if she formed a connection with her patients, if she knew them.

Even if things went badly, it gave her peace to know them just a little bit.

"Does it matter?" Emile asked.

She nodded, their eyes locking. "To me it does."

His eyes twinkled over his mask, and she knew he was smiling at her. "I forgot."

"What?"

"The connection you need and the peace you bring."

"It helps."

"Indeed," he whispered. "Thank you for reminding me."

"You're welcome, Doctor Moreau."

"Of course, Doctor MacDonald. Jasmine is Twin A and Ayesha is Twin B."

"Pretty names," she murmured.

Once again, looking into his eyes, she felt like she could see the old Emile again, staring at her across the operating room. It was like she'd been transported back in time, standing in front of the boy she'd been in love with all those years ago.

"Very pretty," Emile said faintly. Then he looked away, clearing his throat and breaking the spell. "Well, let's get ready."

Chloé approached the operating table and looked down at the babies. Her heart melted because they were so cute, so small and fragile.

She did love children. Sometimes she yearned to be a mother herself, but when would she have time? And there was a small part of her, deeply buried in the far corner of her heart, that was terrified at the prospect of having a child.

Of losing that child.

Her throat tightened as she thought about the parents of these twins, because she clearly remembered the pain and worry that seemed to be permanently etched on her own parents' faces every time Immi was in the hospital.

They'd come to visit Immitaq. She had rallied yesterday, battling her heart disease and they'd all been so hopeful.

But now Chloé knew. Even though she wasn't in the room with her parents, she could see them through the glass windows of the private room Immi's doctor had pulled them into.

Her heart sank.

The pain that had been gradually aging their mother, but had been partially held back, now erupted like a dam inside her had broken, flooding her face. Her father was no longer his jovial self. That was something she and Immi so loved about him—the way he made their days brighter. Now it was like every ounce of joy had been sucked out of his very being. His smile was replaced by pursed lips. His sparkling dark eyes devoid of that twinkle.

Chloé stared down at the book she'd brought for her sister, but she knew then Immi would never read it. In her heart, she knew that her twin, her other half, was gone.

She also knew she had to be the joy for her parents. She had lived when Immi hadn't. The least she could do was make sure she never added to their pain. So she swallowed her own.

Her parents needed her to be strong for them, even if it felt like she was crumbling; even if she barely knew how.

She was certain about one thing. She never wanted to feel the agony that her parents were going through.

"You ready?" Emile asked, interrupting her thoughts.

"Yes," Chloé said, smiling brightly from behind the mask and tearing her gaze away from the twins on the table. "Ready when you are, Doctor Moreau."

Emile was slightly surprised when Chloé just seemed to zone out while staring at the twins. He wasn't so shocked that she wanted to know the twins' names. He'd forgotten that sweet part of her. Maybe he'd buried it away deliberately, because there was no place for that kind of softness, not in his father's hospital. At one time, he'd liked to build up that personal connection with all of his patients, too, but once he'd stepped into his father's shadow, he'd had to lock away those bits and pieces of his personality.

Emile had known the twins' names, but sharing them with Chloé had felt special; it had changed the energy in the operating room to something hopeful.

Beautiful even.

Observing surgeons didn't usually ask for those kinds of personal details. They came to watch the procedures. And his father had *never* been one to form any kind of connection with a patient.

Not on that kind of level.

Everything in his father's life was business.

Cool.

Aloof.

Even his own private and familial relationships.

When his father had come to play the role of guest surgeon at the hospital in Toronto where Emile had been doing his residency, he'd rounded with Emile and had not been pleased to see that his son had picked up that less than desirable habit.

"What're you doing?" his father demanded.

Emile was shocked. He'd been thrilled when his father took time out of his busy schedule as a visiting surgeon to do rounds with him, but now he'd pulled Emile into a meeting room. It seemed like his father was angry.

"Well?" his father asked again. "What're you doing, Emile?"

"Speaking to my patients?" Emile responded, confused.

"You're being too personal with them."

"Are you suggesting I be mean or cold with my bedside manner?"

His father's eyes narrowed. "No. You can be friendly, but don't make it personal. They're patients, not friends."

Emile was still confused. "Father, I guess I don't quite understand what you're getting at. I know they're not my friends."

"You're too chatty. Too friendly." His father frowned. "Do you want to one day be head of cardio at Hôpital de Ville-Marie?"

"Of course."

"You say that with hesitation."

"Father, I was pleased you came to see me. My attending is happy with my work…"

"That doesn't matter. What you need to do is keep patients at a distance. You can't get too attached."

"I guess I don't understand, Father."

"You are their doctor. Their surgeon. Their life is in your hands. You're a professional, not their friend. They need to know you deserve their respect."

"I don't agree. They trust me."

Without even contemplating the fact that Emile could be right, his father shook his head. "You should've done your residency in Montreal. You're learning too many bad habits here. Hôpital de Ville-Marie is your legacy, a family legacy, and you will squander your chance to take your rightful place if you continue acting this way. Don't you want to make me proud?"

And that was the crux of it.

Emile shook the memory of his father out of his mind. He couldn't let it get to him. One of the reasons why he was one of the best cardiothoracic surgeons in Montreal was because he *did* have that personable connection with his patients. His patients all adored him. Frankly, it made him a better surgeon. It was one small piece that he kept from his time with Chloé, who was always so joyful and caring. Sometimes he liked to think that holding on to that empathy kept him connected to her, especially on days that he missed her.

His staff, on the other hand, might find him as cold and distant as his father. But to run his unit efficiently he had to be strict. What things would slip through the cracks if he really let down his guard?

He'd been out at lunch when those scans came in. A good chief of cardio would've been in radiology watching as the scans were being done. But instead...

Emile looked across the operating table at Chloé. Her dark eyes from behind that bright blue mask. Her dark lashes fanning her face. Her silken hair tied back under the scrub cap.

In that brief moment of admiring her, it felt like no time

had passed. That he was still that young resident in Toronto, head over heels in love with her. The happiest times of his life.

Why had he thrown it all away?

But looking at Chloé, her accomplishments, her happiness, he just knew he'd made the right choice. This place and the person he'd become... Eventually, it would've ruined her and their love.

That, he could not bear.

Focus on the surgery, a little voice reminded him. *No time for doubts. Or for reminiscing over something you can't have.*

How quickly he was forgetting himself when he was around Chloé.

He had to shake all those thoughts out of his mind. His resident was reading off the information about the patients, about the operation they were going to perform, as Emile turned to the scrub nurse.

"Scalpel," he requested.

His preferred blade was handed to him and he set to work, because he was a surgeon first and foremost, living in the shadows of his family, and these little lives were in his hands.

Later, he could mull over the ghosts of his past, but nothing was going to change.

Chloé's home wasn't in Montreal and never would be. And that, as far as he was concerned, was for the best. She wanted a life he couldn't give her. Couldn't want for himself.

CHAPTER SIX

"Come closer," Emile motioned to Chloé. She stepped forward. "I know I shouldn't ask a surgeon of your caliber to hold a clamp…"

"I would love to. Just like old times." Chloé stepped up and held a clamp where he instructed.

"You and Doctor MacDonald used to work together?" the resident on her left asked. Dr. LaCroix, Chloé remembered.

Emile shot him a "no small talk during surgery" look and Dr. LaCroix looked away.

"Don't be so grouchy, Doctor Moreau," Chloé answered brightly. "We did, in fact, Doctor LaCroix. We were residents together."

Emile groaned, but couldn't help smiling under his mask. "I forgot how you like to chat in theater, Doctor MacDonald."

"I do."

They shared a warm look across the table. He was half expecting her to start telling embarrassing stories about their days as residents, but she didn't.

He wouldn't mind reminiscing with her, just not around others. His residents didn't need to know about his personal life.

The operation went off without a hitch. He and Chloé worked seamlessly—which shouldn't shock him. When they were residents, they had always worked well together. But it was like no time had passed at all.

Sometimes, back then, they would butt heads, but for the most part they thought very similarly when it came to surgery and medicine. He'd forgotten what it was like to work with her and how much he enjoyed having her across from him in the operating room. He could get used to it.

She knew him before. She saw him as more than the head of the department here. He didn't have to earn her respect.

No. Don't think like that. I can't.

Emile had Dr. LaCroix close, and Chloé left the operating room while he worked on his operative report. Then he made his way to the post-anesthesia care unit to make notes on the twins' chart for the neonatal intensive care unit. He left detailed instructions for the nurses for the twins' post-op care. Jasmine and Ayesha were still under sedation and intubated so that they could fully recover. And he hoped that in a year they could be strong enough to be separated.

I wish Chloé would be here for that, too.

For a brief moment, he considered inviting her back.

He *tsked* under his breath and finished up his notes, annoyed that he was letting himself think like that again. Thinking of excuses or reasons to bring her back into his life.

Chloé was needed here to help with Céline and they had agreed to be friends. Nothing more. It didn't have to be complicated.

The only risk was to his heart. Being around her made him forget himself, transported him right back to who he used to be, the man who had loved her so much.

Did you, though? If you loved her, you wouldn't have let her go.

In Emile's eyes, letting her go was the best thing he could've done, because at least now he wasn't holding her back—from her work, from everything she wanted.

"Father?" he asked, *walking into his dad's study.* Even at

eighteen he felt like a child. His father was sitting in the dark staring at a photograph of Emile's mother.

"What is it?" his father asked. There was a clink of ice and Emile knew his father was drinking scotch, like he often did. There was a sense of sadness in the air.

"Why don't you call Mother?" Emile suggested.

"And why would I do that?"

"Because you miss her?"

And in one moment of clarity, his father's expression softened. "Oui. I do, but we're too different. It was better to let her go. I loved her and set her free."

"Why?" Emile asked.

His father shrugged and then looked away. "I love the hospital more."

And that was what Emile had done, too. It was for the best. For the both of them.

"Hey."

Emile turned around to find Chloé standing there. She had her coat on and her purse over her shoulder.

"You heading home?" he asked.

"Well, my home here in Montreal, yes." She grinned.

If only your home was here. A pang of longing hit him. But would having Chloé here really change anything in the grand scheme of things?

It wouldn't. Emile's stance on marriage and kids remained the same.

Why?

"I see," he stated, unsure of what to say or what to make of the emotions churning inside him.

"How are the twins?" she asked.

"Sedated, but their vitals are strong."

"Good. Thank you for allowing me to attend their repair today."

"Thank you for your help in the operating room." He set the chart back down at the nursing station for the NICU.

"I didn't do much," Chloé remarked.

"You did. It's easy to work with you. I'm glad that hasn't changed. Although, you had me worried."

"About what?"

"What were you going to say to Doctor LaCroix that might incriminate me?"

She chuckled, pink tingeing her cheeks, and tucked a strand of hair behind her ear. "Well, I'm going to head off. Céline is starting immunotherapy tomorrow and I want to get here early."

"What time does the immunotherapy start?"

"Six. Just after rounds."

"Well, then I think I'll be there as well. I would like to be there when immunotherapy starts. If I ever encounter heart cancer in a pediatric patient, I would like to know how to tackle it."

"You mean without having to call in the reserves?" she teased.

He smiled. "*Oui*. I suppose so."

They fell into step as they were leaving the NICU, not saying anything but walking in companionable silence, nothing like the awkwardness from before. Usually, when Emile was moving about the hospital, he was marching at top speed, always on a mission. He didn't really take strolls and definitely not with beautiful women. There was no time for that in his life.

Not that he would call walking through the hospital a stroll.

"What're your plans for dinner?" he found himself asking. He almost couldn't believe the words he was hearing, or that he'd been the one to say them. They just came spilling out of him before he had a chance to really think about it.

"I don't know," Chloé said. "I haven't had a chance to go

shopping yet, so I was going to see what was around the residence hotel. Worse comes to worst I would have dinner in the hotel restaurant. Why?"

"Would you like to grab a bite to eat with me?"

What're you doing?

Emile didn't know, and judging by Chloé's stunned expression, she didn't, either. Apparently, he was having some kind of out-of-body experience.

But maybe this would be for the best; just bite the bullet and socialize. She had said friends were social. Dinner was social.

"Dinner?" she questioned.

"As friends," he reiterated. "I want to be your friend, Chloé. We were friends once before."

Chloé blushed again, then shook her head. "I want to be your friend, too, Emile. I enjoy spending time with you and I was glad when you reached out to me about this case."

"Good. I'm glad you want that. And of course I reached out to you. In this case, with respect to Céline, you are the best."

"I appreciate your frankness."

He cocked an eyebrow. "Really? Then you have certainly changed because in the past you didn't always appreciate that."

Chloé chuckled, and the awkward tension caused by the surprise dinner invite melted away. "Well, we're both older and wiser. Well, you're older."

He chuckled, unable to help it. "So, do you want to have dinner with me tonight? There's a great little restaurant down by the river."

"I would like that. It's a beautiful night and I would like to take in more of Montreal. Besides, I was going to take you up on the offer to go to Quebec City soon. Seeing how we're going to be friends, I thought it might be nice."

"*Bonne.* I'm glad for that. We can go this weekend if you're free?"

What are you doing? Dinner is one thing; a weekend getaway to another city is different.

"I am free. Unless something changes with Céline's case and I'm needed here, but that will most likely be the case the closer we get to surgery. Now might be the best time to go, when we're just starting out with her treatment. Would we have to stay overnight?"

"No. It's only three or so hours to Quebec City. But we can discuss all the details at dinner. How about I pick you up about seven at your hotel?"

Chloé nodded. "That sounds great. I'll see you then."

"Indeed."

Chloé walked away and Emile stood there for a few moments watching her, before the realization hit that he'd actually made a date with her.

Not a date. A friendly dinner between colleagues. He'd have to convince himself of that fact. Even if he'd never been out for dinner with anyone he'd worked with before.

He spent the next couple of hours trying to talk himself out of picking up Chloé. He half expected her to text him and try to get out of it herself, but she didn't. Finally, he just told himself to get over it. He truly did want to be her friend. And he'd enjoyed his lunch out with her.

A little too much. It had made him grapple with all those feelings he thought he'd locked away. But he wouldn't let that happen again tonight.

When they'd gotten back to the hospital after their lunch, he'd shut her out. Yet, try as he might, he couldn't keep away from her. It was clear he was lonely and the idea of having Chloé in his life in a platonic way was tempting.

It doesn't have to be more than that.

When he got back to his family's home, where he now

lived, he realized the empty halls echoed a bit more than usual tonight. Most nights it didn't bother him, but right now it did.

Of course, it always was empty. Especially after his mother left. When it was just him and his father.

"You're too much like your father," his mother chided gently.

He briefly looked up from his work. "How so?"

"I've come to Montreal to visit you, but you're always working."

"I'm a surgeon."

"I know," his mother sighed sadly. "Why don't you take time off? Come to Beaupré for a break."

"Maybe."

Only he never had. He rarely saw his mother. He made sure she was taken care of, but time was not something he could give to her. There was an estrangement there. Why didn't he visit her? Why was he so afraid to leave the hospital work behind?

Because it's my life.

Now it was just him in this echoey old house, and always would be. Because the work that meant he never saw his mother would never allow him to get married and have kids, either.

It cut him to the quick to think he was like his father; scared him. But then again, if he wasn't like him, Emile wouldn't be where he was now—wouldn't be the surgeon he was.

He was still mulling this all over in his head, when he realized with a jolt that he was pulling up to Chloé's hotel. It was like he had left the house and driven over in a trance.

But all those trepidations melted away the moment he saw Chloé, standing outside waiting for him. Like a beam of light at the end of a dark tunnel.

She took his breath away.

Just for a second. Just like the instant he'd seen her when she first entered the hospital, and time had stood still. Like she was frozen in a moment from their youth, when they had been so in love. When he'd been so happy.

Now he took another chance to watch her, taking it all in. She was wearing a flowy, flowery dress, sandals and a denim jacket. She looked chic and adorable. Perfect for a sultry summer Montreal night.

Emile smiled as she seemed to almost float toward the car. As much as he liked her in scrubs, she was gorgeous in a dress.

A dangerous thought. He had to be careful. He couldn't let memories or loneliness suck him back into thoughts of something more than friendship.

That wouldn't be fair to either of them.

This is exactly why I needed to keep my distance from her.

Too late for that now.

Chloé opened the door and slid in. The scent of her vanilla perfume wafted over Emile and he fought the urge to bury his face in her neck, her hair, to get lost in her arms like he had done so many times before.

"Thanks for picking me up, but I could've taken a taxi or something to the restaurant."

"It's not a problem," he replied, tearing his gaze away from her and gripping hard at the wheel. Friends out at dinner, nothing more. He had to keep replaying that mantra over and over in his head.

"Still, I could've met you there."

"It's kind of hard to do that when I didn't tell you where we're going," he said, smiling briefly.

"You didn't?" She glanced at her phone, scrolling. "Oh, you didn't. So where did I get that idea from?"

"Did you have a place in mind?" he asked, curious.

"Poire Romantique?"

"How do you know about *Poire Romantique*?"

"Well, I thought you told me." She shrugged. "So who knows where I got that from. Perhaps Céline's mom mentioned it when I stopped by to check on her before I left."

"That would make sense."

"Plus, I really like saying that name, *poire romantique*. Is it super exclusive or expensive? Is that why the premier recommended it?"

"Not really, but it's trendy. Hard to get into, but we can try, if you like," Emile stated.

"Well, where were you going to take me?" she asked.

"Does it matter now?"

"Sure it does." She smiled brightly at him. "Maybe I would like your place better?"

He chuckled. "And if you don't, I'll never hear the end of it."

"Ah, there's the old Emile," she said brightly.

"What do you mean?"

"You're so serious these days."

He bristled at her tone. "I run a department at the hospital. It's not a joke."

"I didn't mean to offend. I get it. I can't even begin to imagine."

"Thank you," he replied stiffly. Although, he understood her reasoning, her point.

It was hard to let loose. There was so much responsibility on his shoulders. A legacy baked into his DNA.

More like a burden.

"So where are we going?" Chloé asked, interrupting his morose thoughts.

"This little bistro down by the water that has an excellent duck confit and plays jazz."

"Oh, that sounds fun!" Chloé settled back against her seat.

"Although, not sure how I feel about jazz. I'm more of a death metal gal."

"It's *light* jazz," he teased, correcting her. "I forgot you liked to head bang."

She stuck up her index and pinky, stuck out her tongue and shook her head, and he couldn't help but laugh.

"Give jazz a chance," he quipped.

"I swear I will."

It didn't take too long to get down to St. Paul Street and he parked the car in a garage. They walked a short couple of blocks to the bistro, *Choisir*. It was a beautiful summer's night. As the sun was setting, lights from the city reflected in the perfectly still waters of the St. Lawrence River. Light jazz floated out from the restaurant, creating an idyllic ambience. Emile couldn't remember the last time he'd really enjoyed himself like this, just walking down by the river on a summer night.

Maybe because I never have.

"This is cute," Chloé remarked as they came up to *Choisir*.

"I'm glad you think so," Emile remarked. He spoke quickly to the maître d' who stood outside and they were led inside the brick building that had originally been an old warehouse. It was warm and modern inside, and yet there was a retro speakeasy feel. It was one of Emile's favorite places, but he didn't often find time to come here.

It was the perfect place to take a date.

This is not a date.

How easy it was to slip back into old habits.

That's because you want to slip back.

Chloé's first impression of *Choisir* was how romantic it was. Nothing about this felt like a meal between friends. Of course, she wasn't exactly dressed for a work dinner, either, but since Emile had mentioned that he wanted to be friends, she'd chosen an outfit that she thought was completely casual, flirty and fun.

Nuka, not flirty. Not with Emile.

Chloé liked to flirt. It was fun. But even an innocent little flirt with Emile wasn't exactly safe. There was always a danger it could turn into something more. Chloé knew that firsthand, because that was what happened last time.

She slid into the booth that was tucked away in the corner. Emile slid in from the other side. The maître d' left them with menus, spoke some quick French that she couldn't pick up and then discreetly left.

The bar looked like a bootlegger's hideout, all exposed brick, dark wood and mirrors. And live jazz in a corner.

"Is this acceptable?" Emile asked, his blue eyes twinkling in the dim light. She'd always loved when they dazzled in her direction.

"We'll see. I mean, *Poire Romantique* was personally recommended to me by the premier of the province. If you can't trust a politician, who can you trust?"

A smile tweaked at the corner of his mouth, just briefly before it vanished. "That's very facetious of you."

"I know." Chloé winked exaggeratedly, then instantly regretted it when Emile didn't laugh. "So, what's good here? I mean you said duck, but I'm not sure I want to eat Donald."

"What?" Emile asked, looking baffled.

"You know, the most famous duck I know."

Emile rolled his eyes. "Seriously?"

"I am being serious."

He sighed. "I forgot how weird you can be sometimes. Maybe I blocked it out."

"Okay, I'm sorry, weirdness aside. Duck confit sounds good, but I was hoping for some fish or seafood. Maybe something French."

"Duck confit is French," he said dryly.

"You're really pushing this duck on me, aren't you?"

"Fine. Foie gras?" he suggested.

"No. I can't in good conscience eat that. And besides, that's still duck, just its liver."

"You caught that, huh?"

"I'm not uncultured if that's what you think. I enjoy wild game and a good Alberta steak."

"Don't like jazz, prefers death metal. Rather have a burger." There was a hint of humor laced in there.

"Steak and hamburger are completely different."

"It's cow."

"Chopped and ground. Different."

"Salad Niçoise with the tuna is good," he mentioned, changing the subject.

"That sounds good." She closed her menu. "What're you getting?"

"Duck." There was a sparkle in his eyes and slight smile curled on his lips, hidden partially by the scruff of a beard he now wore.

Aloof, grumpy, whatever the others in the hospital called him, whatever he tried to be at work—deep down, Chloé could see that there were still pieces of the Emile she used to know; little glimpses that snuck out before he could quickly lock them away again.

The Emile she'd used to love.

Nuka, don't think like that, eh? Immi's voice warned in her head.

Her time here in Montreal was limited and she couldn't fancy herself falling for Emile again or give up on her goal and her commitment to Nunavut. She didn't want others in the north to face what her parents had, to have someone else lose their Immitaq.

Her whole career was centered around that goal and she

couldn't walk away, just like she knew that Emile couldn't leave Montreal. It wasn't going to work for them.

It was annoying how easily she could be swayed by just a conversation with him; how much it made her want to allow those walls she'd built up to slip.

"*Bonjour*, I'm Henri and your waiter for this evening. Can I bring you some wine?" Henri asked, interrupting her train of thought.

"*Oui*, we'll have a bottle of your Crément de Loire, Clos de Quaterons Chenin Blanc," Emile replied.

"Of course, monsieur." Henri scurried away.

"That sounded fancy," Chloé remarked. "White wine?"

"Champagne or something similar to champagne. It's *bulles*, or bubbles. I thought it might be nice to celebrate the successful procedure on the twins from earlier."

She nodded. "That's a good reason to celebrate."

Henri returned with their bottle on ice. There was a loud pop as he opened it and poured the sparkling wine into two glass flutes. "Are you ready to order?" he asked, placing the bottle back into the silver bucket.

"I think so," Chloé remarked.

"What would you like to order?" Henri asked.

"I'll have the Niçoise."

Henri nodded and turned to Emile. "Monsieur?"

"Duck confit." Emile handed him his menu.

"Very good. I'll return soon." Henri disappeared again.

Emile picked up his flute of *bulles* and held it up. "Cheers to our successes, both today and to come."

"Indeed." Chloé's hand shook slightly as their glasses clinked. She took a sip and then set the flute down on the table. "So, immunotherapy and chemo starts tomorrow for Céline."

"I saw the orders."

"I'm hoping that by the end of the month I can do the surgery." She fiddled with the fabric napkin on the table. "That being said, I have a patient from the north who I need to see. I was wondering if you'd had a chance to email the board about bringing my patients here?"

"I did. The premier also heard and said to do what it took to make it happen. They're quite willing to bring patients from Nunavut to Montreal."

"Good. I'll make the arrangements tomorrow, then." There was an awkward tension that fell between them. Suddenly, she didn't know what to say. "I was so shocked you asked me out to dinner."

"Trust me, I was shocked, too."

"Then, why?"

"Are you complaining?" he asked.

"No. Just…curious."

He nodded. "So am I."

She laughed nervously. "Well, we're off to a great start. You're just agreeing with me and we're not really talking about anything."

There was a brief half smile, one she always used to love, one that made her weak in the knees.

"Well, what do you think of my choice compared to the premier's?"

She looked around again. "This is a very cool spot. Trendy, you might say."

"It is indeed. It's one of my favorite places, but I don't come here often enough."

"Why not?"

Emile shrugged. "No time. I don't make time, I suppose. Work is my life."

"I hear that." And then even though she didn't want to ask, she couldn't help herself. Maybe it was the bubbles talking. "So, no girlfriend, no dating?"

"No one." There was hesitation. "And how about you?"

"No. I'm very single. I guess work is my life, too. How sad is that?" Their eyes locked across the booth.

"I don't think it's sad," Emile said. "Look at what we do, the lives we save. I do love my work."

She smiled. "So do I, but don't you ever... I don't know, get lonely?"

She didn't know what she was hoping for with that line of questioning. Maybe *she* was the one who was lonely, though she never let it show. She was the master of a brave face, had been ever since they'd lost Immitaq, and her parents were so broken. Her happy face made everything okay.

And she'd gotten so used to it.

It was a bit nerve racking to sit here and let it slip, even a bit, to talk about loneliness with Emile.

"Yes, but my life does not allow me to devote time to a family. I won't do that to anyone." Emile looked away then, turning his head to look at the band playing in the corner. His lips pressed firmly together.

She'd definitely triggered something, but she didn't know what. She could recall him saying many times that he didn't want a family, didn't want kids, when they were residents. He'd told her he could never commit to that, even though he knew it was something she wanted.

Yet, back then he'd wanted her.

Until he hadn't.

The pain she felt at the memory of the breakup was fresh and startling, enough to steal her breath.

She had to be more careful here tonight.

For the rest of the dinner she steered the conversation toward work. There were no more personal discussions and Chloé was relieved. It was easier to block out all those old feelings about Emile when she could keep him at a professional distance.

When the food came, she kind of regretted not getting the

duck because it looked amazing, but she enjoyed her salad nonetheless.

When dinner was over, they split the bill, like friends would do. Chloé reflected that she would eventually have to find a place to pick up groceries; her hotel suite had a little kitchen and she really couldn't eat out every night for the next month. Even though she wouldn't mind coming back to *Choisir*.

"So that wasn't too bad, was it?" Emile asked as they strolled at a leisurely pace back to where his car was parked.

"No. It was wonderful."

"Even with jazz?" A smile curled on his lips.

She laughed softly. "Yes, even with jazz."

As they walked along the city streets, she could hear the sound of a ship in the distance. For a brief moment, it reminded her of home, of the remote village along Hudson's Bay they'd lived in before they'd moved to Iqaluit. The big cargo ships would come in near their house, laden with supplies that couldn't be flown in, and it had been so exciting to watch them carve through the icy waters.

"You're smiling. What're you thinking about?" Emile asked.

"Home."

"Oh?"

She nodded and pointed over her shoulder toward the water. "The ships on the river. It reminded me of the ones that came up to the little inlet where I lived when I was a kid. Immi and I…" She trailed off, thinking of her sister. "We'd all be excited."

Emile didn't question her about Immi, and she was relieved. She never told him about her sister, and she didn't want to talk about her tonight.

"Would you like to take a walk down by the river?" he asked.

No.

A moonlit walk with Emile didn't seem very smart. But instead of being smart, she said, "Sure."

Emile placed his hand on the small of her back, guiding her down a side street toward the promenade that overlooked the water. His touch sent a shiver of anticipation coursing through her, her body coming alive at such a simple yet intimate movement. The river was still, but they could see the moving lights of one of those big ships coming in.

Chloé leaned over the railing, drinking in the fresh air. The St. Lawrence was where fresh water from the Great Lakes met with the ocean, so there was a hint of brine on the air.

"I wonder where they're going," she said out loud.

"Nunavut," Emile remarked.

She glanced up at him. "Really?"

He nodded. "Did you not know that those ships from your childhood came from here?"

"I was eight. I wasn't really tracking it."

He smiled. "I suppose not when you're that young."

"We were more concerned about who in town would be getting a new truck or toys or something."

"Hmm, growing up here I never really thought of waiting for a car to come in on a ship."

"I guess not. You have access to the Trans-Canada Highway. Nunavut does not."

Emile leaned over next to her. They were so close, their arms almost brushing as they stared out over the water.

Chloé felt exposed talking about her past like this, when he was so silent. "Tell me about your childhood," she said.

"Why?" he asked, cocking an eyebrow.

"You never really told me much. All we did was study and make out." Heat flushed in her cheeks. That last part was just blurted out, without her conscious permission.

Oh, Nuka.

Emile grinned. "Those weren't terrible days."

She groaned, straightening up. "I'm so sorry."

"For what?"

She shot him a look. "Seriously."

Emile laughed then, out loud. "It's okay, Chloé."

"Is it?"

He stood in front of her, his hands resting on her forearms. He stared deep into her eyes and suddenly she wasn't embarrassed anymore. Instead, her body reacted to his touch, to his smile, to everything.

"Those were some of my favorite days," he said softly.

"Mine, too," she whispered, her heart racing.

Emile reached out and gently ran his knuckles over her cheek. She closed her eyes, reveling in his touch. The warmth. The heat. Her lips parted, and then she felt his mouth against hers. Just a light brush first, and then something deeper as his arms wrapped around her. She crushed him to her body, her fingers trailing in the hair at the nape of his neck. Her body thrumming happily as it remembered his kisses, even after all this time.

Emile froze in her arms. Then he stepped back. "I'm sorry."

"For what?" she asked. Though she didn't know why. She knew she shouldn't be kissing him, either, but her body longed for more and she wanted to be back in his arms, even if it was wrong.

"That shouldn't have happened," he said quickly. He wasn't looking at her. His body rigid like he'd locked down every ounce of softness.

"Well, it did."

He shook his head. "We're working together. This can't happen."

It was like he was angry with her, which hurt for a moment, alongside the sting of rejection. But he was right. This couldn't happen again, and Chloé *knew* that. Nothing had really changed. He was here; she was needed up north. He didn't want kids; she did.

Even if it hadn't happened for her yet.

She pushed that thought away. She still had a lot of work to do before she settled down. She was doing something with her life and not squandering it.

And if she let a kiss that could go nowhere happen again or, worse, if she allowed herself to hope for anything more, she would be wasting her time. Time best spent on her work.

"You're right," she said, finding her voice. "It won't."

Emile nodded, but still wouldn't look her in the eye. "I better take you back to the hotel."

"I think that's wise."

They walked quickly back to his car. In silence.

Chloé was so mad at herself for falling so fast into that trap. It hurt to drag herself back out, just like she'd known it would, but she had to put on a brave face, press on. She was stronger than heartache.

What she had to do was pretend like this night had never happened. For Céline's sake and for her own.

Emile dropped her at the hotel and she quickly went back to her suite.

As much as she tried to sleep and put that amazing yet regret-tinged kiss out of her mind, she just couldn't. She spent the night tossing and turning again, replaying it over and over, wrestling with all the emotions that Emile could easily stir up in her.

When she got up the next morning, she had made the resolution that she wasn't going to go to Quebec City with him this weekend. He kept saying that he wanted to be friends and she'd thought she wanted that, too, but she was finding it too hard. Whenever work was off the table, other things began to creep in, like that perfect, terrible kiss.

There was no way she was going to put her heart on the

line like that again. Even though she'd absolutely *loved* it. She couldn't be foolish or selfish.

When she got to her office, she sat down with a sigh. At least, burying herself in work would help her to ignore all these racing thoughts. Medicine grounded her completely. All she had to do today was focus on that and get her head on straight.

"Chloé, I hope I'm not disturbing you?"

Chloé groaned inwardly as the very man she was trying to avoid this morning was standing in her doorway. She hadn't even heard him knock. "Ah, Emile. I just got in and was about to go over Céline's chart from the rounds this morning."

She was hoping he'd take the hint and leave her to work, because right now she didn't really want to see him. What she needed was space.

"I'll just be a moment. It's about this weekend…"

"You don't have to say any more," she responded quickly. "I have to run back to Ottawa for some things I forgot. Hopefully, we can go to Quebec City another time."

She was giving him an easy out. It was for the best to put some distance between them. It was the only way to keep things professional in the long run.

Emile looked relieved. "Oh good. I was coming to give you my regrets about it. I have some work I need to do."

"No regrets or apologies needed. We both have busy schedules."

An awkward tension fell between them. Chloé hated it. Emile was barely looking at her, yet he still lingered, like he wanted to say more, but didn't speak.

"So," she said, hoping her voice didn't break. "Work."

"Indeed. Well, I'll leave you to it."

Just as Emile turned, she got a buzz on her phone. It was about Céline, who was starting her chemotherapy. Emile glanced at his own phone, obviously getting the notification, too.

They exchanged a worried look.

There was no time for personal weirdness. All that could wait. Chloé jumped up, grabbing her white lab coat and stethoscope and following after Emile quickly. They didn't say anything as they ran through the halls, heading to the pediatric oncology department where Céline would be receiving her treatment.

Agathe, Céline's mother, was pacing outside the room. A code blue had been called and residents were working on Céline.

Chloé entered the room, clinging on to her calm, drowning out the excitement around her so she could focus.

"Give me an update," she shouted over the throng.

"Cardiac tamponade," a resident stated. "Patient's heart rate went up after her first infusion of chemotherapy this morning. Patient complained of shortness of breath. We did an ultrasound of her chest and saw the fluid."

Chloé studied the images quickly and then leaned over Céline, who was on the stretcher, unconscious. It was cardiac tamponade during the night that had killed Immitaq. There had been no one there to help relieve the pressure of fluid in the pericardial sac, and her heart couldn't pump under the pressure of the fluid buildup.

She listened to Céline's breathing and noticed the bulging neck veins. The heart was beating fast still and she would have to work quickly to get the fluid out from around it.

"What do we do?" Chloé asked Dr. LaCroix, the resident who had done the ultrasound.

"Pericardiocentesis," Dr. LaCroix stated.

"You're correct. I need an operating room booked stat. Start Céline on a course of antibiotics. Doctor LaCroix, you're the one who caught the tamponade—I want you in the room with me while I perform it."

"Yes, Doctor MacDonald," Dr. LaCroix answered.

"Have Céline down to the OR in twenty minutes. This needs to happen now." Chloé stood up and headed out of Céline's room where Emile was speaking to Agathe.

"Well?" Agathe asked, her face pale. "What happened? I thought the chemotherapy was supposed to help her."

"It will," Chloé responded calmly. "Due to the severity of her cancer, the chemotherapy caused fluid to build up in the pericardium, the lining around her heart. That fluid buildup was making it hard for her heart to pump blood adequately. With your permission I would like to take Céline into the operating room and perform a pericardiocentesis to drain the fluid from around her heart so we can continue treatment."

Agathe nodded, her eyes filled with unshed tears. "Do what you have to do."

"I'll have the consent forms drawn up," Emile stated firmly, disappearing.

Agathe ran her hands over her face. "This shouldn't be happening."

Chloé reached out and squeezed Agathe's hand. "No. It shouldn't be. Not to someone so young, but unfortunately it's common in patients like Céline. At least we caught it—sometimes people aren't that lucky. Or they don't have access to the health care or hospitals. Remote communities up north."

She hadn't meant to say that, but all she saw in this moment was Immitaq.

"Please," Agathe whispered. "Help her."

"Try not to worry about Céline. I will take good care of her and I will let you know when the procedure is done."

Agathe nodded again.

Chloé made her way to the operating room floor. Céline

was already in the operating room and prepped, ready to go. Chloé would review the chemotherapy dosing with pediatric oncology after she did the procedure and decide whether or not she would have to adjust Céline's dose. Cardiac tamponade didn't just happen spontaneously; it had probably been building up since her last scan. She was just glad to be here to catch it and treat it.

As she took a deep breath, she closed her eyes and saw Immi's smiling face. A face so like her own. One she missed. Her other half.

She'd do this for Immi.

Emile got the consent forms for Chloé to do the procedure on Céline.

He'd only gone to her office this morning to call off the Quebec City trip, and had been pleased when she was the one to cancel first. After dinner last night and that kiss, it had become apparent to him quite quickly that being social with her outside of work was just going to be too difficult.

Every moment he spent with her made it far too easy to slip into old habits. So easy to forget to keep her at arm's length. Mostly because he didn't want to.

That kiss had been everything. She'd tasted just as sweet as he remembered. But it had also been a mistake. It had been so hard to end it, but he'd had to step away.

It was for the best.

After he dropped her off at her hotel he'd gone back to his home and just thought about her all night. Once again, not getting any sleep. Ever since he called her to come in and deal with this case, he hadn't been sleeping well.

Just talk to her.

What was he going to say to her? *I don't want to hang out with you outside of work because I can't stop thinking about you? I've never stopped thinking about you?*

He scrubbed in and headed into the operating room to check on how the pericardiocentesis was going. It was hard seeing young children as heart patients, but to see Céline as a heart patient with cancer, especially such an aggressive one, was even more difficult.

The fluoroscopy was up and running and Chloé had just gotten the drain inserted into the pericardium.

"How is it going?" Emile asked.

"Good. I'm glad Doctor LaCroix here was able to spot the cardiac tamponade when he was checking over her vitals after her round of chemo."

Dr. LaCroix briefly looked up at her. "Thank you, Doctor MacDonald."

Emile glanced at him. "Well, I'm glad to hear that."

Dr. LaCroix nodded and continued his work.

Chloé looked askance over him. "I think it's a job well done for your residents."

"*Oui*," Emile agreed, but he didn't say anything further. His father had taught him that you train the best surgeons in this program by being cool and distant, not so heavy on the praise. When Emile had come here after his residency in Toronto, he'd had to shake a lot of bad habits.

Even though his father was gone, the surgeons his father had trained still treated Emile the same cold way his father had treated them, the way his father would treat him. Emile knew that he had a reputation, a family legacy to live up to.

It was why he'd worked so hard to become the youngest head of cardiothoracic surgery in this hospital. He was always striving to make his father proud. But it was hard to make someone who was no longer alive proud.

"Tough crowd," Chloé muttered under her breath.

Dr. LaCroix chuckled, but only for a moment before he caught Emile's eye again and went back to his work.

"Are you going to adjust Céline's medications?" Emile asked, ignoring the slight barb from her.

"I will get the fluid tested and make sure there was no infection that caused the fluid to build up around her heart, but yes, most likely. I want to avoid this happening again. I need her heart as strong as I can get it to do the surgery. Cardiac tamponade is an unwanted complication."

"Indeed." Emile watched the fluoroscopy images as the fluid was drained slowly away. There wasn't much he could do in this moment. "How are her vitals?"

"Improving," Chloé offered. There was a hint of hope, but also a bit of sadness in her voice as she said it. "Kids are resilient."

"They are."

"No matter how hard my sister's treatment was..." She trailed off and he could see the bloom of pink flush in her cheeks. She cleared her throat. "Anyway, yes, kids are resilient."

The comment caught him off guard. A sister? He could tell by Chloé's reaction that she hadn't meant to let that slip out.

"I didn't know about your sister," he said tentatively. "Does she have heart troubles?"

"Had," Chloé replied stiffly. "Had a sister."

Then before Emile could ask anything else, she moved closer to Céline and continued her work on the delicate procedure. Just from her body language, he knew that the conversation was closed.

He was shocked. All through their residency and their time together, she'd never once mentioned her sister.

Had a sister. There was pain in those words. One he'd never heard in her voice before.

It was obviously a sore spot. But still, why had she hidden that information? Why hadn't she talked about it with him before?

Was it really so surprising? There were things about his personal life Emile had never told her. Things he kept hidden and didn't want to share. When they'd gotten together in the first place, both of them had known that they were going in different directions, and so why open up?

What they'd had together had been fun and easy. It was never supposed to be more. Even though, at points he'd wished it could have been. Still wished it, sometimes.

"Well," he said, clearing his throat. "I would like to be kept informed on Céline's status. Let me know when the procedure is done so I can inform her parents."

"I'll keep you updated," Chloé replied brightly. "Another thirty minutes and the fluid should all be drained and we'll have her in recovery."

Whatever sadness that had passed over her when she talked about her sister was now gone. There was no need to dive deeper or get to know her any further. She clearly didn't welcome it, and there was no point.

Emile left the operating room, scrubbed out. He was working on his notes, waiting, when Chloé finally came out and found him.

"Well?" he asked.

"Céline is on her way to the PACU. I've sent the fluid off for testing. Shall we go tell Agathe and Tomas the good news?"

"Oui."

They found Céline's parents in the waiting room. They both stood when Emile and Chloé entered.

"She's in recovery," Chloé announced. "She's strong and I've sent the fluid off for testing. Once we have those answers we'll adjust the treatment."

Agathe and Tomas hugged each other.

"When can we see her?" Tomas asked.

"Soon," Emile responded.

Agathe relaxed and straightened her sweater. The worried

mother, transitioning back to put-together politician. "Doctor MacDonald, thank you," she said. "You're clearly talented."

"Flattery is not needed," Chloé stated. "It's nice, but not required."

"Oh, when I see talent I take hold of an opportunity," Agathe explained. "Earlier you mentioned something about northern communities."

Chloé's eyes widened. "I did."

"We have a remote northern Quebec community that is struggling right now. We can't keep staff. We fly surgeons up there when we can. There are several heart patients waiting. When I was sitting here, I was thinking about that. I would like you both to go up there to help."

"I would be happy to give up a few days to visit your patients up north," Chloé responded enthusiastically.

Agathe smiled. "You would?"

Chloé nodded. "I'm from a remote community, although my family lives in Iqaluit now. It can be hard to keep staff and sometimes the infrastructure doesn't support it. If I can help out while I'm here, then I would love to."

"How about you, Doctor Moreau?" Agathe asked. "Can the hospital spare you for a couple of days?"

Emile totally understood why Chloé would agree to that, and part of him yearned to do the same. But he wasn't sure how he felt about being in a remote community with just her. Riding in a bush plane with just her.

At least it's only for a day, to see some patients and assess them. That's it.

"Of course," he said, but not with the same enthusiasm as Chloé.

Agathe nodded. "I'll arrange it and let the community know. Having two cardiothoracic surgeons of both your calibers up there attending to the community would be a huge boon. And as you're familiar with northern communities, I would love to get a report on what the government of Quebec could do to further strengthen our communities up there."

Chloé gave Emile a strange look, but she was still smiling. "Well, I'm going to go check on Céline. I will send a nurse out to get you both when it's okay to see her."

"Yes. I better go on my rounds." Emile went in the opposite direction. He was still in shock that he'd agreed to go up north with Chloé.

He shouldn't have done it. He had too many responsibilities here. But it was something he'd always wanted to do.

It would only be for a day or two. Max. I can handle that.

As he was thinking about it, a charge nurse in the PACU came rushing up to him. "Doctor Moreau, your assistant Donna has just phoned about an urgent call."

"An urgent call?"

The nurse nodded. "Your mother is in the hospital."

"My mother?" he asked, confused.

Why was his mother in Montreal? He hadn't seen her in five years. She didn't like coming to the city and he didn't go visit her.

"Donna is on line three."

"*Merci.*" Emile quickly ran over to the nursing station desk and picked up the phone. "Donna?"

"Doctor Moreau, your mother has been admitted to the cardio ward and she's requesting to see you. She's on floor four in room 104B."

"I will be there straightaway." Emile hung up the phone. Of all the things he'd thought he would have to face today, his mother being admitted to the hospital was not on his bingo card.

He sped quickly to the private room where his mother had been admitted. He didn't even knock, just barged into her room, startling the nurse who was taking her vitals.

"Emile," his mother said, surprised. "You scared us."

Not a word about "I haven't seen you in a long time" or any explanation about why she was in Montreal. All she did was chastise him about startling her.

"What're you doing here, Maman?"

His mother looked so small in the hospital bed. Her long white hair braided over her shoulder and her blue eyes, which usually sparkled, were dull. There were dark circles under her eyes. She gave off the appearance of being frail, which was never a good sign.

"Well, that's a pleasant way to say hello. I haven't seen you in five years and this I how you greet your *mère*? Just barging into her hospital room and asking her what she's doing here?"

Emile sighed and glanced at the nurse.

"I'll be back later," the nurse said, discreetly exiting.

Emile crossed his arms and watched her leave. "Maman—"

"You scared off that poor nurse," his mother chastised.

"Maman," Emile stated firmly. "I mean, what're you doing in Montreal?"

"I was in town for an art exposition. Some of my work is being featured at a gallery and I collapsed. My heart was racing and they couldn't bring it down, so I was brought here where a cardiologist had me admitted. Then I had you paged, as you're a heart doctor."

Emile sighed and pulled up her chart. "I can't be your heart doctor, though. Besides, I'm a surgeon. I don't even know if you need a surgeon."

"Oh, I do," his mother said offhandedly. "Something about a block in an artery? I don't know. I lived with your father for many years and I could never keep up with the medical terminology. Just like he had no interest in my art."

He softened as he flipped through her chart. He could see the note from her physician in Beaupré that she did indeed need an angioplasty and that her doctor had recommended it a year ago. Her arteries were blocked: the procedure would allow the surgeon to widen the arteries and improve blood flow, not only to her heart but also to other parts of her body. He wondered if she was having any kind of numbness or tingling.

"Maman, Doctor Boulanger said you needed an angioplasty a year ago, but you didn't have it done? Why didn't you tell me?"

His mother shrugged. "I feel fine. Besides, you're always working. I didn't want to burden you."

Instantly, he felt crushing guilt. "Maman…"

"Emile, I'm fine. I'm not angry at all. You don't have to fuss."

Emile took a deep breath. "You're clearly not well. I'm booking you in for an angioplasty."

"I thought you couldn't do my surgery?"

"I can't, but I can have another surgeon here at the hospital perform it. It's a minimally invasive procedure. You could've had it done in Beaupré or in Quebec City. When Doctor Boulanger told you to."

"Well, I'm here now." His mother smiled. "It is good to see you. Still married to your work, I see?"

Emile grunted, but then smiled down at her. "I'm sorry I haven't been out to visit."

"You're like your father that way."

"So you tell me," he groused. "Well, I'm going to find a surgeon to help you. You're admitted, officially."

"So much for the gallery," she sighed sadly.

Emile felt a pang of sympathy for her. He bent over and kissed her quickly on the head. "I'll come by and visit you later."

"I would like that."

Emile stepped out of the room, texted Chloé to call him and scrubbed his hands over his face, leaning against the wall for a brief moment to catch his breath. Right now he couldn't keep his emotions under control. He felt like he was spinning like a whirling dervish. His phone buzzed and he answered it.

"Hey, Céline is waking up," Chloé said, bubbly. "I'm very happy with her recovery."

"That's good," he said.

"So you wanted me to call?"

"*Oui.*" He cleared his throat, hoping his voice didn't break, because in that moment he just couldn't control his exhaustion.

"What's wrong?" Chloé asked softly on the other end.

There was a part of him that didn't want to tell her, but this was his mother, and Chloé was a good surgeon. If he couldn't do the angioplasty, he could have one of the best cardiothoracic surgeons in Ontario and Nunavut do the procedure.

He trusted her.

What he wanted to tell her was that he needed her. He needed a good surgeon and he needed a friend. But he locked that all inside, didn't let it out.

"Would you come up to floor four, the cardiac ward? I have a case I need to discuss with you."

"Sure. I'll be there soon."

Emile ended the call and tried to collect himself.

Not just a good surgeon, not just a friend. He needed *Chloé* in this moment. As much as he didn't want to, he did need her. Now more than ever.

CHAPTER SEVEN

Chloé was surprised by Emile's call. Especially after she had just seen him. Her first thought was to wonder why he needed an update so soon. Then she thought maybe he wanted a chat about going up north, since Agathe had kind of surprised them both with the offer. Chloé had been shocked that he'd actually said yes.

Then she'd heard his voice over the phone. He'd sounded completely distraught, completely unlike anything she'd heard from him before, even from their residency days. She couldn't help but wonder what was up.

She hoped it wasn't about her admission in the operating room. He'd seemed so concerned about that.

She really didn't want to talk about her late sister with him. She was still kicking herself letting that bit of information slip, because she didn't tell anyone about Immitaq. That was her burden alone to bear. Anytime she'd tried to bring up her sister as a child, it had always brought so much pain to her parents that she'd just learned not to talk about it. There was no need to upset them.

The only person she talked to about Immi was herself. There was no reason to hide behind a mask of happiness when she was alone.

Yet, seeing Céline there, going through the exact same thing that had killed her sister, it had been so hard not to think about Immi. She'd slipped up and couldn't be more annoyed with herself.

If Emile wanted to talk about Immitaq, she would just have to put a stop to it. It was too personal. She'd never shared it with him back when they were dating, and she wasn't going to open up about it now. It was too intimate.

The last thing she needed to do was have him think differently about her. He seemed to view emotions as a weakness, because he was so good at locking them up tight, and she didn't want to appear vulnerable in front of him or have him think that somehow she wasn't strong enough.

But why had he sounded so lost on the phone? She wanted to reach out and comfort him, like she did when her own parents were in pain.

Slippery slope, Nuka. Slippery slope.

When she found him at the nursing station, she actually took a step back. He was slouched in his chair, his head in his hand, aimlessly staring at a chart. He seemed distraught. Not his usual collected self. It threw her off. She'd never seen him like this.

He looked up and just appeared to be exhausted. "Oh good. You're here."

"Of course I am. What's up?"

He handed her a chart, his mouth set in a firm line. "Take a look at this."

Chloé cocked an eyebrow but opened the chart on the tablet he handed her. She quickly scanned the assessment with imaging.

"What do you think?" he asked, his voice quiet.

"I agree with this diagnosis. An angioplasty should be done right away."

"And the patient waited a year!" Emile snapped, in a strange burst of emotion.

Chloé looked again. "Indeed, that was kind of ballsy of her, given her age of seventy-eight."

"It was foolish," he seethed, running his hand through his hair. He was really worked up. Angry almost, which also seemed not like him.

"Marguerite Angenoux. Do you know her? And by that I mean personally?"

"I do. She's my mother."

Now it was Chloé's turn to be stunned at brand-new information. "Your mother?"

Logically, she knew Emile had a mother; it was just that he never mentioned her. Or if he did, it was rare. She had a vague recollection that she'd come up in conversation the other night, but from the way Emile had spoken of her, Chloé had thought she had passed.

"She divorced my father when I was young," Emile said, "and she moved out to Beaupré. My father had custody of me. My mother is a…a free spirit."

"Oh really?" She tried to say it in a way that wasn't facetious, but she couldn't help but think of all those memes of a surprised feline because she felt just as shocked as that ridiculous cat. She had a hard time picturing Emile being raised by a flower child.

Emile sent her a quelling glance. "Don't sound so surprised."

"You just never talked about your mother much." Chloé scrolled through the chart again. "So, what would you like me to do about it?"

"I would like you to do the angioplasty."

"Me? Any surgeon here could do that surgery. A resident…" She trailed off as Emile crossed his arms and glared at her in frustration. "Right, not a good idea. Sure, if you want me to do the angioplasty, then I can do that for you. Tomorrow. I see the cardiologist who admitted her has started all the correct pre-procedure medications and she's on blood thinners, so yeah, I can do the angioplasty early tomorrow, if that's okay with her."

"It's okay with me," Emile stated quickly.

Chloé grinned at him. "Ah, but is your mother of sound mind?"

"Well, that's debatable, as she waited so long to get the angioplasty," he groused.

"Oh my, we're grumpy," she teased. "I need to call you Oscar."

"Chloé," he said in exasperation.

"I'm sorry."

"So you'll do it?"

"I have to get her consent," Chloé stated again. "So, I really do think I need to meet her."

"You want to meet my mother?"

She smiled brightly. "Well, if I'm going to perform her angioplasty then yes, I probably should meet her. Ah, she's in room 104B. Perfect."

As she headed in the direction of the room, Emile came running up beside her and grabbed her elbow, pulling her around. "I never told her about us."

"Us?" Chloé teased, which just made Emile frown.

"Chloé," he warned.

"Relax, we're friends, right? Colleagues. I'm just that particular colleague you've seen naked."

She probably shouldn't have said that, but she always did enjoy teasing him. It was a coping mechanism she used to lighten the mood. And the mood definitely needed it right now.

"Chloé," he sighed.

"Don't worry. I'm a surgeon and I'll be professional. I'll take care of your mother." Chloé knocked on the door and opened it when she heard a faint voice telling her to come in. Emile followed on her heels.

Emile's mother had his blue eyes and the same smile. She was smiling now, but looked so exhausted resting against the pillows, slightly elevated in the hospital bed. Instantly, Chloé could see there was some swelling in her hands, possibly from arthritis, possibly from the blockage.

"Hi, Madame Angenoux. I'm Doctor Chloé MacDonald. I'm a surgeon and a colleague of your son's."

"Oh, it's a pleasure to meet you. Please call me Marguerite." She held out her hand and Chloé took it, gently shaking it, feeling the swelling there.

"And you can call me Chloé. I like a bit of informality with my patients." She could practically hear Emile's teeth grind.

Marguerite smiled brightly and then glanced over at Emile. "I like this surgeon."

"Mother, Doctor MacDonald would like to perform your angioplasty tomorrow morning," Emile said tightly.

Marguerite turned her attention back to Chloé. "How long will I be in the hospital for?"

"A couple of days, and then your son can take you home. But then I would like to see you in a week, just to check up on you postoperatively." Chloé stood up. "Can I listen to your chest?"

"Of course." Marguerite tried to sit up but struggled.

Chloé helped her and then listened. Her breath was labored, but her chest sounded clear, just not her heart. "Thank you, Marguerite."

"So this checkup. If I go home to Beaupré, it's quite the trip to come back in a week. I don't drive and I think the train might be too difficult if I'm recovering from surgery."

"You're right," Chloé agreed. "Well, since I'm a visitor here for a short time and you're the mother of a friend, I think I can make the trip out to see you myself."

"A house call?" Emile asked, stunned.

Chloé shrugged. "Sure. Why not? I do them all the time

in Nunavut. Sometimes, it's just easier to go to the patient rather than dragging the patient to the hospital."

Marguerite beamed brightly. "Oh, I like her. And Nunavut? How exciting. I used to study the artwork of Kenojuak Ashevak when I was in university. I met them once when they came to Ottawa."

"How exciting! I do love Kenojuak's works," Chloé stated.

"I think it's quite all right if you perform the surgery. You're much more personable than my late husband and my son, who hasn't visited me in five years." Marguerite looked at her son pointedly.

Emile groaned and rolled his eyes.

Chloé laughed quietly. "Is that true, Emile?"

"I'm a busy surgeon and head of a department at a busy hospital."

"Yes. We know," Chloé stated.

"I'm only teasing, Emile," Marguerite said, winking at Chloé.

"I think your son might've reminded you that you should've had this taken care of a year ago," Chloé said gently.

Marguerite sighed. "I know, but I was busy and it just seemed like a nuisance."

"Now you sound like your son," Chloé said lightly, making Marguerite smile.

"Maman, your health is not a nuisance," he said firmly, with a hint of tenderness.

Chloé nodded. "I have to agree with your son on this."

"My apologies then for being such a trouble." Marguerite sighed, leaning back.

"Well, it'll be taken care of now," Chloé said softly.

"Thank you both." Marguerite nodded.

"I'll see you tomorrow," Chloé said.

"Get some rest, Maman." Emile opened the door and they left Marguerite's room. As he shut the door, Chloé stifled a grin.

"Well, for being your mother, she's not what I expected," she said.

"And what did you expect?" he asked with an exasperated tone.

"I don't know, someone not so…friendly and agreeable. Then again, you did say she was a free spirit. Still, I see some similarities."

"How so?"

"She's stubborn. So are you. She waited a year and is only here because she collapsed."

"I see your point."

"She's lovely, though, Emile."

"She's only nice to you because it's you and not me." He let out a sigh. "She's very well liked. It was my father who was a bit cold and aloof. I honestly question why those two got together in the first place."

"Chemistry?" she suggested.

Emile made a face. "I don't want to think about my parents having any sort of chemistry."

She laughed. "I'm sorry. Like I say, she's lovely. I don't mind doing the angiogram."

"I appreciate it. Truly, I do."

They both started to walk away. Chloé could tell that he was bothered by something, yet not telling her what it was.

The weirdness about the kiss from last night, meanwhile, seemed to be a forgotten point on his side, and that was fine by her. It was just best to pretend it didn't happen. Except, it was a hard thing for her to forget, because she kept seeing it in her mind.

She could taste it on her lips. Her blood heated.

Nuka, stop!

"Hey, family is complicated," she said, breaking the silence. "And the angioplasty will go smoothly. From what I can tell by just glancing at your mother's chart, besides the blockage, she's in fairly good health. A couple of days to recover here and then you can take her home. I don't recommend sending her home on the train."

"Agreed. I will take her home."

"Do you want me to help?" She couldn't believe the words were coming from her mouth, but now they were out there. Even though they had both *just* agreed to cancel their friendly trip to Quebec City, here she was now offering to help take his mother home, which was on the other side of Quebec City.

Nuka, this is not keeping your distance.

Emile raised his eyebrow in surprise. "You would help me do that?"

She shrugged. "It's an excuse to see more of the province."

"What about the stuff you needed to attend to in Ottawa this weekend?"

She worried her bottom lip and grinned. "It was an excuse?"

Emile chuckled. "So was mine... I thought it would be better."

"This is foolish, though. We can be friends. I want to be your friend, Emile. You asked me to help out with your mother and that's what friends are for. Let's forget last night happened." Not that looking at him now, so worried about his mother, was helping with that resolution. It was a little glimpse of that tender side of Emile. The one she'd loved once.

His expression softened for a moment again. "You're right. I would appreciate the company on the drive to Beaupré."

"Great. Then it's settled. I'll add your mother to the operating room schedule for tomorrow morning and then this Saturday we'll take her back home and get her comfortable."

"That sounds good."

"I'm going to head down to oncology and talk to them about Céline's chemotherapy and make sure pathology is rushing the test of that fluid we took from her pericardium. I'll talk to you later." Chloé quickly scurried away.

She was pleased that he'd asked for her help with his mother and that they were both able to admit that they'd been giving each other excuses on why they were backing out of the weekend day trip to Quebec City. It was apparent they were both on the same page about their feelings toward one another and the need to just keep everything platonic.

The problem now was: Why did that thought just sting a little bit?

Thankfully, Chloé was able to focus on her work the rest of the day. She was able to adjust and order another round of chemotherapy for Céline, then get Emile's mother on the operating room schedule for six in the morning. For the rest of the day she focused on her reports and didn't see Emile again.

When she got back to her hotel that night she ordered in dinner and finally had a good night's sleep, which she'd been desperately needing ever since she'd arrived in Montreal.

She was at the hospital again bright and early with Dr. LaCroix, ready to tackle the angioplasty procedure. After she scrubbed in, she headed into the operating room where Marguerite was waiting. Emile was nowhere to be found, which was a bit strange.

"Good morning, Marguerite. How are you feeling this morning?" Chloé asked brightly.

"Tired," Marguerite replied. "A wee bit nervous."

Chloé leaned over her. "We're going to give you something to relax you, but really this procedure is routine."

"I was married to a surgeon for many years. I know routine doesn't mean safe," Marguerite corrected.

Chloé winked. "You caught me on that one."

Marguerite chuckled softly. "It's okay, *ma chouette*. I understand the risks. Doctor LaCroix explained them."

"Good. I'm glad. So, we're going to get this angioplasty over and done with, then you can recover in your room for a couple of days. I'll make sure Emile visits you more than once."

Marguerite laughed again. "That, *ma chouette*, would be a miracle. Though he did come to see me this morning."

"He did?"

Marguerite nodded. "At five. He woke me up, but I was glad to see him."

"I'm sure you were." Chloé was glad he'd been there; she'd assumed he hadn't visited yet. It pleased her to know that he wasn't so cold to everyone.

"Well," Marguerite sighed. "I'm ready."

"I do have to ask one thing," Chloé said. "Isn't *chouette* an owl?"

Marguerite smiled. "It's a form of endearment. Besides, I do adore owls and you are quite the pretty one."

Chloé's heart melted at her sweet words. "Well, you're my owl, too."

"Doctor MacDonald, are we ready?" the anesthesiologist asked.

"Yes, inject the propofol please and then we'll start the procedure," Chloé instructed.

"Yes, Doctor MacDonald," the anesthesiologist responded.

While the medication was taking effect, Chloé went over her instruments, and Dr. LaCroix readied the fluoroscopy so they could watch blood flow. When Marguerite was finally sedated enough, the anesthesiologist injected a numbing agent into Marguerite's upper thigh. Then Chloé made the tiny incision to access the arteries and insert the instruments to guide her to the blockages.

There were a few places where the plaque had built up enough to block some of her peripheral arteries. No doubt they were causing numbness in her legs, and if left untreated could lead to gangrene. Using the balloon through the catheter, Chloé was able to clear the plaque and increase blood flow.

There was a large blockage near Marguerite's heart that took several attempts to clear. Once Chloé had managed it, she then inserted a mesh stent to keep the artery from narrowing again. As she placed the stent she looked up into the gallery, where a few medical students had been watching, and she saw Emile.

At first, she didn't recognize him, because he wasn't dressed in his business attire or his white lab coat. He was wearing a blue sweater, which brought out the color of his eyes in contrast to his dark hair. He was staring down at the procedure intently and she could see the concern in his face. It was almost human. Almost like the man she once knew, the man she'd fallen in love with.

The man who broke up with you. The man who said he never wanted a family, remember?

Chloé ignored that logical thought. Right now all she saw was a concerned son.

She smiled up at him. When their gazes locked, even though he couldn't see her mouth from behind her mask, he did return that smile. A tender look could so easily have made her melt, but she had to focus on finishing the procedure.

After placing the final stent, she removed the catheter and had Dr. LaCroix close the small incision. As the nurses and Dr. LaCroix got Marguerite ready to move to recovery, Chloé sent a thumbs-up to the gallery and left the operating room to scrub out.

By the time she was finished, Emile was outside the scrub room waiting for her.

"How did it go?" he asked, his arms crossed. She couldn't help but stare at his muscular forearms, just for a moment.

"Textbook. You watched it."

"I did." He swallowed hard. "I couldn't sleep last night. I was worried about her."

"Of course, she's your mother."

"My father never let these things affect him," he groused.

"Do you know that for sure?" Chloé asked tentatively.

"I do. He wasn't the warmest man. My maman always said I was like him."

Chloé could detect a bit of bitterness in his voice as he said that, and she reached out and squeezed his shoulder. "Hey, it's okay."

"What is?" he asked.

"Whatever it is you're feeling."

Emile took a step back, his spine stiffening, and it was like she could visibly see his wall going back up again. "I'm feeling gratitude toward you for doing that procedure for me."

"I'm glad. I'll go check on her later." Chloé walked away from him. There were times she thought Emile might open up to her, share what he was feeling with her, but then there were times he closed himself off.

She should just put distance between them on her part, too.

It wasn't as though they were romantically linked anymore. They couldn't be. They wanted vastly different things. She shouldn't really be bothered by it.

But she was.

Nuka, you're asking for trouble.

CHAPTER EIGHT

A couple of days later

HONESTLY, EMILE HAD thought that Chloé might actually back out of taking his mother home to Beaupré. After their brief discussion outside the scrub room, he'd barely spoken to her since. He'd see her passing in the halls or in Céline's room, but it had been all business between them.

Every time he saw Chloé interact with a patient, it just melted his heart a little bit, but it also reminded him to give her the distance. When he had listened to her talk to his mother, when he'd watched her do the angioplasty, it had been hard for him not to let all his old emotions surface again. To think about how much he'd been in love with her.

It was a losing battle.

It was impossible not to be enchanted by Chloé. All his staff adored her. A lightness had descended upon the cardio wing and it was all her.

Watching her click so instantly with Marguerite had also triggered a bit of guilt, because he hadn't really connected much with his mother. He was always so annoyed when she said he was like his father, but in that way she was right.

It was funny; he'd used to think being compared to his father would be a compliment, something that would make him happy, but it really didn't.

That alone was making him question a lot of things, things he wasn't ready to deal with.

Nothing in his life was going to change. How could it? If he'd distanced himself from even his own mother for the past couple of years, how could he possibly entertain the notion of having more with someone like Chloé? Someone so warm and open? Someone who dreamed of a real, happy family?

He couldn't. She deserved to have everything she ever wanted and those were the things he just couldn't give her.

Why not?

Emile ignored that niggling thought, yet again. It had seemed to creep up more and more in his mind since she'd come to Montreal. It was testing his resolve.

Making the past three hours trapped in a car with her even harder.

But it was also nice to have Chloé there, chatting and spreading sunshine. It had been far too long since Emile had an enjoyable car ride like this. His mother's surgery had been no picnic, but now it was a gorgeous day for a trip. Chloé and his mother talked, mostly about art and other things. It was nothing too deep, but Emile could see that his mother was enjoying herself.

It made time pass quickly.

"Oh wow!" Chloé gasped from the backseat.

"What?" Emile asked.

"I think she's looking at the falls, Emile," Marguerite answered. "You should pull in to the turnoff. I wouldn't mind the small break to stretch my legs."

"Very well." Emile merged into the correct lane and took the turnoff for the Montmorency Falls. He hadn't been planning to play tourist today. His plan was to get his mother home to Beaupré, get the nurse he'd hired set up, then head straight back to Montreal. But now he thought it might be nice to visit the falls. He couldn't remember the last time he had seen them.

He paid for parking and they all took the short walk from the parking lot to the area with a view of the water. The roar got louder the closer they approached. Marguerite was moving a bit slowly and sat down on a bench instead of climbing up to the viewing platform.

"Are you okay, Maman? Shall I stay with you?" Emile asked.

"You two go, get closer and see if you can spot the white lady," Marguerite insisted.

"We'll be back soon." Emile kissed the top of his mother's head.

Chloé was snapping a picture with her phone. "White lady?"

Emile rolled his eyes and smiled. "It's a legend of a woman named Mathilde and her betrothed, Louis."

"Really, that's all you're going to tell me?" she asked sarcastically as they made their way up the steps closer to the falls.

"I can give you scientific facts. Montmorency is taller than Niagara."

"That is interesting," she agreed, but sounded bored. "Now, tell me the ghost story."

Emile groaned. "Don't tell me you're into that nonsense?"

"Sure. It's romantic, I assume, unless Louis threw her off the ledge or something?" They stopped at the edge of the platform after climbing up the steps.

"No, he didn't throw her over the edge."

The mist was causing Chloé's hair to curl. It was kind of hot and humid out, so it was nice to have the cool rush of water fanning their faces. Chloé closed her eyes and sighed.

"What was the sigh for?"

"Just enjoying it. It's beautiful," she murmured.

"*Bonne*. I'm glad." And Emile was enjoying it, too. He relaxed for a moment, then remembered he had to keep his wits about him. Last time he'd relaxed around Chloé, he'd kissed her. And now, as he watched her with her eyes closed enjoying the spray of the roaring falls, he desperately wanted to kiss her again.

"So," she said, spinning around to face him. "This white lady story. Tell me about it? Are you hesitating because it's a murder mystery or something?"

"I told you he didn't murder his wife."

"So then why the delay?"

"I can't quite remember all the details. But Louis and Mathilde were set to marry when the British invaded. Louis joined the militia and was killed. Mathilde was so distraught she donned her wedding dress and threw herself into the falls. Legend is you can see her falling."

"Oh, that is tragic." Chloé turned and squinted. "I can see a rainbow, but no star-crossed lovers."

"You sound disappointed in that."

"I am. I one hundred percent believe in the supernatural and spirits."

"You do?" he asked in disbelief.

"Why is that so shocking?" There was a hint of amusement in her voice. "Remember I like death metal."

"You're a surgeon. A woman of science..."

"So? It's not all just about facts. It's about beliefs." Then she reached out and placed her hand on his chest. "About what's in your heart, Emile."

His body reacted to her delicate hand on his chest, the mist in the air, the warm breeze. It made his heart beat just a bit faster. Even the talk about nonsensical legends was making him forget about the barriers he put up. It was just so easy being with her, talking and joking around. He gazed down into her dark eyes, staring at her long, dark lashes, her slightly parted luscious lips, and fought the urge to kiss her.

Instead, he reached out and tenderly brushed away a strand

of her hair. Her cheeks turned pink, and she quickly removed her hand.

"We better get your mother home," she said. "I know it's warm, but I don't want her to catch a chill with all this mist in the air." Then she was rushing past him and down the stairs, breaking the spell.

Which was a good thing.

He had to remember that.

They got his mother settled back into the car and continued down the highway. The chatting had slowed down as his mother was resting, her face rather flushed. Emile was worried that the stop at Montmorency had been a little bit too taxing for her.

It was lunch time when they pulled into Beaupré. His mother's home was a little chalet, painted blue, that sat across from the river. The yard was overgrown with hostas and other blooming wildflowers. What had been a white picket fence the last time Emile was here had been painted over in rainbow colors. It was definitely the home of an artist.

Once they got his mother settled inside and in her bed, Chloé took her temperature.

"Fever?" Emile asked from the doorway, hovering.

"Mild one. I saw there's a hospital in Beaupré, which is good. Do you know any doctors there, maybe a nurse we can hire to check in on her later?"

Emile nodded. "I do. I already arranged that."

"He's very efficient, my Emile," Marguerite responded drowsily.

"Well, I'm still going to give you some Tylenol and I'm not leaving until your fever breaks," Chloé warned. "Even if I have to take the train home."

Marguerite chuckled as Emile groaned. "I won't leave, either," he stated.

"Well, I'm glad to hear it," Marguerite said. "You better not abandon *ma chouette*."

Chloé shared a tender look with him and then placed a cold, wet cloth on Marguerite's forehead. "You need to rest."

She administered some Tylenol and made Marguerite comfortable while Emile called his friend about the arrangements. The nurse he had hired to check on his mother next week would stop by later tonight instead, and Emile was hoping the fever would break before then so he and Chloé could get back to Montreal at a decent time.

When he finished his call, he found Chloé wandering in his mother's front room, staring at all his mother's paintings on the wall, including one small portrait she'd done of Emile. There were also several photographs on the mantel of their times together in the country. Those happy memories that he clung to when he was younger. The summers he'd gotten to spend with his maman were the favorite he'd ever had.

He hadn't thought of them in years. And the last time he spent a summer here had been so long ago now.

"You were cute as a kid," Chloé remarked. "Such chubby cheeks."

He laughed softly. "Yes, well, I seem to have outgrown my baby-fat era."

"Indeed. Don't worry, I had very chubby cheeks while…" She trailed off, her energy shifting to sadness again. He was certain that she had been going to mention her sister but had stopped herself.

"You keep doing that," he remarked.

"Doing what?" she asked, absently still staring at the paintings on the wall, but he knew that she wasn't looking at them. She was far away.

"Changing the subject from your sister."

"Ah, you caught that."

"I did, but I also didn't want to pry."

She sighed. "It's okay. I don't know why I don't talk about it more."

"Yes. I didn't know you had a sister."

"A twin, in fact." This time her smile was a bit wobbly. "You've heard of twin-to-twin transfusion syndrome?"

"I have. It's where one twin receives too much blood."

"My sister Immitaq was that unfortunate twin. I have a mild murmur, but Immi suffered with heart problems most of her life." Chloé drifted off again, quiet, her hands wringing together as if she was thinking of something.

He'd never seen her like this, this raw, vulnerable side to her. Instinctually, he just wanted to pull her into his arms and hold her.

He wanted to tell her not to blame herself, but she was a heart surgeon; she would know it wasn't her fault. There was no logic sometimes when it came to emotions. He knew that better than anyone.

All he could do was let her process it out loud to him. All he could do was listen.

And provide distraction, if she needed it. "I think I'm going to walk to the village and get a bite to eat. Would you like to come for a walk? We can bring back my mother her favorite food. By then her fever should be broken and we can head back to Montreal."

Chloé nodded, her smile brightening. "I would like that."

Chloé was appreciative that Emile wanted to change the subject. She was still in shock that she had brought up Immitaq to him, but there had been no point in hiding it. For some reason she was feeling Immi's presence strongly today, although her usual voice in her head was quiet.

A walk would definitely take her mind off it and help her regain control of her emotions. The last thing Emile or Marguerite needed to see was her sad. They had enough on their plates. She could control her own grief. No one else had to be burdened by it.

There was no reason to be sad or bring anyone else down.

After letting Marguerite know where they were going, they headed out. She followed Emile down the road, walking along the river that eventually flowed into the St. Lawrence. The whole rue was tree lined and full of quaint homes, similar to Marguerite's in some ways but also vastly different.

It was a short jaunt to the neighborhood *boulangerie*. Chloé's stomach growled at the smells that were wafting through the open doors from people who came and went.

It was so crowded in there, Chloé sat outside while Emile ducked in and made the order. It wasn't long before he had a bag filled with fresh bread and some sandwiches.

"That smells so good," she remarked as they strolled back to the house.

"It does. It's my mother's favorite place. I haven't been here since I was a kid."

"I'm surprised you stayed in Montreal and didn't stay with your mother."

He shrugged. "I was going to school in Montreal and she didn't want to pull me out. That and my father had more sway and won custody."

"That must have been so hard."

"It was," he said stiffly.

"Well, I thankfully didn't have to deal with that. Custody battles and the like. Just a lot of relatives. I'm practically related to most of the village I came from or at least, they're all involved in our business."

He chuckled. "I don't know what that's like."

"Intrusive," she groused and it made them both laugh. "I'm sorry you had such a hard childhood. You never mentioned it when we were together."

"You can't put all that blame on me. You never told me

about your sister or your large intrusive family. I had no idea you were a twin."

"Touché. I guess I can't really complain about that. We didn't really talk much about our personal lives now that I think about it. What did we talk about when we were together?"

"Sex?" he teased, winking at her, which made the butterflies in her stomach do a little backflip.

Her cheeks heated and she nudged him slightly. "Besides that."

"Work, mostly. We were residents in a busy Toronto hospital. We had charting and rounding. We were trying to get all the experience we could so we could make our dreams come true."

"So our relationship back then was superficial?"

His eyes widened. "I didn't think so. I was in love with you."

It came out so quick. He looked a bit stunned at himself.

The admission caught her off guard, too. It shouldn't, though, because she'd been in love with him, too, all those years ago. They'd just never verbalized it before.

Actually, there were times when she wondered whether she ever had fallen out of love with him. The few times she'd gotten involved with someone else, it hadn't lasted long. She'd always blamed it on her commitment to her work, but now she couldn't help but wonder if there was something more there.

There can't be more. Don't get caught up in a romantic ambiance of a quaint Quebec town.

Damn him and his dishy good looks, his French accent and this beautiful place. It was those good looks and accent that had swept her off her feet last time. She did always like the broody heroes.

Back then she'd believed a bit in fairy tales, but that had never been in the cards for her or Emile. And for so long afterward, she really just couldn't see herself having that dream with someone else.

It was just easier to be alone and focus on work.

I was in love with you. That was what he'd said. And while the past tense hurt, it was a good reminder.

"I loved you back then, too," she said. "I guess we were young and dumb. We both had aspirations and dreams and they didn't mesh. I don't regret our time together."

They'd stopped in front of his mother's house, and there was a moment when their gazes locked. Chloé realized that her heart was racing and her body trembled in anticipation of something that she wasn't going to let happen.

She couldn't let it happen. The last kiss had been a mistake. They'd moved on. She couldn't let it happen again.

If she ever did want a family, she had to let Emile go.

"Why is it when we say we're going to be friends, we skirt this dangerous topic?" he asked, chuckling.

"I don't know. I think, in spite of my bright attitude, which drives you nuts, we get along well together." She let out a little breath of relief, glad that it was light again and they weren't talking about love and the heartbreak of when it all ended. Levity was so much easier.

"That is true. Your cheerfulness drove me squirrelly. Always so happy and eager, bleh." He winked and she punched him in the arm. She liked being able to mess around with him again.

"Let's go check on your mother and get back to the city. I need to get some distance from you and your snark," she teased.

"Fine."

They headed back into his mother's house. She left Emile in the kitchen and snuck into Marguerite's room.

She was resting comfortably and opened her eyes slightly when Chloé came in.

"How was your walk, *ma chouette*?"

"Pleasant, or *bonne* as you might say. We brought you some

lunch, but I just want to check your temperature. If you're fever-free, I'll bring you some food. Then after we eat, we'll head back to the city."

Marguerite sighed. "I wish you could both stay. It's nice to have the company."

Chloé smiled and took her hand. "I wish I could, too, but there's a little girl in Montreal with heart cancer that I was brought in to treat. I have to check on her."

"I understand. That is important."

Chloé used the digital thermometer and found that Marguerite's temperature had returned to normal. "That's good. You're fever-free. Emile has hired a nurse to check on you. No heavy lifting for ten days. I don't want you to hurt your small incision, but you can walk around and rest when you need to. I'll be back within the week to check on you."

"That sounds good." Marguerite closed her eyes and Chloé slipped from the room as Emile brought a tray with a sandwich and a small pastry.

"How is she?" he asked.

"Her temperature's normal. No fever."

"Good. I left you something to eat in the kitchen."

"Thank you."

Emile slipped past her into his mother's room and she sighed. There was a part of her that wished they could stay here, too.

Emile seemed so comfortable here. Probably because he was out of the shadow of his late father's legacy. Here, he didn't seem so closed off or guarded. Here, it was like he was his real self, just like the man she thought she used to know.

The one she missed the most.

The car ride back to Montreal was silent. Chloé was mulling things over in her head and trying to battle a bunch of emotions. She was also still grappling with the realization that she told him about Immitaq.

Usually, they didn't talk much about Immi in her family, because it always made her parents get maudlin. Luckily, Chloé had always been right there to make them happy again. Making jokes eased the tension.

Immitaq had always been a delight to her parents. Chloé had had to work hard to be like her sister, to bring them some of the joy that Immi's absence had snatched away. It was her duty, just as saving lives was her duty now. If they hadn't been twins, if there had been more specialty care for twin-to-twin transfusion syndrome available, Immi would still be here.

A tear slipped from her eye and she brushed it away quickly, hoping that Emile didn't see it. That was something else she had learned not to do—cry in front of others. She was so glad he hadn't pressed her on the topic.

"That's it." Emile turned on his blinker.

"What?" Chloé asked, shocked.

"Well, we're in Quebec City. It's three o'clock and I think you need to see it. I know we said we weren't, but we're here. Unless you really want to get back to Montreal."

"And if I did really want to go back to Montreal?"

"It doesn't matter. I'm making a decision and we're going to Quebec City."

Chloé laughed, startled out of her moment of sadness by his unprecedented behavior. "Okay, you're the boss."

He nodded. "That's right. We're going to walk around the *Chateau Frontenac*, then we're going to go down to the old part of the city and find a quaint little bistro to have dinner. Maybe ride the *funiculaire*, or walk the *Plains d'Abraham*."

"Whoa, you've got this all figured out, eh?" she teased.

"Not really. Usually, I do like things planned, but we're going to wing it. No reservation, just fun."

"Okay. I like that."

"There's a hint of nervousness in your voice."

"Is there?"

"Just a bit. Trust me, it'll be okay. I know my way around *Petit-Champlain*."

"And where's that?"

"The old part of the city, below the chateau."

"Sounds good. I guess I have nothing to do but trust you." And she was tentatively excited about the prospect. Despite always thinking of herself as such a cheery person, she couldn't actually remember the last time she'd let loose and just thrown caution to the wind. The last time had definitely been with Emile, but that time it had been her instigating it.

"Why are we getting on a ferry?" he complained.

She grabbed his arm. "We're going to the Toronto Islands!"

"I understand that, but why?"

"It's our day off?"

"Why are you saying that in the form of a question?" He frowned and crossed his arms.

"Because you didn't seem to understand that it's our day off, it's a warm summer's day and there's a nude beach on the island."

One of his eyebrows quirked upward. "Are you saying you want to go nude bathing?"

"I am." She grinned.

"Well, then." He rushed forward and scooped her up in his arms, flinging her over the shoulder and carrying her toward Queens Quay. "Let's go!"

"You're smiling again. That's good. What were you thinking about?" Emile asked.

"That trip to the Toronto Islands."

His brow furrowed and then he laughed. "I forgot about that. The skinny-dipping incident."

"Well, it's technically not skinny-dipping when it's an adult nude beach. And you didn't even take off your shorts."

"I remember you did, though."

"Heck, yeah. It was a hot day and I was there to swim. You can't swim in my hometown unless it's an indoor pool. No one swims in the water off Baffin Island unless you're swimming for your life."

"I can imagine. Well, there's no nude bathing in the city."

"That's okay. I haven't prepared myself properly. Things have to be waxed and prepped. Some bits wobble now that I'm older."

Emile sent her a look of disbelief that made her laugh.

He navigated his way to a parking place above the *Petit-Champlain* area. They walked along cobbled streets toward the Chateau Frontenac where the staircase headed down to a place steeped in four hundred years of history, pausing to admire the view from the top of the cliff. It was a bright, sunny afternoon and as they approached the railing overlooking the older part of the city, Chloé could see the bends of the St. Lawrence River, the large ships traversing the blue water and the islands connected by bridges. It was similar to Montreal, but also not. It was old European here.

The *Chateau Frontenac* rose high behind them, with its red brick and green shingled roof, like it was standing guard over the city.

The brightly colored homes and narrow streets below them looked like they'd been pulled straight from the French countryside. It was so out of place in Canada, or the places Chloé had been to, which were all more reminiscent of frontier buildings than this quaint, old-world charm.

"What do you think?" Emile asked.

"It's beautiful." She leaned against the railing, drinking in the air.

"Well, my favorite bookshop is down in the old part of the city and there are many great places to eat."

"Well, let's go to the bookshop and then sit outside to eat and enjoy this nice weather."

Emile nodded. "That sounds like a very good plan indeed."

Without thinking, she held out her hand and he linked his fingers between hers, like it was the most natural thing in the world. It just felt right. It felt like she belonged.

That was always the problem with Emile, why the breakup had been so hard, because when he was gone it felt like a piece of her was missing. She should let go of his hand, but it was comforting to hold it.

Emile led her down what he said were called "the breakneck steps," though there was nothing sinister about them, and they descended into the lower part of Old Quebec. The streets were narrow and the stone buildings were close together. Signs of various shops hung along the street, *patisseries* and coffee shops that had wonderful aromas wafting from them. Every which way Chloé turned her head, there was something new to look at.

Emile didn't let go of her hand and she didn't pull away as the streets were crowded with tourists and locals.

She was used to the Byward Market in Ottawa and Toronto from her days of residency, so the crowds of people didn't faze her, but she really didn't want to get lost here.

"You doing all right?" Emile asked, pulling her closer as they dodged some oblivious tourists.

"Fine."

"Well, not many people frequent this bookshop, save locals and people from Quebec. It's mostly French editions."

"I don't care. I can't wait to see it."

Emile smiled and they stopped at the end of a smaller alleyway where a sign read *Livre Poussiéreux*. He opened the door and a bell rattled above them.

"*Bonjour*," a man said from behind a counter. "Can I help you find anything today?"

Emile spoke with him quickly in French and the man nodded and went back to his task behind the counter.

"What did you say to him?" Chloé asked.

"I told him we were locals." Emile winked. He let go of her hand and they wandered through the antique used bookstore. It was piled high with volumes of dusty tomes, like something out of an old fantasy novel. Books upon books and even one of those rolling iron ladders as the shelves against the back wall reached almost to the ceiling.

At that moment Chloé almost felt like busting out into song from her favorite cartoon princess movies.

Emile had disappeared, but returned with a book tucked under his arm. "Well? What do you think?"

"I think there must be more than *this* provincial life," she teased, quoting a line from one of the songs.

Emile groaned. "And I'm *la bête*, am I?"

"Could be. What did you get?"

He glanced down at the book. "An old book from a polar explorer who then wrote fictional stories of characters in the north. I loved his books as a child, but my father threw them out when I was in university. I've been trying to track them down ever since."

"A polar explorer?"

"I was always fascinated with the north."

"Really?" she mocked. "I hadn't noticed."

He rolled his eyes. "Come on now."

"It's funny how you ended up in the southern part of Canada."

"My family has been working and running that hospital's cardiac wing for generations. It's hard to walk away from a generational expectation." There was a slight hint of bitterness in his voice.

She softened her joking then, because she couldn't even begin to imagine the pressure he felt growing up. There were deep wounds, too, generational scars, that ran deep in her family. Ones that rippled through the fabric of their community still. And then there'd been so much pain after losing Immitaq. But despite all of it, Chloé had really been surrounded by warmth, affection; she'd never lacked love from her family.

For that she was grateful.

"I'm starving," she announced, changing the subject. "Buy your book and let's get something to eat. Walking past all those coffee and pastry shops was too much a temptation for me."

Emile chuckled. "*Oui.* That sounds good."

They paid for his book then he led her out of the small side street back onto the main rue, where there was a little bistro. It was tucked beside an elevator that went on an angle up the side of the cliff.

"The *funiculaire*," he said, pointing to it.

"Can we ride that back up when we're done?"

"*Mais oui.*" He grinned as she clapped her hands in delight.

They ordered a light supper and some freshly ground coffee. Then they sat there, just enjoying the sights and sounds of Quebec City, laughing and talking about nothing in particular. Just like they always had done in the old days.

If this was friendship with him, Chloé could be happy.

Can you?

When they finished their early dinner, they walked hand in hand to the *funiculaire* and got their own little elevator to ride back up the cliff, slowly, overlooking the charming lower city and the St. Lawrence River.

"Your home province is very beautiful," Chloé sighed. "I can see why you love it."

"I do love it. But I have always wanted to go to Nunavut. Tell me about it."

"Tell you about it?" she asked. "You never wanted to know before."

"Well, it's clear we didn't really talk about much. So…" Emile nodded and leaned closer. "I want to know. And not the facts about populations and infrastructure. I don't want to hear about the things that you have to tell bureaucrats and politicians. I want to see it through your eyes."

The way he said that to her, so low and husky, made her pulse quicken. He was asking her to describe the place she loved most of all in a deep and intimate way. One she hadn't shared with anyone else.

Usually, when people asked her about the north it was about: *What can we do there? Where can we eat or stay? What are the activities and the history?* Touristy things. In meetings, it was about funding, lodging and trying to attract medical professionals up there.

She was always trying to sell the place. And she got the hint that Emile didn't want to be sold on Nunavut; he wanted to see it through her eyes. It touched her very deeply.

"Well, it's like nowhere else on earth. No, there's no lush greenery where I come from, but the rock and the ice, it's stunning. But in the summer out on the land the lichen, moss, berries like Crowfoot and the purple saxifrage. It blooms in color. Everyone thinks the tundra is a barren wasteland, but there is life there. In the autumn, when it gets dark again, the aurora will come out and paint the sky with vibrant colors." She closed her eyes and thought about the last time she'd really taken a moment to view them, to listen to them. "The best thing I love is the sense of community there. You have to rely on one another to survive."

"It sounds wonderful."

She nodded. "It is."

Their gazes met and her pulse began to race as she stared deep into his eyes. She was losing herself again. He leaned closer, then touched her face, running his thumb over her cheek and over her lips. She trembled with anticipation, remembering how his kisses made her feel.

But she couldn't let this happen.

He wants different things. I want things he can't give me.
And she doubted he'd ever change his mind.

Except, she was so weak when it came to him. All she could remember was the good times. How he always felt like home.

He's not, though, Nuka.

It was true. So when his other hand slipped around her waist, she put her hands on his arm.

"Emile," she whispered. "We can't."

He sighed, all the intention leaving his frame. "I know," he agreed, his voice laced with disappointment.

She stepped back. Her body was still thrumming all over with anticipation, angry that she was ignoring what she really wanted.

The *funiculaire* stopped and the doors opened.

Emile looked away and they quickly disembarked so the passengers that were waiting to descend could board.

They didn't say much as they walked quickly back to where they parked, but she could feel the tension in the air.

That had been far too close a call. She couldn't let it happen again.

Her time with Emile had an end date. When Céline's case was over, Chloé would head back to her work between Ottawa and Iqaluit and he'd stay in Montreal. She hadn't managed to change him all those years ago. There was no way she could now.

And even if she could change him, she couldn't change the world. There was too much work still to be done for her to be thinking about happily-ever-afters with anyone, least of all Emile. There were so many people like Immi out there who needed her.

What about what I need?

She pushed the thought away, furious that she'd let it in. It was selfish and she was satisfied with the course of her life.

So despite her body's demands, she was *glad* she'd had the strength to push him away.

Are you glad, Nuka? I don't think you are.

"I'm sorry," Emile said when they were away from the crowds. "I got carried away."

"So did I," she said, relieved that he'd been the one to bring it up. "We can't let that happen again. I don't want any weirdness between us when we go to do Céline's surgery. What we have now is nice."

He nodded. "Agreed."

They stood there for a few moments longer. God, she hated awkward silences.

"So, should we head back?"

"*Oui.* We better get going."

"Thank you again for showing me around Quebec City and your mother's town. I did have an amazing day."

Emile smiled at her but the smile didn't reach his eyes the same way it did before. "I am glad."

They headed back to his car, still silent. The spell that had been woven over them was broken. Now they were worlds apart in the same country.

It was for the best. Maybe it wasn't fair, but life wasn't fair.

Chloé knew that. As much as she'd loved fairy tales when she was younger, sometimes there just couldn't be a happily-ever-after for everyone.

Sometimes, for some people, there was only an ever-after.

And she was one of them.

CHAPTER NINE

Two weeks later

CHLOÉ WAS FEELING so much more confident about driving around Quebec, that when she went back to Beaupré to check on Emile's mother, she was able to manage it herself. Marguerite's doctor insisted that he could do the check-in, but Chloé had made a promise to Marguerite.

She'd barely seen Emile since Quebec City.

They'd passed each other in the hallways and had a couple of quick meetings about Céline, but that was it. At least there was good news about Céline, who was doing very well on the new course of her chemotherapy; the latest scan looked promising and the tumor was shrinking.

It wouldn't be long before Chloé would be able to perform the surgery and remove the tumor. She was planning a meeting to go over the procedure with the surgical staff that would be involved. Due to the size of Céline's heart, the surgery would be tricky and she wanted to make sure that everyone in that operating room knew what they were up against when the time came.

Emile wasn't the only one to blame for the avoidance game that seemed to be transpiring in the halls of Hôpital de Ville-Marie ever since their ill-fated almost-second-kiss in the *funiculaire*. It had taken Chloé a lot of willpower to remind him that they couldn't give in; even now she caught herself replaying the moment in her head, over and over. And the less she saw of him now, the easier it was to stick to her resolution.

She'd done the right thing in the moment; she had no doubt of it. Only now they weren't really speaking beyond work. And the truth of the matter was she missed him.

She might not be able to have a romantic relationship with him again, but she did miss the camaraderie and the rapport.

And she didn't want to fly up to the remote community of Aivik Bay on Hudson's Bay crammed in a small bush plane with someone she wasn't talking to, because it would be 100 percent awkward.

She picked up the list of supplies that the hospital provided for the community. There was a nurse practitioner up there, and specialists often flew in for checks, especially in good weather. If there was something serious, that specialist could make the suggestion that the patient be flown down to the city. It was similar to the setup Chloé currently had with Iqaluit.

She went through the notes that had been sent over and read reports from the nurse practitioner, who mentioned a few causes for concern with respect to cardio patients who needed assessment about possible surgery. That would be where she and Emile came in. They could assess and deem if it was necessary.

If they could keep their heads on straight and act normal. Or normal-*ish*.

She set down the list and took a sip of her coffee. It was four in the morning and their flight was leaving at six with the estimated time of arrival of seven-thirty to get their day started. They weren't going to be leaving Aivik Bay until nine at night. It was going to be a long, long day. And she'd made sure that her own supplies consisted of a small overnight bag, just in case they got stuck up there. She'd learned that when traveling to remote communities, it was always best to be prepared.

"Are the supplies almost loaded into the transport to the airport?" Emile asked, coming into her office. He was dressed in jeans and a polo shirt with a light but warm jacket, but she didn't see a duffel or a knapsack. Only a leather messenger bag that looked too nice to travel up north. Actually, it looked like it hadn't been much of anywhere.

"Is this your first time doing a round up north?" she asked carefully.

"*Oui.* Why?"

"You don't have an overnight bag." She nodded in the direction of the messenger bag.

He cocked an eyebrow. "Why would I need an overnight bag? We're just going for the day."

"Something could happen."

"It's summer. I doubt there will be a snowstorm."

She narrowed her eyes. "How very stereotypical of you. You know, even though where we're going is above the tree line, it's farther south than Yellowknife and it's summer."

"But Yellowknife has trees!" Emile stated, all proud of himself.

"Yes, but…the tree line in your lovely province ends at the fifty-sixth parallel and not above sixty."

Emile blinked a couple of times. "Why are we discussing parallels and tree lines?"

"Because you seem to think it's snowing where we're going and it's not. Plus, making assumptions."

"I never said it was snowing." Emile scrubbed a hand over his face. "Why are we talking about snowing? It's summer and I don't know what could possibly waylay us. We're going up for a day. I don't need an overnight bag."

"Okay, suit yourself." Chloé took another sip of her black coffee. "Look, I think we need to talk more about what happened a couple of weeks ago on the elevator thing."

"The *funiculaire*," he corrected.

"Now who's being pedantic?" She smiled slightly.

"My apologies. What about it?"

"We've been avoiding each other. I say *we* because I'm just as much to blame."

"I've been busy," Emile stated. "But I do see your point."

"I don't want our trip up to Aivik Bay to be weird. I like working with you. When we do Céline's surgery at the end of the month we need to work together seamlessly. So no weirdness. We've got to move past it, all of it."

Emile sighed. "You're right. We do and I'm sorry that I've been avoiding you."

"You are not the only one to blame in that, *ma chouette*. Like I said, I was avoiding you, too."

He cocked an eyebrow. "Owl?"

"Not appropriate? Rats. I thought it was a friendly endearment."

"Not for me," he snickered. "I agree, though. We'll move on and just forget about it."

"That's all I ask."

She picked up her overnight bag and they walked together to the waiting transport.

It was a slightly rough ride from the hospital to the airport in the transport van to where the charter planes were. Chloé was used to riding on bush planes, but she saw Emile frown when he watched as a tiny Cessna with floats was being loaded with the supplies and he realized that was how they were getting north to Aivik Bay.

"You look a little green," Chloé teased gently.

"I've never flown on a small plane like this. I mean, I've read about them."

"It'll be okay. I've flown on worse-looking planes in my life. Think of it as an adventure, something you've always wanted."

He nodded. "You're right."

"Good."

Once everything was loaded, they boarded the plane, put on their noise-canceling headphones and the engines roared to life. Chloé sat across from Emile, their knees almost touching in the small enclosed space as the plane taxied on the runway then took to the sky.

When they were in the air, she just relaxed and enjoyed watching the scenery through the window. The city gave way to rolling hills and countryside, which then turned into boreal forest with flowing rivers. Before long, the tree line disappeared and she could see Hudson's Bay like a big blue shimmering sheet north of them.

The plane finally made its descent toward a sandy beach at the edge of the bay and Chloé could see the familiar sight of a remote northern community clustered together. There were boats on the water and dirt roads that connected the homes. The rocks outside town were blooming with purples and greens. Metal modular homes, some painted in vibrant colors and others in that familiar shade of bright green, dotted the landscape. There were solar panels, trying to soak up and take advantage of the longer hours of daylight this far north. As they got closer, she could see kids on their bikes, racing toward the airport at the edge of the community, wondering who or what was coming into town. Up on a hill she could see a white picket fence marked by white crosses, a typical cemetery. All the communities were so different, yet they were also the same, with the rugged land of the north connecting them all.

"Welcome to Aivik Bay," the pilot said over the radio. "We'll be making our landing in five minutes. Tray tables up!"

Chloé laughed at the sarcasm. She leaned over and tapped Emile on the knee. "What do you think?"

He nodded. "It's just how I pictured it from the books I read as a child, but better."

"And first bush plane ride?"

"Fine." He smiled, but it was a little strained.

She gave him a silly and encouraging thumbs-up, which made him groan, but he relaxed and this time when there was a twitch of a smile, it was genuine and not forced.

The thought of him being happy with a northern community actually gave her a sense of pride, because she always did love her home, where she came from.

Nuka, maybe he'll move north with you? Maybe it doesn't have to be so black-and-white?

Chloé shook Immi's voice away.

There was no time to entertain a notion like that. She'd closed that chapter. And she had work to focus on. She was going to show Emile the north and how worthwhile it was to give yourself to something greater and make your own legacy.

Whether he would listen or not, that was up for debate. Emile had always stated Montreal was his legacy. No family, head surgeon. He'd done those things. She doubted he'd change now. He was so stubborn in that regard.

Emile hated that he'd been avoiding Chloé since Quebec City, but the truth of the matter was he couldn't stop thinking about her. When she was with his mother, she'd been so sympathetic and gracious. She hadn't even chastised him for not visiting Marguerite. He'd been grateful—he was busy enough doing that inwardly himself.

Emile knew she'd gone down to Beaupré again to do the checkup, because since the health scare, he'd been checking in with his mother more. And he'd been enjoying it.

Pieces of himself he'd locked away in order to carry out his father's legacy were bubbling up to the surface. Being with

Chloé in Quebec City, laughing and enjoying a tranquil moment, had just reminded him of something better.

He hadn't meant for their near-kiss to happen. He wasn't sure what had come over him, but he had been utterly lost in the memory of the softness of her lips.

Even though he'd known it was wrong, a bad idea, he just hadn't been able to keep himself from slipping his arm around her waist. Only when she'd stepped away had he come back down to reality and realized his mistake.

Chloé didn't want him. And that was okay. It hurt, but he shouldn't be surprised. They'd always wanted different things in life. Things he couldn't give her. He didn't want to ruin that dream for her.

If having her in his life in this professional capacity was how it had to be, then so be it.

It was for the best, and that was what he had to keep reminding himself.

When they got off the plane, they were greeted by a crowd of people, but a red-headed woman with a knitted cap and a smattering of freckles stepped out of the throng to welcome them.

"Doctor MacDonald and Doctor Moreau, I'm Janet Hobbes and I'm the registered nurse in Aivik Bay. Thank you for coming up here. There's a couple of outlying communities that are sending patients in by boat once they heard you were here today. We have a small clinic/hospital here in Aivik Bay to work with and these other communities are part of our catchment. I only mention it because they weren't in my initial report."

"The pleasure is ours," Emile stated. "We brought supplies as well from Hôpital de Ville-Marie."

"Excellent," Janet said excitedly. "Hey, Jerry and Carl," she called to two men, "get the quads ready and take the supplies being offloaded to the clinic, yeah?"

"Yeah, yeah," one of the two said, waving. "We've got you, Janet."

"It's a short walk," Janet stated. "I hope you don't mind. There's not a whole lot of vehicles around here, although there's hopefully going to be a ship making its round with cargo in a couple of weeks."

"It's not a problem," Chloé stated. "I get it can be hard to get vehicles up here. I'm from a small community on Hudson's Bay originally and now my family is in Iqaluit."

Janet beamed. "I did wonder. Your tattoos are a giveaway."

Emile followed behind Chloé and Janet as they chatted. Behind him, some kids were following along laughing. He glanced back over his shoulder and they all froze, eyes wide.

If he was his father, he'd just ignore them, but then again, his father would never have come here. So instead, Emile smiled and winked, making the gaggle of children laugh.

It warmed his heart to see them so happy. He remembered those days when he hadn't had a care in this world.

It actually made him feel a little lonely, thinking of the life he'd never have.

The family he'd never have.

"We don't get a ton of visitors here," Janet remarked, spying the children.

"I gathered," Emile stated. "It's fine."

"Here's the clinic. The first patient that needs to be seen by a heart specialist is coming at eight, I think, and then it's a fairly steady stream. I'm so glad there are two of you. I hope this will be okay? It's a long day. Also, I may still need to see emergency patients. This is, in fact, our hospital, too."

"Don't worry about that," Chloé stated.

"You're sure it's okay? Some visiting doctors get weird," Janet said.

"More than okay," Emile reassured. "It's why we're here."

The clinic was a white-and-red building at the edge of

town, close to the water, which would be good for those coming by boat. It was built on top of a rock outcropping, but part of it was elevated by stilts because of the permafrost in the ground. They clambered up the steps and Janet opened the door to the clinic, flicking on the lights.

Emile wandered around and peeked in the back. It wasn't big, and there were two exam rooms. He was pleased to see a small ultrasound and X-ray machine. There was also a well-stocked medicine cabinet.

"I'm so looking forward to working with you both today," Janet said. "You can leave your coats and gear in the staff room. A couple of the elders are going to bring lunch and dinner to you both."

"They don't have to do that," Emile said, but he was appreciative.

"No, they want to. Besides, there's no real restaurants in town. Home-cooked catering here."

"That sounds great," Chloé stated.

Emile followed Chloé to the staff room where they stored their gear.

"You ready for this?" she asked. "It sounds like it's going to be a jam-packed day."

"More than ready." And he was. He couldn't remember the last time he was actually excited to do clinical work. For so long he'd been bogged down with the running of his department. He was involved with surgeries, but there he usually knew what to expect.

Today, what would be walking through the door would be the unknown.

Almost like the time he'd done rounds in the emergency room when he was an intern. When he was exposed to all the departments of medicine.

It would be a long day, but this was what he actually loved about being a doctor and he was glad he was here for it. In a way, he was living out a long-standing dream, without having to give up work in Montreal.

It was only a taste, but he'd savor it.

Janet hadn't been kidding when she said the patients would be hitting the clinic like a tidal wave. It wasn't just people from Aivik Bay, but from other smaller communities that were farther up the coast. Emile prescribed medication, and there were a couple of patients he saw who needed surgery, so he was able to fill out the proper requisitions to have them flown down to Montreal as soon as possible, so that he and his staff could do the procedures. Anytime Chloé had one of those requisitions to fill out she sent the patient to him, because she didn't have the authority to refer to Hôpital de Ville-Marie.

They had a brief respite at midday when they were brought a potluck lunch, complete with bannock, which Emile had never tried before. Everything he ate was delicious and very much appreciated.

Eventually, there was a lull and he had a moment to breathe. He thought he'd try to have a power nap, but found sleep wouldn't come; he was running on endorphins and enjoying remote medicine. Still, it was hard to keep his eyes open.

"Here," Chloé said, coming into the room he'd been hiding in. "I brought you a coffee because you look like you're dragging."

"You made me coffee?" he asked.

"No. Uh, Janet did." Then she looked askance as she took a sip.

Emile was hesitant, but it smelled good. He took a slug and then winced as the bitterest, strongest, *thickest* coffee he'd ever tasted slid down his throat. He cursed. "What is that?"

"Strong coffee," Chloé chuckled. "This stuff will keep you up for a week!"

"No doubt. *Merde*, that's what it tastes like." He took another sip. As much as he wanted to pour it down the drain, he could use the boost to keep going. They still had hours before they got back on the plane to Montreal.

"Do you know what *merde* tastes like then?" she teased, a twinkle in her eyes.

"No, but if I had to guess—this. Why are you drinking it so easily?"

Chloé sat on the edge of the desk he was sitting at. He couldn't help but admire her long legs as she crossed them. As much as he was trying to ignore how close she was, he did remember how nicely they'd once wrapped around him.

This is what got you in trouble the last time.

"I'm used to this stuff," Chloé said. "This is the kind of stuff my *ataata* would brew up when we were at our cabin. Kept you going and in the winter keeps you warm."

"I'll take your word on that." Emile set the mug down, nudging it away.

"Doctors?" Janet said, poking her head in. "We have our next patient. She's...not well. It was a long trip by boat."

"Is she in the waiting room?" Emile asked, standing up.

Janet nodded. "She is."

Both he and Chloé got up and walked out to the waiting room.

The patient was a young girl, maybe no more than thirteen. Her breathing was labored—Emile could hear the raspy gasps for air across the room. She was lying on the floor, her head in her mother's lap.

Chloé's demeanor changed instantly. She froze in her tracks, her eyes locked on the young girl.

"Doctors, this is Immitaq Peever. She's from Kamik, farther north."

As soon as Janet said the name, Emile glanced over at Chloé. She had gone pale and looked like she was staring at a ghost. Immitaq was the name of her twin, he recalled, the one who passed away.

"We heard there were heart surgeons coming here and we decided to make the trip. We couldn't afford a plane trip, but we have a boat…" Immitaq's mother stated.

"There's no need to explain," Emile said, kneeling down. He smiled at Immitaq. "I'm Doctor Moreau. Can I listen to your heart?"

Immitaq nodded. "Okay. Just give me a moment and I can get up."

"No. You stay there." Emile looked up at Chloé. "Can you pass me a stethoscope?"

"Yes," Chloé stammered. She handed Emile a stethoscope and then knelt down on the other side of Immitaq, helping her mother to raise the girl up so that Emile could listen to her heart from her back.

He frowned as he heard the beat. It was quick, like there was a blockage, but there was no way to get an angiogram done here, if that was what she needed. At least there was an ultrasound so he could take a look at her heart.

"I would like to do an ultrasound of your heart, so we're going to have to get you up and into an exam room."

"Her father can carry her, but he's down on the beach," Mrs. Peever stated.

"I can carry her. If that's okay with you, Immitaq?" Emile asked.

"Yes." Immitaq nodded.

Emile stood and then reached down to scoop the young girl into his arms. She was light and it was clear she was losing weight, but there was swelling in her face, so she was retaining fluid. Chloé went ahead of them and got the exam room and ultrasound ready. Emile laid the girl on the bed.

"I'm going to step out and Doctor MacDonald and your mom are going to help you get into a hospital gown. Doctor MacDonald is going to do the ultrasound of your heart and I'm going to watch the monitor."

Immitaq nodded. "Okay."

Emile stepped out of the room and waited until he was called back in. Chloé was still a bit subdued, but she was chatting to the patient and her mother while she got out the ultrasound jelly. Emile turned off the lights and they turned on the ultrasound.

"This will be cold, Immitaq," Chloe remarked as she spread the gel and then placed the probe. She was watching the screen along with Emile. "Can you hold your breath?"

Immitaq held her breath.

Emile could see there was a blockage, but there wasn't anything they could do about it up here. Immitaq had to get down to Montreal and have an angioplasty.

They finished with the ultrasound and then Emile pulled Chloé out of the room. "She needs to take our plane," he stated. "I need to get her to Montreal and another surgeon can do the angioplasty."

"Do you think she'll make it there?" Chloé asked. "She's showing signs of a blood clot."

"They have the medication to set up a thrombolytic therapy. We can get her an IV and then transport her down on the plane with her parents. It's a short flight."

Chloé chewed on her bottom lip. "It's worth a shot. It's a good plan, but it means we're stuck here overnight. I doubt they'll get another plane up here in time."

Emile sighed and then shrugged. "It is what it is. I can sleep in these clothes."

A soft smile hovered on Chloé's face, her eyes full of tears. "See, you tempted fate with that fancy messenger bag."

He rolled his eyes. "Let's get this treatment set up. You

talk to Immitaq's parents and I'll make the arrangements for the flight and her being received in Montreal."

Chloé nodded. "Okay. And then we'll finish out our day. I get the sofa in the staff room."

He just chuckled and left to make the calls he needed to make while Chloé handled the treatment. Immitaq would have to be on the IV drip for the rest of the day and then she could take their plane this evening.

Emile had no problem getting the staff at Hôpital de Ville-Marie ready for his patient. Dr. LaCroix would wait and arrange everything with the surgeons on duty.

Janet was very helpful setting up the IV and getting Immitaq comfortable. Once the drip was in place there was nothing more for them to do but continue to see the patients that trickled in as the day waned.

Emile watched the clock, though, waiting for that flight to return. And he could see the concern etched in Chloé's face, too. The ghosts haunting her.

What he wanted to do was take her in his arms and reassure her that *this* Immitaq would be okay, but he couldn't. Frankly, it was amazing that the girl was alive and he knew that Chloé knew that, too.

When it was finally time for Immitaq to get on the plane, Emile carried her out to the waiting ATV, which had a wagon secured to the back to pull her and her parents to the airport. Once he was sure she was settled, he followed on foot to get the whole family safely on the plane and place the drip in Immitaq's arm.

In fact, he ended up carrying her aboard himself.

"Here you go," he said, gently sitting her down in the plane. He checked the IV was secure, belted her in, then tucked a blanket around her.

"I don't like flying," she said, her voice weak.

"Neither do I, but it's a short flight and you get to see

Montreal and the hospital where I work, which has the most amazing children's ward." Emile smiled at her. "Your own television and there's gaming systems. You'll feel better in no time."

Immitaq's eyes lit up and she nodded. "I am excited to see the city."

"I'll come and see you there tomorrow, eh?" Emile said warmly.

"Okay."

Emile climbed out of the plane where Immitaq's father was waiting.

"Thank you, Doctor Moreau, and thank Doctor Mac-Donald, too, yeah?"

"I will. My staff is prepped for her. You and your wife can stay with Immitaq tonight and then we'll get you both set up with lodging for her post-operative care and recovery."

Mr. Peever nodded and followed his wife on the plane.

Emile gave instructions to the pilot, who said he would return in the morning to bring him and Chloé back down to Montreal. Emile stayed until the plane took off. Watching it leave safely gave him a sense of hopeful relief. When the Peevers made it to the hospital, he would get a call from the staff there and a status update.

As he watched the plane recede into the sky, Emile thought back to the argument he'd had with his father about being too friendly with patients. Now it seemed trivial.

It had been good to have that moment of connection, like a part of him that had been asleep for so long was waking up. This feeling was why he'd become a doctor. In that instant, he felt he understood Chloé a little better and remembered his own dreams about remote medicine. The ones his father had quickly quashed.

Today had been one of the most exhausting and rewarding

ones he'd spent as a doctor in a long time. There was a part of him that could see himself here, in a place like Aivik Bay.

I want to stay.

The thought surprised him. How could he walk away from Montreal now? There was too much responsibility waiting for him there.

He swallowed down his doubts, like he always did, shook his head and headed back to the clinic, eagerly awaiting the call from Dr. LaCroix to let them know the Peevers were all okay.

As he climbed back up the steps, Janet came running up to him. "I have a place for you and Doctor MacDonald to stay," she said breathlessly.

"Oh? I assumed we'd sleep in the clinic."

"Well, you can, but the couch is really uncomfortable. There's a guest lodging. It's small, but the community would like you two to stay there for the night. Everyone is just so grateful for what you and Doctor MacDonald did for the Peevers."

"Well, that would be most agreeable," Emile said, because he didn't relish the idea of sleeping on the floor.

"And dinner will be delivered there. There are no more patients. I can't thank you and Doctor MacDonald enough," Janet gushed.

"Well, I'll have to talk to my board of directors, but I would actually like to make it a quarterly trip if I can. It's too long for some of them to wait at the moment." All he could think about as he spoke was Immitaq, how urgently she'd needed help. What if the premier hadn't asked them to come up here today? Emile shuddered to think of that reality.

Janet's eyes lit up. "That would be amazing."

Emile nodded. "I'll keep you posted."

He headed into the clinic where Chloé was slouched in a waiting-room chair. She looked tired, but there was also a hint of sadness there. And he knew, without a doubt, that everything that had happened with that young girl had her thinking about her sister.

"Chloé?" he asked gently.

She sat up and plastered a wobbly smile on her face. "Oh. Hey."

"You okay?"

"I'm fine."

"You don't…"

"I'm fine!" she insisted, but again, her smile didn't reach her eyes. It was forced, like she was putting on a brave face. And she didn't need to do that with him. "So, am I taking the couch tonight?"

"Janet found us accommodations. So grab your stuff."

"What accommodations?" she asked quizzically.

"A place they offer to visitors as emergency shelter. It's got to be better than that couch."

Chloé laughed softly, perking up. "You're probably right."

They collected up their belongings and followed Janet to a little house in town.

"We use this for visiting elders, but since we have none with us today, the community would like to offer it to you both since you gave up your ride home." Janet opened the door to the home.

"It's not locked?" Emile asked, curious.

"No. We don't lock doors around here. We always offer a place to shelter," Janet explained.

"That's very generous," Chloé said. "To offer us a place to stay."

"It is," Emile agreed.

"There's food waiting for you in the kitchen. Just relax. There's a large solar flare projected tonight so maybe the aurora will come out, but it's weak in the summer. Not much night up here." Janet waved and left.

Chloé walked inside and Emile followed. It was a small home; everything was in one room. A tiny kitchen in the corner, a couch, wood stove and one bed in the corner.

"Still want the sofa?" he teased.

"Nope." She winked. It appeared that she was coming back around. She set her knapsack on the bed and then sat down next to it. "That was a long day."

"It was." He sat down on the couch. "Do you think we'll see the aurora tonight?"

"If you can stay up late enough for it. The sun won't set for a while and when it does, it won't be for long." She started fiddling with her thumbs and he could tell she was lapsing into melancholy again.

"Look, I know that the young girl affected you."

Chloé nodded. "She did. She reminded me of my sister, but I guess you figured that out."

Emile got up and sat next to her. "Tell me about her."

"What is there to tell? She died." She tried another of those horrible forced smiles.

"You always have to put on a brave face?" Emile asked.

"What do you mean?" Chloé asked, her body going rigid.

"You're a sunshine personality, for sure."

"Is that a bad thing?"

"No. But... How do you really feel?"

Chloé stood up and began to pace. "I survived. Immitaq didn't. *My* Immi didn't. And just seeing that young girl with the same name...it was all too much."

"No doubt."

"I try to be happy a lot of the time because it helped my parents. They were so sad... It was the least I could do."

"The least you could do?"

She shrugged. "Sure. I didn't want to burden them. If I was happy then they didn't have to worry about me. I got good grades, made them laugh... It was easier on them."

"What about you?"

"What about me? I lived." She brushed away a tear quickly from her cheek. "If doctors like us had been up there when Immi… She might be still alive."

Emile stood up and pulled Chloé into his arms and she sobbed a bit, clinging to him. "It's okay. I've got you."

"I'm glad," she whispered.

Maybe it was his turn to cheer her up.

"Shall we eat something, maybe go for a walk?" he suggested.

"I would like that."

"Good."

As much as he wanted to stay here and hold her, he knew that would lead to something else. Something they'd both agreed could never happen, that Chloé had stated plainly that she didn't want.

The truth was no matter what he told himself, Emile did want her. Her humor, her charm, her strength and optimism. Everything he'd never had when he was growing up. He was falling in love with her again, or maybe he never really stopped.

What he was sure of, though, was that she just saw him as a friend. She'd made that clear, so he'd resist holding her, comforting her, even though it was all he really wanted to do.

She deserved to fall in love with someone who could give her everything she wanted. As much as Emile wanted to be the one to do that, he wouldn't risk failing, risk crushing her bright personality and having their love turn to bitterness like his parents' had.

He wouldn't do that to Chloé.

She deserved better than him.

CHAPTER TEN

WHEN CHLOÉ HAD seen that young girl with the same name as her sister, suffering from a heart disease, she'd frozen. It was like her whole world had gone still. And it had taken all of her strength to keep up a brave face for as long as she had.

Emile had really taken the lead on the whole thing and she was so thankful for that. He'd stepped in, where she faltered.

And it had been so kind of him to offer up their seats in the plane. His softer side, peeking through again.

There was a part of Chloé that wouldn't relax until she knew that the young girl was safe in Montreal and was on her way to recovery. This Immitaq's case was just a reminder about why Chloé did what she did, why she was so passionate about her work. Especially when she thought about the fact that if they hadn't come when they did, Immitaq wouldn't have lived much longer.

Thinking of it like that had saddened her all the more. How many lives had been lost because the right doctors weren't there?

When Emile had pulled her into his arms, she'd known she should step away, but she couldn't. It had felt so good to be comforted and wrapped up in his arms. She could've stayed there forever.

It had been a relief when he'd been the one to break the contact and suggested that walk…but also not so much.

She'd wanted more.

She wanted the physical connection with him. What she didn't know was how she was going to ask for that or what kind of can of worms it would open up. She'd pushed him away in Quebec City. They'd both agreed that it had been the right thing to do.

Only right now she didn't care about the right thing. She just wanted him, and the sense of security he offered. She was being haunted tonight and she needed to chase the ghosts away.

"Come, you need to eat," Emile said as he dished up some of the fish and potatoes that had been provided for them. "It looks good. What kind of fish is it, I wonder?"

"Arctic char," she replied offhandedly. "It's one of my favorites."

"Well, you need to eat something. It's been a long day. You can't just exist on lunch, which was hours ago, and that sludge you call coffee."

Chloé laughed, but it was still laced with some sadness. At least he'd made her laugh. Sort of like she'd always done for her family. It was nice to have someone do that for her. "You don't like camp coffee?"

"No offense to *ataata*, but no." He grinned, handing her a plate.

Chloé sat down at the table across from him. The food was home cooked and it had been awhile since she'd had it. It was a comfort.

"This is good," Emile remarked.

"Nothing like a fresh catch."

"Agreed. So walk after? Or... When does the sun go down here? Are we too late? It's about nine o'clock."

"Not until near midnight and then maybe sort of dusky. We're nearing the solstice. Longer days for sure."

Emile's eyebrows rose. "Wow."

"You know for someone who reads a book series set in the north..." It was a gentle tease.

"It was a long time ago that I read those, and they were mostly set in the winter, so give me a break."

She chuckled. "Okay, just a small one."

"Thanks."

They shared a smile; that made her heart skip a beat. Companionable silence. It was comforting.

"I want to thank you for the hug. I... It meant a lot." She reached out and took his hand. Emile didn't pull away; instead, he gave her hand a squeeze.

"That's what friends are for."

She nodded slowly. "Right."

They finished their food and then cleaned up the dishes so they could leave them tidy for the elders. Then they headed outside, where the sun was hanging low, but still bright. A perpetual twilight. It reminded Chloé of summers out on the land with her father and with Immi.

Summers were always Immi's favorite. They would pick berries and make jams. Then Chloé would pick the purple saxifrage and put it in Immitaq's hair.

"What're you thinking about?" Emile asked as they walked down along the beach. The water was calm. There was just a gentle lapping against the sand and the rocks. There were a few fishing boats out on the water still, taking advantage of the longer daylight.

"My sister. She loved summer," Chloé sighed.

"Your sister sounds lovely. It was just me and my father."

"Tell me about him. I only saw him the one time when he came to speak at the hospital and he seemed kind of formidable."

"That is a nice way of saying it," Emile groused. "He didn't show affection. My mother did. Now I think... I think I wish I could've lived with her, but it was impossible. My father had so much more sway."

"I'm surprised he never remarried."

"Me, too," Emile admitted. "Then again, work was his life. It was the reason my parents split up. My father's work came first. Always. And my mother couldn't compete. I like to think that maybe he didn't move on because he still loved her, but then again, I don't know if he really loved anything but the hospital."

"I think he loved you. He must've."

"He never showed it," he said moodily.

"And your mother never remarried."

"Ah, that's because she loved my father. She waited for him to come back and he never did."

Chloé didn't say much, but she thought on that statement. Thinking of Marguerite waiting for her ex-husband to return tugged at her heartstrings.

Was it really work that was keeping Chloé from dating, from having a family, the way she'd always claimed? Or maybe, just maybe, was she just waiting, too?

Waiting for Emile.

"Well, I'm sorry your mother loved and waited."

"So am I. It's why I don't want a family."

"You're still so sure you don't want kids?" she asked.

"No. Not with my work. My childhood was lonely. I won't do that to a child." His expression hardened for a second then he looked at her tenderly. "What about you? You always said…" He trailed off.

"I do want kids…but work…" It was all an excuse. There were so many real reasons. She wanted love and marriage, but she was still nursing a broken heart from all those years ago. She was afraid of having a child who had problems like Immitaq. And she'd spent so many years dedicated to medicine and to saving people like her sister, that she couldn't selfishly give it up to start a family.

Maybe if she had a partner who was supportive, she wouldn't have to walk away. Maybe she could make it work.

One thing she knew; that partner wouldn't be Emile. His work always came first. He'd made that clear, even just now.

They didn't say anything further. They just stood there on the beach, staring out over the water.

"What're those?" he asked, pointing.

She turned and saw jets of air and then the white back slip above the surface of the bay and she smiled. "Beluga, I suspect."

"A whale?" he asked, his voice awed.

"Sure, they come up into the Hudson and James Bay all the time in the summer."

"Amazing." They shared a grin.

"You look like a child on Christmas morning," she chuckled.

"It's been a dream of mine for so long to see a wild whale and up north." He whispered those words, the wonder apparent in his voice.

Her heart was beating quickly. She leaned into him and he wrapped his arms around her. She rested her head against his shoulder, just reveling in the feeling of being close to him, because that was all she wanted right now.

She just wanted to be close to him again, even just for one moment. Even if it couldn't happen again, she wanted to be with Emile.

Even though all logic told her she shouldn't.

His phone vibrated. He pulled it out, answered and put it on speaker. "Doctor LaCroix, what's the status?"

"Immitaq Peever had her blockage, the clot, removed. She's stable and Doctor Rosenbaum thinks she'll make a full recovery."

"*Bonne*, keep us posted." Emile ended the call.

Chloé let out a breath of relief. "That's wonderful."

"It is indeed."

"Thank you for supporting me today," she murmured. "It means so much."

"Of course. Thank you for bringing me up here and getting a taste of your world. I had no idea."

"And what do you think?"

"You're doing amazing things. I wish..."

Her breath caught in her throat. "You wish what?"

"It doesn't matter. I'm just glad I'm here with you."

Chloé shivered and she took Emile's hand. "Let's go back. I'm tired."

"Me, too."

They walked slowly back to the cabin. She was trembling with anticipation, because she knew what she wanted to ask him. She wanted to let him know what she needed. And tonight she just needed *him*.

She needed touch and warmth and, above all else, him. She just wanted to be held in his arms and to forget everything else. Forget the pain she buried away; forget that she always had to be the bright light for everyone else.

She just wanted her old Emile, the man she'd never really stopped loving. Deep down she knew it wasn't just geography separating them, but a desire for different things. He didn't want a family and she did, eventually. She couldn't give that up, couldn't give up any of her dreams, but she could have this one night with him.

Once they were inside, she stood there, suddenly so nervous. She hoped he would say yes, but she would understand if he didn't. So much water had passed under the bridge since they'd been together.

"I'll take the couch," he remarked, but he seemed to linger as if he wanted the same thing, too. As if he also felt the magic that was electrifying the air.

"You don't have to." It was barely a whisper.

"Pardon?" he asked.

"You don't have to take the couch. In fact, I would..." Her face heated with a flush.

Emile took a step closer and he brushed his knuckles over her cheek, causing her blood to burn. "You would what?"

"I would like you to kiss me," she murmured.

"You pushed me away last time."

"I know. It was hard to do that."

"Chloé, are you sure?"

She nodded. "Positive."

"I don't know if it's wise."

"I don't think it's very smart, either, but the truth of the matter is I want to be with you, Emile. I know that we can't have forever. We work so far apart and we're on different paths, but I would like one more time. Just one more moment with you."

"I would like that, too," he said, his voice deep and laced with promise. "Only if you're sure."

"I've never been so sure about something in my entire life."

Even though she always put on a brave face, right now she felt completely vulnerable. And she needed that, too. She was tired of being the rock, and her family wasn't around. She needed to feel and let go. She'd opened up a part of herself to Emile, the grief that she didn't share with anyone else. With him she could be free.

Emile had always been her safety net. Most of the time she was putting everyone else first, like she'd done most of her life. Tonight she wanted to be selfish and indulge in the one thing she wanted and could briefly have.

Him.

"Chloé, should we really?"

"Do you not want to?"

"Oh no, *ma chere*. I do. More than you know, but I don't have a condom."

"It's okay. I'm on the pill. This is what I want, Emile. I want to be with you tonight. I want you to make love to me one more time."

She couldn't really believe that one more time would be enough, but it would have to be.

Emile drew her into his arms and kissed her again. Just like he had after their dinner at *Choisir*, down by the river. This was what she'd wanted when they were at the *funiculaire*, but she'd stopped it. Tonight this ride wasn't stopping.

She wrapped her arms around his neck, pressing her body against him. Annoyed that there were so many layers of clothes between them because all she wanted was nothing so he could touch her. Possess her.

Emile's hands slipped under her shirt, cupping her breasts. His hands hot on her exposed skin made her nipples harden, his fingers lightly trailing over her. Then he scooped her up and carried her a couple of steps to the bed, setting her in the middle, where she proceeded to sink into the old mattress.

She screeched with laughter.

"*Merde!* Are you okay?" he asked, humor lacing his voice.

"Yes," she giggled. "It was just unexpected."

He grinned. "Well, I see one more problem with this whole thing."

"And what's that?"

"We're both still dressed," he pointed out, the huskiness in his voice making her heart skip a beat as he pulled off his shirt and she got to drink in the sight of his muscular chest.

Her blood thundered in her ears, her body fizzing with anticipation as she quickly took off her clothes, until nothing was between them.

Emile sat down on the bed, pulling her close, trailing his hands over her body, making her ache for more. He pressed kisses against her neck.

"I remember our first time together like it was yesterday."

"Me, too," she whispered as his kisses traced lower down her body, along her collarbone, over her breasts, his tongue circling her sensitive nipples.

Chloé lay back against the bed, the air crackling with a burning fire of need. His lips trailed down her belly. His strong hands on her hips as he held her in place, exactly where he wanted her. The moment his lips kissed her lower she cried out, spreading her legs wider. Her body trembling, begging for him to claim her.

Her legs shook as he pleasured her with his mouth; she was so close to giving out under the absolute heady pleasure of bliss. She didn't want this sensation to stop, but if she didn't put a stop to it, she'd come, and she wanted to come around him.

The first time back with him, she wanted him inside her.

"Emile," she moaned. "I'm so close."

"So?" he teased.

"Oh, God."

"Tell me what you want," he murmured against her thigh.

"I want you to take me."

Emile shifted his weight, leaning over her as she wrapped her legs around him. She reached down and stroked his hard length. If he could tease her then she could torture him just a bit, too.

"Chloé, I…" He trailed off and moaned. "When you touch me like that… It's too much."

"Good."

"You're such a tease."

"As are you. I want you, Emile." She kissed him.

The head of his cock pressed against her. He thrust quickly, sinking into her, filling her completely and in exactly the way she wanted. She let out a moan of pleasure, remembering how good it felt and how long it had been.

"*Si serré*," he moaned.

"What?"

"It doesn't matter. Move with me." It wasn't a request; it was a command and she was more than happy to oblige. He moved slowly, sensuously, so she could match his rhythm, loving the feeling of them being in sync as she urged him to take her harder and faster.

A coil of heat erupted deep inside her. He reached between her legs, touching her, stroking her as she moved. She was so close. She arched her back as heady pleasure washed over her, burning through every nerve ending and fiber in her body. Her body squeezing around his thick, hard length as she tipped over the edge into joy.

Emile cried out, quickening his pace as he came, too. Holding still for a few moments before he slipped out of her, then falling beside her with a contented sigh. She rolled up next to him, tucking her head under his arm, his fingers stroking her back and her hand on his chest. She could feel his heart beating under her fingers.

This was home. It always had been.

Except, it couldn't be.

This was just a fleeting moment in time. There was an end date looming.

What did I just do?

She'd set herself up for heartbreak.

That was what she'd done.

Emile couldn't believe what had just happened and how much he'd missed being in her arms. No one had ever held a candle to Chloé and there were so many nights he thought back to their most intimate moments, missing her.

Longing for her. As much as he always tried to deny it.

She was snuggled up against him and he just breathed in the scent of her, trailing his fingers over her soft, silky skin. He was trying not to think about the fact that she would leave him again. They wanted different things. She wanted a family and he couldn't give her that. How could he keep her from fulfilling her dreams? Instead of mulling it all over or thinking about the end, he just focused on this moment with her back in his arms. Which he'd savor forever.

"What time is it?" she asked softly.

"I think midnight. Nope, I was wrong. It's one in the morning." Had he really been just holding her while she slept against him? Time was slipping by so fast.

She sat up. "Want to see if the northern lights are out?"

"I would rather stay in bed," he teased.

"I would, too, but you said you've never seen the aurora and now is your chance." She clambered out of bed and started pulling on her clothes. He watched her, enjoying his view and not wanting this night to end.

"Why don't you look and tell me? Then if it's not out there, you can come back to bed. We have an early flight tomorrow."

She rolled her eyes and smiled. "You're hopeless. Besides, you need a couple of minutes to let your eyes adjust to the darkness before they appear."

"Fine."

"For someone who said he's never seen the northern lights you're being awfully curmudgeonly about it."

He chuckled softly. "Fine, if you insist."

"I do." She grinned smugly.

He got out of bed and pulled on his clothes. "If there's no lights out there, then you owe me."

"Oh?" she teased. "And what will I owe you."

He pulled her close and kissed her playfully. "I think you know."

"I think that can be arranged. And if I'm right, then you'll owe me something for all this trouble you're putting me through."

His pulse kicked up a notch. "Oh? And what will that be?"

"We'll discuss that later." She opened the door and they stepped outside onto the small porch, shutting the door. They walked down and went around to the side of the building so they wouldn't be under the porch light. It still wasn't fully dark outside; Emile had never experienced anything like it. He'd read about it, sure, but seeing it was something so completely different.

In the sky there were a couple of stars that were bright enough to withstand the dusky midnight, but not too many.

"I see nothing," he groused.

"Look up toward the north and let your eyes adjust," she chided. "Also, stop complaining."

He smirked but did what she asked, staring at the dark sky, waiting for something. Then it was as though the sky filled with pale smoke that moved like water. The longer he stood there and stared, the more brilliant the colors became. They burst in pinks and reds, like a shimmering ribbon above them. It wasn't as bright as he'd seen in photographs, because it wasn't fully dark, but it was still mesmerizing.

"C'est incroyable!"

"It is, right?" Chloé beamed. "So beautiful."

His heart was so full and they shared a tender expression. "Not as beautiful as you are."

"Emile," she said softly and leaned her head against his shoulder while he wrapped his arm around her, just as they had earlier, but somehow so much closer after everything they'd shared. He didn't want to let her go. "What is going to happen when we head back to Montreal?" Chloé asked.

"Nothing will change. It won't be weird. I promise."

"Oh." There was hesitation in her voice. "Good."

"I care for you, Chloé. We'll be okay."

What he wanted to tell her right then was that he was still in love with her, that he never really had fallen out of love with her.

Only, he couldn't say those words. He still wasn't enough for her, and he never wanted to make her unhappy. This was all they could share together.

Nothing more.

* * *

The plane landed in Aivik Bay early the next morning. It was the same pilot. Emile had been getting updates about Immitaq Peever through the night, and she was doing well since her angioplasty. Chloé had been getting updates about Céline. She was done with her chemotherapy and the scan was showing good margins to do the surgery.

It was just a matter of when. They wanted Céline to be strong enough to withstand the long procedure, and the team had to be ready. When they got back they'd have a lot of work to do.

It felt good to focus on patients instead of talking about what had passed between them last night. It had been magical, the whole night, but both of them knew there was no future for them.

When they landed in Montreal, they parted at the hospital to clean up, before heading back later in the day. When Emile got to his father's house, his house, it just seemed even more empty than before.

It was a beautiful home and had been in the family a long time, but he couldn't help but think about that little cabin up in Aivik Bay or the crammed medical clinic where he worked in tandem with Chloé. And then he thought of walking in Beaupré with her.

Everywhere she was, she lit up the room and he was going to miss her when she was gone.

You don't have to miss her.

He shook his head. There was no way he could ask her to stay in Montreal, not when she clearly loved her work between Ottawa and Iqaluit. And it was important work, just like his work in Montreal was. As much as he wanted her to stay, to have a surgeon of her caliber on his team, he couldn't ask that of her.

She deserved her happiness.

She deserved her life, not to be chained to the same place he was. She deserved a family.

It wasn't her duty to stay here, but it was his.

CHAPTER ELEVEN

A week later

ONCE THEY GOT back to the hospital Emile went to check on the Peevers, and Chloé went to see Céline. It was then she had to throw herself into the planning of the surgery. It was hard to believe that a month had passed since she'd come to Montreal and reconnected with Emile, but only a week since they'd deeply connected again.

At least, that was how she saw it.

True to Emile's word, nothing had gone weird between them, and she was very thankful for that. They were professional and friendly. It was like their night of passion never happened

That was what they'd agreed, but in truth, she now missed him more than ever.

She missed being in his arms, kissing him, waking up next to him. The bed at her hotel was lonely.

And she wanted more of him.

Which was exactly what she'd been afraid would happen.

I could transfer to Montreal?

Maybe she could still do her rotations in Iqaluit from Montreal? Maybe the board of directors at Hôpital de Ville-Marie would allow that? But it would be tricky. Ottawa and Iqaluit worked together and right now, she had an awful lot of funding helping her work between the two hospitals.

There was nothing really tying her to Ottawa, just the proximity to Iqaluit and the rapport. The real problem was Emile's steadfast determination on the topic of kids. He had made it very clear that he didn't want a family or a relationship because work came first. She also knew how scared he was of it, because of what happened between his parents. Chloé understood it; she didn't have to like it, but she understood it all the same.

Was family something she was willing to give up? Chloé wasn't sure. If she really wanted marriage and children, despite all her fears about illness and juggling work, she would've found someone else, but she hadn't.

She just didn't know, and it was all so confusing. Her brain was working so hard to try to figure out a way to make it work so that she could stay with Emile. But would he even *want* her to stay? When they'd gotten together that night it was on the promise that it would just be for one night, and with the assumption when the time came she'd leave for good. And he certainly hadn't hinted that she should stay and work at the hospital...

Nuka, you can follow your heart.

Chloé let out an exasperated sigh in frustration. She hated all this wishy-washy nonsense. All this thinking and worrying over something she walked away from years ago.

Except she wasn't sure that she ever actually did walk away.

As she sat there at her computer mulling all this over, she got a ping that the latest imaging and lab work for Céline had come in. She quickly chased those thoughts away and pulled up the information.

Céline's blood work looked good. She was stronger than she had been last week. Her prealbumin was high and white cell count was manageable and the tumor hadn't grown again in the past seven days, which meant the surgical margins were good. Now was the perfect moment.

It was time to do the surgery.

She sent the files to the team who would be joining her on the surgery and then got up to make her way over to Emile's office. Usually, he'd be walking the floors and working with patients, but she knew he had several meetings today so maybe he'd be easy to find.

As she walked through the hallway, she passed the paintings of his ancestors. All the Moreaus that had worked and bled for this hospital before Emile. Their sour expressions. Once she'd thought they were just stoic, but now she got the feeling they were dour, looking down at her. She felt bad that Emile had to deal with this indignation every day.

This judgment.

Why did a bunch of dead ancestors hold such sway over him?

And looking at Emile's father's portrait, she couldn't help but wonder what the senior Dr. Moreau had really felt.

Did he have any regrets about pressuring his son, for breaking Marguerite's heart? And why did Emile want to make *this* man so proud?

She shuddered and quickly made her way over to Emile's office.

Donna was working on her computer as she approached. "Doctor MacDonald, he asked me to send you in once you arrived."

"How did he know I was coming?" she asked, puzzled.

Donna smiled. "He received the files on Céline and he's expecting you."

Chloé laughed. "I don't suppose you can book me an operating room time for tomorrow?"

"Already done. I emailed you and the rest of the team."

"Perfect, Donna. You're a gem." Chloé knocked and then stepped inside Emile's office. "Hey, you all ready?"

"Glad you're here. I had Donna book the operating room,"

Emile said, looking up from behind his desk. Behind him were windows that overlooked Montreal. It was a stunning view and she was a bit taken aback as she realized that in her month here she hadn't actually been in his office. Emile had come to hers, or she had spoken with him in the hall.

He looked over his shoulder. "What?"

"I just realized I haven't been in your office before. Jeez, I have a little hovel in the corner and you have a penthouse."

Emile shrugged. "It is a nice view, but I barely spend time here. So, are you ready to do this surgery?"

Chloé nodded. "Have you called Céline's parents? I would like to go over the procedure with them this afternoon."

"I have," he stated. "Only because I was talking to Agathe about Céline when the information came in. Parliament is on a summer break, so she is here already. If you want to go down and talk to them, there's no time like the present."

"Good, because Céline will be in the hospital for a bit longer. I want to make sure she gets one more round of chemo after she heals from surgery. Just so we can make sure we kill off all the cancer cells." Chloé hesitated for a moment, wondering if he'd ask her to stay and see that through.

But Emile didn't respond. It cut her to the quick.

She cleared her throat. "I will leave post-operative instructions for her care, as I'm just here for the surgery."

A strange look passed across his face, almost like he was surprised, and she wondered if he had been expecting her to stay, after all. "I appreciate that."

Ask me to stay. I'll consider staying if you ask me to stay. She kept those thoughts to herself.

Instead, she asked, "Are you ready for this surgery?"

"I am. It will be long, but I'm glad it will be done for Céline. It's her best possible chance."

Chloé nodded. "It is."

"Well, let's go down and speak to Agathe and Tomas." He stood up and grabbed his white lab coat.

Suddenly, things were awkward again and she didn't know why. Maybe it was all in her head, because her own stupid heart was involved now. And she was realizing that even despite her best efforts, she loved him and wanted to stay here with him. After this surgery was done, it was going to be so hard to get into her car and drive back to Ottawa.

They made their way down to the pediatric ward and sure enough, Céline's parents were in her room. Agathe was pacing. Just from watching them through the window, Chloé could see the look of worry etched into their faces. The same expression that her parents had worn so often when Immi was sick in the hospital or faced yet another surgery.

It wasn't new on Agathe's and Tomas's faces, but today it was hitting harder. Perhaps because Emile knew about Immi, and Chloé didn't have to paper her own pain and trepidation over with laughter and happiness.

She was feeling a lot of emotions today. Even though the margins looked good, the tumor had shrunk and Céline was strong, there was always the unknown. The small percent of uncertainty she couldn't control.

"Hey," Emile said softly. "This will be okay."

"Of course," she agreed quickly. "Why wouldn't it be?"

"You're thinking of your sister again, aren't you?"

She smiled slightly. "I am. I'm glad I don't have to try and hide it from you."

I can be myself around you. I don't have to make you happy. But she didn't say that out loud, either. How could she be a burden to him? He had a lot to shoulder here, too. Sure, he'd seen that side of her, the grief, but how long could he really tolerate it?

All he knew before was her sunshine. That was what people were drawn to. Maybe if he'd seen the real her all this time, he'd have grown quickly tired of her.

Emile smiled at her, encouraging her. "Let's go give Agathe and Tomas the good news."

"Yes. Let's do this." She took a deep breath, steeled her resolve and locked away everything she was feeling, to plaster that bright sunshine smile on her face. Céline's parents needed that brave face from her. They needed her confidence.

As they walked in, Agathe stopped pacing and sat down next to her husband, clutching his hand. Céline was sleeping in her bed, still holding a tablet where she'd been playing some kind of game. Chloé could still hear the music from it. It was precious.

"Well?" Agathe asked. "She had scans early this morning and blood work."

"She did. She's ready for her surgery," Chloé stated. "I'm going to start her on preoperative antibiotics and no food or drink after midnight."

"It's tomorrow?" Tomas asked.

"*Oui*," Emile answered. "We want to make sure we get a head start and not give the tumor time to grow. It was aggressive when you brought Céline to us, so we don't want to give it any more chances."

"That's understandable," Tomas stated, and he squeezed his wife's hand.

"What time tomorrow?" Agathe asked, her voice shaking.

"Seven in the morning," Chloé responded. "It will be a long procedure. It's open-heart surgery and then Céline will be in the intensive care unit for a couple of days, sedated and intubated to allow her to heal. It will be a hard procedure."

A tear slipped from Agathe's eyes. "I understand. It's the only way, right? We can't shrink it any further."

"You're correct," Emile responded. "The chemotherapy did work on shrinking the tumor, but it will grow back and spread. Once it spreads to other parts of her body, there's not much hope."

"This is our time to take care of it," Chloé reiterated. "It's hard, but she's young and kids bounce back incredibly fast."

Tomas nodded. "Okay. How long will the procedure take?"

"About six hours," Chloé stated.

"That's a long time," Agathe murmured.

"It is, but it's complex. After her surgery and after she heals, we'll put her on one last round of chemotherapy to really make sure we've killed off as much of the cancer cells as we can. Once that's complete, she'll be able to ring the bell and go home," Chloé said, smiling as brightly as she could muster.

"Home?" Agathe looked down at her daughter and smiled tenderly. "That's always been my hope. Thank you, Doctors."

"Don't thank us yet. I'll send down a resident to go over the paperwork and talk about the risks with you," Emile said. "But I'm pretty confident that those won't be an issue."

"If you need anything else, please let us know," Chloé added. "We'll see you both tomorrow morning."

Chloé and Emile left. She glanced back to see Agathe and Tomas hug. A sob welled up in her throat watching them. They had each other to lean on. Just like her parents had. Despite everything, Céline was a lucky girl.

"Well, now we should go over the procedure with the team and then you and I both need to get some good sleep tonight," Emile remarked.

"Agreed. It's going to be an early day tomorrow." She worried her bottom lip. "I can't believe my time here is almost done."

"Me either, but you'll be glad to get back to your own hospital and your apartment, *non*?"

Well, that is a finality.

"Sure," she said, hoping her voice didn't break. "Well, let's go assemble the team and go over the plan of attack."

He nodded. "*Bonne.*"

Chloé couldn't let herself think about her own feelings or her heart or anything like that right now. Céline was counting on her. She wasn't going to let that little girl not have a chance at life. She'd been brought here to Montreal for this.

This was what she did best.

This was her life. And it would have to be enough.

Nuka, I'm right here with you. I always am.

Chloé took a deep breath and closed her eyes to calm herself. Hearing Immi's voice in her head was a good thing. She always took it as a good sign. So she focused on that.

Céline was prepped and ready to go. The surgery had started.

Emile had made the first cuts and Chloé was waiting to do the delicate work on the heart, which couldn't happen until Céline was on the bypass machine.

Chloé had actually slept that night. Maybe it was because she had *finally* allowed herself to come to the full realization that this was all she'd ever have with Emile. That it was okay to move on.

Even though part of her really didn't want to.

Focus.

This was her big moment. So many surgeons would be watching and learning from her. She opened her eyes and looked up at the gallery. It was packed with residents and interns who weren't part of this surgery.

She wasn't used to working in a jam-packed operating room. A gallery was fine, but she didn't want to have extra bodies in the operating room with her. This was a delicate procedure. She tore her gaze away from the crowds and instead focused on Emile's work. It was always calming watching a skilled surgeon at work, and Emile was no exception.

She stood there, patiently waiting. Ready to go.

"Okay, put her on bypass and start the clock," Emile stated. Their gazes locked as he stepped back. "She's ready for you, Doctor MacDonald."

Chloé nodded and stepped up to the table. "Scalpel."

The scrub nurse placed what she needed in her palm. They had practiced the steps, the instruments were ready and now it was time for her to take this tiny nonbeating broken heart and repair it. Remove the cancer that grew in there and give the little girl a chance at life.

Right here with you, Nuka. You've got this.

Chloé didn't even think about the clock that was counting the time. There was only so long Céline could be on the bypass machine. Only so long it would be safe.

Emile was close to her. Watching her.

"I'm right here," he whispered in her ear. "You're doing beautifully."

"I hope I'm giving enough instruction for everyone," she said out loud. "Sometimes I think in my head, but I don't know that I'm actually talking out loud."

"Yes, Doctor MacDonald. You are," Emile reassured. "All you're missing is a bad pun or a dad joke."

She smiled to herself and continued the work.

She knew the steps like clockwork in her head and she wanted to make sure she was imparting her wisdom on everyone here.

She made a cut and exposed the tumor. "See how the tumor has shrunk? It will be easier to get better margins now and allow the muscle to repair."

Chloé carefully excised the tumor from the heart muscle, making sure she got it all and placed it into a bag for pathology.

Once she was sure all the cancerous material was removed, she began to repair the muscle and put the heart back together.

If only someone could put *hers* back together.

"Clamps, please," she asked.

Emile reached down beside her and clamped an artery so she could stitch it back up. As she continued to drone on about the repair, she felt lighter, because the surgery was going well. Once she went over her work with Emile, she laid down her instruments.

"Everything looks good. Let's bring her off bypass and check the flow for leaks," she asked.

"Yes, Doctor MacDonald," Dr. LaCroix stated. The machines flicked off; the clamps were removed.

Please. Chloé said a silent prayer, the way she always did when she'd completed heart surgery and they were checking for leaks.

The heart pinked back up and there was a beat. A steady beat with no leaking, no bubbling, just a heart.

There was clapping and Chloé smiled under her surgical mask, breathing a sigh of relief.

"She's all yours to close up, Doctor Moreau," Chloé stated, stepping back from the table.

"Excellent job, Doctor MacDonald," Emile said and he got to work closing up Céline. Chloé checked the clock and was relieved to see that it hadn't taken the full six hours to remove the tumor.

You never knew until you opened the patient up. She had explained that to Agathe and Tomas, but she was glad Céline's tumor had shrunk so much and Céline didn't have to be on bypass for any longer.

She took another shaky breath. She felt like crying.

Tears of relief, but also of mourning that her time here was over.

Emile and his staff could handle her post-operative care. There was no need for her to stay.

Unless Emile asked.

Nuka, would you stay, though?

Could she give up the thought of kids for a chance with Emile? Her career for him?

She still wasn't sure. She was in love with Emile. She just wasn't sure if that was enough, because to be with him meant sacrificing so much.

Even if he did ask her to stay, there was always a chance that they would just drift apart. Hospital came first for him, and her work was important, too. She couldn't ask him to give up a piece of himself for her.

That was not how love worked. Love meant supporting your partner, not giving up on yourself.

Emile didn't usually follow his patients from the PACU to the intensive care unit, but this time he had to. He was still in awe from the surgery and the fact that little Céline, with such a big tumor, was still alive.

He was also in awe of Chloé's skill. The surgery and her teaching had been recorded with Agathe's and Tomas's permission; they wanted others to learn. And Chloé removed the tumor with such care and talent.

She had left once he'd finished closing, but as he followed the gurney to the intensive care unit, he found her waiting there.

"Vitals good?" she asked as Céline was wheeled into the ICU pod.

"Stable," he replied.

Chloé smiled; he could see the exhaustion in her face. "That's great news."

"Shall we go tell Céline's parents?"

"You haven't spoken to them yet?" she wondered out loud.

"No. We both should do that. Besides, it's the best part of the job."

Chloé nodded, beaming. "Yes. Let's do that."

They walked in silence to the waiting room. It was hitting him that soon Chloé would leave and there was nothing he could do to entice her to stay. The board would do anything they could to keep her here in Montreal, but he knew how much the north meant to her.

After going to Aivik Bay with her, he understood why she did what she did.

Just like she understood why he did what he did. The legacy of his family here in Montreal and the benefits of this hospital.

They were on different paths, the ones that they'd always been on.

It was breaking his heart, because he did love her, but his commitment was to this hospital. He wouldn't get involved with her and ruin what they had, just like his father had ruined his own marriage. He wouldn't hurt her like that. He couldn't do that to her.

If he was in a different place and didn't have this burden of a family name looming over him, if he knew how to be a good father and husband, then he could give her more. He could have that life with her.

He just didn't know how.

So as much as he wanted to ask her to stay, he just couldn't.

Céline's parents were in a separate waiting room, because the last thing Agathe needed was people bugging her about the government. Agathe and Tomas stood when they entered, and Emile could see the dark circles under their eyes.

"She made it through and is in the ICU," he stated.

Agathe gasped, covering her mouth as Tomas wrapped his arm around her.

"I removed all the tumor. Pathology is checking the mass. I think she'll require one more round of chemotherapy to make sure all the cancer cells are gone. First, she'll be intubated and in the ICU for a couple of days," Chloé explained. "It all looks really promising, though."

"I can't thank you both enough. When can we see her?" Agathe asked.

"I'll take you now," Emile offered.

Agathe and Tomas both thanked Chloé and left with him. At the door, Emile looked back at Chloé and sent her a congratulatory smile, trying to boost her up as he walked away. He wanted to see her off, but first he had a duty to his patients like he always did.

When Agathe and Tomas were settled in the ICU he did a quick check on Céline, then, happy with her progress, he made his way up to Chloé's office, knowing that was where she'd be.

When he got to her office, her door was open and she was packing up her computer.

"You're heading out?" he asked, trying to swallow the emotions that were crying out in him, telling him to beg her to stay. Not to leave. To give her everything she wanted, only he couldn't. He was fighting inside.

There was no way he would hurt her like his father did to his mother. It would be too cruel; to know he'd crushed her beautiful soul by not giving her what she needed—by stopping her seeking it with somebody else, because he selfishly wanted her.

And Emile wasn't cruel. He wasn't coldhearted.

He had to let her go.

He'd rather do that now than have her hate him down the road.

"Tomorrow. One more night in the hotel." She smiled, but the smile didn't reach her eyes.

"Your hospital will be happy to have you back."

"Indeed. Thank you again for allowing me to see a couple of patients here in Montreal. I appreciate that."

He nodded. "Of course. The board…"

"Yes?" she asked.

"The board and Céline's parents were thankful for all you did."

She nodded her head. "It was my pleasure."

Stay. For me.

Only he couldn't get those words out. He couldn't say them. He wasn't going to trap her here with him. She could be free; he couldn't. How could he break her heart?

He didn't even know how she felt. Neither of them had expressed love, not here in the present. He wasn't even sure he knew how to show it. His father never had. All he had taught Emile was devotion to work. And he had once promised his mother love, but it had just turned to sadness and bitterness.

The idea that Emile might do that to Chloé tore at the very fibers of his soul. He just couldn't risk it.

"I hope…" he managed. "I hope we can work together in the future again sometime."

Their gazes met, her eyes sad. "That's it?"

"Is there supposed to be something more?"

A strange expression crossed her face. "No. I guess not."

"You belong in the north and I belong here."

"Why?" she asked. The smile was gone. Her lips set in a thin, firm line. No twinkle in her eyes. Already, he could see he was diminishing her light and he hated himself for that.

"My family."

"What family?" she asked sadly. "All I see are people who caused you misery hanging from the walls."

Emile frowned. "That may be so, but I am not the only one clinging to a past, to a duty."

Her eyes widened in shock, before they narrowed. "You're right. My work in the north is because my sister died due to lack of care. Every life I save is another Immitaq. Your father is dead. You can't earn his love and respect now," she said firmly, with a hint of bitterness.

He didn't want them to part ways again in an argument.

He regretted that the last time when they'd broken up. He wasn't going to let it be like that again.

"I can't give you what you want, Chloé."

"And what's that?"

"A life. Family. My work comes first and you know this."

"I suppose I do. I'm glad you know what you want." There was a hint of bitterness there, too. It tore at his heart, but this was better.

You mean easier.

He shook that thought away. "It was a pleasure working with you again, Doctor MacDonald." He turned and left her.

It was the hardest thing he'd ever done, walking away from her again. With each step, his heart tore open.

He hated himself for hurting her again.

This was why he hadn't wanted to get involved with her. It was why he wanted to keep his distance.

The problem was he could never resist her. How could he resist someone he loved so much?

CHAPTER TWELVE

One week later

CHLOÉ HAD BEEN gone a week. And like a fool, Emile walked by her office every day.

He was barely sleeping, because he couldn't stop thinking about her. He missed her, but he'd pushed her away for her own good. There was no way he was going to take a chance on love and ruin it like his father did. He'd seen firsthand how it nearly destroyed his mother. There was no way that he could do that to Chloé.

She was too nice, too happy. She was all things good and bright. How could he dim that light?

In spite of all the hardships that she'd endured and the pain of losing her twin, she saw the brighter side of life.

He was too afraid of turning into his father.

Haven't you already?

Céline was doing well and responding favorably to the chemotherapy, but seeing her or Immitaq Peever reminded him of Chloé. She was now everywhere in the halls of the Hôpital de Ville-Marie. Every day he still walked past the dour faces of his relatives, but now looking at them just made him so angry.

Angry that they had trapped him here.

Trapped him in this legacy that he wasn't sure that he wanted anymore.

All his life he'd been told he wanted this to the point that he believed it. Now he wasn't too sure.

What am I doing?

Every day since Chloé had left, he'd grown more frustrated and angry at himself.

Finally, he decided to go against the grain and take a day off. He packed a small bag, got into his car and headed to Beaupré, to the only person who would understand what he was grappling with.

His maman.

Driving to his mother's home, he recalled the laughter the last time they drove there. Chloé's sense of wonder over the falls. The moments they'd shared in Quebec City. Just every joke, every conversation. How much she'd loved every little bit of his home, making him see it through new eyes.

Now this drive didn't seem so magical. Instead, it hurt.

When he pulled up to his mother's house, Marguerite was outside, puttering around in her front garden. She seemed surprised when he parked the car and got out.

"Emile?" she asked, stunned. "It's the middle of the week."

"Can't I visit you during the week?" he asked, amused.

"You don't usually. You're always busy with work." She pulled off her gardening gloves. "Are you okay? Where is *ma chouette*?"

"Chloé returned back to Ottawa. Her rotation in Iqaluit was starting and she had to go back." What he didn't tell his mother was that he'd pushed her away.

Her mother looked crestfallen. "I'm happy she's doing her work, but I'm sad her visit here was so short. I adore her."

"I noticed, given what you call her." Emile locked his car and headed over to his mother, kissing her on the head. "How are you feeling? I hope you're still taking breaks?"

"I'm not an invalid, Emile. And yes, I do take rests. Would you like to sit down?"

Emile nodded and took a seat on one of the white rattan chairs on her front porch. He could hear the river babbling across the road, the birds trilling in the air. So different from the city. He'd forgotten how much he loved it out here, the summers he spent here with his mother.

It was nice to take a moment and breathe. He realized he hadn't done that in a long time.

"So, why have you come?" his mother asked.

"Do you not want me here?"

"Oh no, I do. I'm glad."

"I needed... I needed to breathe." What he needed was Chloé and a life with her; he needed the sunshine back in his life, but he didn't know how to say it. He didn't even dare to dream it.

"You love her. Don't you?" his mother asked, taking the seat next to him.

"What?" he asked, stunned.

His mother looked at him with reproach. "I know you, Emile. You love her. You always have."

"And if I did? She works too far away. She won't come to Montreal."

"Did you ask her?" his mother asked.

"No. How can I ask her when her life is up north? She's doing something good there."

"I agree," his mother stated. "You can go on rotation there, too, you know."

"I can't do that. I'm head of cardiothoracic surgery. I have a legacy to uphold."

"Whose?"

He sighed and scrubbed a hand over his face. "Father's."

His mother shook her head. "You don't have to live up to him. Why are you trying to earn his love? He loved you, Emile."

"He didn't love me, Maman. How could you say that?"

"He loved both of us." His mother's voice shook.

"If he loved both of us, then why did you leave?"

Marguerite sighed. "I left because yes, he loved his work more. Because he was living up to his father's expectations. Always chasing that love. Just like you, and I hate seeing you doing the same."

It felt like everything Emile thought he knew came crashing down. That was not what he expected to learn about his father. It wasn't the man he thought he remembered... But it sounded exactly like the man he'd become, too.

They weren't totally the same. He valued his connection with his patients; he was opening up more. He had pushed Chloé away for her own good so he wouldn't hurt her like his father had done to his mother.

I still put the hospital first.

In that way they were the same. But what if it didn't have to be like that? What if Emile could have more?

"How can I walk away from the hospital?" His voice shook as all the probabilities played around in his head.

"You don't have to. You just have to walk away from the head of cardiothoracic to take up work in Iqaluit. Can you do that?'

It was a fair question.

Could he? It wasn't like he was leaving Montreal or his family behind here, and he would be working toward something he'd always wanted. Freedom, love and doing what he was passionate about.

Being up in Aivik Bay had been amazing. It had given him that thrill like the one he'd felt when he first started medicine.

Maybe he did deserve more than somebody else's dream. He deserved happiness, and going after it didn't make him less of a surgeon.

"Well?" his mother asked. "I'm sure the hospital will let you do rotation up north."

"I can, but that's not all."

"What, then?"

"Chloé wants a family, marriage, children. How can I give her those things? Look how..." It was hard to finish the sentence. It was hard to speak because it seemed so obvious, suddenly, that it wasn't enough justification to push Chloé away.

He loved her. Could he rise above his father? The idea terrified him, but he wanted that life of love and joy with Chloé.

"How you were raised?" Marguerite asked quietly.

"*Oui*." His voice shook.

"It's my greatest regret I didn't fight harder for you. Your father had more money and sway, but you can break the pattern, Emile. I know I say you're like your father, but there's me in there, too. If you were truly like him we wouldn't be having this conversation."

She was right. If he was truly like his father he wouldn't be here. He wouldn't miss Chloé so much.

"Do you still love him?"

"I did, but it was better we were apart. We were so very different. I don't regret it, though. I had you."

It warmed his heart to hear her say that.

"Chloé and I are different, too."

"Not that much."

Emile nodded, swallowing a hard lump in his throat. "I want to be happy, Maman."

She smiled and placed her hand on his knee. "You deserve to be happy, Emile. Go and find your happiness. You deserve love and you won't get it from someone who is no longer here, but I want you to know that he did love you. He loved you very much, even if he couldn't show it. I do, too, even though I wasn't there."

And that was the crux of the matter. He *could* love Chloé. He knew that in his heart, but he needed to show up for her. He needed to demonstrate he would be her partner. That he was there.

Was he scared? Yes, because he might've already blown it, but he had to take that risk and show her he was here for her.

He loved her.

And he wasn't going to leave.

Emile leaned over and kissed his mother on her head. "Thank you."

"If you're looking for my blessing regarding *ma chouette*, you have it. Just in case that wasn't clear." His mother winked.

"No, not clear at all," Emile teased.

Marguerite smiled. "Now, I believe you have decisions to make and probably travel arrangements? If you have the wedding in Iqaluit, I am quite willing and able to fly up there."

"Good to know, Maman." He got up and headed to his car.

"One more thing," his mother called out.

"What's that?"

"Give her my love. I can't wait to see her again."

"She might turn me down."

"She won't."

Emile nodded. "I'll tell her. I'll call you later, Maman."

It was scary, giving up the legacy that had been instilled in him his whole life, but when the decision had been made it felt as though a huge weight had been lifted off his shoulders. And for the first time in a long time Emile finally felt free.

His only hope now was that he wasn't too late.

That he hadn't hurt Chloé too much, and that he still had a chance with her. Even if it took him some time to convince her, when he got to Iqaluit and declared himself, he wasn't going to let her go for a third time.

This time, he was playing for keeps.

He was playing forever.

One week later

"You have been kind of down since you came up here. Thought summer was your favorite time to come here?"

Chloé looked up at her *anaana* and realized she had been just sitting there, staring out through the front window of her parents' home, holding her cup of coffee, not drinking. It was cold now and a bit congealed because her mom had made her father's special camp coffee.

"How long have I been sitting here?" Chloé asked.

"Since I poured you that coffee," *Anaana* remarked, giving her a knowing glance.

"The coffee may have turned into some form of blob-like life," Chloé joked halfheartedly.

Her mother snorted. "I wouldn't be surprised. What's eating you?"

"Sorry, just lost in thoughts."

"You've been lost in thoughts since you got off the plane a week ago," *Anaana* stated. "What's going on with you? Usually, you come here for your rotation and you're so bouncy and happy…"

"I don't have to always be happy, *Anaana*," Chloé snapped. She sat down her coffee mug and rubbed her temples.

"Hey," *Anaana* said, sitting across from her. "What's going on with you? You don't usually get snippy."

"I'm sorry. Just…tired. A couple of weeks ago I was in Montreal and doing a complicated surgery on a child and… just tired."

It was a lie, but she didn't have the energy or the need to burden her mother. She didn't want to be a hardship to her parents. Ever. And swallowing her emotions was habit.

Nuka, you can talk to Anaana.

"Chloé, somehow I don't believe you," her mother said gently. "Tell me."

"No. I don't want to…"

"Don't want to what?" *Anaana* asked.

"Upset you." Her lips trembled. "I'm happy and bubbly because…I didn't want to worry you ever."

"What're you talking about?"

"*Anaana*, when Immitaq…" She swallowed the lump forming in her throat, trying to hold it back. All those years of grief that she had to keep bottled up. All the times she didn't talk about Immi to her parents because she didn't want them to be sad, it was all about to erupt out of her again.

This time she wasn't sure that she could hold anything back. She'd been bottling her grief for so long and her bottle was filled. It was overwhelming how completely the emotion consumed her.

Nuka, tell Anaana.

"When Immi died, I made a promise to myself to never cause you or *Ataata* any kind of pain or grief. I wanted you both to know that I was okay."

"Oh, Chloé," her mother said softly. "You didn't need to do that. You were a kid and…"

"*Anaana*, no, it was okay." She brushed away tears.

"No, it wasn't. I was the parent. You weren't and that wasn't your responsibility. So I'm sorry that you felt it was."

Chloé began to cry then. Full-on ugly cry. "Everything I do, my work, it's so others don't have to go through what you and *Ataata* had to. I'm saving others."

"I know," her mother's voice broke. "And I'm so very proud of you. But this isn't your burden to bear."

"How could it not be?"

"What do you mean?"

"I survived."

Her mother's lips trembled and she held Chloé's face, bringing her forehead to hers. "And I'm thankful every day you did. The way you use your life to heal makes me so proud. I want you to live the way *you* want, though."

Chloé closed her eyes. Hot tears rushing down her cheeks. "I'm trying."

Her mother let her sit back. "I think that something else is bothering you. It's not just Immi. So tell me. I'm here for you. I'm your parent, tell me."

Chloé sighed. "It's Emile. I saw him again and…I'm still in love with him."

"And that's a problem?"

"He is so tied to Montreal and the hospital where his family has worked that…I think he's afraid of love. Afraid of hurting me."

"That sounds slightly familiar."

Chloé looked at her mother. "What do you mean?"

"You were so scared of hurting us you've been bottling up your emotions for so long. Afraid of having any kind of happiness, because you've dedicated your life to saving Immitaq."

"Yes," Chloé whispered.

"Immitaq is gone," her mother said. "You are still here and you deserve happiness."

"I know," Chloé said. "The problem is…" Now she was talking she couldn't hold any of it in. "He didn't want me. He said he can't give me what I need."

"Are you sure about that?" her mother asked.

"He didn't ask me to stay." Chloé felt the tears slip down her cheeks and she brushed them away. "I love him, *Anaana*."

Her mother got up and held her and she clung to her. "I know you do, and you should fight for what you want. You deserve it. And you don't need to hide your emotions away anymore, Chloé. Not from me. Promise?"

Chloé nodded. "I promise, *Anaana*. I don't know what the next steps are, though."

"I can't tell you that, but I can tell you, you'll be late for your clinic if you sit around here any longer."

Chloé chuckled through the last of her tears. "Okay. I better clean up. I'll see you later tonight?"

Anaana nodded. "Take *Ataata*'s ATV. He won't miss it."

"I thought he wanted to take a load to the dump?" Chloé asked.

"He'll survive. He just goes out there to hang out with Jerry Aglook."

"Remind me later to talk to Jerry about his French words. He gave me bad advice in school." Chloé was feeling much better as she washed her face.

"And that surprises you?" *Anaana* asked, making her smile.

She grabbed her jacket and her briefcase and headed outside. Her *ataata*'s ATV was ready and waiting. She took his helmet and climbed on it, starting the engine and driving toward the hospital.

She waved at a few people she knew then parked the ATV in the parking lot, leaving the helmet on the seat, knowing it would be safe.

She really didn't know what the next steps would be, but she knew she was going to tell Emile how she felt and go from there. If he still didn't want her, she could move on and heal. Right now, she had to focus on her clinic work.

She headed inside, trying to get to her office when she saw the chief of the hospital approaching her.

"Ah, Doctor MacDonald, I have great news. There's a new doctor here scoping out our hospital. Wants to be part of the cardiac rotation program and we really want to have him."

"Great," Chloé said brightly.

"Would you show him around? He says he knows you."

Her heart skipped a beat. "What?"

"From Montreal. A Doctor Moreau," the chief stated.

"That's impossible. The Doctor Moreau I know is the head of cardiothoracic surgery at Hôpital de Ville-Marie. There's no way a head surgeon could be part of this rotation."

"He was head, but now he's just a surgeon there," the chief stated. "The new head sent him a recommendation. So can you show him around? Convince him to join?"

"Sure," Chloé said, stunned, and took his file. She headed

into her office, her pulse thundering between her ears as she opened the door. Emile was sitting there waiting for her. His eyes lit up when he saw her.

"Emile?" she asked, surprised. "What're you... Why? I have so many questions."

Emile grinned. "I'm sure you do. *Oui*, I'm here about joining the rotation program, though I have some stipulations about that, and I am no longer head of cardiothoracic at Hôpital de Ville-Marie. I stepped down and became an attending. So I have more flexibility."

"Why?" Chloé asked, shutting the door behind her.

"Because I can't do this program being the head."

"I understand, but...what are you doing here?" Maybe she should've drunk that coffee.

There was a nervous energy emanating from him, something so unlike him. She felt like she should sit down, only she couldn't, too nervous herself.

Emile ran his hand through his hair, making it stand on end. Then his gaze locked on to her and his eyes twinkled. He smiled at her tenderly, just like he used to do. "I'm in love with you, Chloé. I've always been in love with you."

Chloé's pulse was pounding between her ears and her heart felt like it was going to bust out of her chest. She couldn't quite believe what she was hearing. It had been what she'd longed for for years, since she left Emile. It was the stuff of fairy tales, a dream. She gripped the doorknob behind her and blinked a few times before she was finally able to speak. "I love you, too. I always have."

Her pulse began to race and all she wanted was to be in his arms, but she still wasn't sure if she trusted him. If this wasn't all a delusional hallucination.

Emile took a step closer to her. "I want to work up here with you. Together."

"We only allow those accommodations for married couples," Chloé stated, trying to still figure out how to read him.

"*Oui*. I understand. Which is why I want to marry you."

She found it hard to breathe, the gasp of surprise catching in her throat. "You...what?"

He chuckled softly. "I said I want to marry you."

She shook her head in disbelief. It was all just too good to be true. "Is that so? What about kids and family?"

"I want that."

"You didn't before." It came out as a whisper. If only it were true.

"I was wrong, but I only want that with you. I can give you that. Let me come up here and show you."

"But I mean...you love Montreal. It was evident. Are you sure you can walk away from that for months at a time?"

She worried her bottom lip. As much as she wanted this, she didn't want him to give up everything, either. He should be happy, too.

Then Emile smiled at her tenderly and she believed him. All the worry melted away as he brushed his knuckles over her cheek. The old Emile was there, in those blue eyes, and she melted from his touch.

"*Oui*. I can. The thing is, I do love Quebec. It's been my life's work. But I think seeing it from your perspective when you were in Montreal was a way for me to let it go, because the truth of the matter is, I love you more. Much more than a legacy or a hospital or a city. I was spending my life chasing my father's love and approval. You were right—the problem with that is he's gone. You're here and I can't seem to let you go. I'm terrified of hurting you or turning into my father, but I think you won't let that happen."

Tears stung her eyes and she cleared her throat, her smile a bit wobbly. "You're right. I won't. And... I can transfer from Ottawa to Montreal. If your new head will have me."

"She will." Emile grinned, so cocky and sure of himself. It made her laugh. Her Emile was back, truly back. He tipped her chin and kissed her gently, making her melt. "So? Does that mean you'll marry me?"

"Since you're stooping to blackmail..."

Emile blinked. "What?"

Chloé grinned, enjoying the torture. "You'll only come here to work if it's with me so I *have* to marry you."

He groaned. "Are you serious?"

Chloé laughed, then sobered up. She thought of her conversation with *Anaana* about hiding her feelings. She didn't have to do that with him. She knew that now. "I will be serious sometimes. But I think I can be with you. You're the first person I shared Immitaq with. You're the first person since her that's made me feel safe."

"I'm glad to hear that."

Chloé kissed him again. "I may not always be bright and sunshiny, though."

"It's okay. I just want to be with you. So, do I have the job?"

She grinned. "Perhaps. I do have to interview you first."

He cocked an eyebrow. "*Chloé...*"

"*Oui*," she whispered.

"And, what about the other question I asked?"

She wrapped her arms around his neck and made a face like she was thinking hard about it. "*Oui*."

He kissed her again, deeply, making her weak in the knees. She was bursting with a happiness she couldn't comprehend. It wasn't a facade she put on to make others happy—she was truly reveling in the fairy-tale moment that she never thought she would ever have. Her happily-ever-after.

"I love you, Chloé," he whispered huskily against her ear.

"I love you, too, Emile. But I also have a *stipulation* before we announce our engagement to the whole world."

"And what's that?"

"You have to take the ATV in the parking lot and drive over to my parents' house and ask my *ataata* permission to marry me."

Emile's eyes widened in horror. "I don't even know where your parents' house is?"

"Just ask people as you drive toward the docks, then they can tell you."

He frowned. "You're not going to make this easy for me, are you?"

"You want to work in the north, this is an initiation like no other." She kissed him again. "Do I have to ask permission from your mother?"

"No, she adores you. She wants her *chouette* to visit her again, and she wants the wedding to be up here."

Chloé laughed. "I think we can make that happen."

For the first time since Immi died, she felt free. Like she didn't have to pretend anymore. She hadn't been sure if she deserved a happy-ever-after, but now she knew that she did.

And she was getting the one she'd always dreamed of.

An equal one.

EPILOGUE

One year later

EMILE PULLED UP to the familiar white house in Beaupré. His mother was outside waiting, sitting on the porch, like she usually did in the summer.

"I wonder if she's been waiting out there since we told her we landed in Montreal yesterday?" Chloé asked, a hint of humor in her voice.

"Of course. Are you surprised by this?" Emile asked, looking through the rearview mirror at his wife sitting in the back next to the car seat.

"No. Not at all," Chloé responded.

"She is not going to sit inside patiently and wait for the arrival of her granddaughter." Emile climbed out of the car and then opened the back door to take out the car seat, which had the most precious bundle in the world inside it.

His daughter.

Chloé got out of the car.

"I'm so glad you're all here," his mother said loudly, rushing down her path, her arms wide-open. "*Ma chouette!* You look wonderful."

"Marguerite, it's so good to see you again."

Emile watched as his mother embraced Chloé, kissing her on the cheek. Then his mother turned to him.

"Is that her? My granddaughter?" His mother's eyes filled with tears.

"Indeed." Emile turned the car seat carrier around so his mother could see the tiny little girl with chubby cheeks and dark hair sleeping soundly. "She apparently likes car rides. She slept so soundly the moment we left Montreal."

His mother leaned over, tears in her eyes. "She's beautiful."

"Let's go inside and you can hold her," Emile suggested.

"I still can't believe you only had her two weeks ago," Marguerite gushed.

"It was a fast birth," Chloé admitted. "She came early and furiously. I had just finished an angioplasty and an hour later I was giving birth on the scrub room floor in Iqaluit. The midwife didn't even have time to get there."

Emile beamed down at his wife. He'd been working in the clinic and barely had time to get there and catch his daughter as she was being born.

"What did you call her again? My apologies, it was hard to hear on the phone when you called and I wanted to make sure that I got her name correctly."

Chloé shared a tender look with him. "Immitaq Marguerite."

His mother brushed away a tear. "I am so happy. So very happy. Let's go inside. I need to hold her."

Chloé wrapped her arm around Marguerite and they headed inside. Emile stared down at his little girl. He never thought he would have a family of his own—he'd thought he'd die alone, just like his father.

He had been on that path.

But here he was. A father, a surgeon, a husband.

It was too much happiness. Something he'd never thought he'd have.

Chloé came back outside. "What're you doing?"

"Just taking it all in." He kissed her quickly. "I love you, Chloé."

"I love you, too, but if we don't take Immi inside to meet her grandmother, your mother will march out here and take our daughter from you."

Emile chuckled. "Good point. Lead on, MacDuff."

Chloé giggled and he wrapped his arm around her, keeping her close. His sunshine, his joy and his love.

* * * * *

If you enjoyed this story, check out these other great reads from Amy Ruttan:

Snowbound with the Single Mom
Their Accidental Vegas Vows
Rebel Doctor's Boston Reunion
Tempted by the Single Dad Next Door

All available now!

MILLS & BOON®

Coming next month

SURGEON'S SECOND TIME LUCKY
Karin Baine

'Now, where do you need me?'

It was the voice behind her which sent chills along the back of her neck, before she turned around to face him.

Time had chiseled his features into that of a handsome, mature man, from the teen she had known, but the swoop of dark hair, deep brown eyes and full smile hadn't changed that much. Harrison. Her ex-husband. Father to the baby she'd lost. The love of her life who hadn't loved her enough to stay. And now he was here, in front of her.

It took a moment for Ruby to compose herself, not wanting to give away the nature of the relationship they'd once had to any of her colleagues. No one here knew of her life before she'd qualified as a nurse, and that was the way she wanted to keep it. Especially if she and Harrison were apparently going to be working in the same hospital from now on.

She saw the moment too when he recognized her, the almost imperceptible sharp intake of breath, and flare of recognition in his eyes.

Continue reading

SURGEON'S SECOND TIME LUCKY
Karin Baine

Available next month
millsandboon.co.uk

Copyright © 2026 Karin Baine

COMING SOON!

We really hope you enjoyed reading this book.
If you're looking for more romance
be sure to head to the shops when
new books are available on

Thursday 23rd April

To see which titles are coming soon, please visit
millsandboon.co.uk/nextmonth

MILLS & BOON

TWO BRAND NEW BOOKS FROM
Love Always

Be prepared to be swept away to incredible worldwide destinations along with our strong, relatable heroines and intensely desirable heroes.

OUT NOW

Four Love Always stories published every month, find them all at:

millsandboon.co.uk

FOUR BRAND NEW BOOKS FROM
MILLS & BOON MODERN

Indulge in desire, drama, and breathtaking romance – where passion knows no bounds!

OUT NOW

Eight Modern stories published every month, find them all at:

millsandboon.co.uk

OUT NOW!

Available at
millsandboon.co.uk

MILLS & BOON

LET'S TALK
Romance

For exclusive extracts, competitions and special offers, find us online:

- **f** MillsandBoon
- **X** @MillsandBoon
- **◉** @MillsandBoonUK
- **♪** @MillsandBoonUK

Get in touch on 01413 063 232

For all the latest titles coming soon, visit
millsandboon.co.uk/nextmonth